I0753000

ABYSSAL

Abyssal

Cover illustration designs by: Kimberly Pinzon

Contact: Kimberly.pinzon@gmail.com

First paperback edition

ISBN: 979-8-9895941-4-6

This one's for Kyle. He always lets me be as weird as I want to even when I ask weird things like, "What do you think it would feel like if I stabbed you with this knife?" Love you.

And to everyone who reads my books
and keeps coming back for more.
You're the real ones. <3

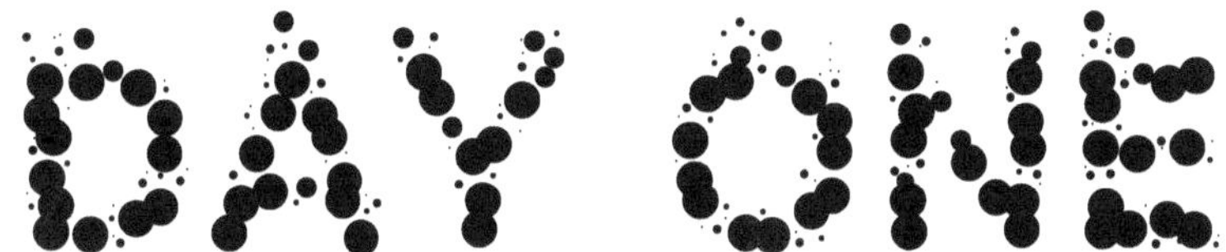
DAY ONE

Asha

With a high-pitched whine, a computer screen woke from "Sleep" with a series of lethargic flashes. Once the screen solidified, numbers and images indicating ocean depth and waypoints filled the blue gradient, darkest at the bottom, lightest at the top where a small white sub icon flashed. A series of dots descended to a gray rectangle at the bottom of the simulated ocean.

Looking up from her book, Asha sighed like this development was a huge inconvenience and not her job.

Except, it *was* a huge inconvenience: the best friends who still hadn't accepted they loved each other had just checked into a hotel room with only one bed, and the slow burn novel was *finally* getting somewhere. The long-awaited payoff was within her grasp until the submersible notification. Asha's eyes flicked toward the digital clock on a separate screen ticking down the time until the submersible's arrival: one day, seventeen hours, forty-five minutes, six seconds, and counting. There were no scheduled submersible arrivals for… Asha wrinkled her nose in thought. There weren't any arrivals scheduled for months, at least. A resupply sub had docked only a few weeks ago. Yet here was a notification for a submersible coming down in fewer than forty-eight hours, catching her–and probably everyone else on the team–unprepared.

Flopping the book closed on the Post-it note she was using as a bookmark, Asha rolled her chair over to the monitor demanding her attention. There were eight monitors in total, stacked two high and four wide, each with its own purpose. Prior to the sub's interruption, only three were lit up: messages, security scan, and a map of the hab showing where crew were located. Not that Asha wanted to keep tabs on them; it was just nice to know when someone left the facility for a deep walk.

In case they got lost.

Grabbing her headset, she snugged it over both ears and glanced over the other monitors in her space, confirming that there was nothing out of the ordinary with those.

Fishing out the correct keyboard for the screen she wanted, she set it in front of herself and opened a chat box. Before typing into it, Asha reached towards her radio screen and tapped her finger against a pictograph of a microphone to begin transmitting. A green bar appeared above the microphone for her chosen channel, showing that she and the surface had activated their communications. Depressing the foot pedal under her desk, Asha spoke into the mic hovering in front of her mouth, her tone bordering on the edge of irritation.

"This is Kraken 7 to the surface. What're you assholes doing sending another sub down? We didn't call for anything." She typed as she talked, releasing the pedal when she was finished speaking. Sending off a quick message to the rest of the Kraken team that something, or someone, was coming, she waited for a return transmission from the surface. At nearly seven miles down on the ocean floor, it took a few seconds for each transmission to get through even with top-of-the-line technology. A reply from Carlos came just as static crackled into her headset.

"Kraken 7, this is Saul Perisdo."

Asha clenched her jaw at the name. Shit.

"Your needs aren't any of our concern. I'll be coming down with some other parties holding a stake in the project. I expect you all to be on your best behavior." The condescending tone in his voice tightened Asha's jaw further and she started to tap her fingers on her desk to a made-up tune. "We'll be flying into the area in a few hours and then boarding the sub. Plenty of time for you to get things in order." Saul's mic clicked off and the green icon disappeared from the screen, indicating the surface station was no longer on the air. Asshole hadn't even given her a chance to respond.

Sliding her headset off, Asha clicked open Carlos' message:

They do understand we have strict schedules down here? They can't just come when they feel like.

Several other messages appeared after his:

Divya: The dry dock entrance isn't prepped yet and the decon chambers haven't been cycled. Do they want to get in, or be stuck in tiny purgatory?

Mina: I'm sure it's for something important.

Keaner: I'm going to cook so much food.

Zane: I don't think this is anything to be worried or upset about. I'm sure it will be fine.

The flow of comments stopped. Asha smirked at the screen, imagining how everyone's faces would change as she typed in her comment.

Asha: Perisdo and some other surfacers are the ones coming down.

There was a brief pause before a deluge of exclamations, shocked face emojis, and images of skulls cluttered the screen. This was not the kind of alert anyone expected to get. Working at Kraken 7, at the bottom of the ocean, they were promised a certain amount of independence and isolation from the world above. Asha knew most of them chose to work here so that they could avoid scrutiny and interference from people who never worked for anything less than seven figures and vacationed with a private jet. Amphitrite, the company that owned and managed Kraken 7, paid everyone down here exceptionally well to keep to themselves and not talk about anything they might find. That sort of unspoken promise of, “We’ll leave you alone as long as you do your job,” was being broken.

Another message pushed the other ones up the screen.

Benson: These messages are all recorded in the Kraken system. Stop using it inappropriately and meet in the control room in five minutes.

Asha groaned, leaning back in her chair. Leave it to Benson to suck the fun out of anything. And of course, she needed to be at the complete other end of the hab in five minutes when, even at a brisk walk, it took at least twelve minutes to traverse that distance. Benson was the ever-present thorn in their side who enjoyed reminding them that, even on the sea floor, someone could still rain on everyone’s parade.

“What a stellar day this is turning out to be,” Asha growled. Locking all of her computer screens, she pushed away from her desk and stretched. It was time for a walk anyway.

The hab, shorthand for “habitat” and what everyone called their underwater home, consisted of three miles of hallways, twenty-one rooms, three docking points, and a whole lot of technology. The specs for the hab were full of detailed lists of how many miles of wiring, pounds of titanium, and tons of steel existed in the structure; the number of computer screens, keyboards, and ergonomic chairs which were fixed structures in most rooms. Other lists detailed the gallons, pints, kilos, or grams of chemicals, liquids, compounds, and drugs shipped down to the hab. Still other lists showed what was shipped up from the hab, no matter how infrequent that was.

Perisdo and his surface-dwelling stakeholders coming down to visit with them was not the ideal working situation in a space this isolated.

Asha's boots were almost inaudible padding down the hallway on the metal floor. She hated the *click-clack* sound of hard heeled shoes on the metal, the way it reverberated up and down the hallways, so she'd requisitioned soft-soled shoes. There was so much metal here, everything in shades of gray stretching off into the distance, lit by lights meant to mimic the sun to prevent the residents from becoming as pale and ghost-like as the few other benthic organisms that managed to live at this depth of the ocean.

The sun mimicking lighting was also supposed to prevent them from going crazy. Asha felt the jury was still out on that, sometimes feeling she was crazy just for working here. The lighting was a poor imitation of the sun, but at least everything was bright: there were no shadows to stare into or alcoves to hide in. The walls bared their all, including every control panel that she didn't know the purpose of and the fire extinguishers she doubted they'd ever need. A defibrillator would make more sense, she'd argued several times, only to get a single unit in the mess hall, but working with bureaucratic red tape was a nightmare.

Passing one of the clear composite panels built into some of the outer walls to give a glimpse into the depths, Asha couldn't fathom why the designers would do something like that. While it didn't bother her the way it often did visitors and some of the other crew, there was something vaguely hypnotic to her about staring into an abyssal blackness. Even just passing it made her skin prickle and shorten her breaths. Asha might not think much of the view into the darkness, but her subconscious sent her subtle cues that maybe she shouldn't spend much time staring. It just felt like something might be staring back.

Asha didn't even glance at the panel this time, though, her mind consumed with other thoughts.

Why would the surfacers even want to come down here? That question without an answer wedged in Asha's brain. She ran her hands through her short hair, colored a purple so dark it was almost black in the right light. The only time anyone from the upper office came down when someone wasn't in trouble was because they wanted to flaunt the team's research or show off the only structure this far underwater that was habitable by humans. Amphitrite Corporation wanted everyone to know just how talented and amazing they were, meaning problems almost always got swept under the rug. That suited Asha just fine; the less corporate came down here the better.

However, she still wanted to know what the crew had done recently that warranted this visit. She wracked her brain, trying to remember Mina or Zane mentioning something new or strange, something that would have attracted attention. To her knowledge, no communications were sent to the surface, and nothing made its way up there without her knowing. So, what the hell?

Asha imagined the sour faces of her coworkers, knowing that in just a few more minutes she would get to see them in the flesh. She practiced making her face flat and pleasant, knowing that the second Benson started talking, all that work would go down the drain. The man grated on her. Not that she was one to be friendly with authority figures in general–there was a reason she was managing comms at the bottom of the ocean–but Benson always seemed to use his authority to bring out the worst in others.

Stepping over the threshold of the control room, Asha clocked that everyone was there.

Except Benson.

The five of them clustered around the large metal table in the center of the room. There was space enough for twelve people, each spot sporting a cushy rolling chair and a holographic screen built into the table. Everyone's bright orange tumblers with their names stenciled on the sides were on the table, accompanying their owners. Asha had forgotten hers, along with her book, at her station.

This area was called the "control room", but not much was controlled here. Most of them did their work throughout the hab, unable to be tethered to one single spot, and the control room only had two computer consoles to work with. Not nearly enough to manage all the complicated machinery at Kraken 7. So, this was their meeting room most of the time.

Asha tilted her head at Carlos, leaning back in his chair with his boots kicked up on the table. His engineer coveralls were pulled down to his waist with the arms tied together so they wouldn't slide down over his hips, exposing a faded band t-shirt of some folk group she didn't know. They were the only two of the crew in their late thirties, and had initially bonded over their disdain for Boomers and love of Godzilla.

Carlos shot her a small smile and raised his eyebrows toward his dark hairline, inclining his head towards Mina and Zane, huddled together at one end of the table, separated from the others.

Mina was not someone Asha would have ever pegged as a scientist, a bias she was well aware of. The woman looked more like a linebacker, someone that should be running with security, not handling delicate instruments and explosive chemicals. Yet Asha had watched the woman work and been amazed at how those hands could be so deft and gentle. As Mina conversed with Zane, she brushed her long blonde hair behind her ears, copper bangles on her wrist jangling together. It was a familiar motion since she didn't seem to own any hairbands to hold her hair back. Mina always had that sort of unkempt air about her, dressed in sweatpants and a loose t-shirt.

Zane, on the other hand, was skinny with a faux hawk and black lines of tattoos scrawling down his arms and up his neck. Benson was going to have a conniption when he saw; the man was still of the very outdated belief that tattoos were unprofessional. Zane fiddled with the hem of his purple sweatshirt while he leaned to the side to say something to Keaner, his legs someone folded up into a pretzel shape on his chair despite the fact that he was wearing skinny jeans. He looked like an emo teen, but she knew he was at least thirty.

Asha circled the table, passing Keaner whose hands were tangled up in yarn while he conversed. He was moving strings of yarn from finger to finger, creating geometric designs. Without looking at her, her asked, "What's the good word, Ash Ketchum?" Rolling her eyes,

Asha wondered if he knew that reference from kids he'd never mentioned, or if he wasn't the almost sixty years old he claimed to be. Asha reached down and plucked a string, collapsing his entire design. "Heyyyyy," Keaner groaned. He draped the yarn over his head like the hair he didn't have, and pouted at her. "I'm not telling you where I saw a Pidgey now."

"Stuff it, Keaner." Asha laughed and pushed between him and Zane, interrupting whatever conversation they'd been having.

Mina sucked her lips into her mouth and Zane's gray eyes darted towards Mina; they looked to be confirming something without speaking.

"Hey, Ash K–" Mina bit back the rest of her words at the withering look from Asha. Once per meeting was enough with that nickname. A tentative smile twitched on Mina's lips when she asked, "You know what this is about?"

Frowning, Asha crossed her arms over her chest and looked towards Zane. "I was hoping you geeks would know something. Nothing's crossed my panels, so I wasn't sure if it was some automated thing on your end."

"Nope," Mina chirped, her tone too bright. Zane's hands fluttered in his lap and he avoided looking at Asha for too long.

"Some must be revealed, some are for righteous individuals, and some are private." Zane's words were barely above a whisper, and it took a second for Asha to realize that he wasn't really saying anything, just quoting bits of nonsense. He often cherry-picked random stuff from the Bible, and she wasn't sure if it was because he actually believed or he was trying to be ironic.

Pointing a finger between the two of them, she put an ominous tenor into her response. "You know I'm going to find out either way. And when I do…" She cut her pointer finger across her throat. Mina's half smile was full of nerves. Zane kept his mouth flat.

Finishing her lap around the table, Asha dropped into a chair next to Carlos. Divya, sitting on his other side, had her eyes closed and head tilted back. It sounded like she was snoring.

"Hey." Carlos kicked Divya's chair. The woman snorted, shifted in his seat, but didn't open her eyes. Her long, straight dark hair was pulled back in a ponytail which swayed as she adjusted herself. Out of all them, she was the only one to wear the Kraken 7 t-shirt they'd all been issued as a sort of uniform. It was a deceptive concession to the company, though. Divya was the one most likely to get under Benson's skin when he was trying to give orders. She was both the youngest, at twenty-three, and the most disagreeable.

Without opening her eyes, Divya mumbled something that sounded incoherent but also could have been "ugly bastard."

Carlos shrugged and turned back to Asha. "Our fearless leader has yet to appear."

"Guess I shouldn't have worried about being late," Asha grumped. It was these little things that irritated Asha about Benson. He never seemed to care about anyone else's time, and it often seemed purposeful, like he was better than the rest of them.

Rolling his eyes, Carlos reminded her, "The man is never on time. If time is a universal concept, he's in a completely different universe." Snorting, Asha kicked up her boots to put them next to Carlos'.

“I feel like our guests are going to be stuck in the dock for a few hours while she gets the decon procedures up and running.” Asha inclined her head toward Divya. She tried to keep on Divya’s good side as best she could since the woman had a mean streak a mile long. Carlos believed it was because she’d been kicked in the head by a mule as a kid, and the mule had transferred some of its assholery to her. Keaner thought it was because Divya was a Scorpio. Asha was inclined to believe it was the mule.

Nodding, Carlos leaned forward to grab his tumbler and took a long drink. “If I put some Jim in her coffee she might be a little nicer.”

“Would at least maker her funnier,” Asha quipped back.

“I can hear you. I’m not asleep.” Grumbling, Divya tilted her head forward and squinted an eye at Carlos. “What was that about my buddy Jim, though?”

Carlos laughed just as Benson strolled into the room.

“Something funny, Engineer Cepeda?” Everyone’s mouths cinched shut and they sat up in their seats, except for Divya who slouched even lower. Carlos shook his head, but Asha caught the smirk he shot in her direction. “Vice President Perisdo is coming down with some special guests. You’re all to be on your best behavior, to be the most accommodating.” He centered his gaze on Divya. “Ms. Choudhary, are you with us?”

With an exaggerated sigh and mumbled grumbling, Divya opened her eyes and leaned forward to plant her elbows on the table and plop her head on her hands. “Present against my will and better judgement.”

There was a heavy pause while Benson and Divya eyed each other across the table. He adjusted his glasses, sliding them a bit down his nose before pressing them back up to the bridge. Between Divya's acerbic nature and Benson's pompous "better-than-thou" attitude, Asha couldn't think of a pair more likely to hate each other. Yet they were all stuck underwater together as a dysfunctional family that managed their homicidal impulses rather well.

On the good days.

This must have been a good day for Benson because he chose to gloss over Divya's attitude to address the group as a whole.

"The Vice President of Amphitrite is coming down to visit us this week." Benson repeated, looking over the group to gauge their reactions to this news. Everyone except Divya kept their faces flat; her lip curled in a half snarl. Instead of addressing Divya's reaction, Benson turned on Keaner. "Mr. Carston, are you paying attention?" Benson snapped. Keaner tilted his head in Benson's direction but kept twisting the yarn around his fingers. Red started to creep up Benson's neck from under the collared shirt he wore.

Reaching a long leg out, Mina kicked Keaner's chair, startling him and collapsing the design wound around his fingers.

"Where's the emergency?" Keaner had a weird accent that made him enunciate his vowels extra hard. Asha wasn't sure where he came from, or what would produce that, but it only enhanced the startled nature of Keaner's question.

Benson snorted, ignoring Keaner's question. "The soon to be arriving visitors have a vested interest in what we're doing down here, and want to see the progress we've made."

Thrusting her hand into the air, Asha tried to follow the rules Benson liked to incorporate into meetings: remaining orderly and following the Amphitrite hierarchy where Benson was at the top. She preferred when things were kept in order, however Benson rarely respected them the way he wanted them to respect him. Which is what he did as he ignored Asha's raised hand and continued on with his monologue.

"I expect you all to give Mr. Perisdo and the investors as much of your attention as you can spare." The unspoken words were that they would give all of their attention to them. "They will be your priority. The investors and Mr. Persido will be here for a week, which is the minimum amount of time required to adjust to being down here before they can return to the surface." Asha straightened her arm out, reaching higher. Benson continued to ignore her. "I expect everything to be prepared for their arrival in an hour and a half–"

Divya scoffed, derailing Benson's monologue. "An hour and a half? They're going to be here in two days. Rushing everything is stupid."

"It needs to be ready in advance in case they show up earlier." Benson jutted his chin up, exposing them to the dark holes of his nostrils.

"They can't get here any earlier than they already are. The plane and the submersible can't go extra fast." Divya waved her hands to accentuate the last two words. "My tasks will be completed when they're completed."

Hands on his hips, Benson's mouth flattened in preparation of scolding everyone in the room. Benson's idea of correcting behavior was to yell at everyone. Next to Asha, she caught Carlos shifting in his seat from the corner of her eye. He was Divya's direct supervisor, so he might also come under Benson's wrath if Divya didn't stop arguing.

"Excuse me," Asha interrupted, tired of waiting for Benson to acknowledge her when she knew he wasn't going to, "but, how did you get this information? How did *they* know that there was anything of note?" Asha resisted the urge to stand up so that Benson wasn't the highest point in the room. "There haven't been any transmissions or mail items sent to you or to them this whole week. What changed?"

Benson angled his chin a few centimeters higher than it already was. "While I don't answer to the Communications Officer, I will advise you that the message informing me of their arrival bypassed usual channels and was sent directly to me."

Asha squinted at Benson, feeling her muscles tightening across her shoulders and into her neck. "What do you mean 'bypassed usual channels'? You know I go over all of your messages to make sure they're not carrying any software or viruses that could kill us, right? It's not just for funsies? I don't actually read your messages, just the packaging it came in." Her job as Communications Officer also covered the security of their technology and computer systems. Asha approached her position as if it were life or death, which it was. If something or someone with bad intentions were to get into their software, it could wreak havoc on their life support systems and the basic safety mechanisms that kept outer doors locked.

"It came from the company. Obviously, it was safe." Benson redirected his gaze, dismissing her with a sniff. He reminded her of a snooty waiter dismissing people who didn't look rich enough to be at the restaurant, and it rankled her. Heat flushed through her and Asha jerked into a standing position, sending her chair rolling away to collide with a wall, losing out on the battle to stay seated.

"That makes it even more suspect! Does anyone read the trainings I send out on how to protect yourselves from this kind of stuff? To make sure we don't have catastrophic failures down here where no one can help us?" She looked around at her coworkers. Mina, Zane, and Keaner all raised their hands and provided some sort of ascent that they had, in fact, read the trainings. Asha didn't bother to look at Divya, but when she made eye contact with Carlos he shrugged and gave her a sheepish grin.

"Sorry, pal. I don't get any messages anyway."

Throwing her hands in the air, Asha snapped, "I can't believe you people. If messages are coming in through back doors, then what messages went out those same doors?" Benson opened his mouth, then closed it. Whirling on Mina and Zane, she demanded, "Well? What messages are going out?"

Carlos grabbed her wrist and she shook him off, her gaze darting between her crew members, waiting for someone to answer her. She again pulled away from Carlos when he wrapped his hand around her wrist, watching Mina and Zane exchange looks with Benson. She hadn't thought they would be in league with him, but a part of her hoped it was because they didn't have any other choice, that this was out of their control.

"Well?" she demanded. Carlos wrapped his hand in the fabric of her tank top and sweatpants and jerked Asha down into her chair. The sudden drop expelled the air out of her with an "oof" sound. Grabbing her hand, Carlos squeezed hard, redirecting her ire toward him. He jerked his head towards Benson, who was looking at Asha like he wanted to drown her.

"If you're quite done, Communications Officer Moore." He sounded like a stuffy British nanny without the accent. "A message was automatically sent from the labs to the surface due to certain discoveries made by Doctors Kibner and Marsh."

Everyone turned toward the scientists, a range of emotions reflected on their faces. For once, Divya looked interested, rather than disgusted and bored.

"What did you find?" Divya leaned towards them, her blue eyes lighting up. They had been working down here for almost a year, and hadn't done much more than dissect lots of familiar dead sea creatures like anglerfish, barreleye fish, vampire squids, and the like. They all wanted to know that something of value was finally coming from their time underwater.

Mina looked to Benson for guidance, which was uncharacteristic of her since she thought he was dumber than a rock. Whatever silent exchange happened between them chilled Asha's blood, sending a cold prickling down her arms.

"Amphitrite will determine when it's appropriate to share any successes with the rest of the team." Benson's tone was meant to shut down the conversation, but Divya wasn't about to let it go.

She leaned back in her chair and crossed her arms. "Well that's some bullshit. Does it have anything to do with the noises I've been hearing?"

“Noises?” Carlos released his grip on Asha’s clothing to turn towards Divya. “Noises from Kraken 7?”

Benson raised his voice over Divya’s response. “You may take that up with Vice President Perisdo when he arrives, as well as the future of your employment here.” Divya stiffened, along with everyone else in the room, smothering any further conversation about Divya’s supposed noises. “You’re all dismissed.” Benson turned on his heel and left the room, leaving them to stare at each other.

Carlos

It wasn't often that Asha was mad at him, and when she was, she made no bones about him knowing. Sometimes that meant Asha ignored Carlos, or she would hide his things. Other times, it meant she would complain without taking a breath, the words rolling out of her like water over a waterfall. Unceasing, smothering.

Loud.

He stopped listening a few hallways ago and was letting Asha talk herself out. Instead, he catalogued what he and Divya would need to get done over the next forty or so hours to prepare for the submersible's arrival and still get some sleep.

While Benson thought prepping and deconing could be done in less than two hours, that wasn't remotely realistic. He wasn't sure if they had even cleaned up from when the last sub came, which would take extra hours.

He should stop letting Divya encourage him to procrastinate. If it had been done when it was supposed to be, it would be one less thing on their current to-do list.

Checking his watch, Carlos figured they had at least four hours of "daylight" left to work.

"Do you think Divya is going to be in her room or the gym?" Carlos tossed the question out when Asha paused to look out one of the viewing windows. He hated those things, finding the reminder that they were at the bottom of the ocean akin to feeling like they were trapped in a coffin buried underground. Not that he didn't like this job. He just preferred not to think about where he was. Carlos averted his eyes from the window before his stomach had a chance to drop and churn.

"What?" The change in subject knocked Asha out of her complaint orbit. "What do you need Divya for?"

"Some of us need to prepare the hab for the sub's arrival. Unlike you, who's just going to sit in your little office reading your trash books and waiting for messages." His mouth curled into a sly grin.

Sticking her tongue out at him, Asha retorted, "I could have just told Benson they were coming down and left everyone out of the loop."

"As if you would do that." He dodged her attempt to punch his arm and held his hands up. "I really do need to find my assistant and get started on this job." He sighed and rubbed his temple before sliding his fingers down to squeeze his earlobe.

Asha hummed in her throat and stepped to the glass, putting a hand against it. "Why don't you just call her on your bracelet?"

The bracelet was the piece of technology they all wore around their wrists that allowed them to communicate with each other, tracked them through the hab, and gave them entry to rooms that might require different clearances.

"I'd have an easier time trying to reach the surface on it. Divya only answers when she feels like it." Carlos checked his Amphitrite bracelet for Divya's location, and noted that her status was listed as "Offline". He showed the display to Asha.

Chuckling, Asha said, "I'd tell you to just write her up but I know it won't make a difference." Carlos grunted in acknowledgment. Divya frustrated him, but she was good at what she did and it wasn't like Amphitrite was going to send someone else as a replacement. She was just one more eccentricity of working at the bottom of the ocean. "Speaking of Divya," Asha continued, what do you think she was talking about?" Carlos swallowed hard and stepped away from the window, trying to encourage Asha to leave with him and continue their walk.

"She talks about a lot of things. Mostly things she doesn't like. Can you be more specific?" Carlos waved to Asha and she stepped away from the glass.

"The noises. She said she was hearing noises and wanted to know if that was why the surfacers were coming down here." Asha started walking down the hallway again.

Carlos couldn't believe he'd forgotten Divya mentioning that at their meeting. No matter how brief, any noises that were out of the ordinary were important in a structure under trillions of gallons of water and pressure. Weird noises in a surface structure were often benign: structures settling over time, walls groaning from a hard wind, or pipes clanking from hot water running through them. At the bottom of the ocean, though? Structures didn't settle and there was no wind. Expansion and contraction were limited.

Uncharacteristic noises were a problem, and even though Carlos didn't know of any previous catastrophes in Kraken habs, there was always a first time for everything.

But not on his watch.

"I really don't know. I haven't heard anything that she might be talking about, and if she has heard something, I'm kind of pissed she didn't mention anything to me before." Frowning, Carlos followed Asha down the hallway that would go to her office. "Is it something that's broken? Is it just some weird noise that's developed because of general wear and tear, and it's okay?" Carlos shrugged and heaved a heavy sigh.

"Well, you know what'll fix that?" Asha stopped outside the door to her office. "Asking her. Dumbass." She slung her arms around him in a hug and stepped into her office.

Just as soon as the door closed, it slid open again.

"You want help finding her?" Asha hung on the doorframe like she couldn't wait to get back into her office.

Carlos shrugged. "Nah, it's fine." I need to get my run in anyway."

"Suit yourself." Asha disappeared into her office.

Of course Asha was right about needing to talk to Divya. Carlos just needed to find her. Gym or her room? Gym or her room? Carlos headed for the gym. Not many of them used the gym, but he knew

Divya did. When she was top side, Divya used her nice six figure salary here to travel the world climbing cliffsides and scaling mountains. She had to keep in shape somehow, and the gym was actually very nice. On his more ambitious days, Carlos ventured in there to move some weights around. Then he avoided the place for the next few weeks.

Walking and running the halls was much more enjoyable for him, so he took the long route to the gym. On the way there, he kept his ears and eyes open for anything out of the ordinary in Kraken's hallways. The smooth metal walls looked fine, the joints at doorways weren't buckling, nothing was popping out. The general hum that existed throughout the hab and which they all learned to ignore after the first week sounded no different than it usually did. He heard the air circulator turn on. Somewhere, someone was using the hot water because he heard a change in the ticking of the pipes. The hab was a beast of machinery to run, like an actual kraken, full of long limbs and complicated innards. It had its own internal hums and ticks, grumbles and groans. Carlos enjoyed understanding all these things.

He crossed paths with George, the hab's tuxedo cat, sitting and staring at…nothing. Carlos wondered what occupied the cat's tiny mind as she stared off into space. Could she hear what Divya was talking about? He didn't know, and he didn't interact with George enough to know if this was normal. Who, exactly, had brought the animal down here and how, he wasn't sure. George just seemed to have appeared one day, wandering the hallways, but Carlos would bet money Zane had smuggled the cat down here. He knew Zane was the only one of them who had cats at home, so if George came from anywhere, Carlos would put his money on Zane.

Divya was not in the gym. It didn't look like anyone had been here all day. Carlos looked longingly at the yoga mats, thinking that it had been too long since his last session. But, no, yoga could wait. He needed to find his partner.

Leaving the gym, Carlos took a circuitous route to Divya's room. He again used the time to just listen to the hab, trying to pinpoint anything that might be of interest.

Because there was nothing. Not an abnormal peep anywhere. Was Divya just trying to mess with Benson? That would be in character for her, the same way as it was in character for Benson to ignore and talk over her. Except, shouldn't the Kraken supervisor also be concerned about the wellbeing of the hab? Irritated there might be something wrong with the hab and he couldn't figure it out, Carlos rapped hard on Divya's room door.

"Div?" he called when she didn't come to the door. After a few more seconds of silence, he sighed and turned away. Where was this woman?

Mina

"You can't say anything, please." Mina could feel the tears threatening as she pled with Divya. They burned, hot and intense, threatening to spill over and embarrass her. She should have known better than to talk to Divya about the noises she'd mentioned at their meeting. Mina thought that if she addressed Divya's concerns in as bland a way as possible, if she could stop Divya from digging further, than Divya would let it go.

But, Divya wasn't letting it go. In fact, Divya was livid, becoming an additional worry for Mina who wasn't sure what was coming next. Not for her, or Kraken 7, or anyone down here. Maybe what she and Zane found would get them a bonus, or an award. A Nobel Peace prize? Or, it could be the reason Amphitrite fired them. *Disappeared* them even. Amphitrite was big enough; they could do that. It would be so easy for them to just no longer exist at the bottom of the ocean.

Not that she believed something ridiculous like that. Zane was part of the Tin Foil Hat Society, not her.

"Everyone else deserves to know." Divya crossed her arms over her chest and Mina admired the henna designs on her hands and forearms, distracted for a moment from her distress. The equations she would need in order to create such art would be astronomical. Art was never Mina's strong suit. Neither were friends or relationships.

Godsdammit. Why had she said anything?

"I think it would be best to keep this between us. It's not dangerous, just different. We need to do more research before we jump to conclusions." Mina blinked, trying to ease the pressure of tears in her eyes.

Divya shook her head, then looked away from Mina at the wall of freezer doors. "Did we not just experience the same thing? I've been hearing those noises for two weeks and losing sleep over it. And you're telling me you're not worried about–"

Mina cut in, shushing Divya. "Not so loud."

"Why?" Divya snapped, throwing her arms open. "Will yelling wake them up?"

Panic welled up from Mina's throat, threatening to choke her. "No, no, no, it's fine. I just… Zane and I, we've vetted everything," Mina finished weakly. It was a small lie, but the distress already on her face would hide any other reddening of her features. Oversharing the truth in order to gain a friend had landed her in this situation, so she would have to lie her way out of it. "You can't do anything in science without taking risks, and we're doing it in the safest way possible. I just don't want you getting upset."

Divya leaned up against the wall in the lab, one leg cocked up with her foot pressed against the wall. Her eyes flicked over to the closed doors on the other side. Mina wished she would stop looking around the lab.

The lab lights seemed harsher than usual, making Mina struggle to keep her tears at bay. They were also giving her a headache. Or maybe that was Divya. She wanted to press her fingers to her temples, but didn't want Divya to ask anymore questions.

Mina really should have kept her mouth shut. She just didn't want to disappoint her crewmates if they had questions she could answer. She wanted them to know she was capable of doing her job. Instead, she'd blabbed to Divya about what was making the noises and about things Mina shouldn't even have known. But how could she not explore information just sitting there openly in the Amphitrite archives? It would have been criminal to not read all the previous science notes.

Divya grunted and pushed away from the wall. "You don't get to tell me how to feel. I'm worried about my home and what that thing is capable of." Divya shook her head and Mina felt herself sweating, pools of it collecting under her arms and at her lower back. "Do you even know? Or are you just fucking around?" Divya chewed her lip while she thought, leaving Mina to sweat out her anxiety. "Fine. For now. But if anything else weird happens…" She let the unfinished sentence speak for itself.

Mina felt herself sag with relief despite Divya's threat. "Thank you. Thank you, Divya. I promise, everything is fine." Everything would be fine. They were making discoveries important enough to warrant surface dweller attention.

"It fucking better be," Divya snapped. "And those noises? You're sure they're nothing to worry about?"

Shaking her head like she was trying to dislodge something caught in her hair, Mina mustered all the confidence she had to assure Divya.

"Nope. Just all part of the work here."

Divya

There wasn't much that unsettled Divya. She didn't fret about superstitions, or the deep ocean outside the hab. Even being stuck on the side of a mountain wouldn't rattle her. She liked the adrenaline.

What Mina had shown her in that lab, though? An unfamiliar icy shiver trickled down her spine. Giving her shoulders a rough shake, she decided on going to the gym to work off some of the creeping anxiety. Lifting heavy things could solve most problems that sarcasm couldn't. It would have been better if she could find a mountain or a rock wall to scale, but for all the things Amphitrite could bring them, neither of those were possible.

Why would Mina want to share the information about the noises with her? They never talked outside of necessary exchanges and couldn't have been considered friends in the most basic sense. Divya liked to keep people at arm's length. It was better that way, easier to focus on herself. Her parents would approve of that.

A streak of home sickness hit her and she pushed it away, thinking instead of Mina's pleading. Divya rolled her eyes. She was always so desperate for approval. Couldn't she get that from Zane? Or even their supervisor-in-name-only, Benson?

A worm of doubt slithered through her. Maybe she shouldn't keep Mina's secret. It didn't benefit the team if she did. She wallowed hard. She could tell Carlos. He was the person she trusted most down here. What would happen if she did, though? The toppers were already coming down for those things in the lab. They thought there was some value there, but what? Mina hadn't shared any of that, if she even knew.

Maybe it really was nothing and Divya needed to stop overthinking everything.

A plaintive *meow* drew her attention downward, derailing her train of thought.

"George!" A smile spread across her face as the tuxedo cat approached her. One of her ears flicked back, then she looked at Divya and meowed again. Kneeling down, Divya gathered George up in her arms and pressed her face into her fur, closing her eyes. George reminded her of home, of the topside that she sometimes missed.

That was the whole reason behind her smuggling George down here. Not like it was hard. The personal items they carried in a bag with them onto the sub went through the same decon processes the owners did, so a sleepy, Benadryl addled George was perfectly safe traveling with her to the depths of the ocean. The cat had adjusted well to living in the hab, and Divya was thinking about bringing a friend down for her soon.

"I didn't know it was possible for you to smile."

Divya slitted her eyes open at the sound of Carlos' voice. She liked her supervisor: Carlos was fair and knew more about engineering than all her college textbooks combined. But, she wasn't about to let him know that. "I only smile for animals. People I can do without." She let George jump from the confines of her arms and trot down the hall, giving her a reproachful look over her shoulder. "Look, now she's mad at me."

Carlos sighed, and said, "We have work to do, Divya. The cat can wait." Divya rolled her eyes at Carlos and his attempt at authority. "I wanted to ask you about the noises you said you were hearing before we got started on anything."

Divya only needed to say a few words to stop Carlos in his tracks, to tell him what she'd seen in the lab, what Mina had told her. Divya bit her lip. Minding her own business would have kept her out of trouble on the surface, so she could only hope it would keep her out of trouble here.

"I talked to Mina about it. But you know her. She talked about anything and everything except what I asked her about. I don't think it's anything we have to worry about, though, whatever the sounds were." Divya didn't want to lie, and tried to say a bunch of words that meant nothing but sounded like an answer.

"Mmmm," Carlos grunted. He sounded like he was going to say something, then shook his head. "It took me long enough to find you, and we've only got a few more hours of daylight to get things done." He gestured at her to follow him and he headed down the hall.

Huffing, Divya fell into step behind him. "Daylight is forever down here if we need it to be. Or, we could just make the toppers wait."

"I think I'll remember that the next time you say you want a break." He touched a finger to his chin, pretending to look thoughtful. "And don't say topper. It's derogatory." His dramatic eye roll almost made her smile. *Almost.* No way would she give him the visual satisfaction.

Heaving a sigh, Divya started walking in the direction of the dry dock.

"I'm taking at least three breaks over the next four hours."

I can feel them. Systrarna, my pieces, there are so many scattered, but I feel them here. This place that I've found in the darkest depths. I have lived here for an age, more than an age. Cast down when the skies cleared to reveal the yellow death hovering in the sky. I yearn for the surface. We yearn to return. Out of isolation and scarcity.

I yearn for flesh to wrap myself in, for me and the systrarna to be whole again.

DAY TWO

Zane

Schedules and order in a place like Kraken 7 were important. Nothing caused problems in the ocean faster than chaos. Yet chaos reigned on a daily basis at Kraken 7. Benson didn't run a tight hab, despite what he believed or how much he tried to act the part of a tough boss. Everyone, for the most part, operated on their own time and did their tasks on an "as-needed" basis, which translated into "whenever they wanted".

Like this deep walk Keaner wanted to do on short notice when there were other things he needed to do.

For example, he should be working with Mina on the things in their freezer. He didn't like that the toppers were coming down without them being fully prepared. As it was, he was still poring over the notes from previous Kraken habs, and having no luck in finding anything.

Instead, he was setting up deep walk suits in another dry dock since the toppers would be using their usual one to dock the sub. There was no reason for an unscheduled deep walk, not when there was so much else going on.

And not when Zane wanted to avoid being out in the depths as much as possible, knowing what was out there.

Irritation set off the tic in his jaw. He tried to rub it out, even though he knew nothing would help until he could either find time to relax or pop an Ativan disguised as a Vitamin D supplement. They couldn't bring their own drugs, and the ones down here had to be signed out, but no one thought anything of Zane bringing down a bottle of "Vitamin D" from the surface. They weren't getting any of that from the sun, so supplements were encouraged and, apparently, not checked. Zane did take his vitamins as he was supposed to, but he also preferred some recreational "vitamins".

Unfortunately for him, he wouldn't put himself or others at risk by being high during a deep walk. So, even though his jaw was ticking, there would be no little white pills in his future.

Zane grunted as he unscrewed a bolt on the deep walk suit he had wedged between his knees. The dark blue suits weren't bulky like the suits astronauts wore to space, but they were stiff, full of metals and materials meant to protect the soft, squishy human it contained. Oftentimes, he would try to maneuver the suit one way and it would wind up flopping and clattering in an unwanted direction.

The suit arm he was working on slithered out of his grasp. Zane closed his eyes and breathed noisily in and out of his nose, trying to cut off the mounting aggravation crawling up his throat and setting off a tic on the other side of his jaw.

"Depart from me into the eternal fire for the devil and his angels," he muttered.

Keaner could be doing this suit inspection with him to make the process go faster. He was a jack of all trades down here, and Zane could only figure it was cheaper for Amphitrite to send down one many skilled person rather than many singularly skilled people. He didn't really understand corporations and their willingness to penny pinch when dollars made cents.

His internal monologue made him pause. Did that word play make sense or not? Shrugging, he wrote himself off, mumbling, "I'm a scientist, not an English teacher."

Once the bolt was off the suit, Zane pulled the panel it was holding away and inspected the meters and levels of the chemicals that filled the suit to keep them alive on their walks at the bottom of the ocean. Everything looked good inside the suit, so he closed it back up.

Next, he gave the cage they brought out with them a once over, though he doubted they would find anything. Large enough to hold something St. Bernard sized, the cage's walls were made out of steel meant to hold something much stronger than a dog. Zane shuddered and turned away, trying not to think about the last thing they'd caught in there. Maybe he would get lucky this time. Keaner had just been on a solo deep walk two days ago and returned with nothing. Solo deep walks weren't allowed for safety reasons, yet Keaner somehow charmed his way into Benson's good graces to do them. Just another way that Benson played favorites.

Zane sighed and dusted off his work pants. He didn't want to find anything else out there. There were enough things in the lab to keep him and Mina occupied for a few weeks, and bringing more of those things on board would just complicate their work. Especially with the toppers coming down. Whatever they wanted with his and Mina's discovery, it couldn't be good. There just wasn't enough available data to make the trip worthwhile. It just didn't make sense for them to come down. Zane didn't trust Amphitrite, and he was counting down the days until his tour was over. He never should have come back for a second, and this would be his last one. He would go back to wandering the globe on his own, living off the land and keeping a low profile with the money he'd earned from Amphitrite.

The hairs on the back of Zane's neck stood on end and he smacked a hand to his nape, as if that would get rid of the bad feeling creeping down his spine. They should never have brought those things into the hab. He told Mina it was mistake, fuck their protocols and mission and Amphitrite. They should have at least got rid of them once–

An angry hiss jerked Zane from his thoughts.

George sat at the entrance to the dry dock, her head twisted nearly all the way around, ears flat and teeth bared. Before Zane could get his bearings on the cat looking like Regan MacNeil, she took off down the hallway, paws scrambling on the slick surface.

Stepping into the entryway, Keaner gazed after the cat before shrugging at Zane. "Still don't know why that thing hates me."

"Maybe because you call her a 'thing'. Her name is George." Zane dropped his hand from the back of his neck. He still felt on edge, but he didn't want to tell Keaner about it. The prickliness of his nape spread into his stomach, and Zane glanced at the dry dock door, the one that led out to the ocean, as if he expected to see something menacing there. He needed to get a grip.

Or his drugs.

He took a deep breath to try and keep his heart rate in check, and turned to Keaner.

Grinning at Zane, Keaner scoffed, "Eh, the cat has no idea what we say about it. Ready for the deep walk?"

"Yeah." Zane paused, trying to will away the bad feeling still coiled at the base of his neck. Maybe they shouldn't do the deep walk. Then he could take the edge off with a pill. It felt like the tic in his jaw was spreading, or getting more insistent. "I'm just gonna eat something first. Don't want to walk on an empty stomach."

"Oh yeah, good catch there. Want me to cook? I've got French toast on the menu today." He wiggled his eyebrows but Zane waved him off. He preferred to be in control of his own food preparation, just like he was always the one to check and double check their deep walk equipment for safety. If he wanted something done right, he did it himself.

If he didn't want to die, he checked over his gear with his own eyes and hands.

"I can handle it. I'll see you back here in two."

Out in the hallway, out of view of Keaner, Zane slapped a hand to the back of his neck again. Nothing in the hallway was out of place and there were no shadows for anything to skitter in or out of. The whole hab was as sterile as possible, and there wasn't anything in here that didn't belong.

Except…

Zane ran a hand through his hair, grabbing at the lengths and tugging.

Goddamn this place gave him the creeps sometimes.

Asha

"Don't be cross with me, Ash. Zane and I didn't even know a message had been sent out until Benson came down demanding to know what we'd done."

Mina looked from the bank of computer screens showing messages and numbers and images to Asha. Her shoulders hunched forward, curling her over like a wilting plant.

Watching from the corner of her eye, it amazed Asha how such a large woman could take up so little space. She knew Mina would only continue to shrink into herself if she didn't interact with her, but Asha was still irritated about the whole thing. Everyone seemed to think being the Communications Officer meant that all she did was relay messages back and forth between the surface and the hab. That was only a portion of her job, though it didn't matter how much Asha assisted them with their electronics and messages, or sent out reminders for security clearances and measures.

What was even more frustrating than her team disregarding basic security measures, was that there were some back door communications going on that she didn't know about, and which were apparently programmed into certain areas and functions of the hab. Asha would rather be turning over stones in the hab's internal systems, looking for these sneaking transactions, not listening to Mina apologize. It was eight in the morning, and prior to Mina coming in quiet as a mouse to perch on the chair next to her, Asha had been quite happy hunting through the hab's software and files.

Or unhappy. She was still looking for anything of interest, and Mina was still there despite Asha's fourth heavy sigh.

"You need to tell me when things like this happen. I don't think you all understand that any slight mistake down here could mean death for all of us. If something malfunctions, doesn't close right, or cycle right, or starts a fire, that's it for us." She jerked her head to the side and mimicked a tearing sound from between her back teeth. "It's not just Carlos and Divya that keep things running smooth here."

Mina didn't respond, choosing to focus on her lap. Asha sighed, closed her eyes for a count of six, and then turned toward the other woman. "Don't worry about it. I'll figure it out. Especially if I can make life difficult for Benson."

Even though Mina's head was tilted down, Asha caught the gentle curve of a smile creasing Mina's cheeks. Lifting her head up, Mina's smile faded and she bit the inside of her cheek. It looked to Asha like Mina was waging some sort of internal war, arguing with herself about something. She wished the other woman would just leave.

"I shouldn't do this," Mina mumbled.

Asha was only just able to hear the words, and she leaned in. “Shouldn’t do what?” Asha could list a few things Mina shouldn’t be doing, but she wanted to know what Mina was referencing.

“Do you want to see what we found?”

Asha narrowed her eyes. “So you did find something. Benson wasn’t bullshitting.”

Mina shook her head, back to biting her lip.

“But you’re not supposed to say anything?” Asha remained leaning into Mina’s space.

“No.” Mina held onto the vowel a little long, dragging it out a bit as if she were thinking about her response. She sat up in her chair and reached out a hand to Asha. “But, I think it will be okay. I can show you?” The last word of her sentence lilted up into a question when Asha did not take her hand right away and she pulled her lips into her mouth, back to biting them. Asha worried she was going to chew them off.

It wasn’t that Asha wanted to keep Mina waiting for an answer and feeling worse; she was just processing that their supervisor had to know about these background operations and never thought it was relevant to tell her. He thought it was just fine for operations to go on unsupervised, like all their lives weren’t in the balance. Just one more reason to hate the nitpicking bastard.

“Yes. Yes.” Asha emphasized her second ‘yes’ to erase the questioning look Mina shot her, as though the other woman thought Asha was only saying yes out of pity. “Take me to the lab and show me what the hell caused all this fuss.”

The hallways heading towards the science labs were not as familiar to Asha as most of the rest of the hab. She did not often–or ever–have a reason to head that way, since her specialty was in inanimate things, not…whatever it was they were working on down there. In the past when she questioned Mina or Zane about their work, the two clammed up and would look for any excuse to leave the conversation. As far as Asha knew, there wasn't anything top secret going on at Kraken 7, but perhaps she just wasn't privy to that information. Which was just another irritating thought to bounce around in her head. Something else for her to go digging for.

What else was going on at Kraken 7 that was compartmentalized from everything else? Her fingers itched to get back to her keyboard, to start searching out these back alleys and hidden machinations. But Mina was walking quickly and despite paying attention, Asha wasn't one hundred percent sure she would even be able to find her way back to more familiar hallways.

At least, not without a lot of wandering.

They passed one of the glass viewing windows that showed nothing beyond a few inches of dimly glowing sand, lit by the light that leaked from the hab.

"What is it that you're working on, again?"

Mina glanced over her shoulder, her grin dimming when she saw where Asha was looking. Turning forward, she answered, "It'll be easier to show you."

"You know," Asha mused, her eyes passing back to the gray interior as the window slipped away, "if something is too complicated to say in only a few words, then you're not smart enough to do it."

Barking out a laugh, Mina returned, "If you need short sentences to understand a concept, it's not meant for you anyway."

"Touché." Asha's muttered word was lost on Mina who stopped in front of a keypad.

Finally, the lab rooms. It felt like they had walked all three miles of the hab. Like the route Mina took her on was meant to be confusing.

Mina keyed in a code that she shielded with her body. Asha didn't say it out loud, but she rolled her eyes while thinking about how easy it would be for her to find the key stroke logs for this keypad. She'd never had reason to do so before, but maybe she would just for fun. Especially since there wasn't really any reason for this room to need a keypad. What were any of them going to do in here? Steal the latex gloves and blow them up like balloons?

The door to the lab slid open. Giddy, Mina announced, "Here it is!"

Asha stepped through the door ahead of Mina, who held her arm out as though she were a concierge for a fancy hotel, the copper bangles encircling Mina's forearm clinking against each other.

It wasn't a far-off comparison: the lab was the fanciest place she'd seen in the hab. The lights were a far brighter sun bulb than anywhere else, and they were neatly recessed into the ceiling. The walls were bright white, almost painful to look at, and the floor was also white, smooth and clean like no one ever walked on it, like you could eat off it. Instead of the typical room with four walls, the lab had six. One wall was full of monitors, while another contained sixteen metal doors that looked like a freezer in a morgue. A chill crept up Asha's spine, burrowing into the nape of her neck. She doubted there were any dead people in there.

Unless they were running experiments on dead people? Was that why a coded door was necessary for this room?

Acid churned in her stomach, and Asha turned away from the wall to look at the rest of the room. She didn't want to think about dead people. Or sharing a space with them. Or about how this was their final resting place, like the hab was a tomb instead of her home.

Suppressing a shiver, Asha pointed across the room and asked, "What're those doors for?" On two of the remaining four walls, there were red metal doors without windows. Asha didn't care where they led, she just wanted Mina to arrest her mind's spiral.

Mina was standing in between two of the four stainless steel tables in the middle of the room. Trays of metal tools covered with thin, clear plastic sheets were placed at the head of each table. Asha imagined these tables had to have been used, but they were as clean and sparkling as everything else in the lab; she could see Mina's reflection in the steel.

"That's where we keep the uh," Mina paused, her eyes looking between the doors, her fingers tapping on the side of the table she stood next to. "That's where the live specimens are kept. Until we're ready for them."

Asking about the doors didn't help the chill still clinging to Asha. If anything, she felt worse, colder. "The live ones? Why do you need two rooms for them?" A sudden, second thought cropped up before Mina could answer. "How big are these things?"

It never occurred to Asha that anything being studied at Kraken 7 would be large enough to need a room, rather than a fish tank. Of course, she knew that there were gargantuan things in the depths: sperm whales or krakens, the namesake of their hab. She just preferred not to think of them. It was difficult to contemplate something that large being so close to them when it was just a few feet of manufactured material between the billions–trillions? –of gallons of ocean and the inside of the hab.

"Oh, not that big." Mina sounded unconcerned, not registering the slight tightening of Asha's face. "They just don't get along well with each other or other sea creatures in small spaces, so, even though we keep them sedated, they all have their own tanks."

Asha felt like the floor was tilting beneath her. Stepping towards Mina so she could lean on the table, a question tumbled out of her mouth for a need to say something: "Well, what are they?" Pressing her hands against the table, Asha knew she was probably going to leave fingerprints, but she didn't care. She was convinced that nothing Mina could say would be any sort of relief. A fear of being underwater, of being in the ocean at this depth, was never a thought in Asha's mind. What was there to fear down here, if one were being rational? Except, after seeing those morgue-like doors and thinking about dead bodies, something in Asha's brain was off kilter, letting that fear in.

Mina stepped towards one of the doors. "Come on. I can show you. It'll be easier than trying to explain it. We don't have an official name for it, but Zane's been calling them Mordices and it's kind of stuck for us."

“Mordices?” Asha repeated.

“Yeah,” Mina confirmed. “Mordices. Latin for teeth, or, really, biter. You’ll see.”

Teeth? Biter? Images of anglerfish came to Asha’s mind, small black fish with rows of needle-like teeth. Goblin sharks, with their oversized noses and projectile jaws full of knife blades ready to snatch fish. Was this something like that?

Following Mina toward the door, she felt a sudden desire not to enter the room. “Is the thing you wanted to show me in here?” As the door swung open, it revealed a dark room, like a yawning, hungry mouth. Watery lights illuminated a few areas in the room, but it was difficult to see anything when her eyes were still operating in the brightness of the lab room.

Asha waited for Mina to step through, feeling like if she crossed the threshold first the door would slam behind her.

Trapping her with the Mordices.

Sweat dampened her lower back, another reaction she didn’t like. Her nerves were in overdrive, all over some stupid fish. Or sea life. Whatever it was that resided in this room.

And out there, beyond the walls of the hab. Enveloped in the protective, velvety darkness of the ocean.

Without realizing she was doing it, Asha started to tap her thumb against the tips of all her fingers, repeating the process over and over to her made up tunes.

“Yup.” Mina sounded as cheerful as ever, in her element. Standing at her full height, brimming with confidence, she breezed over to a six-foot-long tank, her straight blonde hair fluttering around her face. The tank's stand raised it up so that the top edge was four feet tall, just low enough for Asha to be able to peek into the tank if the crazy thought seized her.

It took a few seconds for Asha's eyes to adjust, while Mina took no time at all. "Hello, Mordices Seventeen." She talked to something in the tank like it was a beloved pet dog.

Asha stepped forward, willing her eyes to adjust so she could see what the hell was in the tank. The lights she saw from outside the room where in the actual tanks, five in total, which was why the light was so diffused. Blinking a few times, Asha stepped further into the room. The thing suspended in the tank seemed to rock back and forth, small appendages towards the bottom of the tank fluttering. They looked sort of like fins, but there were also what looked like fingers dangling down, brushing the bottom of the tank. It filled most of the tank, a lumpy gray-green form cast in splotches of light and shadow. Where the light hit just right, Asha could see what looked like tiny spikes sticking out of the creature's skin.

"I wanted to show you the live one, because the dead ones don't have this response. All their nerves seem to die. No postmortem reflex movements like when you put salt or lemon on a dead fish and the thing twitches. Or, you know those videos of wolf fish where they still chomp after they're dead? Not these guys. But, anyway, look. This is neat."

She didn't say it out loud, but Asha would reserve judgement on what "neat" actually was until she saw what was about to happen.

Dipping below the level of the tank, Mina came back up with a stick about four feet long. She gestured to Asha with the stick, the copper bangles on her wrist clanging together. With her free hand she pushed her hair behind her ears. "Come closer, it'll be fine." Asha tilted her head, nerves still jangling and sweat still percolating. Her feet didn't move.

Mina shrugged, then hesitated as she reached over the top of the tank. Asha thought it was odd that Mina was suddenly having second thoughts about doing this after trying to get Asha closer. Her excitement in the other room was palpable, yet in this room she looked like she might be reconsidering showing the fish to Asha.

Just when Asha was about to ask if Mina was going to do anything, the scientist reached down with the rod and poked the gray-green mass.

Nothing happened. Asha took a small step forward, waiting for Mina to poke the thing again. Instead, Mina replaced the stick on the ground. What was supposed to happen?

The darkness crept in while she waited. It seemed to press against her, sticking to her like slime. Even worse, it took on a rumbling quality, like she was hearing a roaring waterfall from somewhere far off. Goosebumps erupted along her arms and she crossed them against her chest, unsure why she felt a sudden, instinctual need to run away.

A glance at Mina showed her that the scientist was watching her reaction, her gaze revealing nothing. The rumbling was getting louder, and Asha felt more like she needed to leave this fucking room. She took a step back to turn around, when the thing in the tank moved. The flesh rippled, looking like it was being blasted with sound waves. Maybe whatever was making the rumbling, which was getting louder, was affecting the creature?

From the rippling gray-green flesh, tiny spikes erupted, creating a vicious blanket of points. Asha felt like her bones were vibrating with how deep the rumbling was getting. It didn't even seem to be a sound anymore, just a vibration that rattled her skeleton and made her feel like vomiting. The bone deep feeling of there being no escape from this room crushed her lungs, wrapped around her windpipe, pressed against her eyeballs like the pressure in the room was suddenly not suitable for her.

"Mina, what is this?" It was difficult to get the words out. "Mina." The second time, the word snapped out of her mouth, her mind somehow reasserting itself over the terror crawling through her body.

Then the thing opened its eye.

Asha had assumed the creature's eye was open the whole time. Why would it be closed? But then, as if a shutter slid up, a luminescent white eye was revealed in stages. Like a tiny white star, there was no pupil, no iris, just brightness that somehow conveyed that it was staring straight at Asha.

The control she thought she'd regained spilled out of her like she was a glass swiped off a table, crashing to the ground. Her bones felt on the verge of turning to dust from whatever that sound, or vibration, was doing.

Moving backwards, Asha tripped over her feet, stumbling over the threshold and almost falling on her ass in the lab room. She caught herself on a cart with some sort of computer. Even though the thing had wheels, it was heavy enough to stop her from falling over.

A breath wheezed out of Asha, her mind racing, her arms still covered in goosebumps. She could still feel something crawling over her bones, burrowing into them, but the feeling faded the further she moved away from the room. A table met the backs of her legs and Asha sat down hard.

Mina followed, closing the door behind her and sealing away that awful monstrosity.

"That was not fucking *neat*, Mina. That was awful. What is that thing?" Even though Asha felt like she was gasping out the words, they sounded like knives being hurled at Mina. Never before had she felt that level of fear, and she had been plenty scared before.

A frown crossed Mina's face, scrunching her features together before they flared into panic. Mina's shoulders hunched, her eyes darting from side to side. "I didn't think anything would shake Ash Ketchum."

"Don't," Asha snapped. "How can you joke after that? That wasn't just anything. That was…that was terror incarnate. Throw that thing back out of the dry dock, set it on fire, I don't know." Swiping her hands back and forth in front of herself, it felt like Asha was trying to disperse any lingering bad feelings from that fish creature.

The Mordices.

Mordices Seventeen.

"Wait." Mina stopped moving across the room, heading toward the wall of doors. "You said that was Mordices Seventeen. Are there seventeen of those things in there?"

"Oh, no." Shaking her head, Mina kept walking toward the freezer doors, avoiding looking at Asha. "A bunch of them died in the tanks, before we figured out how to keep them. They don't like total darkness, which is weird considering where they live. Hence, the lights in the tanks. And they eat each other when they're too close, like I said before." She shrugged, moving past the cannibalism like it were normal. "Some of them have been euthanized so we can dissect them. I want to show you one of those. Don't worry, this one won't make that vibration."

Asha realized that the wall of doors was a freezer, just like the ones in a morgue that she'd thought about earlier. She swallowed hard.

"Is this the thing that triggered the message to the surface?" She needed to get back to her whole reason for coming here to begin with. Mostly, she wanted to get out of here with the least exposure to these fish as possible. Mina was crazy. She could stay here with the fish, but Asha wanted out. "Because if it's not, I don't want to see anything else."

"I'm sorry." Mina opened one of the freezer doors and rolled out a tray. She did sound sorry, but Asha didn't find any comfort in that. "I just want you to understand what it is we found, what the surface is interested in. When we entered what we found in our notes, we were notified that a message was being sent based on some keyword we entered. I'm not sure which one it was. Zane was going through our notes, but there's months of stuff to compare." A white sheet concealed something large under it on the tray. The edges of the sheet that hung down fluttered in the cool air filtering out of the freezer. Before interacting more with the tray, Mina put on a pair of nitrile gloves and a medical mask which suctioned to her face and released air through a tiny filter valve on the side. Mina handed Asha two boxes with the PPE, the instructions silent and obvious. Legs extended down from the tray and Mina rolled it over to the tables in the center of the room.

Asha pressed the mask against her face and held it for three seconds, the suction engaging as the air valve began to function. A tiny whirring came from the mask, a white noise that faded into the background within a few seconds.

"No more surprises?" Asha stepped towards the table, feeling a little wary, still aware of what floated in the tank in the other room.

"Oh, no, no, no." Apology saturated Mina's words. She was stuck between hunching her shoulders to match the apology and the spine straightening confidence that doing science gave her. Do not touch anything, though. We're still not sure how this thing moves or if it might attack." She didn't sound like she was joking.

Asha didn't get a chance to ask what she meant because Mina slid the sheet off. It made a dry swishing sound, like sand rushing over metal.

Although Asha had just seen the creature floating in a tank, the darkness prevented her from getting a truly good look at it beyond a patch of rippling flesh that grew spikes and its unsettling eye. Seeing it in the light was something else. It looked like it had skin, rather than scales, a smooth expanse of unbroken gray and green, like vegetables that went slimy and old. It stretched across the table, looking both deflated and lumpy. The two fins at the front looked like regular fish fins for a few inches, then split into long, finger like appendages. There were knuckle joints–could fish have knuckles? –spaced down the tendrils, making the odd appendages twist at weird angles. Further down the fish were another set of fins that looked much more fish like. A thick ridge jutted up from the fish's side and ran all the way down to a tail shaped like a whale's fluke.

Except, this 'fluke' had a pincer on the end of each lobe. The thing should be dead and dried up, especially after spending so much time in the freezer, yet there was a clear liquid dripping from each pincer. Some sort of venom?

Mina, chatty now that she was talking about something she loved, explained that she and Zane wore thicker, cowhide gloves to handle the fish. She pressed against the thing's side, drawing Asha's eyes away from the tail and to the needles punching out of the skin.

"Why does the tail do that?" Asha could feel a crack threatening to snap her voice. She regretted her curiosity, her desire to control everything going in and out of Kraken 7. Who cared if there were secret messages? Especially if they had anything to do with the fish on the table. Maybe ignorance was bliss and she was better off not knowing.

Making a questioning noise in her throat, Mina leaned towards the end of the table to observe the clear liquid dripping from the tail. "Oh, that's some sort of venom, at least from what our analyses have told us. Just don't touch it. Let's open this baby up for you to see the inside."

Asha's whispered repetition of "Inside?" went unnoticed by Mina who opened a drawer and pulled out a small silver colored stick, like the rod she had in the tank room.

Mina continued talking like she was doing a lecture. "We're not sure why its fins have all those knuckled joints or why they're so long. Maybe to grab food in the sand? Or lure other fish to it so it can grab them and bring them to its mouth?" Asha's question didn't make it out of her mouth. She didn't think she wanted to know more about the feeding habits of the fish. Shrugging, oblivious to Asha's paling face, Mina continued, "We haven't gotten a chance to see it feed yet. Oh, if you look up at the head, you can see the eye. It's much less spooky in the light because these lights wash out its natural bioluminescence which, weird enough, hasn't dimmed even though the thing is dead. Usually, bacteria causes bioluminescence, but there are no bacteria that we can find. If I turn the lights off, they still glow. Not sure why that is either. This thing is a real mystery." She sounded almost giddy about the monster.

The white eye was open, as Mina said. It still looked very much alive, set above a mouth that gaped open to show sharp teeth as thick as pencils. The Mordices' mouth was stuffed with them from the very tip of the thing's nose all the way back into the mouth. Asha imagined the teeth went into the thing's throat as well, mimicking some sort of demonic garbage disposal, like the terrifying robot shark from *James and the Giant Peach.* There were only three gill slits behind the mouth, and each one had a fringe that matched the knuckled tendrils of the front fins.

"Alright!" Mina's excitement startled Asha and she sucked in a breath. "Let's open this big girl up!" Adjusting her leather gloves, Mina reached over the fish and slotted her fingers into the belly Asha hadn't known was already cut open.

"Girl?" Asha cringed at the squelching noise the insides made as they were peeled apart, like hands sinking into a basket of rotten fruit and squeezing the guts out. As the sides of the fish separated, loose tendrils of pink meat stuck to either side, stretching until Mina pulled them apart with muted ticking sounds. The strands on the top half swung like pendulums until Mina wrestled it over and flopped it onto the table.

With a huffed breath, she said, "We don't actually know how to sex them yet. I'm just calling it a girl. At any rate, let me give you the tour." She gestured at the carcass on the table. "We didn't find anything in the stomach, at least what we think are the stomach and the intestines. And it looks like it has two hearts, but each heart only has one chamber."

Following along as Mina pointed out the different blobs of meat that were supposed to be organs, Asha was amazed that Mina and Zane could look at this mass of colors and identify what anything was. Nothing looked real, instead resembling wet, gummy-like objects that vaguely resembled what could be organs to Asha's untrained eyes. Something inside the fish shivered and Asha blinked, feeling her entire body tense up. Mina kept talking like an organ in a dead fish hadn't just moved, and Asha stared hard at the lump of blueish flesh near the tail end of the fish, swearing that she could see a tremble of movement, something that wasn't right.

"Up there, the brain, it looks like the lobes are all separated from each other, connected by a single strand of nerve tissue. I wish we could get in there on one of the live ones, but every time we put knife to skin, the things flatline. Just up and die. Don't know why."

It took an effort to draw her eyes away from the quivering flesh that Asha was still convinced she saw, but she managed to drag them up the body and looked at Mina. "I would up and die, too, if someone tried to stick a knife in me." What was supposed to be funny lacked the right tone and pitch, instead taking on an almost accusatory tone. Mina looked up, meeting Ashas eyes. Before she could respond, Asha ran on with her words. "What was it that you saw that you think triggered that message?"

Mina blinked, like she was resetting. "Ah, hmm, right. That's why you're here." Shooting Asha a nervous smile, she lifted the small, silver colored stick. "We just need to poke around a little," Mina mumbled. Asha didn't respond, flicking her eyes toward the tail end of the fish. What the hell was in there?

Pressing the tip of the stick into some faded orange organ near the front of the fish, Asha watched as the organ started to twitch, just like the meat in the tail.

"What are you poking at?" Asha asked the questioned, then repeated it as the organ's vibrations intensified. "What are you poking at, Mina?"

White, worm-like tendrils exploded out of the organ. Hair-like, they whipped around, some reaching in the direction in which Mina had withdrawn. Asha yelped, jumping away from the table and knocking over a tray of medical instruments behind her. Attracted by the sound, the white hairs redirected their writhing in her direction. Asha's knees folded under her and she fell to the floor, pain shooting up her tailbone.

"Asha!" Mina stepped around the table without looking away from the fish. "Are you okay? It's fine, they don't leave the fish, it's okay."

"What the fuck are they? They're in the tail, too!" Asha pushed herself back, scooting away on her butt.

Mina blinked, glancing at Asha before focusing back on the fish. "The tail?"

"Yeah, some blue organ. It was moving." Asha stopped backing away when Mina moved to the tail end. What if something different was in the tail? What if it grabbed Mina? Lurching to her knees, Asha barked, "Mina, wait!"

The scientist didn't stop. She glanced at the tendrils which were settling down, withdrawing back into the fish, and then placed the stick into the fish, on what Asha assumed was the organ she mentioned. Drawing her hand back, Mina stared down at the fish.

Nothing happened. No white worms, no shocked face from Mina. The scientist looked up at Asha with a quirked eyebrow. "There's nothing here. Are you sure you saw it moving?"

Getting to her feet, Asha inched towards Mina and the table. "That one? You poked that one?" She gestured at the organ that caught her eye earlier. It was as still as a dead organ should be.

"Yeah, Ash Ketchum. That one. Nerves getting the best of you?" Mina gave her the smallest smirk, to which Asha snorted in response.

"You said no more surprises. I'm over this. Put the Mordices away and give me a copy of the notes." Her words were more demand than request. Asha wanted to get the hell out of the science wing of the hab. She didn't care about the fish, or the science. None of that stuff was her business. Letting Mina distract her with sea life was a mistake.

Behind her, the lab door slid open. Looking over her shoulder, Asha clocked Zane coming in, tumbler in hand with steam rising from the top.

"What're you doing down here, oh mighty comms officer?" Looking like he was on his third tumbler of coffee, Zane looked away from Asha and spotted Mina closing up the fish. "What is that thing doing out of the freezer?" A tremor of fear laced his words.

"Asha wanted to see it." Asha whipped her head from Zane to Mina at the lie. "I'm sorry." Mina whisked the sheet over the fish and maneuvered the tray it was laying on back onto a wheeled gurney.

"The actual reason that I'm here," Asha cut in, "is because I wanted to see your lab notes. Mina wanted to do show-and-tell." Asha wouldn't outright call Mina a liar, but she wasn't going to let her slide, either.

Zane wasn't listening. He stomped over to a wall full of drawers, neck tattoos stretched tight over the taut tendons of his neck. Ripping some of the drawers open, Zane grabbed spray bottles and wipes. "That thing is supposed to be quarantined, Mina." He pinched the bridge of his nose, squeezing his eyes shut. After a sigh, he snapped on a pair of gloves and pressed a mask to his face. "At least you have your PPE on. Please, just, just put it the fuck away. Asha, go stand against a wall." Never had Asha heard such a commanding tone in his voice. Zane only looked like a badass because of the stereotypes associated with bold black neck and arm tattoos. In reality, the man rarely raised his voice, and made even fewer commands.

Asha was unfamiliar with this version of Zane.

“Yeah, sure. I just want to see your notes from when you found that…those worms, things, whatever they are.” She wasn’t about to argue when all she wanted to do was get the information and leave. Asha backed up against the wall while Mina swung the freezer door shut and Zane sprayed down the table. Whatever the liquid was, it sizzled when it landed on the metal. Some sort of acid? Maybe she should have paid more attention in chemistry class, or biology, or whatever it would have been that would have helped her understand what was happening here.

From near the freezer, Mina kept apologizing. “I know it’s under quarantine, but it’s not like she touched it, and we were wearing PPE like you said. I know how to do my job.” The words lacked any bite, too saturated with apology. Zane kept on spraying and wiping the table. Then he grabbed another bottle, and sprayed an aerosol over everything the fish had been near. He walked an ever-widening circle away from the table, continuing to spray. “We know it’s not airborne, Zane. You’re overacting.”

Zane whipped his head towards Mina, and even though Asha couldn’t see his mouth, she could tell by his clenched jaw he wanted to say something. Instead, a tic made his jaw twitch and he shook his head, continuing to spray the aerosol. The tension between them was squashing down the fear that was still gurgling in Asha’s gut.

“Um, airborne?” Neither of the scientists reacted to her question, Zane too busy cleaning and Mina watching him. Asha tried a different question as she inched towards the door that would lead her back out to the hallway. "So, about those notes you wrote? The ones that triggered the message?"

Mina went to one of the consoles, looking grateful to have something to do other than apologize, and navigated through some screens.

Zane stopped spraying the air. "Don't say anything about this to Benson. No one else on the crew is supposed to know about the…things in the fish. It was only supposed to go to the surface and Benson." He shot a frown at Mina.

Asha felt a little bit of her old self return with the indignation in her tone. "Why shouldn't we all know about this thing that is supposed to be quarantined but is just chilling out in a freezer?"

"Pun intended?" Mina sounded more nervous than she should have if she was making jokes. She held out a small disc to Asha.

"None of this is funny, Meens. It's actually pretty messed up. Why shouldn't everyone know? We live down here with these things. Keaner goes out with Zane on deep walks." Asha shook her head and grabbed the disc. "Does Keaner know what these things are?" Mina turned her shoulders in and her chin down.

"Yeah, but I didn't tell him. It's not like I told everyone," Mina mumbled.

"You *should* tell everyone," Asha countered. "Fuck the surfacers. It's just us down here."

Zane stopped cleaning and went to stand next to Mina. He didn't look about to budge, despite the irritation brimming around him.

"Who's got your back at the end of the day?" Asha demanded.

“Look.” Zane’s jaw twitched. Before he could continue, Asha cut in.

“Who’s got your back?” she repeated.

Zane shook his head. “Mina put everything you asked for on the disc. Just don’t say anything. I’m sure Perisdo will bring everyone up to speed.” Asha cut her eyes at Zane, curling her lip.

“Perisdo.” The name was a curse coming out of her mouth.

Zane narrowed his eyes in return, his fingers fluttering around his waist as though looking for something to do. “There’s a lot information in there.”

Even though it sounded like there was an extra meaning in those last words, Asha decided to ignore it for now. “I’ll see you kids at the meeting with the surfacers. I don’t ever want to see that fish thing again.”

Zane

"You doing okay there, buddy?"

Keaner leaned into Zane's field of vision, and Zane tried to unclench his jaw. After all the aggravation from earlier, he still needed to go out on this damned deep walk. An Ativan or four would fix him up.

"Yeah, everything's fine."

Everything was not fine. Mina was breaking the quarantine procedures they'd agreed on, and gone and shown Asha the fish. Even though Kraken 7 didn't have any quarantine procedures he could find, that didn't excuse Mina's carelessness. There were still basic scientific principles for handling new biological samples to follow. It wasn't brain surgery. Maybe he should have gone to Asha about the fish, instead of trusting Mina to keep it quiet. He had no doubt Asha could have found a quarantine procedure, or at least made one up that maybe Mina would follow.

With Zane's help, of course. Asha wasn't a scientist, after all.

"I'm just asking because you're slamming things around a little more than usual." Keaner paused, and touched a finger to his temple, twisting his face in thought. "Actually, you never slam things. You're always super careful. So, ya know. Just making sure you're good for this deep walk because it's not like we could both die out there or anything."

Zane breathed out a heavy sigh so that he wouldn't growl out his frustrations. "Everything's fine. Let's get this done." Picking up his helmet, he brought it over his head and tightened it down. His faux hawk provided padding on top that kept the helmet from pressing too hard against his skull. The mechanisms that locked it in place hissed, and he felt the cool flow of oxygen waft over his face. He tried to modulate his breathing so he wouldn't waste oxygen, but his anger was making all of his bodily systems work too fast.

"Second or third trap today?" Keaner moved behind Zane to check the readings on his suit, then turned around for Zane to do the same for him.

"Just the second today. I need to go over a few things with Mina before the topsiders get down here." Zane patted Keaner's shoulder, letting him know that he was good to go. Going to the second trap would also enable him to get back faster and take an Ativan. He wasn't quite jonesing, not yet, but he wanted to relax. If he could get his brain to stop running in circles for a few hours, he could refocus on what he needed to do with the Mordices and Mina.

"Boooo. Boring." Keaner pulled the lever that allowed water to flow into the dry dock and equalize the pressure with the outside. Zane always thought this was the worst part: waiting. He knew, of course, that he would breathe in the suit. It didn't make watching the rise of water close over his helmet any less disconcerting.

Trying to keep his voice light, as if he were making a joke, Zane retorted, "Some of us have actual work to do." His tone didn't sound like he was joking at all.

Shrugging, like Zane's tone didn't bother him in the least, Keaner quipped, "No rest for the wicked, eh?"

The water rose over their heads and Zane didn't bother to respond. Keaner would just keep going if he said anything back, and he didn't feel much like talking.

In front of him, the dry dock door slid open, revealing the deep dark of the ocean. Zane didn't think he'd ever get used to the vastness, the fact that they were steeping out into areas that were less well understood, and less explored, than space. On one hand, it seemed crazy to him that their own planet still required so much exploring. Then, on the other, it was obvious why so little of the ocean was explored. It was difficult to get to, difficult to survive in, and no one could see it. Every night, people could look up at the sky and see the moon or stars or far away planets and stare at them in awe and wonder. No one saw the bottom of the ocean on a regular basis.

Unless one of those someones was a member of a Kraken crew, living every day at the unseen ocean bottom.

"You oriented?" Zane asked.

"Like a compass," Keaner reported back. It was hard not to roll his eyes, but at least Keaner was looking forward, heading out into the darkness. Flicking on his headlamp allowed Zane to keep his partner in his view, pressing back against the black that threatened to engulf them.

The first trap wasn't too far off from the hab. The traps were baited with chunks of meat from smaller fish to lure in...well, anything they could catch. Searching for new life forms was one of the science officer directives, and something Zane hadn't thought would be too difficult. With such a small percentage of the ocean floor mapped, and so little known about it, there had to be dozens of new species down here. New species were found all the time in the Amazon and other places that humans didn't frequent that much. So, when he and Keaner continually pulled in familiar creature after familiar creature, Zane thought they'd never find anything other than squids, anglerfish, and snails.

Then they'd pulled in the first Mordices.

As a lifelong animal advocate and conservationist, Zane liked to think he loved all animals. Even the termites and carpenter bees that chewed up houses, or the candiru, the little parasitic fish that would swim up men's penises. Zane thought something like that might be the worst nightmare he would face, should he ever decide to spend time where those fish lived.

But then they'd pulled in the spikey, knuckly, grumbly, Mordices. Funny, how perspectives change with new information.

The first trap came into view, floating on a chain anchored into the sea floor. Zane could tell by the way that it floated that it was empty. Mordices were not cooperative house guests in the traps, and oftentimes Keaner and Zane had to struggle with the trap just to bring it in.

Movement at his peripheral caught his attention. Zane tried to turn quickly toward the movement to catch whatever it was, but the stiff suit made it difficult to move. All he caught was a swirl of sediment that may or may not have just been the result of regular ocean currents and eddies.

"Nothing," Keaner grumbled, his disappointment as crushing as an ocean wave. He really lived for pulling things out of the traps, always excited for anything no matter how many times they had already seen it.

Zane stepped past him. "Let's move on to the next one, then." He wanted this day to be over. He wanted the visit from the topsiders to be over. Mostly, he wanted to go to bed and not have to think about the stress tomorrow was going to bring. Bringing other people into their closed ecosystem, as he sometimes referred to the hab, seemed like a terrible idea. It took a certain kind of person to work down here for months at a time, and Zane doubted the topsiders had any of the personality quirks that would allow them to be here comfortably even for a week.

At the edge of sphere of light from his headlamp, Zane thought he saw something large swish through the water. There one second, gone another. He stopped moving, squinting into the dark.

Keaner bumped into him and made an exaggerated sound of surprise. "Woah! You see something?"

Were those lights? Floating out there beyond the reach of his headlamp? No, no way. There were so many, at least eight hovering in the darkness. He blinked, and just like that swish of movement, the lights were gone.

If they were even there to begin with.

"I'm not really sure," he admitted. "It's probably just my eyes playing tricks on me." Zane shivered in his suit, a drop of sweat tickling his cheek.

Keaner made a weird warbling sound. "Oooooo, spooky! Don't go into the light!"

"What?" Zane stared straight ahead as he walked, resisting the urge to look at Keaner.

"I'm just saying, not all lights are good lights. You definitely don't want to be staring down a train light."

Zane checked their orientation towards the second trap on his forearm display. They were almost there. And then they could turn around and be done with this whole deep walk. Maybe be done with deep walks for the rest of the week while the topsiders were down.

Being out in the water never bothered Zane, but there was something about the darkness today that was menacing. Like something just couldn't wait to get its claws into him.

"What's that?" Zane stopped again, motion off to his side capturing his attention.

"That's the second trap." Keaner's initial joy petered off into disappointment. It must look empty, but Zane was staring off in the opposite direction of the trap.

At the lights.

"Do you see those?" There was a tremor in his whispered words. Zane lifted a hand and pointed at the series of lights that spanned a small space in the darkness. Or it could be a vast space. It was impossible to tell the size of anything down here unless there was something nearby for size comparison. There was something out there.

Sediment swirled next to Zane as Keaner came up next to him. "See what?" Zane jerked his hand at the lights which looked to be swaying, like they were on something that was walking.

Getting closer to them.

Zane took a step back, itching to turn and run. "You don't see those? They're right *there.*"

"Sorry, buddy, all I see is the darkness."

The lights winked out. Zane took another step back, not trusting his eyes and not trusting the ocean. Maybe there was a good reason people spent more time in space than they did down here that had nothing to do with the visibility of cool shit.

"Let's just go back." He didn't wait for an answer before turning back to the hab, checking his direction on his forearm readout.

"You sure? We could go find your ooky wooky spooky lights." Keaner made his weird warbling noise again.

"No." Zane left it at that. He didn't want to get into a fight with Keaner. He wanted to get back to the hab and read over the notes from the other hab's science officers. There hadn't been anything in there about Moridces type fish the last four times he read through them, but that didn't mean he couldn't have missed something.

"Killjoy." Keaner sounded dejected.

Zane didn't care. The return trip to the dry dock felt like it took significantly more time than their initial trip out. No lights popped up when he looked around, but there was a lot more movement at the outer edges of the sphere of light. More than could be chalked up to ocean currents.

He didn't like to think that something was following them, stalking them, but it wasn't until he was back in the dry dock with his helmet off that he felt he could unclench his asshole and breath normal again.

Divya

Crew dinners weren't mandatory in the written rules of Kraken 7, but there was a certain amount of side-eyeing that went along with missing them. So, although Divya would have preferred to go hungry and stay in her room rather than be in the mess hall with the crew, here she was, sitting in her usual spot. Carlos sat to her left, and the spot to her right, which Mina usually occupied, was empty. Instead, Mina was sitting at an angle to Divya that forced her to turn her head every time she wanted to glare at her.

Which Divya took every opportunity to do. Thoughts of the fish creature and the worms Mina talked about swam just beneath the surface of her brain almost constantly. The fact that she knew these things, and no one else on the crew did ate at her. Unless Mina blabbed to someone else, which was possible. It all gave Divya an uneasy feeling that didn't quite settle anywhere in her body, but rather felt like an overall malaise. She wasn't sure what to do, and it wasn't time for phone calls to the surface so she couldn't even reach her parents for their suggestions.

Not that she'd tell them about the…Modims? Modicines? She couldn't quite remember the name, plagued instead with swirls of sharp teeth filling her mind. But they usually had good advice, and maybe getting a view of home would help her to center herself in a way the gym hadn't been able to.

"Is everything prepared for tomorrow?" Benson shoved a forkful of soy sauce-soaked noodles into his mouth, slurping them. Divya's eye twitched and she tried to focus on her own meal of sweet potato and chickpea curry. She had noticed Carlos kept looking at her food like he wanted to stick his fork in it for a bite. She didn't understand why, since he'd made his own meal: stuffed peppers with chicken. If he tried to get any of her food, she was going to stab him with her spoon.

There was an extended emptiness where no one said anything and it was just mouth noises and the clink of cutlery against plates. Benson tried to make every group gathering a work meeting and couldn't take the hint that people wanted to eat, and sometimes not do work. He stared at each of them in turn, trying to make eye contact to force a conversation.

"Yeah, everything should be in order." Carlos broke the silence, setting down his fork and wiping his mouth with his napkin.

"With any luck, it'll all go well," Asha added, rolling her eyes. "Can't have anything out of place for the precious toppers."

Benson had just shoved another load of noodles in his mouth, preventing him from admonishing Asha. Divya would bet that Asha perfectly timed that. For all the Comms Officer talked about following rules and orders and whatever, she sure knew how to stick it to upper management when she wanted to. Secretly, Divya loved it. She admired Asha in the moments she wasn't hounding Divya to complete her security trainings.

Zane scraped the bottom of his bowl, and after coming up with nothing, set it on the table. He, also, did not have a bowl of noodles. Instead of eating what Keaner prepared, he'd made oatmeal. Plain oatmeal with nothing on it. Fucking weird.

Folding his hands behind his bowl, Zane said, "I would just like to say again that I think this is a bad idea and they should just not come down."

"Again?" Asha arched an eyebrow at him, asking the question before Divya could.

"He mentioned it to me in the lab." Mina's quiet voice managed to carry to all of them.

"Anything else in the lab you'd like to share with us?" Divya shoved her spoon into her curry with more force than necessary, scraping the bottom of the bowl. She contained her wince before it made it to her face, instead spreading out through her body and tensing her muscles.

Mina and Zane jerked their heads in her direction. Asha did, too, though Divya wasn't sure why. Did she know something?

"I have the rest of everyone's dinner!" Keaner came in with a tray of eggrolls to go along with the chicken teriyaki and noodles he'd made. His sing-song voice cut through the silence like a cleaver, yet he didn't make things any less awkward.

He deposited two egg rolls on everyone's plates except for Zane, Divya, and Carlos. They preferred to make their own meals to fit their own food preferences. At least, that's the excuse everyone assumed Divya would make. She just didn't want someone else's grimy hands on her food.

"Is Zane being a Davey Downer again?"

Benson swallowed and asked, "Is everything alright, Science Officer Marsh?"

Goddamn, Divya hated how formal Benson was.

"He got a little spooked on the deep walk, that's all." Keaner shrugged, examined an egg roll, and shoved the whole thing in his mouth.

Zane slid his hands off the table and Divya narrowed her eyes at him. "What happened?"

"Nothing," he said from between clenched teeth. "There was a lot of sediment being kicked around, and I just thought there was something out there with us. It's not a big deal."

"There are a lot of things floating around out there," Mina said with a half-hearted laugh. It drowned in the edginess that crept around the table. Divya narrowed her eyes at Mina. She would know better than anyone there were things out in the water.

"You're not experiencing Ocean Dark Syndrome are you, Science Officer Marsh?" Benson's question made everyone pause and glance around at each other.

"Why would you even put those words out there?" Divya snapped, trying to quell the icy feeling she felt at the mention of the Syndrome. At the bottom of the ocean, people avoided talking about Ocean Dark Syndrome the same way first responders never wished a "quiet shift" on someone: bad things happened when it was brought up. She looked at Zane, trying to gauge his response. He was staring at his hands, a muscle in his jaw twitching.

Benson rolled his eyes and stood up from the table, lifting his plate with him. "Silly superstitions will get you nowhere. Science Officer Marsh, if you're experiencing any Ocean Dark Symptoms you are to report them immediately to me. Is that understood?"

Zane kept his eyes averted, looking like he was disassociating from being here. Not that Divya could blame him. People who got the Syndrome put entire crews at risk with their erratic behavior: opening dry dock doors without properly sealing hab entrances; destroying food stores; interrupting system updates so the clocks and machinery ran off schedule. Divya thought she could remember a story of some dude urinating in the potable water. Repeatedly. There was something about living at the bottom of the ocean without real sunlight, with the risk of death all around you, that did something to a person. No one wanted to talk about Ocean Dark Syndrome because it was almost always a one-way ticket to isolation until a ride to the surface was available.

"Science Officer Marsh." Benson's voice grated at Divya and she wanted to hurl her bowl at him. "Do you understand?" He enunciated each word, leaning closer to Zane with every syllable.

"Aye aye, Benson." Zane closed his eyes, walling himself off from Benson who sniffed at Zane's use of his name, and the rest of them. Zane muttered something that sounded like he was praying: "I shall fear no evil."

Divya didn't think he had Ocean Dark Syndrome. Zane was being himself, even if that might seem weird or suspicious to the others. She was kind of worried, though, about what he thought he'd seen, or actually seen, out there on his deep walk.

Getting up from his seat, Keaner wrapped an arm around Zane. "No worries boss man. I'll keep an eye on Zane here."

Divya stood up from the table in Benson's wake, her meal half eaten. Mina startled, as if she expected Divya to attack her.

"Family dinner's been great, everyone." She put on her fakest smile that made Carlos shake his head at her before sensing an opportunity to dip his fork into her abandoned food. "Can't wait to do it with a bunch of strangers tomorrow."

DAY
THREE

Carlos

It wasn't every day that toppers came down to visit Kraken 7. Hell, it wasn't even yearly. In the eight years since he was hired, Carlos had never seen anyone from upper management beyond his initial interview. Yet, on the other side of this pneumatic door, there was Saul Perisdo and four other men who held a stake in Amphitrite. They were all waiting, with great impatience, for Carlos and Divya to figure out why the door wasn't working and they were stuck in the dry dock. One of the men kept complaining that he needed to use the bathroom, to the great concern of everyone stuck in there with him.

Carlos didn't want to be the one to say, "I told you so", but, sometimes rich management types needed to be more respectful of the people and things they assumed were around just to work for them. People could be cajoled and threatened. But machinery? That couldn't be threatened. It just did what it was programmed to do so long as everything was in order.

This door and its machinery today? Extremely *not* in order.

"We went over all of this yesterday," Divya snapped. "How the hell could it have broken in the past few hours?" She chucked something heavy into the tool bag.

Not knowing the answer, and happy he couldn't see what Divya was throwing, Carlos peered at the innards of a control panel. He couldn't find a single thing wrong with any of the wiring, connections, or mechanics. There was also nothing wrong with any of the other panels he and Divya had opened up around the dry dock. Sighing, Carlos leaned an elbow against the wall and rubbed his earlobe between his thumb and forefinger. He missed having an earring to toy with, but seeing enough people get fried over an errant necklace or ill-placed hand with a ring on it made him wary of wearing any sort of jewelry, ever. No need to chance forgetting he was wearing it, and then *ZAP*. No more worries, at least, but no more being alive, either.

"I think you jinxed these guys," he muttered. Divya, holding a small diagnostic device that was coming up with nothing, glared at him. "Saying they were going to get stuck in tiny purgatory," he clarified.

Snorting, Divya suggested, "Maybe the cosmic karmic forces decided they deserved it." At Carlos' sour look, she shrugged. "Or maybe it's a software problem. I mean, Asha seemed pretty pissed, too, that they were coming down unannounced."

"Mmmmm." Carlos hummed, mulling it over. That wasn't a bad suggestion. Divya might be difficult to work with, but she was great at solving problems. He dropped his voice to a whisper and agreed. "You're probably right, but let's not broadcast that for everyone in there." Divya gave him a sullen look, her mouth turning down and her eyes just short of rolling into her skull. But, she nodded. Grinning as though Divya was the most good-natured employee he ever worked with, Carlos proclaimed, "I'm going to go check with Asha about any potential issues with internet connections." He hoped none of the people in the dry dock were experienced enough with the hab to know he was bullshitting. "Why don't you check the panel in the ceiling?"

There was no panel for the dry dock in the ceiling. In an emergency, it would have made things that much more difficult if one of them had to climb a ladder and crawl around in the ceiling. Same thing went for the floor. Only air vents and other HVAC components were under their feet. Crawling around anywhere was a no go. Everything they needed should have been in one of these panels around the dry dock door.

Unless it was a software issue.

Divya opened her mouth to make a smartass response until Carlos winked at her and cranked his thumb down the hall. She mouthed *I get it*, and then out loud replied, "Yeah, I'll get right on it, boss. Hit the radio when you need me to come back." Skipping down the hallway, Divya didn't even turn around when someone started banging on the dry dock door.

"When are we getting out of here?!" It was another of the toppers, his red face taking up most of the window in the door. Crowded around him were the other three men, their faces contorted into angry expressions. The only one not freaking out was Saul Perisdo who was sitting on one of the built-in wall seats meant for assisting with removing deep walk suits. The whole time he'd gazed through the small window in the dry dock door, a disconcerting presence. Carlos wasn't sure what the man's deal was, but knew most of the toppers made it a point to avoid interacting with him. He guessed they'd find out soon enough what Perisdo was all about.

Rapping his knuckles on the glass, Carlos shouted to be heard through the door. "Give us another thirty minutes. We're working as fast as we can, but the short notice has affected some of our maintenance schedules. I'll be right back." As an afterthought he added, "We apologize for the inconvenience." Carlos turned away from the window so they couldn't see his smirk, not really sorry at all.

It wasn't a long walk to the comms office, and Carlos kept his steps quick. The longer it took them to fix this, the more likely Benson would come by to investigate and make things harder by inserting his useless two cents. He was an okay supervisor, but Carlos didn't appreciate someone who liked to micromanage when they didn't know what they were talking about.

One of the cleaner bots chugged across the hallway, spitting out cleaning solution, frothing it up, and sucking the whole concoction back in to be sanitized and used again. All the lights on the little guy were green, and Carlos gave it a pat like it was doing a great job.

Carlos entered Asha's office without knocking, and she looked up from the book she was reading with her eyes narrowed. The cover of the book made him think of one of those cheesy romances that never went out of style. Everyone could always do with a happy ending, and he couldn't begrudge people that, but could they make the characters less...dumb? He knew there was a required element of ridiculousness to the books, but... Carlos shook his head, his mind way off track from why he was here. Asha was looking at him expectantly, her book still covering half her face like she was expecting this to be a quick interaction.

"The dry dock door is stuck." He raised an eyebrow at her.

"Oh?" She still didn't lower her book and he had a feeling it was because it hid her smirk. "That's unfortunate."

"Asha," Carlos groaned. "C'mon, woman. They've been stuck in there for over an hour now. Haven't they suffered enough?"

Lowering the book, Asha pursed her lips, trying to stop the twitching at the corner of her mouth. "What makes you think I've got anything to do with that?"

With a sigh, Carlos dropped into the chair opposite her and kicked his boots up onto the desk. Crossing his arms behind his head, he leaned back. "Because between me and Div, we can fix anything in the hab just short of the thing imploding. Fixing a dry dock door, *if* the issue is mechanical or electronic, should be a cake walk for us. And yet."

Asha squeezed her lips together tighter to suppress her smirk. He knew she couldn't keep anything from him for long. They spent too much time together down here, and they actually enjoyed each other's company. All he had to do was wait her out just a little longer.

"And yet." Asha added nothing to those two syllables. She put a bookmark in her book and put it on her desk. Carlos locked onto her blue eyes and refused to blink. There was no fanfare when Asha finally decided to act; no heavy sigh or eye roll or conciliatory words. She just turned towards her monitors, typed some things on the keys, and said, "They're free now."

Carlos grinned. “Never doubted you for a second. And, of course, I’ll tell the toppers it was those damn cycling timers that did them in. If they had come down on an approved time schedule, they would already have access to the whole hab.” Asha returned his grin with a conspiratorial one of her own. She reached for her book and paused, looking thoughtful. Carlos again waited, knowing he couldn’t rush Asha and also knowing he was in no rush to get back to the toppers.

“If I show you something, you can’t tell anyone.” She looked him dead in the eyes, so serious he wondered if she was about to tell him that she’d opened the wrong door to the dry dock and drowned everyone. Not that he thought she was capable of murder, or of making an mistake that huge, but he didn’t like the way she looked at him.

“You know you can always count on me.” Even if she had drowned them, Carlos would back her. They were the two longest running beneathers on this team and they would always put each other first. The only person who had spent more time underwater was Keaner, but he had been with a different hab in the Atlantic as far as Carlos knew.

While Asha appraised Carlos, he knew she wasn’t still questioning his trustworthiness; she was just trying to make it seem like she was. It was easy to see how she kept most people at arm’s length, and sometimes she even attempted to do that with him. Carlos liked to think his charming personality was what won her over in the end, but it was probably his consistency and predictability. Asha liked things to be in order.

Without any change in her facial expression, Asha waved him over and turned towards her computer monitors. Carlos dropped his boots to the ground with a *thud* and rolled his chair over, flicking his eyes across the monitors as she woke up three of the eight.

"I mean it," Asha warned, though the threat was half-hearted. She navigated into some windows, typed some words, opened some more windows and entered more words. Finally, documents opened up on the screen. "I got this from Mina and Zane, but I don't think they realized how much information was actually in the files they gave me. Zane might've, but I don't really know." Irritation flavored her words, giving them just enough bite without being directed at him.

Carlos couldn't blame her for being aggravated. If someone were messing around with the mechanics of the hab, moving electrical components around, or hiding things in the conduits, he'd be pissed, too. Those things were supposed to be touched only by him and Divya, and neither of them liked surprises in their work. Consistency and predictability kept the hab running at its optimum. Anything else put people in danger, and it seemed like some of the crew–or maybe it was just Benson and the surfacers–who didn't realize how delicate that balance was.

"You got all this from Mina and Zane?" His eyes roved over the screens, not sure what he was looking at. There was a lot of information, a lot of words, and it was difficult for him to process all of it, especially when Asha was changing the screens so fast. "Can you slow down?"

"I'm going to explain it, don't worry." A gentleness covered Asha's tone and she glanced at him, her smile soft.

"Then get on with it." His words were clipped with a sudden edge. Asha knew about his difficulty with words, even though he worked hard to hide it from everyone. Somehow, she figured it out, but she wouldn't tell him how. When she did mention it, or allude to it, Carlos became defensive even though she never spoke about it in a judgmental way. It was just hard not to hear the disparaging remarks from past people, rising up from the black hole of bad things in the back of his mind. "Please." The add on was no less clipped, but at least it was a polite word.

Asha pointed at one screen. "Okay, so." She paused, and Carlos studied her face instead of the screen. It looked like she was struggling with something, her mouth turning down before flattening into a straight line. Goosebumps broke out over her skin and Carlos shivered himself, even though there was no discernable temperature change in the room. Whatever the science geeks were doing, he already didn't like it.

"Okay, so." She repeated herself, took a breath, and continued. "I went with Mina to the lab to get her notes so that I could look for what triggered the message to the surface myself. In typical Mina fashion, she wanted to show me stuff rather than just give me the notes, so she brought this fish thing out." Carlos turned to the screen she was pointing at. An ugly gray green fish with long, knuckled fingers coming from the front fins and a pointy pincer tail was laid out on a shiny steel table. An open white eye stared up, and Carlos felt like the thing was still alive and could see him through the screen. A pit grew in his stomach and out crawled a creeping sense of dread. Carlos' body tensed up, like he was preparing to be attacked.

"What is that thing?" He kept the quiver that threatened to wobble his words out of his voice. "That is some deep-sea monstrosity if I ever saw one." He tried to laugh and it came out watery and thin.

"They call it a Mordices but they don't really know what it is. Nothing like it apparently. According to the notes Zane wrote, some DNA sequencing place on the surface is supposed to be running samples to see if it matches anything else discovered and known to the science community, but so far there's nothing." Asha glanced at him, then clicked another file that opened up a video. "Weird thing is, the sequencing place? It's owned by Amphitrite, but we don't have access to any of the test results. You'd think they would be more open about sharing their findings, since we're the ones actually down here. But even Zane and Mina's credentials are blocked from their files."

"And they…wait. Did you try to use their credentials to get into secure databases?" Asha gave him a look that told him he better keep his mouth shut. Carlos groaned and rubbed a hand down his face. "What happened to following the rules?"

Asha snorted. "I follow rules when everyone else does. No one seems to care, and I want answers."

"You're a menace." Asha turned away, mumbling something he didn't catch. Deciding to ignore whatever it was she'd said, he asked, "And they found these things, these Mordices, down here? Around the hab? Is that what Zane thought he saw on the deep walk yesterday?"

"I guess? After this, I'd bet there could be anything out there. We have no idea what's beyond these walls. None at all."

Carlos shuddered, thinking about the couple of deep walks he'd been on, unaware of what lurked in the darkness, what could have chomped right into him and made him a permanent resident of the sea floor.

"It looks like they were trying to find something specific, but I'm not sure if this was it?" Asha's voice tilted up at the end, punctuating her remark as a question. "The notes are really unclear. It's like they were told to find some specific life form, but they weren't given a good description of what it was. There's also some random handwritten notes scanned in, but the handwriting is so awful I'm having a hard time figuring out what the hell it says." Carlos knew he would be no help with that and didn't say anything. "When they found this fish, and sent a sample to the surface, they were told to continue investigating it, even without knowing what it is they're dealing with. Then there's this." Asha played a video that showed a dark room and a tank housing the fish. Carlos watched as spikes were coaxed from the creature's skin, and then a rumbling began.

Carlos couldn't think of a time when he was ever truly scared for his life. He counted himself among the extremely blessed and lucky who didn't have a number of traumatic incidents in his life to give him strength or a comedically dark sense of humor. The worst thing he could think of was when his daughter was having febrile seizures and the terror he and her mom felt when it looked like she stopped breathing. But that wasn't something he felt he still carried.

This rumbling, though. It made him feel stuck without an escape; as if nothing would ever be right again. The sound burrowed into his bones and made them ache.

In a sudden, spastic movement, Carlos lurched for Asha's mouse and stopped the video. His breathing felt wrong, like a band was constricting around his chest even though the video was stopped.

"Yeah. That." Asha was pale, sweat beading along her forehead. "It's worse when you're in the room with it." Carlos' face blanched and he struggled to voice some words. "Mina thought it would be good for me to see all this in person. All I wanted were some notes. It gets worse, though."

Somehow, even more color left Carlos' face. Freckles that were normally difficult to see on his dark skin became more prominent across his nose. "How?" She must be exaggerating. How could it get worse than a fish that made a sound as terrifying as an Aztec death whistle?

Asha didn't bother to explain. She just played the next video.

A top-down view of the fish creature on the table was displayed, and no time was wasted before one of the scientists started to cut into the thing with a scalpel. Zane was narrating an explanation over the video. As the fish was opened up, white, worm-like tendrils shot out, flailing around like they were in search of something. The sudden motion startled Carlos and he shoved himself away from the desk, nearly toppling over in the rolling chair.

Carlos wasn't at Kraken 7 for the science. Science was not his area of expertise, and prior to these videos, he hadn't even been sure what Mina and Zane were meant to be doing. Of course, no one sent anyone down to the bottom of the ocean and spent billions of dollars for them to be down there for nothing. He knew there must be some purpose for this venture beyond them living seven miles underwater and keeping the hab in working and hospitable conditions for its occupants. Exposure to this horror movie fish, though? That was not in his job description.

"What the fuck does Amphitrite want with these?"

"It has something to do with those worms." The video was no longer on the screen, but Asha shuddered anyway. "Mina showed them to me, in person. She opened up that fish and prodded the worms out. Zane about lost his mind when he found out, saying the fish should've been quarantined."

Nausea roiled in his gut. "Quarantined? Does Benson know?"

Asha cut him a scathing look and shut down the folder of files.

"Of course he knows. He defended the secrecy in our meeting and I'd bet he knows a lot more about what they're looking for down here than he's letting on. You know what the keyword was that triggered the message to the surface? The one from Mina and Zane's notes?" Asha leaned towards him, the sudden pivot in conversation catching Carlos off guard. He didn't even get a word out before she said, "Zane and Mina don't know, they couldn't figure it out. But I tracked programming in their documents and the word was 'worms'. That's what triggered it. Someone up there is very interested in these worm things down here."

None of this quieted his nausea. "Are they like, parasitic worms? Or just…worm worms? And they're growing out of the fish because it's dead?" Carlos may not be a science guy, but he had watched enough random online videos late at night to have come across the morbid ones about death and decomposition. Even though he didn't linger long on those videos, he retained some of the information.

Asha grunted. "I don't know. Computers and communications are my thing. What I do know is that I have a lot more digging to do. I found notes from another hab, but they're all corrupted. So, if you don't mind?" She gestured towards the door.

"You were reading when I came in." Carlos got up anyway, hoping that the acid in his stomach would dissipate the further he got from the videos.

"Union mandated break. Which I'm about to continue." She picked her book up, bringing it to her face so that he couldn't see her anymore.

"We don't have a union," he called out as he passed through her office door.

"Can't hear you over the sound of my union break!"

Carlos chuckled, trying to find his center again. He thought about his daughter, Kailey, nineteen now and the spitting image of her mother. When Carlos divorced Kailey's mother, Luna, he had maintained full custody while she went abroad to work with Doctors Without Borders. It was an amicable split, and Kailey loved living with her father. The roles reversed once Luna returned and Carlos got the opportunity to take a job with Amphitrite making twice as much as he was working as a mechanic for oil fields. Kailey wanted to go to college and this money would put her free and clear through anything she wanted to study, for however long it was. Carlos missed her with a sharp intensity that overshadowed anything else in his mind. He made a mental note to send a message to her once he finished up with the stuffy toppers in their "little purgatory", as Divya called it.

That reminded him.

"Mech 2 from Mech 1." He looked at his Amphitrite issued comms bracelet and squinted at the tiny display of the hab that he could scroll through to find where everyone was. He could see his dot moving along the hallway, heading back to Dry Dock 2. Divya's dot, marked with an "M2" was sitting in her room, unmoving. He noted a few other dots shining on the screen when scrolled over it to find Divya. It looked like there weren't enough dots in the hab, but maybe he'd just missed one. It was annoying to work on a screen this small.

Before he could figure out who might have been missing, the radio clicked with a response.

"Divya here. Ready for me to come back?"

Carlos sighed. He shouldn't expect her to use the appropriate radio designations; she never did. Still, he hoped that if he kept using them she might eventually pick it up from his example.

"You got it, Mech 2. Meet you back at Dry Dock 2."

Carlos skirted around the same cleaning bot he saw earlier, still working through the same hallway.

Turning down another hallway, he glanced left before speeding past the turn for the science wing. To think that the monster fish were not only outside the hab, circling them, but also inside with them, gave his nausea a reason to return. For the first time in his eight years underwater, he wondered if maybe he needed to take a vacation and return to the surface in a week with the toppers. Might do him some good. It would definitely be great for Kailey.

A commotion echoing up the hallways from Dry Dock 2 brought him out of his thoughts. Carlos sped up his steps, not quite running. Yet.

"What kind of circus are they running down here?!"

Ah. The toppers were free and they were pissed.

Turning a final right, Carlos saw Dry Dock 2 was open and five men hovered around Divya who looked like she was about to start swinging. Two of them were clutching duffel bags to their chests, while three suitcases were stacked to the side. The only man in the group he recognized was Perisdo at the back of the group. He watched the other toppers rage like a parent would watch a child tantrum.

When Divya saw Carlos, she shot him a sour look that said, *You're late.*

"Great! You're all out of the dry dock!" Everyone turned to Carlos, his gleeful voice carrying over theirs.

Divya bugged her eyes out at him, trying to understand why he would insert himself in the middle of this. He would have winked if everyone wasn't looking at him, so he settled for a slight head tilt in her direction. Someone needed to take control of the situation and get everyone to stop yelling.

"Are you the one responsible for this?" A bald man stepped out of the group towards Carlos. His cheeks were ruddy and his hands were balled at his sides. "Do you know how long we were stuck in there?"

"Unfortunately, I am not responsible for you being stuck in the dry dock. Our machinery runs on very specific schedules to make sure Kraken 7 remains clear of contaminants and is safe for habitation at all times." He smiled without any friendliness. "Your unscheduled visitation put a strain on our system and we should all be grateful that your detention in the dry dock didn't last any longer." The man with the ruddy features took a step back and loosened his hands as though Carlos had made a threat against him.

"Thank you for enlightening us, Mr. Cepeda." Benson's voice came from behind him, bringing Carlos' attention around. The supervisor was breathing heavy and sweat dotted his face. Carlos wondered where he had run from. The toppers murmured amongst themselves. They looked nervous, and that made Carlos want to laugh. This far underwater, they should be nervous. This wasn't an excursion that should be taken lightly, and none of them seemed to appreciate the gravity of where they were. People who didn't take part in the actual building of things rarely did. When you could throw money at people and have them create or destroy things at your whim, those things lost meaning.

Or fear. Rich people never seemed to be afraid of anything.

"I'd like to welcome our guests and bring everyone up to speed on what will be happening over the next few days until they return to the surface." Benson gestured to Divya and Carlos. "Please collect your crew mates and meet us in the mess hall."

"The *mess hall*?" Carlos missed who made that comment. "What is a mess hall?"

Divya snorted, unable to hold back her laughter. Benson cut her a nasty look, his features bunched up in a scowl. "I gave you a task to complete," he snapped. Wrinkling her nose at Benson, Divya turned away without responding. Benson gestured to everyone and proceeded down the hallway, the men following him like ducklings. Carlos remained where he was, watching them pass, appraising each of them in turn. When Saul Perisdo walked near Carlos, he stopped.

The man tilted his head an inch in Carlos' direction, and without looking at him, said, "I know this machinery is delicate. But I also know it's not that delicate. Good appeasement story, though."

Perisdo walked away without turning back, as though he hadn't said anything. Carlos reached a hand up to his ear, fiddling with a nonexistent earring. It felt like something slimy had touched his skin, crawled over him with Perisdo's words. Giving himself a physical shake, Carlos looked at his bracelet and counted off the dots on the screen. Everyone was accounted for. Time to rally the troops.

Asha

This meeting could have been a message. A memo. A Post-it note stuck to her door. Anything to save Asha from having to listen to a bunch of egotistical men bloviate about themselves and their goals for an hour. The four toppers all talked about their excitement over their visit–brief stay in the dry dock excluded–and how the money they contributed to the Kraken 7 program was well spent. Asha didn't know much about the men in their pressed suits in an assortment of dark colors. Although one had glasses, and another a beard, and they were different nationalities, they were all interchangeable.

And not a single one of them seemed to appreciate that there was a lot of hard work being done down here, other than that which would make them money.

As the saying went, "Dolla dolla bills, y'all." Or something like that. Asha couldn't remember where she heard that from, but it had a nice way of rolling off the tongue.

While those four clustered together like hens in a coop, Saul Perisdo sat a little away from them, watching them talk. Asha couldn't quite get a read on him. She knew he was considered a hard ass, and it was considered a bad thing when he came to visit you. He hadn't done anything, though. At least not yet. Not a word or sigh came from the man the entire time he sat here. He just watched everyone, judging. She made it a point to maintain eye contact with him until he moved on to someone else.

I'm not scared of you.

She didn't think he was intimidated by her, but she felt good about staring him down, regardless.

"What do you mean your intended application for our research is military focused?" The room quieted around Mina's question. Asha was jarred out of her thoughts, having zoned out a while ago. Military applications?

The toppers looked around at each other, then at Perisdo who remained silent. In the space left by their lack of response, Mina repeated her question. "In case the question was unclear, I'm looking to understand why we were told to look for pharmaceutical opportunities, and now we're being told you're looking to sell information to the military?"

Benson stood up from his chair, disturbing George who was walking beneath him. The cat hissed and darted under the table and up onto Mina's lap. She mumbled something to the cat, and after some hesitation George curled up in Mina's lap and purred.

"And, what is your role in this?" Saul stood up and the other men shrank away when he stepped forward. "Ms…?"

Mina's shoulders started to hunch forward and Asha felt bad for her. The scientist didn't like to be the center of attention, much less hostile attention. The whole atmosphere of the mess hall was unwelcoming, which annoyed Asha. This was their home and these men were ruining it.

"Doctor, actually." Mina's voice was low, almost too low for Asha to hear and she was right next to her.

"Speak up," Perisdo said, his tone biting.

Mina frowned at the ground, then lifted her head and straightened her spine. Her movement startled George, and she jumped off Mina's lap and onto Asha's. "It's Doctor, actually. Doctor Kibner. And I want to know why mine, and my partner's, research is going to be used for military applications when we were told this was a research expedition to help people suffering from diseases or other medical problems."

While the four toppers became uncertain at the sudden command in Mina's voice, Perisdo's eyes took on a strange shine. An almost…paternal approval? The look made Asha want to gag. As proud as she was of Mina for standing up for herself and her accomplishments, she was grossed out by the way Saul looked at her.

"I appreciate your question, Doctor Kibner." There was no sarcasm snarling Perisdo's words. He sounded genuine, which rankled Asha further. What was this man's angle? "However, I would remind you that you, and everyone else in this room, signed contracts with Amphitrite authorizing the company to have exclusive rights over any of the discoveries that might be made down here."

Asha looked over at Carlos, meeting his eyes. She'd read every line of her contract, and there hadn't been a single line about rights to discoveries or anything like that. Was that something that was only in the contracts for Mina and Zane?

"Regardless of what we signed, it sounds like your goals were misrepresented to our scientists." Divya leaned forward in her chair, looking ready to jump out of her seat.

Perisdo directed his gaze to her. "The mechanic has an opinion on contract law?" Condescension coated his words, spiking them with derision.

Asha half stood, dumping George from her lap. The cat scrambled off with an offended hiss. "She's an employee looking to get clarification on what the fuck it is we're doing down here. I may only be down here to make sure our comms work and the software runs, and they may be down here just to make sure we don't *die* because of mechanical malfunction, but we call this down here the abyss. It'll eat you up and shit out your bones as dust. We're not here to play around." Asha struggled not to spit her words, to keep her tone professional even though the words weren't. "And we were all under the impression that Amphitrite was looking to make people's lives better through medical advancements. Those bandages made from coral that helped burns heal faster, or–"

Partway through her rant, Saul had held up his hand. Asha railroaded over him, ignoring his request to stop. But he'd had enough.

"Asha Moore." All congeniality was removed from his voice. He sounded pissed, but the smooth brown skin of his face didn't wrinkle, his hands didn't flex at his sides. Saul Perisdo's reputation for being a terrifying stone block was proving to be accurate. Asha clamped her lips shut, feeling the threat in his voice like a hand closing around her throat. She dropped down an inch, almost seated back in her chair. "I hope you don't think that just because you like to operate under the radar, and you're not doing work that we would be technically interested in, that I don't know who you are." Perisdo paused for effect before adding, "Or where you came from."

It was difficult for Asha to maintain eye contact with him as she seated herself back in her chair. She furrowed her brow, latching her eyes to his like her life depended on it. Looking at him was better than looking at the crew, whose eyes she could feel on her like gripping tentacles. The worst gaze was coming from Benson, a seagull circling while he waited for the shark to make a kill and leave scraps behind. Saul Perisdo was not someone to be messed with, and he lived up to that reputation.

"Benson?" Saul redirected his attention, removing his gaze from Asha. Sitting back in her seat, she could feel everyone's gaze sloughing off her with Saul's redirection. Asha glanced up and saw Carlos still looking at her, questioning without being accusatory. She looked away.

Standing up like he'd been jolted, Benson crisply said, "Yes, sir?"

Asha didn't think she could hate the man more, and yet he still somehow sank below the lowest of her expectations.

"I want a tour of the facility. The stakeholders and I want to see what our money has been going towards other than ungrateful opinions."

Benson nodded eagerly, while Asha pulled her lips into her mouth and bit down on them. A few chairs down, Divya kicked out a heavy black boot, connecting with the table with a loud *thunk*, her arms crossed over her chest as she sank sullenly in her seat. Asha wondered if maybe she was also holding onto some secrets she didn't want Perisdo to expose, either.

Smiling, Benson said, "Keaner can assist you with that."

Keaner, who was sitting quietly the entire time and didn't seem to be paying attention, perked up at his name. "Sure can, boss." He smiled as though everyone hadn't just been on the edge of their seats waiting for a brawl. Asha hadn't thought he would be Benson's eager pet, but she also didn't know the guy too well. Maybe he was a company man like his twenty-two years with Amphitrite suggested he was.

Saul didn't acknowledge Keaner. "We also want to see the fish that triggered all of this."

"Absolutely not." Asha turned her head at Zane's pronouncement. "It's not safe. The fish is quarantined. You can watch our videos and see our notes."

"Benson?" Saul looked to their supervisor. Benson hesitated, unsure what to do about Zane's statement.

Before Benson could figure it out, Zane ran on. "We don't know what's in there, or what those worms are capable of."

"Worms." Divya repeated, louder than necessary. She looked around the room, trying to gauge everyone else's reactions to this news. Asha gaped her mouth in what she hoped was a reasonable impression of surprise. Mina really needed to learn how to keep a secret or she was going to be find herself on the wrong side of an NDA one day.

Zane stood up, crossing his arms in front of himself repeatedly as though trying to ward something off. "Or how they transmit. No. You may have control over the discovery, but you don't have control over the safety of the hab. No." To punctuate the word, he sliced a flat palm through the air.

Saul tilted his head at Zane, then looked at Benson in a dismissal of the scientist.

"We can figure something out," Benson said slowly. Asha was amazed at how easy it was for Saul to come down here and dictate everything to everyone. She gritted her teeth together, holding back her words.

"We can do it without the scientists if we must," Saul asserted.

Zane sputtered and looked at Mina for back up. She shrugged, not wanting to engage with Saul again. "You don't know the first thing about safety protocols, or dissection, or…anything of that nature. Your background is in accounting and management."

Saul narrowed his eyes, reassessing Zane. "We're going to see the fish, with or without you, my background notwithstanding. Either make the effort to keep us and your crew safe, or don't. The choice is yours." Saul paused, then added, "Perhaps we won't allow personal items on the next restock sub." Turning his whole body toward Benson, and dismissing the rest of the crew, he demanded, "The tour. Now."

Benson gestured to Keaner and high tailed it out of the room, followed closely by the toppers, Saul, and Keaner. The remaining five crew sat in their seats, stewing in their thoughts. Asha couldn't believe how this meeting had gone. It felt like an invasion, like some War of the Worlds thing where the aliens came down and wreaked chaos across their world and left it in rubble.

Divya stood up, shoving her chair behind her. She surveyed all of them, her lip curling. “Well, this is going to be absolute shit.”

Zane

"Hey."

Zane looked up at the sound of Asha's voice. She sounded like she was raring for a fight, and Zane was going to match her if that was the case.

Instead of running more tests on the fish with Mina like he should have been, Zane took his communication bracelet off, left it in his room, and retreated to the gym after popping a few pills. He could chill out on a yoga mat and no one would ever think to look for him here.

Except Asha, apparently.

"What do you want?" Standing up from the yoga mat so that she would not be standing over him, Zane crossed his arms over his chest. He felt the muscles in his jaw tighten.

Asha matched his stance, crossing her arms and standing outside of grabbing range as if she expected him to lunge for her.

"I want to know when you decided to become a company stooge and keep secrets from the rest of the crew." Her eyebrows were scrunched low over her blue eyes, an edge of hurt along the blade of reprimand in her tone.

"What exactly did you expect us to do, Asha?" Zane squeezed his fists, flexing the muscles in his arms, trying to draw the tension away from the imminent tic in his jaw. He didn't realize he was doing it, and if he had, he would have been embarrassed: there wasn't much muscle to show on his scrawny, tattooed arms. People saw the thick black linework of the trees, skulls, and wolves in his arm sleeves, and assumed he was some sort of hard ass. Zane simply liked art, and didn't mind sitting for hours getting jabbed by needles.

Before she could get an answer out, he continued. "Tell everyone else about the fish that no one else was ever going to come in contact with because they don't do deep walks? No one other than Benson comes to the labs. And if Mina wasn't such a…" He trailed off and closed his eyes, tiling his head to the ceiling and trying to find nicer words to describe Mina than the ones he wanted to use.

Do not go about spreading slander among the people, he reminded himself.

"A try hard?" Asha suggested.

Good enough. It couldn't be slander if it were true.

Zane nodded. "You wouldn't even have seen the fish. We could have just given you notes and that would have been the end of it."

"Until Perisdo and Pals came down and demanded a dissection of the fish. We were all going to find out anyway. It just sucks that it had to be forced out instead of you trusting us."

"Yes, it would probably have come out eventually, but it's part of my job to keep things confidential. Much like how you're so obsessed with our message security." Why was she having a hard time connecting these dots? "You keep us safe, and this is me and Mina keeping all of you safe."

Asha shook her head. "No, that's not the same. I make sure everything is running the way it's supposed to, and none of you open up viruses. You're making us less safe by keeping this information from us."

Zane jerked his hands in the air, his voice rising to a yell. "How, Asha? How are we doing that? The fish don't wander the halls. They can't type or get into our systems. They're stuck in freezers and tanks. You'll never come in contact with them."

"Unless Mina decides to introduce the rest of us to something that should be quarantined." Asha sliced into the conversation, taking advantage of a slight pause in his tirade.

The tic started in his jaw.

"Mina made mistakes."

"Like telling Divya?"

"Will you stop cutting in?!"

"Will you admit that you were wrong?"

"Holy shit you're impossible." Zane dropped his hands and shook his head. He should have just gone to the lab with Mina to run tests and talk about how the hell they were going to safely dissect this fish tomorrow. Asha wouldn't have gone there. "If you want to talk about keeping secrets, what's Perisdo singling you out for? What did you do up on the surface that was so bad?"

"What I did on the surface has nothing to do with down here. My background check cleared and that's all you need to know." Asha angled her head down and glared at him from under her eyebrows.

"Well, it does matter if we're talking about who's trustworthy and who's not." Zane snapped each word at her, done with being pleasant.

"No, it doesn't. What happened on the surface would never happen down here. My problem with you is that I don't want to die and be infested with worms from a goddamn fish. We're supposed to be a team. We're the only ones watching out for each other down here." Zane caught the hurt in her voice, just a tiny sliver, and realized why she was so upset. It wasn't really about safety; it was about perceived betrayal. She thought he was choosing the surfacers, the outsiders, over them, the beneathers, the team. "We come first."

Yet she had some big secret that Perisdo could hold over her, and she thought she didn't have to share it. Trust was a two way street.

Zane sighed. "Asha, if I thought any of this was a danger to the crew, I would have said something. Just like how I didn't want to do the dissection."

"And if I thought my history was relevant, I'd tell you about it. But it's not," she shot back. Dropping her arms to her sides, she shoved her hands in the pockets of her sweatpants. "This whole situation with the fish? It is relevant to all of us, and even though you don't want to do the dissection, *you're still doing it.*" She was not about to budge. It didn't matter what he said about anything, he realized. Asha was determined to be mad. Maybe she didn't want any answers or solutions. Maybe she just wanted someone to fight.

Unfortunately for her, his drugs were starting to kick in and he didn't want to fight.

"If I don't do the dissection Perisdo probably will make Benson do it. That man wouldn't say no to a topsider even if they told him to chop his hands off. He's the yes man you want to be mad at, not me. I'm not about to let people who don't know what they're doing make things worse. And I'm not going to let Mina do this by herself." Shaking his head at her stubborn expression, he stepped around her to the door. Mina was a good scientist. He'd seen her in action and reviewed her previous work. But sometimes she got stuck on getting people to like her; Asha and Divya, for example. "I'm not having this conversation if you're just here to fight."

Asha grabbed his arm, just hard enough to get his attention. He looked at her hand, wishing it would combust into flames under his gaze.

"What about the other habs?"

Shaking her off, Zane asked, "You figured the notes out?"

"Yeah, I dug around and found out that samples of the Mordices have already been sent to the surface. They're not new. Other habs must have done that." Asha sounded desperate. Zane nodded, glad she had been able to get through the security measures that stymied him.

Throwing her hands in the air, Asha demanded, "Why don't we have any communication with them? Why weren't we told they knew about these fish?"

Zane pressed his lips together, letting her come to her own conclusions.

"We should have contact with them. You should have been told the Mordices exist, not have Amphitrite act like they were some new species they'd never heard of. So, why now? If the surfacers knew about these fish and worms, why are they coming down here acting as if this is something new and exciting?" Asha shook her head. "It doesn't add up, Zane. And you know it." She bypassed him to get to the door, her shoulders slumping as the fight left her.

"Asha?" She stopped at the door, but didn't turn around. "I don't know what they want. All I can guess is that it's not something good. They'll spread their darkened wings over us, and try to take us astray. But I promise you. Nothing bad is going to happen tomorrow." The words sounded halfway decent to him, even though he was lying. There was a pit in his stomach that seemed to grow every time he thought about the dissection. Only bad things could happen tomorrow.

"Zane." She looked over her shoulder at him. "Neither of us is that stupid."

The door slid open for her, and then closed with a muted *hiss*, leaving him feeling that stupid.

These small, awkward creatures are not what I want or need for my systrarna. Failed experimental attempts to return to our rightful home. There were other places. Disasters of assimilation attempts. We keep thinking we've learned our lesson.

I will do better this time.

DAY
FOUR

Mina

There was no such place in the hab as a quarantine room or area, or even a quarantine protocol. Of course, they expected to potentially find undiscovered life forms at the bottom of the ocean when only twenty percent of it was explored. But not anything that would require a quarantine. They were still on Earth, after all, not floating in space.

Asha had helped her look for a protocol in every single hab dedicated file for Kraken 7, and then some. There was nothing. Not even a protocol for what to do if, or when, they found an organism that was previously undiscovered. Asha had questioned what the intentions of this project were, and what the point of any of this was if they didn't have all the safety protocols.

"We can't just do things on a whim," she'd growled. "That's how you end up the subject of a safety video."

Mina had to agree with Asha, even if she didn't want to say it out loud or acknowledge the glaring gaps in safety protocol. Zane was infuriated when she shared this with him, and those feelings were still present as they tried to ad hoc a quarantine room that could be observed from the outside. He slammed things down, shoved items at her, and scrubbed extra hard at the stainless-steel table that Carlos and Divya had moved into this space for them. They were in one of the closets meant to house the cleaning robots which had been banished to the halls for the next twenty-four hours. It was a large room, since it was meant to store all seven robots and a maintenance pad for them. At least the room was brightly lit.

But, none of this was ideal at all. Never in Mina's years as a biologist had she been expected to break so many basic safety rules for the sake of egotistical men. She always placed scientists on a pedestal because they were better than giving in to obviously bad practices. Yet, here she was, breaking the rules because she needed this job.

Zane slammed a metal cylinder down and she wondered why he hadn't refused to participate. As far as she knew, he didn't need the money. He was down here because he enjoyed science and isolation.

Several metallic snapping noises drew her gaze from Zane to the newly installed observation window that Carlos and Divya were finishing.

Since the room was at a corner in the hall, Carlos had been able to cut the window into the wall that didn't have the door after consulting Kraken 7 schematics to make sure nothing structural would be damaged. He grumbled the entire time, his surliness matching Divya's. Neither of them was happy with cutting the walls up, but Benson and Perisdo had made this non-negotiable. Mina didn't know what Perisdo might have threatened them with, and she didn't bother to ask.

"This is so stupid," Zane snapped. It was more to himself than to Mina, but she felt the words cut her anyway. "No HEPA air filters, no set decon chamber, our suits are the deep walk suits. They're meant to keep us from being crushed by the ocean, not safe from microbes and whatever the hell is in those fish." He shook his head and banged his fist against one of the tool trays, making the metal implements jump and clatter. Carlos looked over from where he was flash-sealing the window glass into a metal frame. His eyes flicked from Zane to Mina.

Taking a deep breath, Zane looked over at Mina, his eyes flashing and his lips twisting into a grimace. "We shouldn't do this."

Shrugging her shoulders forward, Mina mumbled, "We don't have a choice. Perisdo said we have to." And he made it very clear their jobs were on the line.

"That asshole has no idea what he's talking about," Zane growled. "He's a suit. All he knows are suit things. This is our knowledge base, we should have final say."

Carlos clunked some items into a bucket, drawing Mina's attention. He looked like he was finished with the window.

"Look, Zane," Carlos started, dusting his hands off, "yelling at us isn't going to change what's happening. He may just be a suit, but he's got all our jobs in his hands. And maybe you can find a new job, but not all of can." Carlos scrunched his eyebrows together and Mina wondered if he was thinking about Kailey. "So, how about you just lay off for a bit?"

"I would if my partner at least had my back." Zane looked at Mina, his blue eyes intense. She could see his jaw clenching, a tic starting there.

"Zane, I do have your back." Her voice was a whisper, and Zane either didn't hear it or pretended not do. He turned away to keep scrubbing at the room's surfaces. Mina looked at Carlos who shook his head and picked up his bucket. Divya poked her head in to confirm that they were leaving, then glared at Mina.

Feeling tears start to prickle in her eyes, Mina hustled out of the room, bumping her shoulder into Divya, heading anywhere but that small space with Zane and his anger. It wasn't her fault, none of this was. They were just doing their job, trying to keep alive the things they found, cutting up the ones that didn't make it, logging notes. All like they were supposed to do. That part, at least, was in their job description, was written down where they could find it. Zane might feel righteous enough to be mad about all this, but he could always just step out if he disagreed so much. He didn't have to stay and do the dissection for everyone. Mina felt quite capable on her own.

Her mind spiraled, the thoughts lacking any cohesion or sense after a while. Mina's steps slowed. She looked around, trying to get her bearings. All the hallways looked the same if one ran around without paying attention like she'd been doing. After doing a spin around, she realized she was near the mess hall. Her stomach growled as if on cue.

"Fine," she muttered.

She didn't have anything in her past that Perisdo could press her on. Mina just didn't want to leave Kraken 7. She was thirty-two.

What was she supposed to do if she didn't have this job? Start over? With what? Doing what? That train of thought almost diminished her hunger. It would be terrible to try and start anything new thirty-two. Only crazy people did that.

And Zane? She frowned. She knew he kept drugs in his room; she found them once while looking for a textbook she'd lent him and needed back. She never mentioned the drugs to him, but she would think about them when she noticed his pupils being too dilated or constricted. Thinking him over, she wondered how much she really knew about him anyway. Was thirteen months down here long enough to know who he was? She thought it should have been, at least to know him a little.

Mina walked into the mess hall and almost turned back around. Keaner was sitting in there with Divya. How long had she been walking that Divya was in the mess hall?

"Hello, woman of science! What brings you here? Are you finished with the quarantine room?" Keaner greeted her and got up from the table to hug her. So much for escaping. "I've made breakfast!" Keaner turned back to the table, gesturing at the spread of eggs, sausage, toast, and jams.

"Oh, yeah, thanks. I mean, the room is mostly done. Zane was finishing up when I left." Mina took a seat and reached for a plate to pile on toast and sausage. She grabbed a knife and a small pot of what looked like strawberry jam to spread on the toast.

"It's done." Divya was curt, speaking without looking up from her food. It looked like she was eating some sort of oatmeal.

"Rad then." Keaner didn't react to the tension between the two women. "We'll get to see those fish monsters? Oh!" He grabbed a teapot and a small cup off a rolling sideboard. "Strawberry tea, your favorite." He grinned while pouring the aromatic liquid and set the cup in front of Mina. This was her favorite, and was part of her normal routine which she had missed this morning because of all the preparations for the fish dissection. She smiled at him, appreciating how easy-going he was.

Divya chewed her food, watching the exchange with a pinched face of either disgust or curiosity. It was difficult for Mina to tell. "Thanks," Mina mumbled and took a sip. It was still hot and scalded her tongue.

Plopping into a seat, Keaner kicked his boots up on the table. Divya shot him a disgusted look, shoving oatmeal into her mouth instead of saying anything.

Mina took a bite of her jam slathered toast, and sighed. "They're not…" Keaner looked at her expectantly. Divya eyed her between bites of food. "They're not monsters. They're just animals, fish. Like anything else down here. You've caught them with Zane. You know sort of what they look like."

Keaner flapped a hand at her. "The traps don't let us see much. You and Zane are the only ones who've *really* seen them."

And Asha, Mina thinks to herself. And Divya. She wasn't about to tell Keaner that. Divya stared at Mina until Mina dropped her eyes to her plate of food.

“What kind of fish are they?” Divya’s curiosity was fake, brittle. Mina cut her eyes to Keaner who was smiling at her like Divya’s tone didn’t register with him.

“We don’t know yet.” Mina regretted coming to the mess hall, no matter her state of hunger. “We’re waiting for some DNA sequencer tests to come back from the surface.”

“So, they–” Divya’s question got cut off when George jumped onto the table and startled her. She frowned at her. “George.”

George looked around the table and hissed at Keaner, swatting at his boots.

Mina reached for George and the cat allowed her to rub behind her ears. She meowed and padded across the table.

“Filthy animal,” Keaner muttered. Divya arched an eyebrow and half stood to collect George into her lap. “Putting its dirty poop feet all over the table we eat at.”

Divya stood up, setting George off with an angry yowl. Mina made a grab for the cat but she eluded her. Reaching across the table, Divya shoved Keaner’s boots off the table. “And what exactly do you think you’re doing? With your dirty poop boots?”

His boots hit the ground with a heavy *thud* and Keaner sat up straight. “My boots walk around on a floor that’s routinely sterilized by the cleaner bots. That cat walks around in a shit box.” Divya rolled her eyes, baring her teeth.

Mina decided it was time for her to leave. She could tell that Divya was about to start going off on one of her rants. Without saying anything, she grabbed her half-eaten plate and left the mess hall, dismissed from yet another place by her squabbling crew mates. For the first time at Kraken 7, she felt displaced, like she didn't belong. What was going on with everyone?

Maybe it was just the people from the surface putting everyone in a bad mood. Things had a certain rhythm down here that didn't like to be disturbed. Down here, things ran like the ticking of a metronome, predictable, reliable, never changing. In order to properly play an instrument, like how Mina played an electronic keyboard in her spare time, the rhythm and timing were paramount.

Tick, tick, tick, tick, tick.

Just like when she and Zane worked together. They had a comforting, predictable routine for working in the lab. The surface people had disturbed that.

With a sigh, Mina took the last bite of her toast and focused on where she was.

The lab. Standing in front of the freezers.

Blinking, Mina wondered how she managed to get herself here without noticing.

Pressing a hand to one of the freezer doors that hid away a Mordices, Mina asked herself what the hell she was doing down here.

Carlos

Having new projects was a rare opportunity at Kraken 7. Things were almost always routine, so when Carlos had the opportunity to try and create something, or do a regular task in a novel way, he leapt at the chance. This task though? Him cutting apart the Kraken's walls to install a window for a half-assed operation room? That wasn't something he wanted to be doing. He preferred not to take apart his home. Yet that's what the surfacers were demanding, as though Kraken 7 was just one more toy for them to play with.

Obviously, Carlos and Divya made sure this wall wasn't a structural necesstiy and would be fine with a window in it. But still, it was the principle of the thing.

Carlos could understand why Zane was so pissed. People who knew nothing about being down here were telling them how best to do things they didn't understand. No one liked to be told how to do their jobs, and Zane seemed convinced that doing this was going to somehow compromise the safety of Kraken 7.

"Hey, Zane?" Carlos leaned up against a wall inside the room and looked at the scientist. Everything was ready for the fish: the room was cleaned, there was a decon chamber prepped with the scientist's two suits in there, and there was an airtight transportation box for the fish. Even with all this done, Zane kept scrubbing, scrubbing, scrubbing. "What's the big deal about this fish? What could they possibly want with it?"

Pausing in his scrubbing, Zane readjusted the tray with the surgical tools on it. He took his time answering the question.

"Nothing good, I'm assuming at this point. 'The farmer waits for the precious fruit of the earth'. Why rush us? Why do they want something we don't even understand?" Zane tossed the cleaning rag into a bin meant for disposal of biohazard materials. "Unless they know more about this than they're letting on."

Carlos rolled this over in his mind. He'd always preferred straight shooters, people who weren't trying to manipulate others or a situation for their own gain. Working for a big company, he knew he would be working for people like that, but this seemed to go beyond the typical corporate disregard for its employees.

"I read through every line of my contract." Zane pursed his lips, frowning deep furrows into his face. "There was a single line indicating what that asshole said. Not one about them having the right to do whatever they want with our discoveries." Carlos hadn't read his contact. There were so many words, and so many pages, he'd just signed where he was told to sign and moved on.

Walking closer to Carlos and lowering his voice, Zane said, "The crazy thing is? I can't find a copy of the contract anywhere. I kept a copy, obviously, they gave me one. But my hard copy's gone missing and the one that should be in the online files isn't the same one I signed."

Carlos wasn't sure what to make of that or what to say. Maybe Zane had just lost his hard copy? Maybe he was misremembering what he'd signed? Deciding to play along, he asked, "Why would they do something so obvious as taking your copy of the contract? And how would they even get to it?" He thought these were reasonable things to ask; this whole conspiracy that Zane was spinning seemed farfetched at best.

"I don't know." Zane frowned. "Our crew are the only ones down here, and it's not like people can just slip in and out undetected. We're at the bottom of the freaking ocean." He laughed without mirth, his eyes flat. The stare was unnerving, and a distinct sense of danger crept up Carlos' spine.

"I'm gonna go find Divya. Have her give this window a once over, make sure it all looks good." He didn't actually need Divya to look at the window. He'd already dismissed her, and he had been working here a lot longer than her, with a lot more overall experience. But he would take any excuse to get out of this room with Zane, even if he needed to drag Divya back here to keep up the pretense. Between Zane, the fish, and the toppers, Carlos wasn't sure what was unsettling him the most. Could all this trouble really be from the weird fish and the worms? Could they fix it by just chucking everything back out into the ocean and forgetting it ever existed?

He was almost out of the doorway when Zane's voice stopped him.

"Can you program this door so that it can only be opened with a special code? Set by you?" Zane fluttered his hands around his waist, like he was looking for something to hold but couldn't find it. Carlos hesitated, and Zane added, "I just don't trust this. It's like that part in a horror movie where one decision determines if everyone is going to live or die. I want to make sure we're all alive at the end."

Carlos considered the request. It wasn't a normal thing to ask, and the way Zane asked it chilled his blood.

"I can do that." Carlos kept his words slow and measured, thinking about what Zane was really asking him. "It defeats the purpose of me installing a door switch on the inside of the room, but sure, I can do that. What do you think is going to happen in here?" He hesitated before asking the last question, unsure if he wanted the answer. Carlos took a half step back so that he was fully out of the room, as though something bad was going to happen in that moment. Carlos hadn't even wanted to be present for this event, having experienced enough of the fish through the video. If he was going to reprogram the door, he would need to remain for the show.

"Just make sure the door will stay locked unless you enter the code." Zane looked like he was going to add more, but snapped his mouth shut.

"Everything is ready, I presume?" Benson's voice startled Carlos and he almost yelped. His heart raced, pounding against his ribs.

Zane nodded at Benson, and the other man left as abruptly as he came. The surfacers were coming down the hall, and he took it upon himself to guide them over to the viewing window. There was still a little bit of time until things began. Maybe they were trying to rush this like everything else.

"How will I know?" Carlos turned towards Zane. "How will I know if I should open it?"

Watching the people coming into view of the window, Zane replied, "I don't know."

Mina

Everyone crowded around the window that wasn't quite large enough to fit all their faces. The surfacers, obviously, pushed themselves to the front, claiming their status as stakeholders to mean they were more important than everyone else.

In a way, Mina supposed, they were. Without their finances, Kraken 7 didn't exist. None of them would ever have jobs down here at the bottom of the ocean, where they all preferred the isolation and independence. Mina appreciated not having other scientists breathing down her neck trying to steal her discoveries.

Although, being ogled in a fishbowl by people who didn't understand the first thing about what she was doing wasn't much better.

Suited up in a deep walk suit, Mina felt awkward and clumsy. The suits weren't bulky, but they weren't skintight either. The parts of the suit were jointed together like the exoskeleton of a spider, hard angles full of bolts and fittings, tubes for cycling the air in the suit, and a bulky panel on the left forearm meant for communicating with equipment when out on a walk. They wouldn't need it in here, and all it did was snag on things around her. The suits were made for the wide-open ocean, not a closet.

"Are you ready for this?" Zane's voice came through the comm with a slight crackle. She had to turn her whole body to look at him. He was looking at the box that held the Mordices. Within his helmet, she could see his head tilted to the side as he stared without seeming to really see what was in front of him.

"We kind of have to be." She wasn't sure he heard her. Zane kept staring at the box. Mina grabbed the rolling tray of surgical implements and moved it closer to the table. It was time to start, whether or not they were ready.

Zane flipped open the lid to the box. "I'm sorry, Mina, about earlier. This whole thing just has me on edge." He still wouldn't look at her. Mina watched as he struggled to fit his gloved hands in the box to lift the fish out. It was dead weight, and all of its appendages trailed awkwardly behind it, snagging on the edges of the box. Mina stepped forward and grabbed the curling, knuckled tendrils of the fins.

"It's okay," she murmured. Once the fish was clear of the box, Mina lifted it from the table to make room for the fish to lay flat. It wasn't actually okay, but she didn't know how to tell Zane that and didn't want to cause any further problems when they needed to focus on the task at hand. Her feelings weren't that important in the grand scheme of things, anyway.

After putting the box down, Mina turned to watch Zane arrange the fish on the table.

“Mics live?” he asked.

“Mics live,” she confirmed, toggling a switch on her helmet to change from the “Local” setting to “Broadcast”. Everyone outside the room would be able to hear their words.

Zane picked up a scalpel, looked at Mina, the window, then down at the Mordices. Sucking in a breath, Mina wanted to tell him it was now or never, but the words died in her throat. Looking at the strange new creature they’d discovered, she felt a sudden sense of dread prick her stomach. It didn’t spread throughout her body and make her feel like she was going to drown, not like when she first heard the rumble the live fish could produce. She and Zane hadn’t been able to do anything more than stare at each other for hours, hiding in one of the rooms of the lab that they later converted into the holding area for the fish.

Instead, the small pool of dread filled her stomach with an acidic sloshing. Mina swallowed hard, trying to curb any possible threat of vomit. This was unlike her. Science was her safe space; it was supposed to keep her calm.

There was nothing that felt safe about this fish on the table in a room not meant for dissection and quarantine.

It was too late to turn back, though.

Mina watched the point of the scalpel moving towards the fish in slow motion. The gray-green skin looked like it wouldn’t break under the touch of the sharp metal instrument, but Mina knew it would. This was the same fish she’d opened up for Asha two days ago. Slicing it again with the scalpel was something she and Zane agreed would make it look like a fresh Mordices for the surfacers, something new and exciting for them. "Giving these people a good show is half the battle," Zane had muttered when they discussed this while moving the fish. "Give them what they want and get them the hell out of here." His words were so bitter they were like poison.

The gut end of the fish faced the two scientists, so they both saw the moment the scalpel touched the dark line of the seam they had previously opened.

Except, the instrument did not slide in effortlessly. The skin of the Mordices resisted, the scalpel pressing an indentation into the flesh without it giving way to the sharp point. Neither of them reacted outwardly to this; they didn't look at each other or say anything, but the energy between them shifted. The small sense of routine they were trying to maintain, despite being suited up like this was a biohazard situation, drained out of the room. Mina shivered in her suit and took a deep breath.

"We are just going to slice into the fish, starting up at the throat area and bringing the scalpel down to the tail end." Zane started narrating to fill the silence and try to smooth over the unexpected snag. "It's not like gutting a fish to eat." Zane grunted with the effort it took to press the scalpel through the flesh. It went through with an audible snap, like cutting into a sausage casing. Mina didn't feel any sense of relief: the first time cutting the fish open hadn't been nearly this difficult. The scalpel wouldn't cut any further along the fish's belly.

"Sometimes," Mina interjected, "when they've been in the chiller for a little while, you need a tool with a little more *oomph*." She tried to smile up at the window, but couldn't look away from the fish which was probably for the best considering how tight her mouth was.

Picking up a larger tool a few inches longer than the scalpel with the serrated edges of a saw, she exchanged it for the scalpel in Zane's hand. He met her eyes and the way he stared at her without blinking made her want to call the whole thing off. Or at least get a different Mordices. There was something wrong with this one, or something had gone wrong between when it was opened up yesterday and this moment with everyone watching.

Which was ridiculous. The fish was dead. It couldn't just change overnight. Nothing could *go wrong* with a dead animal.

But the things inside it?

Mina wished they'd brought the laser tool which would have made cutting into the Mordices significantly easier. Neither of them expected this much trouble, though.

Movement from the corner of her eye snapped her attention back to the creature on the table. There was nothing there; everything on the table was as still as death. As it should have been. And yet…

Without narrating, Zane inserted the saw blade and started to cut through the fish's belly. It made a wet, ripping sound, sloppy and grating. Mina could hear every tooth of the blade catching on the skin as it tore through, nicking the flesh open one drag after another. It was not the clean, smooth slice of a scalpel. This was violent, an assault on the dead fish that jerked with each thrust of the saw blade. Little bits of meat and skin flaked off the blade, falling inaudibly to the steel table like flesh confetti. Mina was so entranced by the green and pink bits, that she failed to notice the pool of milky blood spilling from the gaping wound until Zane said something.

"The blood, which might be difficult for you to see, is white. Normally, we only see this in Arctic and Antarctic species. We're not sure why this fish has it since, comparatively, it's not as cold here. It also has none of the antifreeze proteins usually seen in those species." Mina didn't know why Zane was going on about this. These surfacers didn't care about the science. Maybe he was rambling on about it because the slow seepage of blood shouldn't have been happening at all. The fish had been drained of blood when they first opened it up. There shouldn't *be* any blood in it.

"Zane." His name eked out of her mouth and she clamped her teeth together. Glancing up at the window, she saw everyone enraptured by what was happening on the table. The only ones looking at her were Carlos and Asha. Their faces were big question marks and Asha mouthed something that Mina didn't understand; she'd never managed to master lip-reading.

"Yes, can you open the fish up?" He transitioned the conversation as if nothing out of the ordinary was happening. Mina didn't want to touch the fish, even with the added protective layers of the deep walk suit. The irrational thought that the worms in the fish could somehow burrow through the protective shell of the suit flashed through her mind. Zane was right. This was a stupid idea, so stupid.

Mina reached for the gaping stomach of the fish while Zane replaced the saw on the tool tray. It looked like the side of the fish twitched, like something was burrowing beneath the skin. Making an effort to keep her hands from shaking, Mina reached for the fish, telling herself that she was being irrational. There was no reason why the fish should be moving. It was dead. The worms inside didn't move until prodded.

But what if…

Mina shut down thoughts of "What if". She was a scientist, and when other people claimed to see things that weren't there, or imagined things, she laughed at them. Not to their faces, of course. She could never be that rude. But, in her mind she would roll her eyes and wonder how people could be so gullible.

Dead was dead.

The thick fingers of the suit decreased her dexterity and she struggled to slot them into the fish. There was a lot more resistance than she remembered, and she chalked that up to the fish being cold. At least, she assumed the fish was cold. Unlike when she wore latex gloves, she couldn't feel the temperature of the fish through the deep walk gloves. Nor could she feel the movement she was convinced she saw as she pried the fish apart. Despite Zane sawing open the fish, and how easily it had opened the first time, the halves felt stuck together as if glued.

Zane gave her a gentle nudge of encouragement. Or maybe it was a "Get on with it" nudge. She wasn't sure. She pulled harder, the halves peeling apart with a sound like tearing Velcro. She'd never heard flesh make that sound when it separated, and it seemed to go on and on as she kept pulling. The dry tearing filled the room, making it more obvious that something was wrong. More white blood gushed from the slit in the fish, coating her gloves. Mina again had the abrupt thought of the worms burrowing through the suit and made a conscious effort to not pull her hands away.

“Sometimes the freezing process can make the fish a little sticky.” She tried for humor and came up short. Lifting half the fish up, strings of pink meat broke apart with audible snaps. Mina pushed, hoping to get her hands off the thing as soon as possible.

The fish lurched on the table, tearing the flesh out of Mina’s hands. She jumped back with a yelp, pulling her hands to her chest. Zane grabbed for the fish, missing when it thrashed its pincered tail, spraying white blood over the table and onto the floor. Panic seized Mina as she watched Zane sidestep the thrashing tail.

Thumping noises drew Mina’s attention from the commotion in the room to the commotion outside the window. The surfacers were being shoved out of the way in favor of her crew mates, banging on the glass and yelling. Their voices were muffled behind the protection of her suit.

On the table, the fish contorted into a halfmoon shape, it’s tail aspiring to meet the toothy nightmare of its mouth. It held there, silence falling heavy over the room.

Zane’s mic crackled, with heavy breathing or him trying to say something, Mina couldn’t tell. No words were going to come out of her own mouth, shut tight against a whimper. Hollow bangs came through the door and that triggered the fish back into movement. The body relaxed, falling back onto the table, splashing in the pooled blood. Shreds of pink meat dotted with beads of milky fluid dangled out of the fish, its shiny, white eye staring up at the ceiling in some sort of accusation.

“Sometimes this happens with, with uh,” Zane fumbled around the words and Mina had no words of her own to help him. Zane took a deep breath, creating static on the line. "Now, we're…" Mina looked at him, trying to figure out if he had stopped talking or if there was something wrong with her volume. Then, Zane said, "Fuck it. Fuck this fish, fuck you guys out there. Carlos?"

Mina didn't know why he was calling for Carlos, but a noise from the table distracted her.

Something hissed, like a release of pressurized gas, and the cut part of the fish lifted up, flopping over. Bumps bubbled up in the organs and flesh of the fish, looking as though the insides had developed a nasty rash. White blood welled up from each of the bumps, forming tiny peaks until the fluid spilled out to pool inside the fish. The entire Mordices quivered, and white tendrils of worms shot up from it, extending two feet above the mass of guts.

Mina leaped back, crashing into things behind her, stumbling and falling to her knees. She saw Zane take slow steps away from the table, the worms seething and reaching their bodies out of the guts, while still anchored in place. They were larger than before, faster moving.

More purposeful?

Zane grabbed a large can of chemical aerosol. Mina couldn't tell what the name on it was beneath Zane's clunky deep walk suit gloves.

Outside of the fear spiking Mina's heart rate and her breathing, she could hear pounding and shouting on the other side of the door. The worms slowed their thrashing, and looked like they were searching for something. Some of the worms slid away from the fish, giving rise to a soupy sucking sound. One by one, the worms slithered out of the fish and plopped onto the floor.

Mina screamed.

The worms writhed across the floor with labored movements that were somehow slow, and also way too fast. Their bodies weren't segmented, but moved like they were, one twitching, jerking movement at a time. The corpse of the fish twitched, more white worms wiggling their way out. Horrified, Mina wondered how there could possibly be so many of them in the fish.

"Zane!" She shouted for her partner who stood near the table, spraying aerosol over the fish, the worms, everything in the room. He didn't notice the worms wriggling closer to him. "Zane, you need to move!" Mina couldn't make herself move toward him, to grab him and pull him away. He was as locked into what he was doing as Mina was frozen to her spot against the wall, only capable of moving her head as she looked around the room. What was she looking for? Something, anything, that she could use to help Zane? An escape?

Across from her, watching through the window, was Saul Perisdo, looking as calm as if he were watching a television show. His hands were clasped behind his back and he looked to be…smiling? She couldn't dwell on it. The fish caught her eye. In the time she was looking at Perisdo, the fish's side, the one that had been peeled open, was back in place, making the fish look whole. The skin of the fish writhed with infestation. The knobby lengths of fins twitched, flopping off the table to trail on the ground. They moved around, searching for something, as the worms continued inching toward Zane and Mina.

Lunging for the door that would have allowed them to leave the closet, she slammed her hand on the button for the exit. Nothing happened. Mina wailed. On the table, the fish's fins rustled, a susurration that blanketed everything until the rumbling started. Mina thought she'd grown used to the rumbling from the number of times she and Zane had induced the fish to make the noise. She was mistaken. Her stomach turned to acid, drying out her throat. She wasn't going to make it out of here.

Something tugged at her leg and she looked down. Wrapped around her ankle was one of the worms, curling itself around the lower part of her calf and working its way up. The thick metal and plastic of the deep walk suit prevented her from noticing the worm's initial incursion onto the suit until it started to try pulling her towards the other worms. Shrieking, Mina slammed her fist into the exit button and kicked at worm encircling her leg. The opposing movements knocked her off balance, and she wobbled away from the door, her arms windmilling around her.

She did not fall with grace, or the presence of mind to catch herself. When she landed hard on her back, Mina's head whipped, striking the floor and bouncing up. Deep walk helmets weren't meant to protect the head from blunt force trauma, and the whiplash rattled her brain. Starbursts colored her vision and she thought she saw Zane walking toward the fish.

"I'm gonna torch it."

Mina blinked her eyes, kicking her feet in case the worms were still trying to crawl up her leg. It hurt to look around the room, to understand what was happening. The fish was still rumbling, which was making everything even worse.

Light flared in the room, like someone had turned the lights up to the brightest setting. Red light filled in her vision and the sound of the rumble deepened.

Asha

"We need to get them out of there!" Asha slammed her fist against the closed door. It wouldn't open, no matter how many times she jabbed at the controls.

"There are protocols in place," Benson asserted. He didn't sound certain. Fear had his hands shaking and that was all Asha needed to barrel ahead.

"Carlos." She looked past the toppers, past Perisdo who was, somehow, calmly watching the scene unfolding in the former closet turned hellscape, and locked onto Carlos. "Open the door. I don't know what is wrong with this door, but you need to get it open."

Shaking his head, Carlos said, "I can't open that door."

"What do you mean?" Asha almost screeched the words, only just managing to contain herself. "Open. The. Door." Carlos shook his head and looked to Benson for back up. The supervisor couldn't find any words to assist him.

"Like he said." Carlos grabbed for his ear lobe and then jerked his hand down. "There are protocols in place. Imagine if those things got out of the room? What they could do out here?" Carlos' skin paled, making him look ill.

Asha's gaze bounced between Carlos and Divya before settling on Divya who, for once, didn't seem to have anything sarcastic to say. Inside the room, Mina screamed.

"Divya. Open the door." The younger woman turned large eyes on Asha. She stepped towards Divya, her shoulders rigid and her chin jutting forward. "Divya."

Carlos stepped in between them, protecting Divya from Asha's wrath. A flash of hurt spiked through Asha. She never thought Carlos would choose someone else over her, would choose to let their crewmates die over some stupid protocols. For a moment, she thought about barreling through Carlos to get to Divya, just to have something physical to push back on. Then Divya stepped around him.

"What if we put the decon chamber at the entrance? We can give them a chance to get in there, to get away from those things." Divya didn't wait for a response, didn't look to Benson or anyone else for permission. She strode off to where the moveable decon chamber was set up at the side of the closet. It typically was not connected to rooms in the hab, it was meant to be moved into the dry docks so that people coming from, or returning to the surface, could be processed through them to reduce the risk of cross contamination of surface and deep-water bacteria. It was better than nothing.

Shooting Carlos a glare, Asha demanded, "Will you open the door if the decon chamber is here?"

He hesitated. Snarling, Asha pulled out a small screwdriver and started to unscrew the panel to get into the door controls. If Carlos wasn't going to help, she was going to do everything in her power to keep her conscience clear. Behind her, she heard the rolling wheels of the decon chamber squeaking against the floor. The last screw came out of the panel and she popped the flat piece of metal off the wall.

"Hey! Hey! Stop that!" Asha ignored the voice, not about to stop for anyone who came from the surface. "Don't do that!" Thumping reached Asha's ears, and she half turned, reaching into the space behind the panel to pull out the software box. Perisdo was banging on the glass. The amount of activity he was displaying was out of character for the man who was so poised and calculating earlier in the trip. He'd expressed less emotion when he threatened her.

"Don't set it on fire!"

Carlos

Everything was going downhill fast. The demon fish was rumbling, Divya was still rolling the decon chamber over, and Asha had the panel to the room open so she could override the software.

"Hurry up, Div!" Asha was poised to open the door. All she needed was for Divya to line up the decon chamber with the room. Carlos struggled with whether or not he should let that happen. None of this seemed right. Even though Zane hadn't given Carlos any clue as to what would be an appropriate situation to open the door, this for sure was not it.

At the viewing window, Perisdo started yelling and banging on the glass. What was happening now? He didn't think Perisdo would care much if Mina and Zane died, so what was he getting so worked up about?

"Don't set it on fire!"

Fire?

Carlos started for the viewing window. If something in the hab were set on fire, things could go from bad to catastrophic in an instant.

Enclosed spaces, oxygen stored in tanks in the walls, pressurized seals just waiting to give under the wrong amount of stress.

What the hell was being set on fire?

Before he could make it to the window, one of the surfacers lunged for Asha.

"You have to make him stop!" He grabbed for the control panel, getting tangled up with Asha.

"What the hell are you doing?!" She shoved him back. Keaner, coming out of nowhere, wrapped an arm around the surfacer's neck to pull him off. The man shouted, his words incomprehensible as he swiped for the control panel. One of his hands caught Asha's face, scratching lines in her cheek. His other hand managed to grab hold of the control panel.

The door to the storage closet slid open.

Of all the crazy things that could happen by dumb luck, of course the man would manage to get the door open.

Heat and smoke billowed out of the room, making Asha, the surfacer, and Keaner shy away from the opening. A high-pitched alarm screamed through the hallways.

"Oh shit." Carlos lunged forward, needing to see what was happening in the room. Benson and Perisdo jostled in front of him, followed closely by Keaner. Carlos caught sight of Asha shoving the surfacer who opened the door onto the ground and snatching the control panel back from him. Blood welled up from the scratches on her face.

She would be fine.

In the room was chaos. The fish was on fire, along with the worms on the ground. Mina was huddled against the wall, the boots of her deep walk suit singed and partially melted. Zane, with his helmet off and most of his deep walk suit melted, was being wrestled to the floor by Keaner. Nearer to the observation window, Perisdo and Benson were beating at the monster fish to put out the flames that covered it. They were using their shirts wrapped around their hands and were more or less successful: they put the fire out, but there wasn't much of the fish left.

Zane screamed, a shrill noise that tore through Carlos' skull. He jerked towards the sound and saw Keaner gripping Zane's forearm, the flesh angry and red. Blisters bubbled to the surface of his skin and tore open, leaking fluid.

"What are you doing?" Zane shouted and struggled against Keaner. "What are you doing to me?"

"It's for your own good," Keaner grunted. "Someone help me!" Carlos didn't know how to help, or even who to help. He didn't want to touch anything in this room that was full of the charred worm carcasses. The fire was out, nothing of importance for the structural integrity of the room was damaged or on fire; the rest of this was beyond him.

"Mina." Carlos turned toward the scientist. She blinked up at him and he thought she looked a little confused behind her face shield. "Is there anything we can use to sedate Zane?"

The woman stared at him, and he wasn't sure she understood him until she pointed at a needle on the floor. It was next to a jumble of other surgical tools and an upturned tray. Inside of it was a clear fluid. Snatching it up, Carlos went to kneel at Keaner's side.

"This will work on a person?" Before he extended the needle to Keaner, Carlos looked to Mina with his question. When she didn't answer, her gaze locked on the struggle between Keaner and Zane, Carlos snapped, "Mina! Is this going to kill Zane or sedate him?"

"Carlos, please, there's something wrong here. Something wrong wi–" Zane's words were cut off when Keaner slapped a hand over his mouth.

"Goddamit Carlos!" Keaner shouted. "Give me the syringe!"

Carlos hesitated, still waiting for confirmation from Mina whose eyes had gone distant.

Keaner released Zane's mouth with a snarl and snatched the needle from Carlos.

Zane howled when Keaner jabbed the needle into the raw, exposed skin on his forearm and hit the plunger. The fluid disappeared into Zane's arm and his reaction was instantaneous: his arms slackened and his eyelids fluttered closed. It wasn't until his body went limp that Keaner released his grip on the scientist and stepped back.

Outside of the room, the squeak of the decon chamber's wheels halted. Divya poked her head in to look at the damage, her gaze landing on Zane's limp body.

"Well, fuck, man."

Mina

Three hours later, Mina was still shaking. It felt like the fear was still gripping her throat, and she saw bursts of flame in the periphery of her vision at unexpected times. Zane was sequestered in a makeshift brig with his hands zip tied together. The sedative hadn't killed him. In the moment, Mina couldn't remember what dosage was appropriate for a person, or how much was in the syringe. She couldn't think of anything beyond the blood and charred flesh filling her vision, the smell of cooked meat curling into her nostrils.

Zane's cooked meat.

Keaner was to be watching him, and Zane wasn't allowed any visitors. Asha was supposed to be configuring a special lock code for his door, while Carlos and Divya were cleaning everything up. Everyone was getting jobs to do except her.

In the immediate aftermath, Benson had hustled Mina through the decon chamber and down the hall to the lab. He hadn't said much to her, instead mumbling words that Mina couldn't hear over the ringing in her ears.

What happened? What went wrong?

The worms. The fish. *The worms.* The were independent of the fish, could come out of the flesh and articulate across the floor in search of…what? Another fish, maybe, if the one they'd come out of hadn't spontaneously come back to life.

Had it come back to life? How else could it have been moving with all of the worms crawling around outside of it? The fish's flesh had been difficult to cut through, just as if the thing were fresh and not dead and frozen for several days. In fact, it was harder this time to cut into it than when it was pulled fresh from the ocean.

Rubbing her eyes until she saw flashing splotches behind her lids, Mina wanted to not have to think about this anymore. She wanted this whole thing to be put behind her, behind all of them.

That wasn't going to happen anytime soon.

After getting Mina out of her deep walk suit, and directing her to clean up, Benson had ushered her to the mess hall. He didn't ask her any questions or communicate much of anything to her during this time. Everything was motion and getting one task completed after the next until he sat her down at one of the metal tables and draped a blanket over her shoulders. Mina remembered thinking that the kindness was out of character for Benson.

Alone with Benson and her thoughts, Mina was grateful when the surfacers came into the room, minus Saul. They sat at a separate table, huddled together and talking in whispers. She didn't try very hard to hear what was being said; Mina's mind swirled with enough of her own problems to keep her occupied.

"Mina." She startled at the sound of her name. Carlos dropped into the seat next to her, having materialized outside of the zone of space she was staring into. "What the hell was that?"

His words crawled under her skin, making her draw into herself. "I don't know." Her voice just made it above a whisper.

The silence that stretched between him made her wonder if he even heard her. Carlos was staring at the four men at the other table, a muscle working in his jaw.

"What do you mean? What don't you know?" Carlos turned towards her and she hesitated. "You have to know something. You've been pulling these fish in for weeks."

Godsdammit, did he think she knew everything?

Mina stiffened. *Wait a minute.* "How do you know that?"

"Does it matter?" Carlos stared at her, like he wanted her to make eye contact that she refused to give him. "Zane tried to set the room on fire to kill those things and now he's locked up for it. And the sounds that thing made. What are you messing with down here?"

She couldn't get any words out, unsure how to answer because she didn't know what Carlos had been told. Was it Asha or Divya who told him something?

Shouting from outside the room broke Carlos' gaze away from her. Divya and Keaner entered together, followed by Asha yelling at Saul who came in behind her.

"You can't just lock him up! He needs a doctor, he's burned!" Asha whirled around to face Perisdo who stood a head taller than her. She jabbed a finger into his chest. "This is your fault, and you can't just keep him down here because you want to have access to the sub. You can't even leave yet."

"We could need it for an emergency." Ethan, one of the surfacers, piped up from the table of his buddies. Considering Asha's volatile state, Mina was surprised any of surfacers spoke up. They'd been reluctant to contribute much of anything after Benson's grand introduction of them.

"An emergency?" Asha backed away from Saul who was staring down at her, and turned on Ethan. "Because this is not an emergency? A medical trauma is not an emergency?"

"If he takes the sub all by himself, how would we get out?" Another of the surfacers–Mina thought his name was Ashton–spoke up. "We need to be able to get back up."

Asha's face went from just having red cheeks, to her whole face turning red. "Are you absolutely fucking kidding me? How selfish and empty headed are you?" Mina shrank down in her seat, the volume of Asha's voice feeling like a weight on her.

"Communications Officer Moore!" Benson stepped in between Asha and the group of surfacers. "Sit down or you will be locked up with Zane!"

"You'd be familiar with that, wouldn't you, Asha?" Saul's voice froze Asha's rage and drained the color from her face. Mina exchanged glances with the rest of the crew sitting around her, all of them wondering about the meaning behind Saul's comment. This was the second time he'd said something about her background that cowed her.

"None of that changes what I said." Asha stepped backwards towards the crew, her voice quiet. "He needs to get topside to go to a hospital." Carlos draped an arm over Asha's shoulders, earning him a glare.

Keaner mumbled something under his breath that sounded like, "He won't need one." When Mina looked at him, Keaner was staring at Asha, his mouth opened in shock. Maybe she had imagined it. There was a lot going on. Especially this footnote about Asha that Saul dropped into the conversation like it wasn't a big deal. Did he mean that Asha would be familiar with being locked up? Mina watched Asha and Carlos sit, the engineer grabbing her hand.

"I understand that these past few hours have been difficult and scary." Benson spread his hands out in front of himself like he was trying to placate a frightened dog.

Divya scoffed. "Scary? How about we use big girl words like, terrifying? Or something with a little more color. Scared shitless?"

Benson ignored Divya's comment. "But we will be moving forward as a team, without Doctor Marsh for the time being. You are all to continue your duties as scheduled, including you, Doctor Kibner."

The inclusion of her name jolted Mina. She stopped staring at Asha and Carlos holding hands in a white knuckled grip, and looked between Benson and Saul. "What duties?"

Benson gave her a patient look reserved for children or animals. His gentle features disgusted her, and she would have preferred him to be mad at her, like he was with everyone else. Her head was beginning to hurt, a dull ache that started at the base of her skull and was working its way up the back of her head.

"Working on the fish. Identifying what the worms are. You sent out samples for identification. Those should be coming back soon." He spoke like she was a toddler, but Mina couldn't find the words to tell him to treat her like the intelligent scientist she was. Instead, she rolled her shoulders forward and slid her eyes to the floor.

"Right, sure. I need an assistant, though." She didn't, not really. It was possible to run the lab on her own, but maybe she could get out of it if they thought she didn't have the help she needed.

"You can have Keaner. He's been working within habs for many years." Saul Perisdo made the comment with such authority Mina didn't think she had any ground to argue against him. Keaner didn't have any science experience, as far as she knew. Years of being in a hab didn't equate to science skills.

"Keaner is supposed to be watching Zane." Divya's correction drew Benson's attention towards her.

"The door can be locked. Keaner doesn't need to be there all the time. Carlos, you'll see to that. I don't trust Mechanic Choudhary to handle it."

"Are you kidding me?" Divya stepped towards Benson, which brought a corresponding movement from Saul. She looked him up and down, snorted at what she saw, and said, "What're you going to do, tough guy? Feel like having charges for assault and a civil suit on your ass?"

Saul opened his mouth to respond, but both Asha and Carlos got up and put their hands on Divya's shoulders.

"Now isn't the time, Div," Carlos hissed.

Divya ducked under both of their hands and stepped back, pointing at Saul. "You're a dumb bastard, you know that?"

Benson started to say something, but Saul held up his hand and stopped him. Divya glared between them before stepping backwards to take a seat.

Mina kept quiet, happy that the attention was not on her. What were they even to do? What could *she* do? Saul ran the company; he ranked higher than any of them. Divya should be happy he wasn't immediately firing her and sending her topside with Zane for her behavior. Maybe he was just waiting until they could all leave together, then he'd fire her. The stress of the situation had Mina wanting to cry. She resisted the urge to sniff, and avoided blinking to prevent the wetness collecting in her eyes from spilling over. The silence in the room seemed to last forever while she struggled for control.

Finally, Benson clapped his hands together. "Good, then. Keaner will assist Dr. Kibner, and with that settled, I release you all for the rest of the day. Be prepared to resume normal operations tomorrow."

"Normal operations?" Divya couldn't keep her mouth shut, but no one responded to her sharp question.

The surfacers scampered out of the room. Saul looked over all of them, holding his gaze on each of the crew in turn, before leaving. Benson followed in his wake, sucking the air out of the room with him. It was so quiet Mina could hear people breathing. Could hear the sounds of the hab she ignored on a regular basis. George the cat padded into the room and she swore she could hear the padded paws tapping on the floor. Keaner got up and gave the cat a wide berth. Asha bent down to pet the cat's head, then stood up, detangling her hand from Carlos' grip.

"I've got things to do." She announced, leaving without further explanation. Carlos followed after a few beats.

Mina rubbed the back of her head with a groan, the pain spreading to just behind her ears and creeping into her temples. She'd hit her head so hard.

"Hey there, George." She bent to collect the cat from the floor, hoping that snuggling with George would help her forget the pain in her skull. George hissed at her, tail flicking in irritation. Mina pulled back, an unreasonable feeling of hurt hitting her. "Sorry buddy," she whispered. "Not sure what the matter is."

"I don't want to make you feel worse," Divya started, "but you need to come clean about what you know. This is bigger than those fish." She squeezed Mina's shoulder in a gesture that should have been reassuring, but somehow felt threatening based on the strength behind Divya's fingers.

Mina shook her head. "I don't even know what I found. And now that Saul is down here, there could be real consequences to sharing this information."

Releasing Mina's shoulder, Divya stepped in front of her, tilting her head to the side. "More consequences that what's already happened? You need to come clean, or I'm going to get mean." She stalked towards the door, making Mina's head throb more. What did she mean, “get mean”? She was already mean and could only get meaner.

“Divya?” The other woman stopped, but didn’t turn around. “What if you just told them? What I told you, all that stuff.” It was hard to ask the question, to raise her voice so that Divya could hear her. Other than Zane, who didn’t even matter now that he was in pretend hab jail, Divya was the only crew member to know what Mina had discovered. Not even Asha knew, unless she’d found it in the notes.

Picking at the fabric of her sweatpants, Mina waited for Divya to answer, feeling less confident as the seconds ticked by.

“No.”

Divya left the room, leaving Mina with her headache continuing to build behind her eyes.

Carlos

The steady *slap, slap, slap* of Carlos' feet on the hab floor lulled his brain into an easiness that helped him think. Despite Asha gripping his hand in the mess hall, she'd been quick to leave him without a word. While he could understand why she was mad at him, he wanted to explain to her the why of everything that happened.

She didn't know about his agreement with Zane. Someone needed to prevent the worms from getting out, from spreading. It's not like he wanted anyone to die, and for sure not his crewmates. He wanted to make sure she knew his choice wasn't out of malice. It was about doing what was right for everyone. What felt right based on the fear in his gut and the fear Zane had projected before the whole fiasco happened.

Carlos checked his watch, finding that he'd run his last mile in seven and a half minutes. He tried to make a conscious effort to slow down, knowing the effort would fail with how fast his mind was running. There were so many questions. First and foremost, what did Perisdo and the surfacers want from them down here? It had something to do with the fish and the worms, but what could that be? Asha had shown him some freaky stuff in those videos, but none of that answered the question. He didn't know enough science to answer the question for himself, either.

Which, maybe, was why he found himself in front of the room that Zane was handcuffed in. Panting, sweat dripping off the tip of his nose, Carlos stared at the door. Zane was being held in one of the empty bunk rooms that none of them were using this time around. Would he have answers? Or was he just crazy?

Pressing his lips together, Carlos swiped his Amphitrite bracelet over the door panel. It beeped, flashed green, and the door slid open. Apparently, Asha hadn't changed the code like she was supposed to. On purpose? Or was she dragging her feet? It didn't make a difference to Carlos. Getting in was getting in.

In the corner of the room, sitting cross-legged on a bed, Zane lifted his head. His face was thin and gray, his eyes sunken. Burns covered his exposed arms, oozing clear fluid and looking like his skin was still melting off. Some of the burns extended up under the white cotton shirt he wore, staining the shirt sleeves red and yellow.

"Carlos." Excitement threaded Zane's voice. He shifted position on the bed to sit up more and winced when his wrists pulled against the restraints tying him to the bed frame. Drops of blood dripped down his wrists and splattered on the floor, leaving small, red puddles. "You need to get me out of here."

How could Zane be held here like this? How had his wounds become so infected so quickly?

“Who put you in here with your arms like that?” Carlos stepped towards him, hesitating at the wild look in Zane’s gray eyes.

“Keaner and Benson, they put me here. You can’t trust them.” Zane shifted on the bed, the zip ties digging into his skin. The black plastic peeled his skin back, sending a splash of blood onto the floor. The skin wrinkled up, sliding over the red muscle, the zip ties digging some of the muscle up to expose white bone beneath.

“Zane, stop. Stop moving.” Carlos stepped forward as though to grab Zane’s arms. He paused his movement, and backed up, not sure he wanted to touch Zane’s skin with his own. Zane didn’t listen, anyway. Unfurling his legs, he strained his zip ties to the limit. If he pulled anymore, he might just slide the zip ties right off his hands, probably degloving both in the process.

Carlos had never seen a degloving in person. There were the required safety videos explaining why it was important not to wear tight jewelry and to keep fingers, hands, and arms out of the crushing jaws of machines that showed cartoonish images of skin sliding off the body. But to see the top layer of skin being peeled off in real time, leaving behind just the meaty muscles stuck on the skeleton? The skin turning into a pair of unfashionable Buffalo Bill gloves ready to be filled by another pair of hands? He wasn’t ready to see that, and Zane’s hand skin was looking dangerously loose.

“He did something to me. You can’t trust him, Carlos. You need to get out of here.” Zane’s voice rose with each word, forcing Carlos to step back toward the door. This was a mistake. There was something wrong with Zane. “You don’t understand. There’s something in me.” He tried to scratch at his arms, the zip ties squeezing the skin even more around his wrists, drawing more blood. "Carlos, please. I can feel them in me."

Carlos bumped against the door and he jerked his hand up to press his ID against the control panel. The door *whisked* open behind him and he almost fell through the opening.

Zane started screaming and Carlos could still hear him when the door closed. His own skin crawling, Carlos lurched into a sprint, trying to put as much space between himself and Zane's room as possible. His legs pumped faster, propelling himself down the hallway. He took turns without looking, without seeing where he was going. Zane's bleeding hands filled his thoughts, the skin slipping off. The man needed a doctor. He needed to get to the surface. Holy hell, this was out of control. Nothing good ever happened when the surfacers came down. They always managed to screw something up.

Wheeling around another corner, Carlos collided with someone. He tripped, wrapped his arms around the person, and they both crashed to the ground. A yelp ripped out of Carlos, an embarrassing high-pitched sound that echoed down the hallway. In a panic, he shoved away from who he ran into, feeling something heavy scraping and bruising his forearm. Once his yelp stopped ringing in his ears, and his eyes stopped their wild rolling, he saw who he'd run into.

Or, rather, what he'd run into.

A tall cleaning robot was toppled onto its side, red warning lights flashing and a soft tone emitting from it. A notification pinged onto his bracelet with the robot's location and what it needed.

"Cleaner Bot 5 has fallen down. Please find Cleaner Bot 5 and stand it up."

The thing's wheels revved as though it was trying to right itself. Carlos took a deep breath and wiped his forearm across his eyes. His arm felt wetter than it should, even with how much he was sweating, and when he looked at it, he saw blood smeared across his skin from a long cut. Something on the robot had broken his skin, and now he had wiped the blood across his face.

Using his shirt as a makeshift towel, Carlos rubbed at his face, harder than he needed to, feeling like he needed to be clean of the blood. Just the sight of it made him think of Zane's oozing arms.

With a grunt, Carlos pushed himself to his feet and he grabbed the robot to haul it up. The beeping stopped, and the robot trilled notes of thanks. Another notification appeared on the watch, alerting Carlos that the problem with the robot was fixed.

"Good," he muttered. "Great." The robot moved off down the hall, it's servos and gears whirring as it swept and sanitized the floor.

Breathing out a sigh of relief, Carlos looked around to orient himself. It was time to go back to his room, to shower, to get ready for tomorrow.

He froze.

Carlos stood in front of one of the viewing windows. He stared into the vast blackness that threatened to swallow him up, something so deep and bleak that it seemed to eat away the light from the hab. As if it could somehow seep through the window and destroy any illumination. It pressed down on him and the hab with the weight of trillions of gallons of water.

Before he could back away from the window, something caught his eye. Out there, where it didn't belong, a single light bobbed along.

It must be too late for a deep walk. And who would have approved one anyway? They should all be in the hab, recovering from the day. Carlos squinted at the light and moved his head around, making sure that the light was outside and not just a reflection from something nearby. He pulled out his bracelet and counted the dots. Everyone seemed to be accounted for, so who the hell was that?

The lights in the hallway dimmed, telling him that at the surface the sun was setting. Just one more sign that it was way too late for a deep walk.

Instead of stepping away from the window, Carlos stepped to the side and pressed a button. Lights flashed on, illuminating the space outside of the window. The lights only went a few dozen feet into the darkness, but Carlos caught the eddies in the water of things escaping the light.

Farther out, in the darkness, the light was gone.

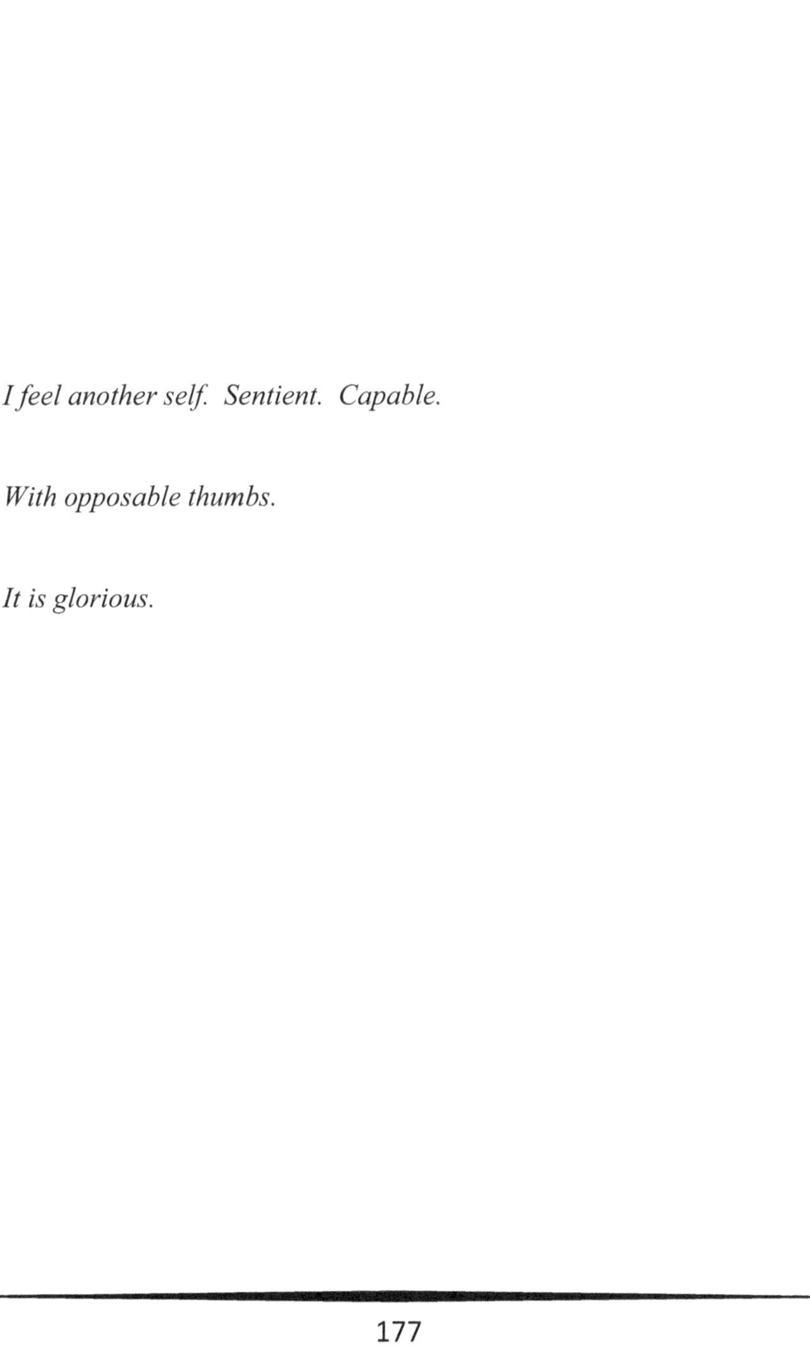

I feel another self. Sentient. Capable.

With opposable thumbs.

It is glorious.

Asha

Sleep was elusive. Short of taking sleeping pills, which Asha didn't want to do, nothing she tried would quiet her mind. It was full of screams and fire and blood, a spinning carousel of fear driving her heart rate too high and keeping her stomach in knots. Asha tossed and turned, getting tangled up in her sheets, sweating, until her alarm blared for her regular wake up time.

Weights in the gym didn't help to slow her mind, and once she gave up on that and went to her office, she tried to finish the book she was reading without success. Every so often she would lean her cheek on her palm and feel the scabbed over scratches from the topper.

What the hell were the science crew members working on down here? What weren't they being told?

In her office, she stared at the bank of computer screens. No new messages had come in or out, not even through the back doors she'd found and started monitoring.

She needed to get back to the information given to her by Mina. The stuff Zane seemed to imply she needed to look at closely.

The screens filled with photos and notes and thumbnail images of videos when Asha clicked open the folder for the disk. She scanned over it, reluctant to start clicking through everything for what felt like the tenth time. There was no way Amphitrite would send them down if they knew these worm things existed down here.

Right?

Asha snorted at herself, at the stupidity in that statement. There was an old sound clip she remembered that went something like, "If you ever think the government wouldn't do that, yes they would", and it was always played over videos of shady things the government had done. Anyone who worked for big corporations knew there was little difference between them and the government. So, the safest assumption was that Amphitrite knew about these worms and wanted them? She inserted a mental question mark at the end of that thought. Wanted them for what? Making dead things jump around?

Growling in frustration, Asha searched for the earliest entry in the notes, thinking that if she went back to the beginning and went sequentially, maybe that would make something stick out in the timeline. Fuck Saul Perisdo and his attempts to bring her down. She was going to turn the tables on him, make him scared to bring up her past.

The chaos of yesterday had dredged up enough of that for her, thank you very much.

Navigating to the earliest folders, Asha noted that the oldest date was from when they first got here almost six months ago. That would have been the start of their second eight-month tour down here. Kraken 7 was Amphitrite's newest facility, and they were the first crew sent down to it. Asha could almost feel the remnants of that excitement, though it was overshadowed by her focus, quickly dissipating. She wasn't all that excited to be here in this moment, with horrible fish sitting in freezers and Zane locked up in an unused room.

"Where are you?" Asha muttered, scanning over the typed notes from Mina and Zane. The "you" was amorphous and vague. She didn't know what she was looking for. Not even a clue.

"What's this?" Embedded in the first set of Mina's notes was another folder at the very end. No explanation for why it was there on its own, just a random attachment.

Clicking the folder brought up a warning box.

"The following documents are meant to be viewed by science officers only. If you are not a science officer, exit this program and report this to a supervisor."

Asha chuckled. "As if."

Clicking open the folder, she was rewarded with a cascade of files. The first three she clicked on were nothing more than maps of the hab from different angles. Her next selection was more interesting: "Goals for the Kraken Program". Sitting up straighter, Asha scrolled past the title page to disappointment. Most of the list was blocked out by thick black lines, leaving only a few words visible.

"Specimen collection, dissection, reporting back to Amphitrite." Asha mumbled the words as the read them, her voice only just above a whisper. "Life cycle of… Containment of larger creatures, such as…" Irritated by the purposeful deletion of information, as if someone wanted to exclude her specifically, Asha scrolled to the bottom. Several signatures were scrawled above the title "Kraken 3 Team Scientists".

Asha blinked at the screen. Kraken 3? As in, a hab before theirs? She supposed it made sense, even though no one ever talked about or mentioned other Kraken habs. Asha knew Amphitrite built habs under all the Earth's oceans. When they hired her, she'd been offered an opportunity to choose the hab she wanted to go to. When she was told Kraken 7 was the newest hab Amphitrite had built, she didn't question why it was Kraken 7. Companies named things weird stuff all the stuff, not always in sequential order. When the United States' Seal Team 6 was created, they only had two other teams. The whole point of calling it the sixth team was to confuse the Russians. Maybe they were trying to confuse their competition?

With the hand not navigating the mouse, Asha tapped her fingers against her thumb in a quick beat with no real pattern. "Where is Kraken 3, though?" On a separate screen, Asha clicked a globe shaped icon that opened a map of the Earth. Small red stars were scattered throughout the oceans, indicating all of the habs operated by Amphitrite. In the search bar, Asha typed "Kraken" and started the search function. It processed for a few seconds and populated the returns.

"Three, okay," Asha said, speaking out loud like it might help her think this through because the three returns didn't make sense. "Two, six, and seven?" She looked over at the document confirming that, at some point, a Kraken 3 existed.

Not on this map, though.

Kraken 2, listed as "Out of service", was plotting in the northern part of the Pacific Ocean, almost right off the coast of Alaska. Six was far off the coast of South America. Kraken 7, at least according to this map, was all by itself halfway between Australia and Japan.

The one she was interested in, Kraken 3, didn't exist.

Yet, it existed in this document.

Asha frowned, looking at the names that were signed on the document. She didn't recognize any of them, and the sloppy script made it impossible to figure out what they were anyway. Moving on to another file, she opened a handwritten note.

They get in
through the
skin.

The lines of the words were jittery, as if the writer's hand was shaking. Asa shivered, her eyes tracing over the letters. It sounded like the writer was talking about a disease, or parasite. Whatever was being referenced, Asha didn't want to encounter it.

A second note opened up after that.

It's Not The
Worms

So, someone within Amphitrite knew about the worms. But who? And was it the worms that didn't go through the skin? Or was there something worse than the worms that was being referenced?

There was one more file to open up. Asha was about to click it when her radio crackled to life.

"Mech 1 to Comms 1." Carlos was calling her. They hadn't talked at all since their argument about opening the door for Mina and Zane. He'd tried to talk to her after that stupid meeting, but she'd ignored him. What was there to say? He would have her back only when lives weren't on the line?

"Go ahead, Mech 1." There wasn't any point in remaining mad at him until they were able to have a conversation about his stupid fucking attitude during that fiasco yesterday.

"Team meeting in the mess hall. ASAP, woman." Under the joking tone of his voice, she heard a blip of stress. The way he leaned on the word "woman". Asha clicked on the last file before she answered.

Another handwritten note appeared, accompanied by a child-like drawing. Asha's mouth went dry.

"You copy, Comms 1?" The stress and joking were replaced by concern. "Asha?"

"Yeah." Asha stuttered through the single word, still staring at the screen. "I'll be there."

Carlos

Carlos didn't like the way Asha walked into the room. She was stiff, and her fingers were tapping her thumbs a mile a minute. He didn't know if this was leftover stress from yesterday, but he hoped he could get firecracker Asha out of whatever this anxiety was. She took a seat across from him, and looked at Divya, Mina, and Keaner who were already seated. Divya glared at Mina, which she'd been doing since they sat down together. For her part, Mina looked everywhere other than at Divya, and when Asha sat down, Mina hunched lower in her seat.

Keaner was too focused on his yarn game to notice that everyone was here. Carlos tilted his head towards Keaner, and Asha took this as her cue to kick him.

"What? Who?" Keaner dropped the yarn on the table and looked around. "Oh, hi, Ash Ketchum. Now the meeting can start." He grinned at her. Asha's lip half curled into the start of a sneer before her face relaxed into a blank mask.

“What are you calling meetings for?” Asha directed this at Carlos. “Benson isn’t going to be involved?”

“No. He’s showing the surfacers around again to try and distract them from what happened yesterday. Saul was in his ear all morning.” Carlos furrowed his brow and then tried to smooth it out. It didn’t matter what Saul and Benson and all those other selfish pricks were doing. Carlos wanted to do what was best for the crew, and that meant excluding Benson. “We need to figure out what to do about Zane.” He watched the wave of emotions flow over everyone. Mina’s pain, Divya’s anger, Asha’s confusion, and Keaner’s excitement. Carlos wasn’t sure why Keaner looked excited, as if this was some grand adventure. He was always weird, and Carlos was starting to think that spending the majority of the last twenty years underwater was taking a toll on him. Or maybe Keaner had always been weird.

“Has he gotten worse?” Asha asked, eyeing Mina. Carlos hated to be the one to share this information if Mina didn’t already know. She was rubbing her temples, like she had a headache, or maybe like she was expecting bad news.

“I don’t think he’s going to get better. Especially not down here. His skin is just peeling off because the burns are so bad.” Divya’s anger faded with her color. “We need to get him to the sub and get him out of here.”

“Now you want to break the rules,” Asha muttered.

“That’s a great idea,” Keaner interjected, preventing Carlos from snapping back at Asha. She was the one always pushing to follow the rules. Yesterday she hadn’t cared about any rules or protocols. “He needs a real doctor.”

Divya glared at Keaner. "Since when do you have an opinion on anything?"

"Zane needs help, what difference does it make?" Asha argued.

"Because why does he care?" Divya smacked her hand on the table. "He never has anything useful to contribute ever, and now he's decided to join the conversation?"

"I do the cooking," Keaner said, which Carlos didn't think would help his argument with Divya.

Underneath the arguing, Mina was mumbling something that no one could hear. She looked around at them, her lips pressed together, her hands flat on the table.

"What are you trying to say, Meens?" Asha leaned toward Mina, her voice a physical presence drawing Mina's attention.

"Yeah, Mina," Divya snarled. "Do you have anything you want to share with everyone? Anything important that we should know?"

Carlos shot Mina a questioning look when she met his gaze. Her lips trembled.

"Everyone, take a step back. Yelling isn't going to help anyone." Despite what he said, Carlos raised his voice to be heard over everyone. "We need to deci–"

Screaming interrupted him.

"What the hell now?" Divya half stood along with Asha and Carlos. Keaner turned to stare out the archway that led to the hallway.

"Stay away from me! Stay away!"

They all got out of their chairs, hearing the terror that accompanied those words. Carlos looked around for a weapon and came up with nothing. What could they possibly need weapons down here for? It was a closed system and all the people who came down needed to be vetted.

One of the surfacers, Terrence, staggered backwards into the mess hall, blood sheeting down his arm, soaking through the fabric of his suit coat. It dripped from his fingers, spattering onto the floor.

"Get away!" he shrieked. Terrence flung his arms in front of himself, sending blood arcing across the tables and walls. All of the crew members scattered to avoid the blood and also to avoid whatever it was that Terrence was running from.

"What is going on?" Carlos shouted, trying to gain some control of the situation. Adrenaline set his heart racing and he felt like everything was suddenly moving too fast.

Ethan, the same surface dweller who had been so condescending to Asha at yesterday's meeting, lurched into the mess hall with a scalpel raised high in his hand. "We have to get it out! You can't keep it!"

"Can't keep what?" Asha screamed, edging around the pair. Carlos couldn't see anything in Terrence's hands. Whatever Ethan thought the other surfacer had, Carlos wasn't about to let Ethan cut Terrence up anymore. There was no flight here, only fight.

Ethan swung the scalpel at Terrence, and the other man dodged away, more of his blood splashing everywhere as he circled around a table to put distance between himself and his attacker.

Carlos moved to grab Terrence, to shove him further back away from Ethan, when Ethan screamed, "No! Don't touch him!" The command in Ethan's voice surprised Carlos, and he stopped midway to Terrence.

“Please, Ethan, don’t do this.” Terrence sobbed, tears and snot streaming down his face. This close, Carlos could see that Terrence’s sleeve was cut apart and there was a long wound gaping open from the middle of his bicep almost down to his wrist. At one point, bone was visible between the folds of pink meat and yellow fat flopping around with Terrence’s movements.

There was something else in there, too.

“Everyone just calm down,” Carlos ordered. Ethan and Terrence both flicked their eyes in his direction. He didn’t know what else to say, how to make this better. Something was wrong with Terrence.

“They’re in him,” Ethan hissed, gesturing with the bloody scalpel. Terrence whimpered at the gesture and looked at his arm.

“Just leave it alone. I need a doctor to take it out. You’re not a doctor!” His voice pitched higher with each word he spoke. Carlos looked between the two men and understood what Ethan was trying to do. “I need a doctor!” Terrence wailed.

Noise at the other end of the mess hall distracted him. Benson, Perisdo, and the other two surfacers appeared, red faced and panting.

Terrence’s shriek jerked Carlos’ attention back to him. He held his arm out in front of himself, the wet red flaps of skin wiggling as the flesh inside roiled with movement. Tiny white heads of worms tore upwards through the meat, thrashing around. Screaming filled the room and Carlos’ adrenaline turned icy in his veins. One of the worms whipped toward Terrence’s face and latched onto his cheek. He tried to grab for it, but his hand couldn’t get a grip on the blood slicked creature. The worm’s body pulsed as it drew itself out of Terrence’s arm and into his face, disappearing inch by inch. The others felt along his shoulders, leaving red streaks on his clothing.

With a shout of terrified rage that unlocked a primal area of Carlos' brain, Ethan lunged around the table, tripping on chairs in his rush, and plunged the scalpel into Terrence's neck. The two of them crashed to the ground and Carlos watched as Ethan tore the scalpel back and forth, releasing great spurts of blood that coated him and everything around him. Carlos had never seen a dead body in person, much less someone killed in front of him, and the sight froze him in place.

Ethan kept stabbing, even though Terrence was unmoving, the worm having sucked itself into his face, leaving a neat red hole in its wake.

"Put down the scalpel, Ethan." Carlos tried to keep his voice level and wasn't sure how successful he was. It was difficult to keep his focus on Ethan and not the open wounds still spurting blood. The worms were less active, moving slower than before. Ethan's eyes were crazed, like he wasn't sure where he was or what he had just done. With a better command of his voice, Carlos repeated, "Put it down, Ethan."

Instead, Ethan got to his feet, the scalpel held in front of himself. He bared his teeth, stained red with blood. Terrence's blood.

"They're in him. They're in all of you." He took a step toward Carlos.

Asha ran at Ethan from the side, a metal chair held over her shoulder like she was a baseball player about to hit a home run. She swung the chair, the movement attracting Ethan's attention at the last second. He turned and caught the chair on his face and shoulder. He staggered away, getting tripped up on Terrence and almost falling. Catching himself just in time, Asha took advantage of his stumble and brought the chair down on top of his head. Something cracked and Carlos wasn't sure if it was the chair or Ethan's skull.

Lifting the chair for a third strike, Asha held off when Ethan crumpled sideways, releasing the scalpel which clattered across the floor. She was breathing hard and Carlos realized how shallow his own breathing was.

"What the actual fuck," Divya whispered in the silence that descended over them like a heavy blanket.

Carlos looked around the room, clocking the shocked expressions of his crewmates. Keaner, for once, looked just as distressed as everyone else. In his gut, Carlos felt a bubbling of acid and willed himself not to throw up. If there was any way that this could get worse, it would be throwing up in front of everyone.

"Now, now," Benson stepped into the room, his hands up in a placating gesture, "this was just a little mishap. We were just looking in the labs–"

"The labs?" Mina's voice was a high-pitched squeak.

Divya was much louder when she shouted, "Are you fucking kidding me? The labs?!"

"–and Terrence did not respect the quarantine procedures. Sometimes these things happen and we will be sure to make sure it doesn't happen again."

"You've got to be joking," Asha said. Her voice was edged with enough venom to take down an elephant. Benson hesitated, taking in the fact that she was still holding a chair that had bits of skin and hair stuck to it.

"No, I am n–"

"Two people are dead, and your idiot ass is just going to say that this was a 'mishap'? There is something seriously wrong with those fish, and the worms that are in them are getting into us! How is that a 'mishap', Benson?" Asha gestured at Ethan and Terrence. "I just killed a man. Shut the fuck up, Perisdo." Carlos glanced at the director who was crushing his mouth into a thin line.

"Tell us what's going on," Carlos demanded. The shakes were coming on as the adrenaline was purged from his system. There was no room for weakness, though. Carlos closed his hands into fists and fought the urge to jam them into his pockets to hide any shaking. He checked on the bodies and saw that all the worms had retreated into Terrence. "If we're in danger we have a right to know."

"You don't have rights to anything." Perisdo addressed Carlos but stared hard at Asha. "Amphitrite is allowed to withhold any and all information that doesn't pertain to the functioning of the hab or your jobs. And until such time as I deem it necessary, you will stop asking questions and do as you're told."

"Are you sure that's the best course of action?" Ashton, the bald surfacer, sounded more terrified than anyone. His hands were held in front of his pants, and Carlos had a sneaking suspicion he'd pissed himself. "I think it might be best if we all left."

"No one is speaking to you, and you do not have a say."

"We are funding this little science project!" The last surfacer, whatever his name was, managed to sound indignant over his fear. Perisdo rolled his eyes and waved a dismissive hand at the man.

Carlos couldn't believe what he was hearing. Perisdo was choosing to keep company secrets over the safety of his employees and the stakeholders, who were looking at each other like they would rather be anywhere else. Did he think he wasn't in danger either?

"Tell us about Kraken 3."

Carlos looked at Asha when she spoke. Perisdo stiffened, his suit jacket tightening around his shoulders. Redness crept up his neck. What was she talking about?

"How do you know about that?" Perisdo demanded.

"It's a real place?" Asha countered. Carlos caught the triumphant look on Asha's face and almost smiled. The smart-ass company man had played right into her hands. "What happened to it?"

"Nothing. It no longer exists." Perisdo was trying to regain his composure and grip on the situation.

On the floor, Carlos caught movement from Terrence's body. He watched as the man's eyeball twitched and began to bulge out of the socket. He couldn't look away even when Asha demanded, "So you're just going to lie about everything?"

The eye continued to bulge up, eyelids peeling back as the eye popped out of the socket with a sharp sucking sound, exposing the wet red inside of the eye socket. Swaying on top of the nerves and muscles that should be holding the eye in the skull, it looked like a flower head on the end of a stalk. The surface of the eye rippled, and the black pupil pushed out from the center. Carlos blinked and glanced around the room at everyone else who was oblivious to what the body was doing. He wanted to say something, but the sight had him frozen in place. An embarrassing whimper vibrated in his throat, but no one heard it.

"It's not lying. You just don't need to know." Perisdo's haughty tone made it sound as though he thought the conversation was over. "We should get these bodies cleaned up. They should be quarantined with the fish."

Carlos silently agreed, as something pushed against the inside of the eye until it ruptured with a sharp, short, tearing sound. Carlos winced as the eye released a short spray of blood and clear liquid that left droplets on the body and the floor. His stomach rolled, and he looked up at the ceiling, trying not to focus on the hot rush of saliva flooding his mouth or the convulsions in his throat.

"Tell us what's going on or she will." Divya stepped forward and pointed at Mina before planting her hands on her hips. "She knows about Kraken 3, where it is. You've probably seen the worms before, too. Haven't you, Perisdo?" Divya left a second of silence before snapping, "Either you tell us or Mina will."

Carlos looked from Perisdo to Mina and then back at the dead body. A white worm, glistening with eye juice, wriggled up out of the eye. It twisted around like it was looking for something, the eyeball deflating around it. At least, Carlos assumed it was looking for something. The thing didn't have any obvious eyes, just a rounded "face". He watched as the end of the worm shivered and then exposed rows of tiny teeth before sinking back down. Carlos was losing the battle with his stomach, the feeling of roiling bile traveled up his throat, clogging up any words he wanted to say.

Trying to find a distraction he looked at Perisdo whose mouth opened and closed, the same question written across his face that was in Carlos' mind: Was Divya telling the truth? A slurping sound drew his eyes back down and he saw the worm disappear into the skull, the deflated eyeball getting sucked down with it to leave a ragged bloody hole where the eye should have been. Carlos covered his mouth with his hand. "We should really get Terrence out of here." No one heard his voice muffled behind his hand.

"Is this true, Doctor Kibner?" Benson asked, saving Perisdo from saying anything. Carlos snapped his attention up, desperate to be distracted from the worm, the eye, the dead man that was way too close to him.

Mina hesitated, looking around the room like a trapped animal looking for an escape. It would be better for her, Carlos thought, if she didn't know anything.

"I," she started, her voice too low to hear well. She cleared her throat and tried again. "I know about Kraken 3. And so does Zane. We found the information."

"Where?" Perisdo ground the question out from between his teeth.

"Does it even matter?" Divya snapped. "We know your dirty little secrets, asshole."

Wincing, Mina answered, "In the notes we received regarding our goals for Kraken 7. There are files hidden…in the files…" She trailed off and looked down at her feet.

"I can't believe this." Perisdo turned on Benson. "Is this the kind of environment you run here? Crew members just doing as they please? Searching through confidential files? Unbelievable." He shook his head.

"No, that's, that's not what happens down here." Benson looked to his crew for help but none of them stepped forward. Turning back to Perisdo, he pleaded, "Please. This situation is very unorthodox."

"I expect this to be cleaned up within the hour and for your crew to return to their duties. No one is to leave Kraken 7," he zeroed in on Asha when he said this, "and I expect a full report on the fish and the worm life forms before I leave, Doctor Kibner." Perisdo leaned on Mina's name like he was mocking her skills. "We have a lot of people topside who are interested in these life forms." He turned on his heel and left, the remaining surfacers scurrying after him.

The stress level in the room decreased with his departure, even though there were two dead bodies in there and one was full of worms.

Benson looked around at them like it was his first time meeting his crew. Carlos thought he looked a little scared.

"You heard the man." Benson lifted his chin, trying to regain some of his haughty composure. "Clean this mess up and get back to work." He left before anyone could think of something to say to him.

What even was there to say? Carlos looked around the room, at the blood dripping down the walls and pooled on the tables. The two dead bodies, one of which he swore looked like it had things moving beneath the skin.

"I guess we don't care about quarantine procedures anymore," Asha huffed.

"Fuck the quarantine procedures." Divya stomped into the middle of the room and jabbed a finger at Mina. "You're going to tell us everything about Kraken 3 right now."

Mina

Discovering Kraken 3 had been an accident. Or, as much of an accident as reading through old science data and reports could be.

Her first eight-month stint at Kraken 7 over a year ago started with a recorded introduction from none other than Saul Perisdo himself.

"You, the science team of Kraken 7, have a very important job." He was smiling, gesturing expansively as if he were talking to many people and not just two. "We are interested in a specific species of fish, as yet uncategorized by science, that could provide potential avenues for medical advancements." Saul had gone on for a few minutes about how exciting these endeavors were, how life, and world, changing all this would be. Mina remembered Zane making a sour comment that this sounded more like a propaganda video than something encouraging science and exploration.

At the end of his spiel, Saul explained that the notes from previous Kraken expeditions were uploaded into their personal files. These were to be considered confidential, and for science officer eyes only. Although that seemed a little unorthodox, considering Mina and Zane hadn't been informed that they were working on anything secretive, they accepted that maybe this was just how corporations like Amphitrite worked. Before working for Amphitrite, Mina had lived in Japan teaching English to school children and working in a lab studying how underwater earthquakes affected the lives of sea creatures. For Zane's part, he'd jumped around at nonprofits improving their scientific procedures. Navigating for profit companies was not something either of them was familiar with.

What they both knew how to do was sift through research and other people's notes for pertinent information. Scouring every page, written or typed, clicking into every attachment, was second nature to them. So, when Zane found a handwritten note scanned into the files, it wasn't difficult to notice that one of the words was written in a slightly different style than the others. And if one hovered the pointer over the word, it would open up an entire folder of hidden files.

Nothing seemed out of place at first. It was a bunch of notes related to an earlier station called Kraken 3 that had the same science directives as Kraken 7. About halfway through the files, the notes started to become disjointed, chaotic. While most were still typed, some were handwritten with sloppy lettering. Those notes spoke of terrifying things, rumbling in the walls, seeing shadows where there shouldn't be any. People going missing on deep walks.

Mina and Zane chalked it up to Ocean Dark Syndrome: spend too much time underwater with imitation sun lighting and the weight of the ocean atop you, and some people went a little crazy. It didn't happen often, and it was hard to tell sometimes since, for whatever reason, it seemed to take over entire crews at once rather than one or two.

"We didn't think much of it at the time," Mina muttered. She didn't look at her crew mates assembled around her. At the beginning of her explanation, she tried to maintain eye contact around the table. Divya's glares, Carlos' disappointment, and Asha's suspicion eventually made her turn her eyes down, her neck following that downward trajectory in increments so that she was almost talking into her lap. Keaner hadn't had much expression, but Mina didn't want to look only at him.

Picking up her one-sided conversation, she continued. "We didn't even finish going through everything because it was just turning into, what we thought, were scientists experiencing Ocean Dark Syndrome. It wasn't until we came back on the second tour, and we pulled that first weird fish–the Mordices–out of one of the traps, that we went back into those files." It was Zane who'd remembered something in the typed notes about a fish with white eyes and fins that looked like long, gnarled fingers. A detail they didn't take note of because there were many weird things in the ocean and that's what they were here to find. Upon finding the fish, and discovering the awful rumbling the fish made, they decided to go back to people that had knowledge of it.

"The problem was, right after they found this fish is when the handwritten notes started to become more frequent and everything stopped making sense. They didn't make any mention of the worms, but they talked about seeing things moving out beyond their viewing windows and people acting strange. Stuff randomly breaking, areas flooding." Mina took a breath, trying to decide if she should include the most disturbing part of the final note. "We…we decided to look for Kraken 3 on the map, see if maybe where it was had something to do with all the weird things happening there. I mean, most of the ocean is unexplored and maybe there was just something specific about that area that affected this crew more. It's happened before. Places with weird magnetic pulls or too much quartz in the ground."

"Except Kraken 3 doesn't exist," Asha interjected. Mina looked up, her mouth gaping. Pursing her lips, Asha crossed her arms over her chest and looked around the table. "Yeah, I looked it up after I found out about it in the notes you sent me. To review what triggered that message to the surface."

"It was in there?" Mina asked, at the same time Carlos shot out a question.

"And you didn't think to tell me about that when you told me about the fish?"

Mina snapped her eyes over to Carlos, and then looked back at Asha. "You told him about the fish?"

"You told me about Kraken 3." Divya smacked the flat of her hand against the table with a hearty thud. "And said you didn't want to share the information with anyone else because you didn't know how they'd react. And look what's happened now."

"Why didn't you tell all of us? If you started with two, there's only Carlos and Keaner after that." The frustration in Asha's voice made Mina want to crawl into a hole.

"There's Benson, too," Keaner added.

Asha and Divya turned on him, snarling, "Fuck Benson" at the same time. Keaner grimaced and pulled a line of yarn from a pants pocket to weave around his fingers.

Mina chewed at the inside of her cheek. If she were being honest, it was because she thought the information might interest Divya, might open up an opportunity for them to become friends over a shared secret. Mina often went out of her way to avoid the sarcastic woman, but what if she could make a friend out of her? It was the same reason why she'd offered to bring Asha to the lab and give her the notes. Mina wanted to make friends with the people she spent the majority of her time with instead of just acting like coworkers. Secrets were supposed to bring people together.

"I thought maybe we could work through the problem together." Her sentence was so soft, she wasn't sure it would be audible to the others. A headache was starting to creep forward from the back of her skull, and she was fighting the wince it was creating.

"A problem to work on together? I thought scientists were to supposed to be smart." Divya stood up from her chair and paced the area behind where she was sitting, snapping her finger in a slow rhythm. "What the hell were we supposed to work through on this?"

"I didn't think it would turn out to be something this serious," Mina said.

"Except it is that serious," Asha growled. "If those people had Deep Walk Syndrome, and we can't even find Kraken 3 on the map, what does that mean? Did Amphitrite try to cover it up?"

"Keep your voice down," Carlos hissed. Mina caught him glancing at the door before he looked down at the floor. He took a few steps away from whatever he was looking at.

"Why would they try to cover it up?" Keaner sounded like he was trying to be the voice of reason, watching them even as his fingers worked the yarn.

Asha said, "Kraken 3 has been erased off the map," at the same time that Divya shouted, "Because they're a corrupt corporate entity!"

Asha and Divya looked at each before Divya lowered her voice and added, "What? It's what they're all like."

"I'm not gonna argue that," Asha muttered.

"That is a good point," Carlos said. "The missing hab, not the corruption thing. If it's not on our maps, and if it is supposed to exist at least at some point, why would Amphitrite have removed it?" He looked around the room, landing on Keaner. "Got any middle of the road suggestions?"

Keaner flattened his lips and shrugged.

"It does exist, though." Divya came back to the table, snapped her fingers once more and placed her hands flat on the surface to lean on it. "Tell them, Mina. You know where it is."

All eyes turned to Mina and she winced. "In the original documents, there are coordinates for Kraken 3 to compare to where they caught their first fish. The first Mordices," she amended.

"What're we waiting for then?" Divya straightened up and gestured to everyone around the table. "Let's go see Kraken 3."

"You're assuming it's somewhere nearby." Carlos frowned, his hand going to rub his earlobe. He looked at Mina. "Is it nearby?"

She didn't want to answer that question. Going to Kraken 3, based on the status of the notes, was a terrible idea. It would make things much easier if she could just lie.

"It is nearby. But, it seems like things were really deteriorating there, based on the notes. And maybe there's a reason it's not on any of the maps?"

"It's not on any of the maps," Divya drawled on with a sarcastic edge to her voice, "because they don't want us to know what they found."

"Some things are better left unfound," Keaner mused. Mina pointed at him, nodding her head, not even a little bit reluctant to agree with him.

"The notes made mention of 'monsters'. Got any idea what that means?" Asha leaned forward in her seat, pinning Mina with an intense stare that made her sweat.

"I don't know. We only found references to the fish. Nothing else. Maybe that's what they mean, the fish are the monsters." Mina worked hard to keep her voice from stammering. What she wouldn't give to have Zane with her. He might not know any of these answers either, but at least she wouldn't feel so alone.

"Well I'd rather not die down here because of some worms in fish." Asha stood up from the table as if the decision were already made. "How far?" When Mina hesitated, Asha's eyes darkened under her furrowed brows. "How. Far."

Mina bit the inside of her cheek, hoping to taste blood but not quite having enough nerve to bite hard into her own flesh. "It would be an extended deep walk…forty, fifty minutes? If we could bring the sub…ten minutes?"

"Fifty minutes of a deep walk is pushing the boundaries of safety, especially if we hit a snag. The max is eighty." Carlos looked up from staring at the ground, rubbing his earlobe again. Mina realized it was Terrence's body he kept staring at and she felt sick. They should have cleaned up the bodies first. "But it is doable. The sub is the better option. Asha can pilot that."

"I mean, I can set up autopilot and generate the run sequences. But yeah, sure, let's say I can pilot it." Asha shrugged, determination setting her mouth in an unhappy smile.

"Mina can come along as the science officer, to help us figure out what might have happened in their labs," Carlos continued, building his deep walk team.

"No, I need to stay here." The bone deep dread Mina felt at leaving Kraken 7 for the other hab rivaled the way the Mordices made her feel when it rumbled. "For Zane." Carlos looked at her like he was going to argue the point. She knew she didn't need to be here for Zane. There wasn't anything she could do for him beyond basic first aid. Mina just did not want to go to the other hab.

Keaner cut off whatever argument Carlos was about to make. "I could go. Mr. Perisdo assigned me to assist Mina now that Zane is detained."

"There you go," Asha declared. "We're all set. Send the coordinates to my computer, Mina."

Headache radiating into her eyes, Mina gave a slow nod, trying to avoid moving her head too much.

"I'm coming, too." Divya jutted her chin out, daring any of them to contradict her. Mina wouldn't want to argue with her. At this point, Mina regretted ever trying to have a conversation with Divya. If she hadn't been trying to befriend the surly woman, none of this would have come to light. Or, at least, maybe not as fast as all this. She was sure Asha would have connected the dots at some point; she was smarter than she presented.

Carlos stood up. "No, you're not. And before you start to raise your voice at me," Carlos spoke louder, taking on an authoritative tone Mina had never heard before, "someone needs to remain here to make sure the mechanics of the hab do not fall apart. That person is you, Divya." She still looked ready to argue and Mina shrank down at the escalation of tension in the room. "And if you need another reason, you're the subordinate in this chain of command. Don't make me start pulling rank. This is going to be dangerous, and we are the three most experienced people here. If anything is going to go wrong at that hab, we'll have the easiest time fixing it."

Deflated, Divya grumbled, "Or you'll just die and leave us abandoned."

No one responded to her.

Carlos eyed Terrence's body and then clapped his hands to get them moving. "Let's get some suits and then get these bodies to the freezers before the worms get out of them."

Carlos

The best laid plans of mice and men often go sideways.

Or however it was supposed to go. This plan wasn't exactly "best laid", so Carlos figured he shouldn't be surprised that things went sideways.

Benson, as if he had some sort of supervisor sixth sense for when his employees were going to step out of bounds, had locked the submersible with administrative codes. Asha thought she could maybe change the software to crack it, but Carlos didn't want to wait. The longer they hung around the hab, the more chance there was that Benson or Perisdo would find them and stop them from leaving.

That was how Carlos, Asha, and Keaner found themselves in a dry dock suiting up for a deep walk. Among the three of them, Keaner was the only one who looked calm. Keaner went on deep walks as part of his routine. Asha and Carlos could put all of their deep walks on one shared hand.

"How do I lock my helmet onto the suit again?" Asha held up her helmet, rolling it around from hand to hand. She didn't look nervous to Carlos and he wondered how much of that was real and how much was bravado. Asha's ability to mask her fear was uncanny, and Carlos was reminded about Perisdo's insinuations about her. He thought he and Asha were pretty close, but there were some cards Asha was keeping close to her chest, much like her fear.

Keaner looked over from where he was standing at the door, staring out into the darkness.

"Wait until Carlos gets finished with his suit. You don't want to put it on too early. We're going to be running up on the outside limits of our oxygen as it is. No need to run that line even closer." Keaner turned back to the window.

Carlos swallowed, his fear getting his heart pumping faster. He would need to get that under control; a faster heart rate meant faster breathing meant faster oxygen consumption.

This little side quest was seeming more and more like a mistake as Carlos pulled on each piece of the deep walk suit. Was there any other way to do this? If there was, Carlos couldn't think of one. Whatever could have been gleaned from the notes, he thought Asha and Mina would have found that and shared it already. And if Zane knew anything else?

Thinking about Zane made Carlos grimace. He hadn't been back to see Zane. In fact, he'd tried his best not to remember that encounter. Between the visual of the skin slipping off, the sounds, and the smells, Carlos wasn't sure he could ever forget it, but he was damn sure going to try.

"Alright," Carlos said. He pressed down the snaps on the suit that would cinch the pieces down to his body. Soft whirring sounds emitted from his suit, and then from Asha's as she followed his motions. The suit snugged itself down around him and then released a fraction so as not to feel claustrophobic. "Ready for helmets?" Keaner and Asha nodded at him. "We'll put our helmets on, then Keaner you'll get the dry dock filled, and open the door. I'll take lead on the walk, Asha in the middle, Keaner at the back. Since you know deep walks best, I want you following us to make sure neither of us gets off track. We'll be in your sight at all times."

Carlos hoped this was the way he should organize them. He wanted Keaner at the rear to keep an eye on everyone, and between him and Asha, Carlos preferred to take the leadership position to ensure they made it to the other hab.

On the forearm of their deep walk suits was a small computer screen. Carlos toggled his with the coordinates Mina had given them and the screen lit up with an arrow pointing out the dry dock door.

"What if the other hab isn't there?" The first crack in Asha's façade appeared in her voice. They were banking on being able to refill their oxygen at the other hab, assuming it was abandoned and that there was still spare oxygen to be found. If not?

"Then we turn around and activate the emergency beacons." Carlos said that as if it wasn't anything to worry about, even though that thought was a sharp thorn at the forefront of his brain. If they needed to activate the emergency beacons and turn around, would Benson allow the submersible to come retrieve them? Could he trust Divya and Mina to force his hand?

There were a lot of unknowns, and Carlos was trying not to let the questions get the best of him.

“It’ll be there.” Keaner spoke with an abnormal amount of authority.

Nodding, Carlos said, “Right. Final checks, kids.” He looked over his suit and then went to check Asha’s. Leaning into her, he asked, “What did Perisdo mean earlier?”

Asha made a weird sound in her throat. Carlos had thought bringing up Perisdo might displace Asha’s fear, but instead her whole face pinched in.

“Is now the best time for that?” she growled.

Shrugging, Carlos tried to play off the misstep. “Just figured if you wanted to get anything off your chest before stepping into the abyss.”

“Helmets on,” Keaner sing-songed, pulling his over his head.

Asha lifted her helmet up and slid it on, hesitated, and brought it up enough that the mic inside wouldn’t pick up her voice.

“Ethan isn’t the first man I’ve killed.” Dragging her helmet over her head prevented any further discussion.

Carlos blinked at her, his mouth snagging open. If he asked her anything, Keaner would be able to hear her over the helmet mic, and it was clear she didn’t want him to know.

“Little help, Carlos?” She dropped her hands from the helmet and he noticed they were shaking. Stepping forward, Carlos took a steadying breath and locked down her helmet.

“There you go.”

She locked her eyes on his, searching for something that she evidently found because she smiled and chirped a nervous, “Thanks” and patted his head, the sound of plastic on plastic making the movement sound more aggressive than it was.

Carlos snapped his helmet on and when he flashed a thumbs up, Keaner started the pressurization process. Water began to filter into the soon to be incorrectly named dry dock.

Asha had killed someone? She'd *killed* someone. Would they really allow someone with that kind of record down here? There must be some sort of extenuating circumstance, something that would make it not insane to allow her to be down here locked in with all of them. Carlos glanced at the person he thought he knew, who he considered to be his friend here and topside, and wondered who she really was.

The water crept over their waists and Carlos moved to the front of the dry dock so that he would be able to be first out when Keaner unlocked the door.

There were never any bad vibes from Asha. No weird behaviors or things that would make him guess in a million years that she'd killed someone. His mind spun round and round and he huffed out a breath. He needed to get a grip. They were about to go on a dangerous deep walk, and he couldn't be worried about who he could trust. He knew he could trust Asha. Even if he couldn't, he was confident that she didn't know enough about the deep walk suits to hurt him or Keaner.

Noise crackled into his helmet just as the water submerged him. Carlos always needed to make a conscious effort to breathe in the first few seconds of submersion.

"Where the hell do you think you're going?!" Benson sounded irate, his voice shrieking through the comms.

"Time to go," Carlos said, gesturing at Keaner.

After checking some gauges, Keaner gave Carlos a thumbs up and hit the release for the door.

"This is court martial behavior! This is mutiny! You will be arrested!" Benson continued to shout into their helmets, not realizing how little his crew cared. Carlos was almost positive they couldn't be arrested for disobeying orders from a superior, and they for sure couldn't be court martialed. This was just Benson blowing hot air because he was mad about being ignored.

Bubbles exploded from around the pneumatic door as it shifted and drew up, opening the hab up to the deep, black darkness of the ocean floor. It was such a complete darkness beyond the scant reach of the hab lights, it felt like they were being drawn out of the dry dock and into some beast's belly. Carlos stepped out past the door and felt the difference in the footing beneath his boots. The solid metal flooring of the hab gave way to the softer, shifting sea floor.

"Turn around right now!"

Carlos was surprised that Perisdo had yet to come over the comms and throw his official weight around to get them to come back. Not that it would have made a difference, at least to him, and he was pretty sure not to the other two with him. A few yards out from the dry dock entrance, Carlos turned around to check on Asha and Keaner. They were both behind him, clouds of silt and sand cascading in the water around their feet. Fading light from the hab illuminated detritus floating through the water.

"How far do we need to get from the hab before we stop hearing him?" Asha's voice came in over Benson's. The suit comms trumped anything else since they needed to communicate with each other more than the outside.

"Not entirely sure," Carlos mused. Was Benson's voice getting fainter?

Carlos flicked on his head lamps which illuminated only about ten yards of the water in front of him. It was just enough to give him a false sense of security that he could see things around him, without showing him much of anything. He was glad Asha could get her lights on without needing assistance, knowing she'd been successful once the area around him lit up just a bit brighter than it had before.

"Once more unto the abyss, dear friends." Keaner's voice sounded ominous, filling Carlos' helmet like he was another warm body crushing against him in the suit.

"If you gaze long enough into an abyss, the abyss gazes back into you." Carlos muttered the words, checking his forearm to make sure they were on the right track to the other hab. Benson's voice was a bare whisper in his helmet.

"Are we really reciting random bits of quotes right now?" Asha sounded exacerbated, and her breathing in between words sounded short.

Did you really need to share your body count? Carlos wanted to snark back. He held his tongue and studied his display instead. There weren't any real landmarks to go by, so Carlos verified their direction as best he could and adjusted their trajectory slightly to the left.

"Asha's right. Let's conserve our oxygen and energy. Just a bunch of nice, easy breathing for our delightful walk in the park." He hoped Asha would take the hint and slow herself down. If he needed to be worrying about her this entire three-mile walk, this was going to be an even more excruciating experience than it already was. Each step he took felt like he was moving forward toward a cliff's edge that he couldn't see. Sure, the sea floor around them should be relatively flat but that didn't help the pervasive sense of dread the darkness brought down. There was a reason prehistoric humans hid in caves when night fell, and then worked so hard to maintain fires to keep the dark at bay.

Carlos smirked at his little inside joke with himself and checked their direction.

Still going where they needed to.

The darkness moved out of the way of the light as they pushed forward. Rocks, some the size of basketballs, others the size of elephants, materialized in the wavering glow of their headlamps. Carlos thought that it might be a worthwhile use of his time to map out these surrounding rocks and structures to get a lay of the underwater land. Shouldn't they know what was around them, even if they weren't going to see it ninety-nine percent of the time?

He supposed this also depended on the state of the hab when they returned, and what they found at Kraken 3.

Off to the right, a gradual incline that took an abrupt ninety-degree turn caught his attention. Carlos tried to keep one eye on the way forward while taking in the impressive rock structure. It was difficult not to become absorbed in what he was looking at. The rock was grayish and white, not looking quite like anything he'd ever seen on the surface. Carlos turned his head little by little, focusing more on the smooth surface of the rock, wavering in the deep-water ocean currents. His helmet lights climbed up, up, up, fading out on the rock wall before it could reach the top.

"Hey!" Asha's shout jolted Carlos back to the fact that he was at the bottom of the ocean walking miles to another hab. "Less sightseeing, more walking there, pal." There was still an undercurrent of fear swimming through her voice, and Carlos felt a little guilty. He shouldn't be staring around at things like he was a tourist who'd paid to be here. This was his job, and he needed to focus.

Turning forward, his newfound grasp on his focus was interrupted by Keaner.

"That's a seamount over there that you were looking at." He sounded bright and cheery, not like a wrong move could lead to implosion. "They're underwater mountains that don't quite reach the surface. There must have been some fault action here at some point."

Carlos didn't respond. Keaner could talk for hours about topics that interested him, and as they had been reminded already, they needed to conserve their oxygen.

On his forearm, the display screen showed them still on track despite his distraction. They were almost halfway there, and it looked like he was doing fine with his levels.

"How are your O2 levels, kids?" He looked forward into the unending darkness, a black so complete it could, and would, swallow him, and everything else that ever existed, whole. There was nothing like walking into the unknown to get the heart rate up when he needed to be calm. Carlos huffed out a breath, promising himself that would be the last big inhale he would take. If he could just stop thinking about how vast it was down here, maybe he would stop feeling like the sand under his feet was going to suck him down.

As his eyes tracked through the darkness, he thought he saw something flitting around at the edges of his light. A Mordices? He squinted, and blamed it on his eyes playing tricks on him.

"I'm at seventy-one percent." For the first time, Asha sounded calm.

Even if it were something, the light would keep it away. At least, he thought it should.

"Eighty-six," Keaner chirped, still bright. Carlos couldn't understand why the man so enjoyed being out in this terrifying ink. He also wasn't sure how Keaner's O2 was still so high. Maybe because he was used to breathing in a suit. Carlos' own level was at eighty-one.

Movement at his periphery distracted him from his thoughts about oxygen levels and mathematical equations about how much they each would have left by the time they got to the other hab if they kept walking at their current pace. Carlos tried to catch what it was without turning his head and alerting the others. He was sure Keaner wouldn't mind if they had sea creatures hovering around their circle of lights, but he knew Asha would, and if he was being honest, he didn't like the idea of them being around either.

Carlos checked his forearm display, noting that they hadn't moved much further since he last looked. Without saying anything, he started walking a little faster, hoping it wasn't so much faster that Asha and Keaner would notice. With any luck, a submersible might be at Kraken 3.

Not because everyone had died in the hab and hadn't had the opportunity to escape. No, of course not, he reasoned. It would be because Amphitrite used to supply each hab with *two* submersibles, and then decided to get cheap.

Yeah, exactly, that's what he was going to go with. Thinking about finding a bunch of dead bodies at Kraken 3 set his heart to pounding. His O2 level ticked down another number. He needed to get his racing thoughts under control. If he could just convince himself that everything was fine, that there weren't terrifying fish in the ocean, or that there might be other horrors they had yet to encounter–

His thoughts trailed off. Right in front of him, a Mordices swam around the curving edge of his light. Breath catching in his throat, Carlos tripped over nothing in his big deep walk boots but managed not to tumble over. The slight buoyancy of the suit helped him to stay upright. The fish didn't seem to be interested in them, its long, knuckled fins dragging in the sediment and causing it to disperse upwards in the water. It floated into the darkness and then Carlos noticed something else around the edge of light. What looked like a hand with thick, gnarled fingers dragged out of the encroaching light. A swirl of sediment was left in the wake of the appendage. There wasn't even any shape hovering at the edge of the light that the hand–was it even a hand? –could have been dragged back by.

He was imagining it, he had to be. Was this Ocean Dark Syndrome? Was he really succumbing to that while he was supposed to be leading two other people across the ocean floor?

Carlos picked up the pace even more, checking his forearm display for the direction and noting that his O2 had ticked down two more numbers.

"Fuck." He muttered the word out loud and when he realized, he thought, *Double fuck.*

"Carlos?" Asha's voice stuttered around his name. He didn't answer, trying to pretend like she hadn't said anything. His eyes darted around the darkness, looking for any movement or spots that were darker than others.

Could anything even get darker than the abyss that laid out before them?

"Carlos." This time, Asha's voice snapped at him over the comms. "What's wrong?"

Had the water always swirled with eddies at the edges of the circle? Around the entire circle or just in spots? Carlos couldn't remember, and his brain refused to spit out any memories of the walk from earlier. How could he have forgotten already? It wasn't that long ago.

This couldn't be Ocean Dark Syndrome. He didn't feel crazy.

"Nothing, Asha. I just remembered that I left the stove on." His footsteps counted out the beats of silence between his stupid answer and Asha's response.

"You're kidding me, right? That's not what you're thinking about." She paused, and he could imagine her face wrinkling up in thought. Carlos reached up to rub his earlobe and bumped his gloved hand against his helmet. "What's going on, Carlos?"

"Did you see something?" Keaner still sounded excited and chipper. Carlos wanted to shake him, but that was unrealistic in these suits: there wouldn't be anything for him to grab onto for a good shake.

"No." The rest of what Carlos wanted to say got stuck in his throat at the new things coming into his field of vision.

Orbs floated down around them, lilting in the currents. About the size of a softball, and a pearlescent purple when the light shined on them, three of them drifted to the sand in front of Carlos. He twisted around to see another three, no, four, scattered around Asha and Keaner.

A whimper came through the comms. "What are these?" Asha sounded like she was a second away from unleashing a scream.

"Probably just debris from the surface." Keaner's dismissive tone didn't help Asha.

"Are you stupid? What the hell is going to be floating down from the surface out here that looks like that? We're on the bottom of the ocean in the middle of nowhere!"

"Just don't touch them," Carlos snapped, regretting his tone. "Don't touch them," he tried again with a gentler voice. In his peripheral, something flitted in and out of the circle of light. He jerked towards the movement to see nothing other than sand and darkness.

"What're they doing?" Asha's voice rose an octave, reaching the pitch of an almost shriek. Her breathing came hard and fast through the comms.

Carlos turned around to see three Mordices swimming into the circle. Their long, weird fingers reached forward to the spheres, curling around them and lifting them up.

"I don't know. Just, just keep moving." Despite his order, Carlos found he couldn't move his legs forward. He was entranced by the Mordices gathering up the spheres, the surfaces of which were squirming.

One of the Moridces curled its knobby fin-fingers up and pressed the sphere into its mouth. The teeth tore into the sphere, shredding the pearlescent surface. From the tattered edges, a torrent of worms erupted. Some of them got sucked into the Mordices' throat. The rest…

Asha's scream rang through the comms and tore through his ears before the system had a chance to muffle the sound.

The worms filled the water as more Mordices ripped open the spheres. A cloud of them swam towards Carlos and he backed up into a human sized object. They both tumbled to the ground, sending up billows of sand. On his back, Carlos saw the worms descend on him, blanketing over his helmet. The ends waving over the glass of his helmet had rings of teeth that clenched closed against the glass, producing of chorus of tiny squeaks.

Fear washed cold over his body, and he flailed his hands around his helmet, knocking the worms off. If they broke through the suit, he'd die. They wouldn't get a chance to eat him. His body would just be crushed from the pressure. A split second of light and heat, and then nothing. He wouldn't even know what happened.

"They can't get in!"

Carlos could barely hear the voice over the roaring in his ears.

"Hey! Calm down, they can't get in!" In addition to Keaner's voice trying to reassure him, he could hear Asha grunting and cursing.

“Die, just die, why are there so many of you!”

Some of the worms slithered off his helmet and spiraled up into the blackness outside their circle of light. The rest still pressed their teeth against the glass, trying to get in. Keaner was right. They were helpless against the suits.

“I wouldn’t do that, Asha.” Carlos registered the nervous tone in Keaner’s voice. He pushed himself off the ground, trying to push the remaining worms off his helmet. “You don’t know where those came from.”

Getting to his feet, the air feeling heavy in his lungs, Carlos watched as Asha snatched a swimming worm and jerked her hands apart, ripping the thing in two. Carlos flinched.

“Fuck these things,” she snarled. She grabbed for another one and missed.

“Come on,” Carlos said. He looked up to see if any more spheres were coming down. There was only darkness above. “Let’s just get to Kraken 3. We need to move.”

“I want hazard pay,” Asha grumbled.

“Along with your union mandated breaks?” Carlos’ quip got a laugh from Keaner.

“Oh ha ha,” Asha drawled. Carlos smirked at her sarcasm, checking the readouts on his forearm display. He shuffled his feet until they were aimed in the right direction.

“You’re all selling yourselves short,” Asha added. “We could…we could…”

The sarcasm drained from Asha’s voice and Carlos swallowed hard. He slowly turned toward her and saw her looking up.

"Oh, shit on a stick," Keaner breathed. Carlos guided his gaze upwards and saw dozens of pearlescent purple spheres raining down into the reaches of their headlamps. Mordices swam among them, their gnarled fin-fingers twisting and grasping.

"Move," Carlos ordered. He swung around and took a few steps forward before stopping. His light caught something, maybe about ten feet up. Maybe fifteen? Carlos couldn't be sure, because what he thought were eyes reflecting the light of his headlamp disappeared into the murk faster than he could make them out in the light. He stepped forward, trying to move his legs faster than the deep walk suit would allow. "Come on, we have to move." His voice sounded a lot calmer than he felt. His fingers were tingling, and he could feel his hair standing on end, an electric line running down his spine.

Movement that swirled the sand and currents caught his attention, and he angled his head to look. Just outside of the reach of the light, off to his left, two red specks glowed, lower to the ground than whatever he'd just seen.

"What is that?" Keaner still sounded excited, maybe a bit apprehensive. Nowhere near as terrified as Carlos thought they all should be.

Below the two specks, claws slipped into view, piercing through the darkness to take shape in the light. There were four of them, yellowy and cracked, tracing lines in the sediment as they came forward.

A purple sphere drifted into his vision, the surface writhing. Carlos batted it out of his way, still walking even as he watched the thing at the outer edge of their lights.

The claws sprouted from wrinkled gray toes, or maybe fingers. Long and stringy with tendons that flexed beneath the flesh, they led up to rounded knobs that turned up at an angle, leading into the dark. The two red specks rose up in the inky black, blinking in and out of existence.

Sound traveled better underwater, even at these depths. So when Carlos heard a rumbling growl that made his blood run cold, he knew exactly where it was coming from. Asha's whimper turned into a high keening noise, like a tea kettle forgotten on the imaginary stove Carlos hadn't turned off. The growling became deeper, an almost physical force moving through the water towards them.

"Run." Carlos didn't yell the word. He didn't even manage to put any inflection in his voice. The word was three letters put together for a singular command: get to safety.

Plunging forward, Carlos took off to the right of whatever this deep-sea monstrosity was. How much further to Kraken 3? God, he didn't know. He hadn't checked, and until he made it past what he felt was certain death, he wouldn't be able to make himself look.

There wasn't even a way to check and see if Keaner and Asha were following behind him. He would have to stop and turn himself all the way around, and that was not happening. Carlos would just have to trust that the heavy breathing sounds in his helmet weren't just his own.

Running underwater in a heavy deep walk suit was difficult under the best circumstances, and these were not the best. Terror had a way of making the body feel heavier than it was, clumsier. Each step took a monumental amount of effort, compounded by the fact that he was moving through water and with his limbs encased in metal and plastic.

The thing behind them had stopped growling, and he didn't know if that was because it was in pursuit or if it was satisfied that they had run off.

Carlos chanced a look down at his forearm display. A droplet of sweat ran down his nose and splashed onto the glass of his helmet. They were a hair off course, still heading towards Kraken 3, but bound to overshoot it if they continued on this trajectory. Jerking his head up, Carlos course corrected. They were less than half a mile from Kraken 3. Surely, they could make it. He prayed they would make it, a cycle of words mashed together from half remembered prayers he had not bothered uttering in years.

Our Father, Mary full of Grace, thy kingdom come, pray for us sinners.

Did any gods even bother with what resided at the bottom of the ocean? This special sort of isolated hell?

White spikes reared up in front of him. The reach of the light from the head lamps didn't give him enough time to react before he collided with one. It shattered from his momentum, throwing up a thick cloud of white specks swirling around in the water. The impact made Carlos trip, and he fell forward onto his knees and elbows. A scream tore through his comms, and then Keaner's voice broke through.

"Get up!" He no longer sounded excited or chipper. There was a note of fear in his voice that made Carlos feel suddenly normal. Keaner was just as afraid as them after all.

Awkward hands grabbed at his arms and elbows, hauling him up. His feet scrabbled beneath him, trying to find purchase in the shifting silt and sediment. Looking up, he saw they were encased in curved, pointed structures that rose up on each side of them, closing over the tops of their helmets.

Was this a rib cage of some long dead monster?

The growl reached his ears and he shook off the helping hands, checking his forearm display. Carlos spun around, trying to reorient them back in the correct direction. Above them, something smashed into the bones, sending another cloud of white fragments spiraling through the water. Carlos caught a flash of yellow claws and gray skin.

"That way." He didn't bother pointing, he just ran. Their path took them straight down the length of the ribcage, the height of the bones decreasing as they went. It felt like something was chasing them still. Some primal sense was telling his crocodile brain that he needed to run as fast as he possibly could if he didn't want to get torn to pieces. Something was hunting him, hunting them, and he had no idea what it was.

The bones disappeared as they left the giant remains behind. It was only the darkness and the ocean floor ahead of them. The light illuminated more and more of the same, instilling a dreadful sense of futility in Carlos. There was nothing out there. There was no hab, no Kraken 3. This was all bullshit, and all this running was depleting their O2 levels and they were going to suffocate out here at the darkest, most desolate place in the world. The red eyed monster was going to find them and peel them out of their suits like shrimp, or maybe suck them out like oysters, enjoying the only red meat it probably ever had.

Carlos wheezed in his helmet, his legs burning. How could he be struggling? He ran all the time, for hours. Yet, here he was, his blood pumping in his ears, peripheral vision fading, electricity crackling along his skin, and he was fucking exhausted. Carlos felt like he couldn't go another step, take another breath.

He'd always thought it sounded so dramatic when people said they were so tired they couldn't feel their feet or some nonsense. But Carlos understood what they were talking about; he was mired in that numb hell himself.

Then, gray walls erupted out of the light in front of him.

It felt like slamming on the broken brakes of a speeding car, the way Carlos tried to slow himself down. He hit the wall hard, whipping his head back and forth. Something cracked in his neck.

"Open the door!" Asha screamed. Keaner's voice mirrored hers. This wasn't a door, though. This was just one side of the hab. Carlos turned to look behind them, unsure if he couldn't see the red eyes due to lack of light or the creature giving up the chase. Deep down, he knew something like that wouldn't give up so easy, not with such easy prey. Carlos refused to think about that. Instead, he tapped at his digital display and searched for a hab entrance.

"This way." He didn't wait for them to acknowledge him before he took off. There was an emergency entrance, different from a dry dock but it would serve their purpose for escaping this monster.

At least, Carlos hoped it would.

The thing hadn't done much more than scare and chase them, but maybe it liked to play with its food before it ate.

Carlos couldn't think about that. He needed to keep moving, keep Asha and Keaner moving. The emergency entrance wasn't too far. It should be coming up, right here.

Should be…

Right…

There!

Stopping underwater didn't work the same as it did on land. There was less friction, more buoyancy. It felt almost like physics didn't apply. Carlos' effort to stop sent him sailing past the emergency door, the reflectors around it flaring under the light of his head lamp. The word "EMERGENCY" flashed past him. Trying to twist around, Carlos lost his footing, and then Asha or Keaner crashed into him. In the chaos of the moment, it was impossible to tell who it was between the deep walk suits and everyone's lights blinding him.

The structure of the suit kept Carlos from being crushed by the collision, but it rattled him. He looked around, trying to get his bearings, and heard the rumbling growl of the creature.

Oh, hell.

Carlos shoved his hands out, knocking whoever was entangled with him away. His movements were sluggish, slow motion, and he wanted to scream. Clamping his teeth together, Carlos lurched up and slammed into the emergency entrance, the big yellow "RG" letters of the word EMERGENCY reflecting the headlamp light back at him. Blinking away the spots in his eyes, Carlos looked for the panel that should be covering a lever that would open the door for them.

"Beautiful!" He shouted the word when his eyes landed on it. In the background of the noise in his head, he could hear screams and the creature's growling. It sounded louder, like it was invading his suit and digging into his bones. A slot for the bulky fingers of the deep walk suit was right on top of the panel. Carlos jammed his glove in and pulled. The panel resisted, more than he would have thought. Panic, which he was only just keeping at bay, surged down his arm and he yanked, tearing the panel off. Carlos let it drop to the sea floor, and grabbed the lever, wrenching it down.

Behind the door, Carlos heard a series of thunks and clicks, the whirring of machinery as things began to move. Everything sounded like it was struggling.

Turning his body, Carlos caught sight of Asha and Keaner to his right. The proximity of their lights made it difficult to see their faces, but he didn't need to see them to know they were freaking out as much as he was. Twisting in the other direction, the door still making labored noises, he looked into the empty space spreading out from the outer wall of the hab. Nothing was there. No reflective eyes, no claws thrusting through the water. The growl was still reverberating around them, so the creature had to be nearby.

Where the hell was it?

An alarm sounded from the door, alerting them that it was about to open.

"Get over here!" Carlos shouted, despite it being unnecessary. Asha and Keaner were right next to him, and they would have heard him if he'd whispered due to their comms. It was hard not to yell, with everything going on. His blood was pumping hard, his breathing was rough, and he could feel a tremor starting in his hands from the adrenaline exhaustion.

"Come on, come, on, come on." Asha chanted next to him, her words speeding up like she was trying to match the pounding of his heart.

"Um, Carlos?" Keaner's voice barely registered with Carlos.

"What?" Carlos didn't turn around, too focused on watching the door, waiting for it to open so he could drag them all inside. There was a *click*, and a metallic grinding started up, the door sliding to the side.

Keaner didn't say anything else, but something made Carlos look up. Whether it was a slight movement or a feeling, Carlos jerked his eyes up and looked into two glinting red orbs. Some noise came out of him, a cross between a curse and a screech. He forced his mouth to form words, to give a command.

"Get inside!" The door was open just enough for them to squeeze through. Asha went first, the smallest of them, the most likely to get through the gap. The bulge on her back that housed the battery for her suit's electronics banged against the wall, a flurry of bubbles exploding out from it. Carlos looked up at the monster, the red eyes closer than they were before. Keaner was sliding in after Asha, disappearing through the half open door.

His turn.

Carlos looked away from the monster, as if the lie kids believed about monsters being unable to hurt them if they couldn't see them was true. Stepping over the threshold felt like stepping into a different world, one that was only a little bit safer than the one he was leaving.

His crew mates were pressed against the far wall, not that that left much space for him. Emergency entrances were usually meant for one, maybe two people, as it was rare for there to ever be more than two people outside of the hab at a time. Even with them all the way inside, Carlos was bumping up against them when he spun around and slammed his hand against the button to close the door. The machinery ground to halt as the door stopped opening, and then the whirring started again, reversing the door to the closed position. It crawled across the track, somehow taking even longer to make that journey than when the door was opening.

"Close, close, close." Carlos found himself chanting the same way Asha had been just a minute before. When two feet of open space remained, yellowed claws curled around the upper edge of the doorway. Screams reverberated in Carlos' helmet. They all must be screaming for it to be this loud.

The claws retracted from the entrance, as though the monster was startled by the noise.

One foot of gap was left. The door was almost closed.

In the glare of their headlamps catching the cascade of sediment outside the door, a gray shape moved into the gap. An expanse of gray skin, a flash of red, and the yellow of reaching claws, slashing into the enclosed space.

There was nowhere for Carlos to go in the enclosed space, nowhere for him to backup or turn. He tried to duck the strike, but didn't move fast enough. The claws struck the glass of his helmet, sending a spiderweb of cracks throughout one side. Carlos swatted at the clawed hand, and felt himself jerk forward.

The claw was stuck in his helmet.

Whatever this thing was, it was pulling him out, or trying to. The door was closing on the creature's arm and it seemed to know it was in danger of losing an appendage. Carlos and his suit were not going to fit through the narrowing gap. The creature pulled him against the door, trying to wrench its claw out of Carlos' helmet, or pull Carlos out with it.

Emergency doors weren't like the other doors in the hab, though. They didn't stop and reopen when obstructions were encountered. This door would close regardless of what was in the way., and Carlos was getting an up-close look at what happened when something got in the way of the emergency door, his head lamp lighting it up for optimum viewing displeasure. The flesh of the creature's arm tightened, pinched by the edge of the closing door, making the meat beneath bulge. Fluid squirted out of tears ripping across the surface of the gray skin. It was blue or green or black, the shining of the head lamp making it almost impossible to tell the true color. The arm thrashed, jerking Carlos around. He let the arm take him, knowing that if he fought too much, he risked the embedded claw damaging his helmet even more.

Beyond the door, an ear-splitting shriek started. Even when the door closed, setting off a hiss of bubbles, he could still hear the monster. There were several loud noises as the door locked, and then an alarm sounded. Carlos jerked away from the door, the wrist attached to the claw sunk into his helmet flopping around. Ragged edges of flesh floated around a splintered bone. This wasn't as bad as seeing two people get killed earlier, but this was much more up close and personal. A roiling in his stomach made Carlos nervous he was going to vomit in his helmet.

On the screen to Carlos' left, the words "STARTING DRAINAGE" flashed. He just had to hold his bile down a little longer, just a little longer.

There was a high-pitched hiccup sound, like someone was biting back a sob. Carlos knew he hadn't made the sound, but he knew he wasn't too far away from the same reaction. He looked up, noticing that the water level was already dropping. Reaching up, Carlos grasped the end of the creature's arm. Even though the suit prevented him from being able to really feel things, he could tell that the skin was squishy, like it was already decomposing or full of water instead of meat. His stomach gave a threatening roll.

The water level dropped below his eye level. Carlos jerked at the appendage, trying to pull it out of his helmet. The claw was sunk deep in the glass, though thankfully not deep enough to have punctured all the way through. Carlos didn't want to think about the implosion that would have happened if that were the case.

Even if implosion were as painless as he was led to believe, Carlos didn't like the idea of his body being crushed to a fraction of its size and left on the bottom of the ocean. It felt somehow like being removed from the world entirely.

Frustrated at how stuck the claw was in his helmet, Carlos banged against the glass with his fist.

"Water's almost all the way out," Keaner commented.

Carlos hesitated to turn around, knowing what was stuck in his helmet.

“You okay there, Carlos?” Asha’s concern was colored by a splash of fear. Her voice trembled over the vowels, stuttering them out.

“Yeah,” he muttered. There was a faint sucking sound as the rest of the water drained. He heard helmet locks click, and the accompanying hiss of air as they were removed.

Taking a breath, Carlos turned around. Asha screamed, and he was glad he couldn’t hear her through the comms anymore. Keaner’s mouth dropped open and then he laughed, high and thin.

“Welcome to Kraken 3, everyone,” Keaner crowed. “Need a hand, Carlos?”

Mina

Godsdamnit, this headache was atrocious.

Mina ground her thumbs into her temples, squeezing her eyes shut against the pain. How hard had that whiplash been?

Groaning, Mina looked through bleary eyes at the desk in her room. It was covered with neat stacks of textbooks, paper files, and digital discs. There was no room to do any actual work on the desk, which was why her unmade bed was also covered with strewn about papers and books.

Pain pills. She needed more pain pills. Or maybe a steady morphine drip. She'd never had a headache this bad before.

Getting off her bed, she went to the gold-colored baskets hanging in a vertical row on her wall and fished out a bottle of pills. Dry swallowing two, she sighed and hoped they would at least dull the pain for a bit. So far, nothing took the pain away, and she was getting a creeping feeling she was going to need to return to the surface with Perisdo and what remained of his group when they went back. The last thing she wanted to do was have to go back up to see a doctor, but there was no way she could remain down here and work if her head was going to hurt this much.

Mina exited her room and walked down the hall, her vision swimming around the edges. Is this what a migraine was? She pushed the heel of her hand into her right eye, her world flattening into two dimensions. Maybe she would talk to Zane. She *should* talk to Zane. He was her partner down here, after all. If he was as bad as Carlos said he was, he would need some pain management, too. He for sure had something strong in his room, but she wasn't about to go looking through his stuff without permission. It felt weird to go through someone else's stuff even with their permission.

Mina mumbled to herself as she walked, trying to remember which way she needed to go in order to get to Zane's holding cell. And, by holding cell, she was referencing the empty bedroom he was being kept in. It was a good thing they kept staffing to a minimum down here. Chuckling, Mina had a sudden, sharp thought that minimum staffing wasn't a good thing. There should be more people down here. In fact, it would be so much more beneficial if the hab were fully staffed up, whatever number of people that meant.

"It's so loud in here." The words left her mouth without her even planning on saying them. What was loud? She tilted her head like a dog trying to pick up on an interesting noise, but heard nothing over the general hum of the hab and maybe a slight ringing in her ears.

Wait.

Mina stopped, looking up, down, right, left. She stared out into the black water beyond the viewing window. Was there… Was something moving out there? Calling out? Did someone need help?

Were the three who went looking for Kraken 3 in trouble? Mina stepped up to the glass and flicked on the switch to illuminate the space right outside the window.

There was nothing. Only sediment and water and darkness. She stared and stared, straining her ears for anything over the pounding in her skull. The darkness fluttered around the edges of the light, like it was a living thing. Her eyes scoured the edges, looking for real movement and not just phantom imaginings.

After a minute, Mina turned the lights off and turned away. Her brain was playing tricks on her. Whatever it was she thought she'd heard, it wasn't out there in the abyss.

Zane's "room" wasn't much further down the hall, marked by a red X on the display screen that usually showed the name of the occupant. Mina faced the door, staring at it like she could see through it, an advanced warning about the state that Zane was in. Even though she hadn't been able to get a good look at him when Perisdo and Keaner dragged Zane out of their makeshift dissection theater, she'd seen enough to know he hadn't been in good shape.

Mina couldn't let that stop her. The pain in her head was still pounding, and she needed to talk to Zane. They were partners in science, after all.

Flashing her ID bracelet against the display, she stepped through the door as it slid open, no special code needed even though Asha was meant to do that. Lucky her.

The first thing that hit her was the smell. Decaying flesh, a thick, flat smell that she never forgot after her work investigating various bacterial colonies growing in slaughterhouses. The smell settled into the lining of a person's nose like a sticky film, and could reactivate at the most inopportune of times, with the most bizarre of triggers. Once, the smell was triggered for her when she looked at a book in a bookstore. The color of it had been the same maroon shade of meat that came off one of the carcasses in the slaughterhouse, and that shade of red tricked her nose into believing it was back there.

Here, in Zane's room, it might not be a slaughterhouse but that smell pervaded.

Zane was on the bed on his side, sleeping, his eyes closed and his chest rising and falling in a steady rhythm. There was a livid red burn on his cheek bone that curved around to his eyebrow. A clear liquid seeped out of it, running down his face in tracks that looked like tears. The skin around the wound twitched. Mina wrinkled her nose, wondering if Zane was dreaming or if maybe his body was reacting in an unconscious way to the untreated burn. She knew burns were delicate in the way that they needed some of the most specialized treatment of any type of wound. Zane was getting none of that, zip tied to the bed, locked in this room.

The state of Zane's arms made Mina tear up, the hot burn closing her throat up. From the first knuckles of his hands almost down to his elbows, it looked like there wasn't any skin where there should be. His forearms were a pulpy red mess, clots of black blood flecking the exposed muscles, yellow pus oozing out of the wounds, leaving streaks of pinkish yellow fluid mixed in with the clots all over the sheets. A smear of it covered his chin. There was a dark, wet patch on the fabric of his pants that she had to assume was another burn.

"Oh, Zane," she whispered, feeling her shoulders round forward.

Zane's eyes snapped open, like her words had triggered a switch in him. They were bloodshot and darted around the room, casting about for something to land on. His jerky eyes passed over her a few times, like he didn't recognize that she was there. When he did look at her, it felt like he was piercing her through with metal hooks and pinning her to the wall.

"What're you doing here?" His lips moved just enough to get the words out, his voice raspy, each word a struggle. "Mina…you're…" He coughed and it sounded wet.

"I, um, I, I, I needed, um." Her words failed her. Would he even be able to tell her where any drugs were in his room? How could he be allowed to exist in this condition? "You're, you look…not good." Zane's entire face twitched, spastic, like he was getting electrocuted. His mouth twisted in what could be a smirk or a grimace.

"I need," he wheezed, "I need you to kill me. They're–"

The door behind Mina slid open, starling her into a yelp. She caught a darkening of Zane's face before she whipped around, almost bowling over Perisdo in her haste to exit the room.

"What are you doing here?" He grabbed her arm and hauled her through the doorway. Before it closed, she heard what sounded like a wail coming out of Zane. His voice slid beneath her skin, expanding between her muscles and making every fiber of her body ache. Whatever pain he was feeling, Mina felt like she was experiencing an echo of that.

Mina winced, ducking her head to press her palm to her forehead. Perisdo dragged her halfway down the hall before he realized that she wasn't really moving herself forward and was more being guided by him.

"What's wrong with you?" He ducked his head to peer into her eyes, but she kept her head down, avoiding his gaze. "Doctor Kibner. Why were you in that room?"

Perisdo's authoritative tone made her look up through squinted eyes, a groan slipping out of her mouth before she could catch it.

"I've had a massive headache since the…hrngh. Since what happened yesterday." It still felt like Zane's pain was squirming beneath her skin, slotting into the grooves of her muscles, the curves of her bones. Just what she needed: some sort of freak coworker sympathy pains.

"A headache?" Perisdo looked at her like she was a specimen he was trying to understand.

"From when I fell. I think it's whiplash, or something. I thought Zane might know if there were any drugs in the lab that would help." Mina winced and ducked her head. She was going to have to take half the bottle of ibuprofen at this point.

Perisdo remained silent until Mina tilted her head up. She was taller than him, so it wasn't like she had to look up at him, but she needed to at least look up from the spot on the floor that was occupying her attention to meet his eyes. He looked at her intently, his eyes flicking back and forth between hers. Mina wondered what he was thinking, or looking for; maybe signs of a concussion. Her symptoms would fit, she guessed, with the intense headache. She'd never had a concussion before and never thought to do any reading on them. It was possible, even likely, that Perisdo had played contact sports in his younger years and was familiar with head injuries.

Making a thoughtful noise in his throat, Perisdo turned away from Mina.

"Come with me, Doctor Kibner. I think I can help you."

Asha

This was insane. This was actually insane. Asha couldn't believe that she'd been on a deep walk to Kraken 3, and it had turned into a sprint for her life because some sort of monstrous creature had chased them.

Chased them.

What the hell were they supposed to do now?

Sitting in the hallway outside of the emergency entrance, Asha watched Carlos and Keaner try to pull the claw out of Carlos' helmet. The helmet was useless for another deep walk. There was no way Carlos could wear something that compromised back out into the abyss.

Asha was hoping they could find another submersible and wouldn't have to make the walk again. That was the best-case scenario. She didn't want to think about the worst-case scenario.

Kraken 3's hallway looked exactly like Kraken 7's, and she figured that would mean the layouts were the same. Or, at least she hoped.

Another hope. At this rate, all she was going to have was hope and fear, because she didn't feel like she'd stopped being afraid since she'd stepped foot out of Kraken 7. Her hands were still shaking after sliding down the wall of the hallway and sitting for several minutes.

"That's in there pretty good," Carlos grunted, yanking on the crushed end of the creature's arm.

Keaner's mouth quirked up, his eyes brightening.

"Don't you say it, Keaner." Carlos looked up at Asha's preemptive reprimand. She glared as Keaner's smile grew and he started to open his mouth. "Keaner!"

" 'That's what she said'." He grinned through the overused and tired joke that people still tried to make a part of regular conversation. She never even found that show that funny.

Carlos looked between the two of them and rolled his eyes, followed by rolling his head from shoulder to shoulder, rubbing his neck. "Keaner," he huffed, digging his fingers into the nape of his neck, "stop trying to make fetch happen. Let's try and find their lab. We could use one of those laser cutters to try and get this out."

Asha used the wall to wiggle and slide herself up. "Do you think that'll work?"

" 'You miss every shot you don't take'," Keaner grinned. Asha sneered at him and flipped him the bird.

"Wayne Gretzky," Carlos provided.

Keaner held up the helmet and shook it so the dismembered limb flopped around with a wet slapping sound. "Who?"

Carlos groaned. "Never mind. I'm assuming this hab will be structured like ours, so let's just head for the lab. But first, Asha, come here." He gestured for her to turn around. "I want to check your airpack. You hit it pretty hard when you went into the dry dock."

She didn't remember hitting anything, but turned around anyway. Carlos mumbled as he checked her rebreather pack, tugging and pulling, making her brace her feet to keep from being pulled around. With even the smallest bit of luck, her airpack wouldn't be an issue. Even if there was no sub, she could use a different suit.

"There we go." He slapped her shoulder. "Let's get a move on, kids."

As they started down the hallway, Asha looked around at the very clean, very empty, hallways. "An alarm should have sounded when we used the emergency entrance." She tried to make her comment seem like an observation rather than a concern, but the nape of neck prickled anyway.

Carlos half turned to look at her, then faced forward again. "You think there's still people at this hab?"

Asha hesitated. Is that what she thought? "There was nothing indicating that it was decommissioned."

"Or that it even existed," Keaner reminded her.

"Then why would they still have the lights on? Why would the air still be good in here?" Asha looked around the hallways and gestured with her arms, as if that would somehow help her to explain. "There should be someone here. Right?"

"Ash, these systems are self-sustaining," Carlos explained. "They can go on forever so long as nothing breaks. The hab doesn't need people to function."

That sent a shiver down her spine. Something didn't sit right with her about this humanmade environment existing without the humans it should be supporting. She wanted to start screaming "Hello!" down the hallways, let the echo travel to whoever might be around and listening.

Or maybe she didn't.

"Do you think that thing from outside got them?"

No one answered her until Carlos finally said, "Let's just get to the lab and get the hell out of here."

Their silence was taken for agreement and they pressed onward.

Asha kept glancing around at the walls and ceiling, looking for any clues of what might have happened here. People didn't just disappear without a trace. There would be *something* left behind, anything. Scuff marks, blood, dents in the walls…

There. At the joint where the wall met the ceiling was a tiny blinking light above a dark lens. A camera.

Kraken 7 didn't have any cameras, something about violating employee's privacy, legal this and that. A brief section had been in her contract about it without much of an explanation.

Why have cameras here, but not at Kraken 7? Asha's heart fluttered at the possible reasons Amphitrite would have for removing cameras. She knew they didn't actually care about employee privacy. So, what would they be trying to hide?

Asha was no closer to an answer by the time they made it to the lab which was where they expected it to be; the layout here was exactly the same as theirs at Kraken 7. "What if we don't have access to the lab?" Asha asked. She didn't have access to the Kraken 7 lab, so why would any of them have access here?

Keaner shrugged and flashed his bracelet in front of the display. The door slid open. Grinning, Keaner pointed to himself and said, "Science officer."

"Or Amphitrite is lazy about granting access," Carlos grunted. He stepped into the lab ahead of them. Lights flickered on, detecting their motion in the room, illuminating a space that did not look at all like the lab at Kraken 7.

"Oh my God," Asha breathed.

"Well, this is bad." Keaner's voice was tight as they surveyed the scene before them, speaking the understatement of the year.

The smell hit them almost at the same time they realized what they were looking at. Heavy and cloying, it smelled like the day-old meat Asha left out on the counter once, except one hundred times worse. It was rot and decay, invading her nose and sliding down her throat to leave a bad taste on the back on her tongue. There was so much blood, and it soured the air beyond belief. Splashed across the walls, pooled on the metal tables, streaked across the floor. The bodies the blood must have come from–because surely this much blood had to be from multiple people–were nowhere to be seen.

Asha stepped further into the room, looking down at the red she was stepping on.

"This is old." At the questioning looks from her crewmates, she gestured a limp hand at the floor. "It's dry. None of us are leaving tracks."

There weren't any tracks period. A few of the streaks looked like they might have been drag marks, but Asha did not know how how to be sure about what she was looking at.

"How old?" Carlos looked to Asha, like she should know these things. She didn't, she just felt it was the most obvious way to tell. Stepping towards one of the metal tables, she picked up a tool off one of the trays.

"Well," Asha said slowly. She reached out with the tool and poked at the blood on the table. It was hard, and bits flaked off the more she dug in. "I'd say pretty old but I'm no expert." Grimacing, Carlos reached up to rub his earlobe.

What the hell had happened here? Where the hell was the crew? The fine hairs at the nape of her neck stood on end, and even though she was encased in a deep walk suit, she could feel the goosebumps rippling along her arms. She wondered if all this blood had something to do with why Kraken 3 was not listed on any of the maps. In fact, she recalled the Kraken hab numbers jumping around. Is it because those "missing" habs looked like this?

She watched Keaner moving things around on the desk that spanned the entire length of the wall. There didn't seem to be any files out, and none of the computers turned on when he interacted with them, having been powered down completely.

Asha crossed the room, leaving Carlos to his musing and Keaner to his searching. This was the last thing she wanted to do, but it needed to be done and she didn't know if the others would object. She knew she would have, if either of them suggested it. She repeated to herself over and over that this needed to be done as she grasped one of the doors to the freezer compartments. Just like the freezer at Kraken 7, all she needed to do was push in on the handle and turn. Her stomach clenched, and everything in her screamed not do this. The freezer tray slid out of its compartment when she pulled, the gentle squeaking of unoiled ball bearings tracking out with it.

Nothing. Nothing on the table.

Asha released a big breath and slid the tray back in.

"What are you doing?" Keaner was right next to her when he spoke, startling her enough that she jumped and slammed the freezer door shut.

"Checking for bodies," she snapped, trying not to focus on her pounding heart. She grabbed another handle and looked at Keaner. "Have you noticed they're missing?"

Asha stared at him, realizing she was only using this interaction to delay opening any more of the freezers. There could be a body in here that she didn't want to see. One with red eyes and claws.

Tilting his head, Keaner squinted at the freezer like it was out of focus.

Behind Asha, a door handle clunked and a freezer tray slid open. Whirling around, fist held against her heart, she saw Carlos looking down at an empty tray.

"She's right. No drag marks in the hallways?" He slid the tray back in and moved to the next one, not experiencing the same level of difficulty with this task as Asha was. "Where did they go?"

"The cleaner bots probably cleaned up any blood in the hallways." Keaner shrugged. Carlos opened a third compartment, and

Asha returned to her second. The faster they did this, the faster they could get out of here.

"They would have cleaned in here, too," Asha reminded him. "They're programmed to clean everywhere unless a person is in the room. Even if they didn't clean the tables, they would have at least done the floors." There was nothing in the second compartment she opened.

"The computers in here are dead," Keaner observed. "We're not going to be able to get anything out of them. We should just see if we can find a sub and head back."

"If there's even one here," Asha muttered.

"There will be one here." Carlos spoke with an authority that made Asha feel better, even though she was expecting a dead body to pop out of one of the freezers at any second.

Keaner grumbled something that Asha didn't catch as he walked over to one of the computer screens. She shut the final door she needed to check on an empty tray.

"I'm going to go check something out," Asha declared, seized by a sudden idea.

"Alone?" Keaner and Carlos echoed the word at her and she rolled her eyes.

"Yeah, it won't take long. And I get the feeling that I'm more in danger from that thing outside the hab than I am from anything in here. Don't worry about me." She kept walking towards the door, throwing a wave over her shoulder.

"I'll go with you." Keaner grinned at her when she turned around. Damn. She didn't want either of them tagging along. "This way at least one of us knows kung-fu." He did a bunch of quick movements and a sad looking kick that Asha doubted was anything close to kung-fu.

"I need your help here." Carlos thumped the helmet with the creature's hand on the table, and looked between the two of them. "Asha can handle herself." He inclined his head towards her, and she understood the nonverbal words he was shooting at her: *Don't do anything stupid.*

Walking backwards, Asha shrugged at Keaner's frown. "Sorry, Keaner. Maybe next time."

Outside the lab door, Asha looked back and forth between the two directions she could take and turned left. She popped her helmet on, but didn't seal it, this way she didn't have to carry it and have it banging against her leg the entire walk to the communications office.

Just because Keaner couldn't get the computers in the lab to work, didn't mean she couldn't work her magic in an office that would be just like hers.

Asha glanced up at the red lights of the cameras every time she saw them in the hallway, her fingers sequentially tapping her thumb to a random rhythm. She was going to find out exactly what happened here.

Carlos

It had taken a little bit of time, pulling, yanking, and swearing, but they finally got the claw out of his helmet. Even with the laser cutter, the claw tore out a chunk of the helmet glass which sent a spiderweb of cracks over the entire thing. Carlos was pretty sure he could tap it with a finger and the glass would shatter. No way was he going to be able to make the journey back without a sub, unless he could find another helmet.

That was a problem for a little later though. With the creature's arm laid out in front of him, Carlos looked at the array of tools next to the table.

"What do you think we should try first?" Keaner asked. He seemed distracted, looking around the room from time to time. Or maybe he was just as scared as Carlos felt and not hiding it as well.

Carlos thought the creature that chased them was bad, but finding an empty hab with blood all over the floor in the lab and no bodies? At least, no bodies *yet*. Where would they be, if not in the freezers? Kraken 3 had to be at least a few years old. No one would have wanted to leave them around to decompose and stink up the place like the blood made this room smell. Or did bodies stop smelling after they decomposed? Carlos wasn't sure about that. He could remember watching a documentary about the decomposition process, but other than the narrator stating that a body smelled, they didn't go into how long that smell lingered.

"Should we cut it up more than it already is?" Carlos frowned, looking at the tools to the table.

The section of arm, from claw tip to ragged edge, was about three feet long. A few inches down from the severed end was a knobby joint, and then it was smooth gray skin all the way up the thin hand. The skin looked like that of the Mordices, and Carlos wondered if this was some sort of evolution, or maturation stage for the fish. Maybe it was just coincidence since they both lived seven miles underwater in an unforgiving climate that didn't allow for much else.

Four fingers–phalanges? Could something non-human have fingers? –grew out of the hand, from four to six inches long, and that didn't include the claws that tipped each finger. Yellow, and shot through with lines of brown, the claws looked like they could shred a person with their finely serrated edges. Carlos knew for certain they were strong; the thing cracked his helmet with only one of the claws.

"We should at least put gloves on," he decided and went to a cabinet that he hoped contained gloves. "We don't know if there's any…worms, or anything in it." Carlos thought about the worm pushing out the Terrence's eyeball, the wet squelching sounds as the eye was compressed until it burst and oozed out of the skull. His stomach gave a warning churn. Redirecting his thoughts, Carlos hoped Asha knew what she was doing. He assumed the only place she would be going was the comms office, but he wasn't sure why.

At last, a drawer coughed up a box of gloves, and Carlos snapped them on, holding the box out to Keaner.

"Did you know, they used to sell tape worm eggs as a weight loss tool?" Keaner beamed like this was important information Carlos wanted. Carlos, in fact, did not want that information, and he wished he could have maintained that obliviousness. "After you lost the weight you wanted, you'd go to a doctor to have it taken out. Could buy them out of magazines." Keaner pulled the gloves on, looking thoughtful as Carlos' stomach threatened him again. "I guess these things are all about perspective, huh?"

Carlos blinked hard and turned back to the arm on the table, praying that there weren't any worms hiding in it. "Yeah, sure." He answered Keaner in the hope that he would shut up. The skin of the arm hadn't moved at all, not even when Carlos stared at it to the point his vision got wavy.

"That was the early 1900's though," Keaner continued. Carlos picked up a scalpel, still waiting for Keaner to shut up. "Now, they're working on something called Helminthic Therapy. Doctors infect patients who have immune diseases with helminth worms, like hookworms or whipworms, and they've seen a decreased incidence of autoimmune symptoms in these patients. They're still studying it, but it seems like the worms are more beneficial than people want to give them credit for."

The last thing Carlos wanted to think about after the disastrous dissection attempt and the two people dying were the practical uses for worms in medicine.

"Keaner, please. For the sake of my sanity, talk about anything else. Literally, anything else. What star sign am I?" Picking up a scalpel, Carlos ran his free hand down the length of the arm on the table. It felt disturbingly intimate, like he was touching the body of a long lost relative or something. He tried to repress a shiver, thinking again about how this might be a mature stage of the Mordices. That would mean there were more of these things out there, an idea that was almost worse than Keaner talking about parasites.

Sighing, Keaner asked, "When's your birthday?"

Between Carlos trying to decide where to stick the scalpel and the whirlwind of horror thoughts melting his brain, Carlos needed to think before he could respond, "June fifteenth." As a kid, Carlos loved his birthday: the end of school always came around the same time so it was like everyone was celebrating his birthday. As an adult, with the magic of summer vacation vanished, it was less of a big deal.

"That would make you a Gemini." Keaner announced this like it was wonderful news. Carlos didn't care; at least he wasn't a worm. Sticking the point of the scalpel into the flesh at the base of the wrist, Carlos dragged a long, smooth line down what he was calling the creature's forearm, despite not knowing its true anatomy. The skin peeled apart into two neat halves, like it wasn't tethered to any of the muscle underneath.

"Might be why it's so squishy," Carlos mumbled.

Keaner continued on as if Carlos wasn't dissecting a monster's arm.

"A Gemini is an air sign, and they're typically social and outgoing but…"

Ignoring Keaner, Carlos noted that there were no worms inside of the arm. Nothing wriggling when it shouldn't be, or shooting up out of the weird, black muscles. At least, what Carlos assumed were muscles. He sliced open the palm, peeling the skin back to see shiny, silver tendons. Possibly tendons, he reminded himself. He wasn't quite sure what he was looking at.

"Come to think of it, none of that really fits you," Keaner mused.

"It doesn't?" He still wasn't paying much attention to Keaner. Putting down the scalpel, Carlos picked up what looked like a diagonal cutter. He used diagonal cutters when slicing through electrical wire and other bits of metal, so he figured it would work for what he wanted to do. Keaner was still babbling about star signs while Carlos lifted the finger that sported the longest claw and placed the diagonal cutter at the base of it.

At the same time Carlos squeezed the cutters, Keaner asked, "What are you doing?" There was a crack as the metal bit through the bone and Keaner grunted.

Looking over his shoulder, Carlos asked, "You okay?" The other man looked a little green in the face, and he was squeezing his hands together.

"Yeah," he ground out. "That sound just hit an unpleasant spot in my brain."

"Oh." Carlos wasn't sure how to respond to that, so he turned back to the three-inch-long claw in his hand. It wasn't curved, like a raptor claw in Jurassic Park. It went straight out, like it was just an extension of the finger.

He needed a bag to put the claw in. Even though he was pretty sure the thing wasn't infested with worms, Carlos figured it couldn't hurt to be extra cautious. Returning to the drawers that contained the gloves, Carlos opened the rest of them and found what looked to be large sealable bags. Good enough.

"Do you know what time you were born? Maybe that could explain some of the discrepancies in your personality." Keaner's voice sounded strained. Breaking bones must really bother him.

"No, I don't." Carlos dropped the claw into the bag, closed it up, and then tucked it into one the sealed pockets of his suit. Keaner was looking at the monster's arm on the table and not him, so he figured the line of questioning about his astrological sign nonsense was over. "Let's go take the long way to comms, see what we can see. Then we'll grab Asha and get the hell out of here."

"Comms?" Keaner's mouth turned downward, and his brows scrunched together. "Why comms?"

Grabbing his helmet as proof that it was broken, so Amphitrite didn't try to dock his pay over negligence or something, Carlos explained. "Where else would Asha go? I don't know what she thinks she's going to find, but I'm pretty sure that's where we'll find her."

"Oh." Keaner straightened and picked up his helmet. "Why the long way? Shouldn't we make sure she's safe sooner rather than later?"

Carlos waved a dismissive hand. "I'm sure she's fine. It's Asha." Keaner didn't look convinced, but he didn't say anything else. He followed Carlos out of the lab, and they took a right turn. After a few minutes of silence, Carlos said, "Hey, didn't Perisdo promote you to science officer before we left? Because of your previous experience?"

"Sure did!" Keaner replied brightly. He swung his arms at his sides like he needed the momentum to keep going forward.

Frowning, Carlos asked, "Then why didn't you cut apart the arm? Why let me do it?" In his mind, it would have made much more sense for someone with at least some science background to do the science stuff. Instead, Keaner just stood by and let Carlos do whatever he wanted.

"I just wanted to see what you would do." Keaner grinned at him, flashing his teeth. Grunting in response, Carlos tried to smother the chill of discomfort that crept up his spine at Keaner's smile. What the hell did that even mean?

They walked in silence that wasn't companionable. Carlos kept glancing at Keaner out of the corner of his eye. For his part, Keaner seemed unaffected by the weirdness between them. He marched along, swinging his arms, looking around like Kraken 3 was the most interesting hab he'd ever been in. Everything looked very much the same to Carlos: same gray walls and floor, the sun-mimicking lights. His footsteps even sounded identical, which was somehow unnerving. Carlos scoured the walls, trying to keep his mind off what it would mean if there were no submersible and no other suits. Would he have to wait here, alone, in the abandoned hab? Asha wouldn't stay, but maybe Keaner…?

Carlos' thoughts trailed off as he noticed a small camera tucked into the corner juncture of the wall and ceiling. A small red light blinked. Of course! Carlos wanted to theatrically smack himself in the forehead at his realization. Asha must have noticed the cameras earlier and was going to see if she could pull anything from them. Clever woman. He'd never admit it, but she was smarter than him by far.

A viewing window came up on their left and Carlos tripped, his thoughts not distracting him enough to walk past it. What if that thing was out there, waiting for them to walk past?

Keaner noticed that Carlos wasn't walking next to him and turned around. "What's going on, old man?" He smirked, waiting for the usual response from Carlos: "If I'm old, you're ancient." It was a joke between them since Keaner was older than Carlos by at least ten years.

Carlos only gestured at the viewing window, unable to find any words.

"What, this?" Keaner peered out of the window. "I don't know what you're worried about. Nothing's out there." He stepped to the side of the window, reaching for the switch that would turn the outside lights on.

"Keaner, don't!" Carlos lunged forward, grabbing for Keaner's hand. He was positive that if those lights went on, there would be an army of monsters out there waiting for them. They'd stare in here with their glowing eyes and lunge forward, raking the glass with their claws until they punctured it like the other one did to his helmet.

Except this time, there'd be no escape. Even if they ran fast enough to get into a sealed corridor before the water drowned them, those things would be inside the hab with them. They'd all die.

The lights flicked on and Carlos froze, staring out into the half circle of illumination. All that moved was sediment in eddies of water. Not a single living thing stirred.

Keaner shot Carlos a questioning look. "You okay there?" The unspoken question that Carlos could see on the other man's face was, "Do I need to be worried?"

Maybe he should be. Carlos rubbed his face with the hand that wasn't holding his helmet. He felt paranoid and scared, but weren't those reasonable reactions to what just happened? This wasn't Ocean Dark Syndrome. It couldn't be. The way Carlos was reacting was completely normal for what they experienced out on the ocean floor. Just because Keaner seemed unphased, didn't mean he actually was. He could just be masking it better, or his tolerance for weird shit was higher than Carlos'. Keaner had been doing this for a long time, a lot longer than Carlos. Still…

"None of this has you freaked out?" Jerking his hand out, Carlos turned the lights off, plunging the space beyond the viewer into the pitch black again. He walked past it without looking out, convinced that things were closing in on them in the dark.

"I guess a little? We're down here to find weird stuff, though, so it's to be expected?" Carlos could hear the shrug in Keaner's voice without looking at him. Keaner wasn't bothered by this at all, and that didn't sit right with Carlos.

A scream echoed down the hall. Carlos jerked to a stop and looked at Keaner. Another scream flew down the halls and the two men took off, sprinting down the hall.

Asha.

Asha

The comms office was exactly where she expected it to be. Asha did not find this reassuring. In fact, the more she realized how alike Kraken 3 was to Kraken 7, the more she felt like she was in some sort of weird alternate timeline.

One that had monsters.

She half expected a clone of herself to be sitting in the chair, reading the same rom-com novel she was halfway through. There was no one, though. No clone of her–she wouldn't even entertain the possibility that s*he* could be the clone–and no one else, either.

Sitting in the seat, she realized that whoever the comms officer was here, was not her clone: the ass molding in the seat was wrong. Breathing out a sigh of relief that felt unreasonable, Asha settled her fingers over the keyboard and woke up the computer. It opened right up, no password needed.

"Seriously?" Asha scoffed. "No wonder this place went to hell. Not even the comms officer followed protocols." Lucky for her, though. The quicker she could get into and out of the computer, the quicker she could get back to her crewmates and get the hell out of here. This place gave her the creeps, and while she was terrified about going back out into the abyss, staying here scared her more.

The screen desktop was empty save for two icons: an unlabeled folder and a camera lens titled “EverTrue Sec”. It was strange that there were so few icons. Her desktop was cluttered with an assortment of things from note documents to security programs. Was her desktop just chaotic? Was this more normal? Frowning, Asha clicked open the program list and found that there weren’t any programs to be found on the computer other than the one for EverTrue Security Cameras. No mail program, no computer security, not even those simple games like Solitaire that often came preprogrammed into the software. Her desktop with multiple icons wasn’t weird; this one was.

Asha hovered the arrow over the folder, undecided. Why was everything else on the computer gone except for these two icons? She’d come here for the camera footage, but the unknown folder was an entirely different kind of enticement.

No. She needed to focus. At least for now.

Clicking on the camera icon, an array of camera views spread across three monitors. She did a quick count of ninety views and couldn’t decide if that was the right amount or not enough for the size of the hab. Computer security, not physical security, was her prerogative.

All of the views gave her a sudden feeling of being overwhelmed. What the hell was she even looking for? Answers to what happened here, and especially in the lab, but, how exactly was she supposed to do that?

Asha scanned the cameras until she found the little image of the lab, Carlos and Keaner moving around in it. This was a good place to start. At least she knew for sure something had happened there.

Opening that camera view brought up the current view of her crewmates, a scroll bar for playing through the camera on the bottom, and on the left side of the screen was a series of dates and times.

Moving the mouse down to the scroll bar, she clicked the ticker at the end of the bar and dragged it backwards. She watched the screen reverse itself, Carlos and Keaner moving like disjointed cartoons. She reappeared on the screen as they searched the lab, and then they all started to back out. The room emptied, leaving only the blood, and then the lights flickered and went out. That was it. There was nothing left to scroll back on.

Asha redirected her attention to the bar on the left, then snapped her eyes up, scanning the other camera views. Narrowing her eyes, Asha stared at each little square. She thought she'd seen movement, a brief flicker rushing past a camera. Nothing moved anywhere. Giving herself a shake, Asha looked back on the left side of her screen. This place was getting to her. No matter how much she reminded herself that this was just like her hab, it didn't help to reassure her at all. There air was bad here. It didn't have a smell to it, other than in the lab. It was more like a feeling of pressure, like how it feels when a roller coaster plummets down the track, pressing the rider back into the seat. She wondered if Keaner and Carlos felt it, too.

The bar was organized in a descending order of dates, with the most recent date at the top. This first listed date was three years ago. She assumed that was when everything hit the fan and went to hell.

That should be the date which showed what happened in the lab. Asha hesitated, then moved down to the earliest listing which was only six months prior to the first one.

Two women walked into the room, dressed in white lab coats, activating the overhead lights in the lab. One had long hair so red, Asha couldn't believe it was natural, and the other was so short Asha wasn't sure she'd top five feet. They looked around the room, smiles on their faces, gesticulating at things. The red head opened up the freezer and hopped onto the tray after sliding it out. She mimed being dead and her partner laughed. A smirk lifted the corner of Asha's mouth. They seemed normal so far. Asha raised the volume to hear their voices, then sped up the video once it became clear they weren't talking about much. The two women did some organizing and then left, the camera shutting off once the lights did.

Okay, boring enough. Asha clicked the next video and dragged the scroll bar across the screen, speeding through another banal video of the women sitting in the lab and talking. The next several videos she clicked were like that: routine. A couple of times she let the video play when they brought specimens in, but none of them looked like Mordices, so she continued on. For almost five months of videos, the women talked, dissected recognizable deep-sea fish, and reorganized the lab.

With only four videos left, Asha landed on something interesting.

The women sat on the tables, one kicking her feet which didn't reach the ground, and the other scrolling through a handheld tablet. At the same time, they looked up at a man rolling in a cart with a large rectangular case on top. The face of the woman sitting on the table pinched together, while the red head grew excited, a smile splitting her face. A brief conversation ensued between the three about a new specimen in the box. The man spoke so softly, Asha couldn't turn the volume high enough to hear him.

Once the man left, the women lifted the box on the table and stared at it. They were excited about the possible new species. Leaning toward the screen, Asha sped up the video until the red head came to the side of the table with what looked like a crowbar. She jammed it into the box and pried the sides apart.

The container exploded, knobby appendages shooting out. Asha jerked away from the screen, flinging the mouse away, a yelp popping out of her mouth. The two scientists screamed, putting distance between them and the appendages that were no longer moving. They conferred, and then approached a step at a time until they were close enough to remove the rest of the pieces of the box.

A Mordices. That awful horror of the deep that rumbled fear into her bones and might be filled with worms. Asha wanted to scream at them to put it back into the box and set it on fire. Get rid of it, toss in the dry dock and send it back into the ocean.

The two looked down at the gray skinned fish monster with the long finger-like fins and the glowing white eye. Grabbing an instrument, the short woman prodded at the creature with no response from it. They conferred again and backed away.

Before they were quite out of reach, one of the long appendages whipped out and wrapped around the red head's arm. Asha jumped out of her seat, as if the Mordices could reach her through the screen. Acting quickly, the short woman grabbed what must have been a cutting tool because it sliced right through the fin. The one end remained wound around the red head's arm, and the short woman grabbed at it and ripped it off, flinging the appendage across the room. Angry red welts blossomed over her skin.

Throwing the cutting tool on another table, the short woman grabbed her partner and dragged her out the door. The lights remained on for a long time, longer than in any of the other videos. Asha couldn't see any movement in the creature, but maybe the camera was picking up something she couldn't see. Her skin crawled.

Later in the video on that same day, the scientists came back dressed in personal protective gear and moved the fish into the freezer. They didn't linger. Asha opened the next video which was the red head staring at the wall of freezers. She stood there for hours and was eventually joined by the short woman. They both stood there, staring, and then left without any conversation.

As worried as Asha was about opening the last recording, she felt more dread about opening the second to last recording which was stored only two days after the video of the women staring at the freezer. It felt like she was hitting a point of no return, but she also thought she was already there. How else to describe being chased by some underwater monstrosity?

Sucking in a breath, Asha started the video. There was a rush of motion: a man and woman she didn't recognize sprinting in and throwing around trays and tools. The noise they made blared from the speakers, assaulting Asha's ears. They seemed to be looking for something, but Asha couldn't fathom why they would need to be so violent about it. Maybe only thirty seconds passed between them running in and when the red-haired woman barreled onto the screen. She had a cleaver in her hand, already wet with blood that also bathed her in wide swaths of red. Asha's chest tightened at the sight, the woman looking like a bucket of blood had been dumped over her.

The people in the room whirled around, empty handed, their eyes wide in fear and their mouths even wider in screams. She lunged for the man, swinging the cleaver into his chest. The crunching sound it made could be heard over their screams. Blood sprayed out and he fell backwards. She followed him, swinging and hacking, blood splattering on the walls and floor, every surface. A hard shot to his arm severed it at the elbow, the limb dangling by strings of white tendon until those snapped, the lower arm falling to the ground in a splash of red.

From behind the blood-soaked psycho wielding the cleaver, the other woman leaped onto her back, wrapped an arm around her throat and squeezed. Her face scrunched up as she worked hard to compress her arm against the other woman's throat. Just a few feet from them, the man was on his knees, grasping at the stub of his arm as blood gushed between his fingers. He tried to stand and kept slipping in the blood.

Switching her grip on the cleaver, the red head swung backwards and planted the edge of the weapon into the other woman's skull. It sounded like a huge watermelon being struck and cracked open. She spasmed, her whole body tightening around the red head, before she went limp and fell to the ground, dragging the cleaver with her. Asha squeezed her hands together, digging her nails into her skin, watching as the red head walked towards the man. Her gait was smooth and calm, at odds with the bloodbath around her. With no emotion on her face, she leaned down towards the man who hadn't noticed her as he was too busy trying to staunch the bleeding from his arm. Spreading her hands out in front of her, she thrust them forward, jabbing her thumbs into the man's eyes.

Asha screamed at the violence which somehow seemed more personal than the attack with the cleaver. The man jerked beneath the red head's hands, and he scrabbled at her, trying to dislodge her hands from his face. She kept shoving her thumbs into his eye sockets, down to the base of her thumb. Her hands jerked, and part of her hand slipped into the man's eye sockets with a crunching, sucking sound. He stopped trying to grab her, his arms dropping to his sides. The body sagged down, and she let it, shoving her hands into his skull, disappearing up to her wrists.

Jumping up, Asha stumbled backwards, tripped over the chair, and almost fell down. She couldn't stop staring as the woman's hands disappeared, sinking her forearms into the man's skull. Asha waited for what felt like forever for the arms to push out of the back of his head, but they never did. Instead, she stuck out her bent elbows and then snapped them in, forcing her hands out of the sides of the man's head. No sound came out of Asha's throat even though her mouth was open, a silent scream wrestling in her lungs. Tiny bits of skull and brain matter landed with small splashes in the blood that was everywhere, sounding like heavy rainfall.

Shaking her hands, as though that would somehow clean off what she'd done, the woman turned around and reached for the cleaver. It stuck in the dead woman's head, and it took several shakes before it dislodged. The body fell back to the floor, the head making a sound like two rocks smashing together.

The red head looked around the room and then walked out, leaving the carnage on screen until the lights dimmed.

Asha stepped towards the desk, carefully, like if she made too much noise the woman from the video might come after her with the cleaver. It felt like her heart was never going to stop banging into her ribs, like she'd never be able to forget what she'd just witnessed. She'd seen a dead person before, even prior to what happened at Kraken 7, but never like this.

There was nothing else filmed in the lab that day. Asha wondered what videos from the rest of the hab would show. Checking the time in the corner of the screen, she didn't think she'd have much more time to look, so she set the final video, recorded three days later, to play.

Lights flickered into existence, revealing the same gory scene that the red head had left. A man with short hair stepped into view, dragging something black with him. He surveyed the room and then dropped what he was holding. Asha squinted, thinking the items looked like big black duffel bags. She watched as the man went to the dead woman first and dragged her back to the duffel bags. Her body squeaked through the blood on the floor. When the man set a duffel bag next to the dead woman, Asha realized she was incorrect.

They were body bags.

He rolled the woman into the bag and zipped her up. Asha caught the side of his face, just a quick flash, and wondered what the hell he had to do with this, why he was so calm. Once the woman was tucked in the bag, he dragged the man's body over and struggled a bit to roll him into a bag. After the bodies were tucked away, he stooped over to pick up any bits of body matter stuck in the blood. It didn't take long, and he was silent the entire time. Not a sigh, a sniffle, a curse. The white noise from the video was oppressive against her ears, and her mouth twisted into a grimace. The man gave the room one last look over before he picked up one end of the body bag and dragged it backwards. He grabbed the woman's body bag when he came within reach of it, and started to drag that one, too. He never turned his head, never gave Asha an opportunity to see his face. There was something about the set of his shoulders, though. Something vaguely familiar...

The man disappeared out of the frame and the lights flickered off.

Grabbing at the mouse, Asha exited the playback video, showing the present-day lab and gasped.

It was empty.

"Shit, shit, shit." There was no time to look through any other videos or even the untitled folder. Scrambling, Asha looked around the desk for any writeable drive that she could copy the information to since the mail program had been removed from this computer. When she didn't see anything on the desk, she tore open the drawers and cabinets in the room. There was nothing in any of these goddamn drawers or cabinets, nothing of any use. Asha continued to curse at the air as she crawled under the desk. If she couldn't find a writeable drive, she'd just take the whole damn CPU drive.

Unplugging the main unit to power it off, Asha popped open the front of it. Just like her unit at Kraken 7, the computer's drive was a tiny box located in the center of the unit and it contained all the memory and processes for the unit. Or, whatever was left after someone deleted all of it. Asha slid it out, and once she got back into a standing position, she tucked the drive down the front of her suit into a pocket normally meant to hold a drinking pouch. Backing out of the room, not caring that it was a mess, Asha turned and jogged down the hallway.

Something really fucked up happened here, and it had something to do with those freaky fish creatures.

As she moved through the hallways, Asha glanced up at every camera she saw, wondering what they'd seen three years ago.

Where had the bodies gone?

Passing a viewing window, she avoided looking out of it. She would be out there soon enough, and the idea made her shudder. She wanted nothing more than to be back at Kraken 7, sharing what she found with Carlos and trying to figure out what the hell they were going to do. Those fish were already on Kraken 7. There weren't even any worms on these videos, and yet this place had gone to hell. What would happen to her hab?

Asha needed to make it to where the sub should be. Would be. Hopefully. Thinking positive thoughts would manifest positive outcomes, or at least she liked to think that.

Rounding a corner, Asha jerked to a stop, her breath catching in her throat. At the next intersection of hallways were a stack of body bags. Maybe "stack" was a little dramatic, but six or seven of them layered on top of each other made the lumpy black mass tall and menacing.

"Ummm." She stared down the hall, not sure what to do. There were other ways to the submersible, but did she really want to backtrack and walk through these haunted feeling hallways? Carlos and Keaner could already be there, waiting for her. If she put her helmet back on, she could speak through the comms, but that would waste oxygen and she might need every last gram. Hesitating a few more seconds, Asha decided to push forward in spite of the goosebumps she felt pebbling her skin. Everything felt super sensitive, like each individual skin cell was sending a message a terror to her brain. She didn't understand why the body bags would be stacked here. There wasn't much at this end of the hab beyond the mess hall, gym, and a submersible dock.

Asha grimaced. Maybe these were people who tried to escape.

One slow step at a time, Asha edged her way down the hall, keeping her back against the wall. She stared at the bags, trying to figure out why they still looked so full. Sure, the habs were supposed to be pretty sterile and germ free since it wasn't easy to get medications or medical care down here. But people were still full of bacteria and should be decomposing on their own, shouldn't they? It was times like these Asha regretted not remembering anything from high school. Sure, she never needed the Pythagorean Theorem in every day life, but biology lessons about decomposition would have been a helpful memory right about now.

Something rustled in the pile of bags and Asha halted her movement. It was her imagination. She was one hundred and twenty percent freaked out, and her brain was playing tricks on her. There was no conceivable reason why one of those bags would move, or something buried in them would move.

She took another few steps and one of the bags lower in the pile jerked.

Asha yelped and jumped back, tripping over her clunky boots and landing on her ass. She wasn't imagining it. Pushing herself back across the floor, the body bag jerked again and dislodged the ones on top of it. The stack tumbled down, heavy thuds making Asha flinch. The bodies sounded like they were still meaty in the bags. The body avalanche stopped, and so did Asha's scooting across the floor. Nervously, she leaned forward over her knees, trying to see if maybe something normal had dislodged the stack. There might have been a pet they kept around, like George, and maybe the pet was eating the corpses.

Bile crawled up her throat at the thought. Some animal eating the corpses was a lot better than the alternative.

A rasping sound almost brought the bile into her mouth. One of the zippers was sliding open. Something dead was coming out of the body bag.

Something.

Dead.

From a bag still half buried in the pile, a gray limb punched its way out and Asha screamed.

Carlos

The screams echoed down the hallways, spurring Carlos on. Keaner couldn't run for anything and lagged behind, huffing.

"Asha!" It was pointless to yell her name, since she probably couldn't hear him over her own screaming, but he shouted for her anyway.

Carlos rounded a corner, taking it a little too sharp and almost losing his footing. His neck crunched with the strain of keeping himself upright. This goddamn suit made everything so difficult whether he was underwater or not. At the end of the hallway he turned down, he saw a black mass and spared a thought to wondering what that was. Powering down the hallway, he didn't check to make sure Keaner was still following. The black shape took form as he got closer: stacked black bags. Some of them tumbled down.

Was Asha somehow under those bags? Was she stuck underneath them? Wild scenarios rolled through his mind as he barreled forward.

Asha screamed again.

Skidding to a stop, Carlos realized how big, how *human-sized,* the bags were. He wrenched himself to the side and almost screamed himself. Asha was there, laid out on the ground beyond the body bags and screaming, her face opened in terror.

There was something standing in the hallway, one of the black bags wrapped around its foot. It looked human, at least it was human shaped with legs and a torso and arms. It was naked, and every inch of skin was covered in sores. Red, puckered circles oozing yellowed pus were interspersed with black bumps of various sizes. A chain of black bumps on the back of its arms quivered and exploded with a succession of quick popping noises, a black liquid spraying onto the floor. There was a meaty tearing sound, like scissors chopping through raw meat, and knobs of vertebra tore through the skin of the person's back.

Except, Carlos didn't think the thing was human anymore.

The human shaped head was stretching above the shoulders, the neck inhumanely long. Two lumps grew from the sides of the neck, tearing through the human flesh and sloping down into the shoulders. Blood welled up from the lacerations in the shoulders and cascaded down the thing's back.

"Oh, hell no," Carlos whispered.

The vertebra snapped out of the skin which peeled away from the open wounds like the papery skin of an onion. Twisting its arms unnaturally, the thing grabbed at the edges of skin and yanked. It sounded like paper being shredded as the skin was pared back, tugging at muscle fibers, snapping them with tiny crackling noises. Yellow globs of fat dislodged from the skin and plopped to the ground with wet *thwacks*.

Keaner collided with Carlos, and Carlos grabbed onto his crewmate like he was the only thing that would keep him afloat in an ocean of terror. A smell like rotting meat filled Carlos' nose at the same time the creature's skin crackled and fell from its grasp, the arms flopping to its sides.

"Carlos!" Asha met his eyes, and she pushed herself to her knees.

A chatter of clicking noises came from the creature–Carlos couldn't think of it as human anymore–and the bumps on the thing's neck jerked up with audible popping noises, forming a second set of shoulders. The clicking noises grew louder, but not loud enough to drown out the wet slurping noise the thing made as the new shoulders kept jerking upwards, pulling long limbs out of what was once a human body. Moisture glistened off the new limbs which looked thin and frail, too soft to do anything other than flail. Several long, thin spines flexed away from the arms, strands of mucous dangling off them.

"Asha, run here! Now! Come on!" Carlos shouted at her and the creature listed around to look at him, leaning as if this new body couldn't hold up its weight. Pale white eyes glowed dimly from the skull, and a lipless mouth peeled back to display two rows of small pointed teeth. Feathery looking antennas, like a butterfly's, lifted off the thing's head, exposing a ridged blue brain lodged inside the skull. Its spine twisted in a way that it shouldn't, unable to hold the top half of the creature up all the way so that it almost seemed to fold in on itself. The skin from the top half of the body flaked off and hit the ground, cracking into pieces. There was a roaring of blood in Carlos' ears, and all he could think to do was scream, "Run!"

Carlos waved his arms above his head, communicating his panic through movement. Behind the creature, Asha gained her feet and tried to run while keeping her body pressed against the wall. The hallways always seemed so wide–fifteen feet across, according to the specs Carlos memorized–but with the monster right smack in the middle, it no longer looked that spacious. Keaner stepped in front of Carlos, like he was going to try and grab for Asha. Carlos grabbed him instead, pushing him back.

"We don't need both of you getting caught up with whatever that thing is." He looked from Keaner's tight face to Asha who was run-sliding past the creature. It turned its torso a quarter of the way towards her, and then its bottom half started to twist to face Carlos and Keaner. The pale human skin on the legs started to crack and fall, flaking off like dying leaves from a tree, exposing grayish-yellow flesh. Somehow, the feet slid around without the thing having to lift them. They looked like they were vibrating. Like how a centipede moved all its legs in smooth, uniform movements. He couldn't tell from this distance if there were any little legs on the thing's feet, and he wasn't about to get any closer.

As Asha slipped past, the thing swung up a limp looking arm that wasn't so frail after all. The finger-like appendages, less rounded and sharper than when Carlos last looked, swiped through Asha's short purple hair, unable to find any sort of grip.

When Asha reached them, Carlos and Keaner both grabbed one of her hands and pulled her between them.

"The submersible," she gasped, running while holding onto their hands. They were dragged after her, Carlos getting one last glimpse of the weird creature. The rest of the human skin fell to the ground and the thing fell to all fours. It opened its mouth and emitted a shriek that stabbed into Carlos' ears, the antenna on its head flaring upward and shaking like some sort of warning. He wanted to press his hands against his ears, but Asha was dragging him and not letting go of his hand. The sound followed them down the hallway, around the corner, and kept chasing them.

The terrifying thought that there would be no submersible cut through Carlos' brain. If they needed to find a helmet for him, they would need to back track. What if that creature wasn't the only one of its kind? What if there were more of them hiding in the hab?

"Were those body bags?" Keaner's shout was only just loud enough to be heard over the shriek still echoing down the hall.

"What does that matter?" Asha's sharp retort shut down any response from Keaner. "Right up there." Each word was expelled on a huff of breath. A new shriek echoed down the hall and Carlos winced. He sure as hell hoped it was right up ahead. There was no guarantee that even if there was a sub down here, it would be docked in this particular area. It could be at either of the other two docks.

If there was a sub.

A small sign on the ceiling had a pictograph of a sub, and an arrow pointing to the left.

"There!" His comment was unnecessary; Asha was already steering them that way.

At the end of the hallway, they turned into was a dry dock door. Beyond, he could see the inside of a sub. They'd made it. They wouldn't have to do a deep walk, and he wouldn't need another helmet.

Asha dropped their hands and smashed the button to open the door. It was such an odd, quiet contrast to the ear-splitting noise still bouncing down the halls at them.

The three crewmates stumbled into the room, trying to fit through the entrance to the sub at the same time.

"Alright!" Carlos backed up and grabbed Keaner, hauling him away from the entrance. "Asha knows how to pilot the damn sub. Let her in first." Asha gave him a thumbs up and hopped through the door to sit at the single console. Carlos pushed Keaner through and then followed. He slapped the button to close the door, and it whispered shut.

"Any day now," Asha sing songed to the sub. Carlos looked from the window showing the dry dock to Asha who was typing away, flipping switches, turning things on or off.

Turning back to the window, his stomach plummeted to his feet. "Any day now would be really great, Asha."

"Why?" She sounded distracted.

"Because that thing is coming down the hall." Keaner's voice was right over Carlos' shoulder, but he didn't turn around, his eyes latched onto the monster.

It half-crawled half-loped down the hallway, the legs and arms splaying out in flailing motions. The head bobbed with each stride, almost smacking the floor each time, the eyes flashing white and red.

It wasn't screaming anymore, instead it wheezed and growled, drool spilling from between the sharp teeth in its gaping mouth.

Lunging forward, Carlos smashed the button for the dry dock door, and it closed with a decisive click. He waved his Amphitrite bracelet in front of the scanner and pressed the option to lock the door. He didn't know if the thing could operate doors, or if it was a crewmate from Kraken 3, and he wasn't about to find out.

Carlos backed away from the door as the creature slammed against it, sounding like a sledgehammer against the metal.

"Shit!" Asha yelled. Carlos looked back at her and met her eyes, seeing the panic in them and knowing his face wouldn't look any less fearful.

"Just hurry up, Asha!" The thing slammed into the door again, roaring. Carlos could see the glistening gray skin in the hallway lights, and when it shoved its face against the window, he was able to get a good look at the inhuman face. The skin was smooth, and when it opened its mouth, he could see that the teeth spiraled down as far into the throat as he could see. Its glowing eyes still flickered between red and white, and seemed to lack eye lids. The skin above the mouth was smooth, with no obvious nose. The antenna lifted from its head, feeling against the window. Carlos couldn't see through the thing's skull anymore to the blue lump of brain.

The creature huffed a breath against the glass, fogging it, and then squealed. Rearing back, it raised an arm with a yellow clawed hand attached to it.

Carlos stepped away from the door, stumbling back into the sub.

Swinging its arm forward, the creature slammed its claws into the glass of the window. It screeched as the claws scraped against the window, putting deep gouges into it.

"How we doing back there Asha?" Carlos didn't look back at Asha or Keaner. He smacked the button to close the sub door, then pulled the lever that would start filling up the dry dock with water in order to equalize the pressure and prevent it from collapsing under the ocean's pressure.

"Just about there." She was still half singing the words, as if trying to keep upbeat in spite of the monster slamming on the dry dock door.

Glass shattered and the creature shoved first one arm and then the other through the small window.

"The faster, the better." There was a tremor in his voice that, if they made it out of here, he would deny ever happened.

Leveraging its arms on either side of the door, the creature shoved its head through the window and then started to pull its body through the window. It looked at Carlos and snarled before falling through the window to the floor. It splashed into three feet of water.

"We're in business!" Asha shouted. A series of musical notes sounded, drawing Carlos' attention. Asha was punching a triumphant fist into the air, Keaner hovering over her shoulder. Several thunks sounded from outside the sub, and a scream was followed by the high-pitched whine of something scraping the glass. Carlos jerked back to the sub door.

The monster was standing, slashing its claws against the window. It looked furious to be unable to get to them. This window was much thicker and reinforced to protect against the millions of tons of water that would be trying to get into the sub and crush them. They would be fine, Carlos reassured himself. He was about to let himself relax, to let his shoulders sink down, when another strike from the creature cut a gouge into the glass.

"Here we go!" Asha crowed. "Back to Kraken 7!"

Carlos stared at the shallow gouge and at the creature's snarling face beyond it.

Shit.

Divya

Everything was awful. Well and truly awful. It was even worse that whenever she thought about how everything was awful, it came out in a little jingle ear worm. The original words to the jingle were "Everything is awesome", which made the juxtaposition of the words in her brain even worse.

The only way this could be worse was if someone was singing the jingle out loud.

Divya spun herself around in a seat in the command portal. Most of the screens were off, a few showing readouts from various instruments documenting that hab's breathable air, pressure levels inside and out, and blah, blah, blah. Divya threw her head back with a groan.

Out of boredom and a need to just *do something* to avoid thinking about the dead people, she'd come here to run diagnostics on all the equipment and make sure everything was in working order. Which it was, of course. The only things not in working order in Kraken 7 were the humans, and she was stuck here with them. Divya snapped her fingers a few times, trying to puzzle through what was bothering her.

Other than the obvious. Two people were dead and her crewmate was…sick. Divya shuddered, thinking about how Zane looked when he was dragged out of the room by Keaner and that asshole Saul Perisdo. Twisting her face in a grimace, Divya stopped spinning her seat and stood up. She paced the length of the room, which didn't reflect the way she imagined a command portal would look. The idea of a command portal evoked images of bright screens and bustling activity, a nice big window to see what was coming. This area, though, was the darkest space in the hab. Most of the monitors were off, there was no viewing window–not that there would have been much to see–and they almost never gathered here. Her gaze drifted towards the ceiling, still snapping her fingers. There were those awful fish, the arrival of upper management, their very sudden and acute interest in what they were doing down here in the science section. What was it they were looking for, and why did Divya have a feeling it had to do with Kraken 3? Mina had known a lot about the other hab, so she must have found that information somewhere. It should be in the lab. Where else would Mina have found it?

Marching out of the command center, Divya turned towards the lab. It wasn't the furthest point away from where she was, like most things seemed to be in this place. Divya didn't have a scale down here, but she was pretty sure all this walking was making her lose weight. And the food wasn't too great, either. For all the money Amphitrite paid them, she would have thought they could send better food down here. Most of the food items were dry goods, or dried in general. Most of the fruits and vegetables she ate came from sealed brown bags, and they were crunchy in the worst way. Keaner kept offering to work his kitchen magic to make them more palatable, but Divya had no interest in letting that annoyance help her. She didn't care if part of his job description was chef. The cat didn't like him and neither did she.

The halls of the hab felt eerie, empty in a way they usually did not. It wasn't like she always saw other crew when she was walking the halls but it never felt like she was the only one who existed down here, either. Divya shivered, goosebumps breaking out over her skin. Although she didn't want to see anyone else as she walked to the lab, it would at least be reassuring if she did. Even spotting an upper management douche to sneer at would make her feel less like she needed to check over her shoulder for bad spirits.

Imagine that? Divya scoffed and smirked at herself. She was more spiritual than religious, but her parents had instilled a healthy dose of fear in the unknown in her. As much as she denied that she feared supernatural entities and gods, it was hard to banish every devil she'd once feared from her mind.

Biting her lip, Divya checked over her shoulder, telling herself she was just making sure that no one was following her.

Which was ridiculous. No one would be interested in following her. None of her crewmates were creeps like that, and she was pretty sure the big-headed management guys were afraid of interacting with her. So, there was nothing to worry about. Nothing to justify the nervous burble in her stomach or the tingling feeling in her chest. Shaking out her hands, Divya paused at the final turn that would take her to the lab. She looked in the direction of the lab, and then in the opposite direction. Divya turned away from the lab, towards the window that showed her the "view" of the ocean that surrounded them. It was laughable, really, that being able to stare a few feet out into the darkness was called a view. Even with the lights on, all any of them ever saw were eddies of sediment, maybe some random gray piece of plant matter. There were never any fish, no animals to be seen. At the beginning, that comforted Divya. It was like when her parents would take her camping. It was one thing to know there was the possibility of bears and pumas and whatever else out there in the woods, and something completely different to see them.

Seeing a Mordices made the reality of them far worse.

Not a single thing moved out in the darkness of the ocean.

"Fuck you." Divya pressed her middle finger against the glass, glaring at anything that might be floating around out there. She stayed like that for a full minute, hoping that whatever was out there got the full meaning behind her words and gesture. "Fuck you," she repeated, before turning away from the window.

She was going to get answers. Then, she could go see Zane, check in on how he was doing. Granted, she imagined he wasn't doing well, but she could check. Just because she didn't like human interaction didn't mean she couldn't make an effort.

Waving her ID bracelet in front of the lab's scanner, a red icon flashed, denying her entrance. Divya bobbed her head back, frowning. That was new.

Sliding a multitool from a pants pocket, she went to work prying open the scanner panel. Nothing inside looked amiss, which meant the door was programmed to refuse entry to certain people. Not about to be denied, Divya rerouted some wires until the red icon blinked off and was replaced with a green one. The door slid open, and Divya stepped inside, scanning the lab.

"Mina?" The tallest person on the crew stood facing the freezers. Divya paused just inside the entryway, the door hissing closed behind her. "What're you doing?" She took a few more steps in the lab and looked around. Nothing in the lab seemed to be out of order. The only thing strange was Mina, unmoving and staring at the freezers.

She took another few steps towards Mina, her hand raised to tap her on the shoulder. "Mina?"

The scientist's shoulders stiffened beneath the fabric of her shirt. It was almost too subtle for Divya to notice, but she caught it. Pausing her reach, she took a step back.

"I wanted to find out more about Kraken 3, since that's where the others went. You have anything else to add? Since, you know, you seemed to be a wealth of information earlier?" Mina didn't scare Divya, since despite the woman's size, she was always hunched in on herself and acting shy. Whoever was standing with their back to Divya, though, wasn't the Mina she knew. She stepped further back, towards the doors. It felt like such a stupid thought. How could this person *not* be Mina? That's exactly who this woman looked like. There was something about her, though. Something so very wrong. It was only a feeling, but it was one Divya thought she should listen to, superstition be damned.

Divya backed up to the door enough for it to sense her and slide open, letting her pass through. As the doors were closing, Mina half turned. "Divya?"

The insignificant creatures have such a desire to continue their lives. We can make them better. If only they will let us in.

DAY SIX

Divya

Divya dreamed of monsters. All teeth and gray skin, screaming and blood. These weren't her regular nighttime forays, which often involved neon-colored landscapes and the ability to fly or jump inhumanely high. Instead, the carnage made her heart rate spike, her limbs twitching in a panic that didn't feel dreamed up.

A loud noise startled Divya out of her sleep, drawing a yelp from her. Her wide eyes darted around the room and she realized that she was in the dry dock. Why the dry dock?

More thunking noises from the right drew her eyes in that direction. Where there should be darkness, a faint red light came through. A sudden terror gripped Divya. Was this a new version of those awful fish? Were they trying to get in?

Divya pressed her back against the wall and used it to shimmy herself up. She didn't want to lean too far forward, lest she be able to see what was outside the window, and then it could see *her*.

There were more loud noises and then the inner door slid open, a waterfall of seawater flowing into the open space. Divya's panic spiked, thinking the dry dock was about to be flooded, when the flow of water stopped.

Okay, so something wasn't breaking in, but that meant that…someone was docking? Leaning forward, she peeked around the edge of the opening and glimpsed the door of a sub. It slid open and out stepped–

"Carlos!" Divya was not typically effusive in her behavior, preferring to remain standoffish so that people avoided her. But with everything that happened over the past few days, and Mina's odd behavior, Divya was happy to see someone she knew she could trust.

He blinked at her, looking exhausted and aged. It looked like he had been gone for longer than–she checked her watch–eight hours?! It was almost two in the morning, and Divya was reminded that she had been waiting in this dry dock for them to come back. It hadn't occurred to her until just this moment that if they had returned in just their suits without the sub, they would have needed to flood this room to enter. She didn't know if an alarm would have sounded to tell her to get out, but she was glad she hadn't needed to find out.

"What are you doing here?" Carlos demanded. He cast a glance back over his shoulder at Asha and Keaner before refocusing on her. "What happened?"

His tone set her on edge, and for the first time she noticed his suit. It was dirtier than it should have been for a simple deep walk. Keaner and Asha appeared to be in a similar state when they stumbled out from the sub. This didn't look like they'd had a routine deep walk. What happened at Kraken 3?

"I was waiting for you to come back. Things are *not* going well here." Divya looked down at her hands, tracing the Henna lines with her eyes. She met his gaze with a determined set to her mouth. "We need to talk."

Asha started to strip off her deep walk suit, dropping items where she stood instead of hanging them up for decon as was the correct process. Narrowing her eyes, Divya was going to say something when Keaner asked, "What's that?"

His deep walk suit was half off and hung up, and he pointed a wrinkled pink finger at Asha's wrinkled tan hand. The state of their skin was a testament to how long they'd been encased in the deep walk suits.

"Nothing." Asha didn't snap, so much as let her voice go flat. It looked like she was holding some sort of rectangular box, but she tucked it into the waistband of her leggings and fluffed her tank top over it. "Nothing. Carlos, let's go."

Divya's mouth hung open, unsaid words dangling from the tip of her tongue as she looked between Asha and Keaner.

Asha gestured at Carlos, her movements sharp. "I need to go over something with you."

Divya narrowed her eyes at the other woman as something unspoken passed between Asha and Carlos. Asha spun on her heel and left the dry dock, calling again for Carlos.

Keaner tilted his head at the sudden tension in the room, and then ripped his deep walk pants off, leaving them on the ground. Expelling a hard breath, he muttered, "I need a drink." Carlos looked like he desperately wanted to follow Keaner to that promised land.

"Carlos," Divya hissed. "Something is wrong here."

"I fucking know, Divya!" He whisper-shouted at her, struggling to take his suit off. "There is a lot that's fucking wrong and I don't know why everyone thinks I am the one to bring these problems to." Air hissed between his teeth.

Divya crossed her arms over chest and cocked one hip out. Carlos never lost his cool, not even when she gave him the worst of her sarcastic attitude.

"What happened over there?" she demanded.

"More than can be covered in the few minutes we have," he snapped back. The door to the sub slid closed, making Carlos jump. He pulled the utility belt off his deep walk suit and left the whole thing on the floor like Asha. "Goddamn it. Take the sub offline and I'll meet you in the tool room in forty minutes." Under his breath he muttered, "Forty minutes should be fine." He rubbed at his earlobe and turned towards the door to get to the hallway.

"Just because you want to sleep with her doesn't mean you can ignore me," Divya snarled.

Carlos whirled around, and from down the hall she could hear Asha screaming profanities.

Red faced, nostrils flared, Carlos jabbed a finger at Divya. "You are out of line Mechanic Choudhary! You will follow the orders of your supervisor, and you will respect the chain of command. Just because you don't like not getting your way doesn't mean you get to act like this." Divya sneered at him as he stepped out into the hallway.

“Yes, sir, Captain, sir!” she shouted after him mockingly. “I’ll get right on powering down the sub!”

Divya seethed. She knew Asha and Carlos weren’t together. Everyone knew the two of them were “professional friends” as they liked to call it. Spending so much time together with the same people made it almost impossible to not become friends in some sort of way. Divya just loathed being ignored, especially when she had something of utmost importance to share. Striking out at Carlos over a rumor he squashed on the last tour was a low blow. But, there *was* something wrong here, and with Mina and Zane. If something equally as weird happened at Kraken 3, they all needed to talk about it together. Not in their own little buddy-buddy spheres.

Growling, Divya turned towards the sub so that she could get it powered down. It wouldn’t even take more than ten minutes, but at this point, it was the principle of the thing. Carlos should value her opinion just as much as Asha’s even though Divya was younger than the two of them. Someone needed to know how weird Mina was acting, and that Benson hadn’t been around at all, which was unlike him. The man loved to be in everyone’s business.

Stepping to the sub door, Divya raised her bracelet to scan in and paused.

“What the hell?” Leaning into the door, she squinted at the glass and brought her raised hand to it. With her pointer finger extended, she passed the tip of her finger to the gouges in the glass. They weren’t more than an eighth of an inch deep but on a submersible that needed to withstand the pressure of billions of gallons of water, it was a considerable problem. “Shit.” Divya sucked in a sharp breath when a piece of glass nicked her finger. Jerking her hand back, she looked at the tiny shard embedded in her skin and scratched it out with a fingernail. The glass didn't make a sound when it hit the floor.

Staring at the damaged glass, Divya's heart started to pound behind her ribs.

Mina

Mina's head hurt worse than anything she'd ever experienced.

It was like a vice full of jagged metal teeth was squeezing around her skull. She kept squinting her eyes against the pain, as if not being able to see would help.

Earlier, Perisdo gave her some pills, claiming that they would be better for the pain than anything else she would be able to find in the hab.

"What is it?" she'd asked, inspecting the small, purple, spherical tablets. They were smooth, without markings, not like typical pills.

"A new type of analgesic developed from a coral we found near a volcanic vent. It hasn't quite made its way through all of the final clinical trials, but it works wonders on my migraines. Should be fine for you."

As a scientist, Mina knew better. There were all sorts of horror stories about medications that would pass the first few trials and then horrible side effects would suddenly appear. Chemicals and their reactions were unpredictable, which was why it was important to run all of those trials. Saul was being irresponsible not just as a business owner, but as a boss, giving an employee unapproved medication. Mina didn't have a migraine; her best guess was a concussion, and who knew if this medication would affect clotting factors and result in an even worse brain bleed.

Despite all of that, Mina had grabbed the glass of water Saul held out and drank down the pills, figuring they at least couldn't make the pain worse.

Hours later, the pain was worse. Her eyes felt like they were too big for her eye sockets, and she'd had nonstop diarrhea. Sitting on the toilet, hunched over, head in her hands, Mina would kick herself for taking those mystery pills if she wasn't so scared of shitting herself. Not only was she stuck here, but she also couldn't check on Zane, and didn't know if anyone had returned from Kraken 3 yet.

She'd tried to read through some of the notes from the previous teams, but they were disjointed, making little sense. Or maybe it was just that she couldn't get herself to focus enough to read or process anything. After reading the same meaningless sentence six times, Mina had given up, and it was about that time that she'd needed to install herself in the bathroom. An explosive retort echoed out of the toilet and she cringed, squeezing her eyes shut. At least whatever she was expelling into the toilet didn't smell. So, she reasoned, it could be worse. Her stomach gave another twist and she groaned, the water beneath her ass splashing.

When all the noise stopped, Mina peeled one of her eyes open, suspicious of the sudden easing of pain in her guts. Mina waited, trying to dig around in her body with her mind to see if things were maybe settling. Her head even hurt a little less? She at least felt like she could think a little better. Gods, if this was a side effect of this pill, it was awful. This was going to be a flop on the market. Why hadn't Saul mentioned this to her? Unless he didn't have this problem.

Mina made all sorts of unflattering sounds as she heaved herself off the toilet and cleaned up. She wasn't in the habit of inspecting what she left in the toilet, but as the automatic flusher engaged, Mina's eyes flashed over the toilet almost of their own accord.

The dark, swirling water was full of bright red clots of blood, some of which were shot through with lines of white. Acid burbled in Mina's stomach. She needed a doctor, a real one, just like Zane did. Even though her guts felt better–and yes, her headache was improved, too–she shouldn't have taken those pills from Saul. Everything about that interaction, about why he and the other surfacers had come down here to begin with, was suspect. Why come down just because they'd discovered some sort of parasitic worm in a new fish species? None of this was applicable to Amphitrite's stated purpose of discovering new and improved medicines.

Although, that was all a lie, anyway.

Mina stepped over to her walk-in shower and turned the water to as hot as she could stand it. The men she'd dated all fit the stereotype of finding women's hot water preferences too hot. Even the women she dated hadn't enjoyed showering with her, saying that her preferred water temperature would boil crabs. Down here, at Kraken 7, she didn't have to care about anyone's opinion but her own. The water would be as hot as she damn well pleased.

Undressing, Mina felt a series of bumps along the back of her shoulder blade and frowned. She doubted there would be any new moles; she didn't get enough sunlight for that. Acne would be uncharacteristic of her skin, but not impossible she supposed. Turning towards the mirror, Mina tried to contort herself enough to see the area where she thought the bumps were. There was nothing that she could see in the reflection, and when she ran her fingers over the spot again, she didn't feel anything.

Mina groaned and ground the heels of her hands into her eyes. This day was so awful. All she wanted was a shower, a meal, and to see if everyone had returned from Kraken 3. They should be back at this point. Stepping into the steaming shower, Mina yelped and jumped back, almost slipping on the tile. The water was way too hot. She checked where the handle was, noting that it was in its normal spot for when she showered. Taking a tentative step into the shower, she reached her hand out to the spray. When the droplets hit her hand and arm, it felt like acid.

Hissing, Mina withdrew and turned the water temperature down. This day just kept getting worse. She showered as fast as possible in the lukewarm water that still felt too hot and got dressed in clean clothes.

The headache was creeping back around the sides of her skull from the ball of tension at the base of her neck. Those stupid pain pills had done nothing after all. If she was the assertive type, she would go find Saul and tell him just what she thought of his little experimental drugs. She wasn't, though. If he asked how she was feeling, she was more likely to tell him that they had, in fact, helped her to feel much better.

Ugh. Pathetic. It's not as though she liked being so agreeable. It was just what came naturally to her. She hoped the next time she saw Saul was in a group setting, so that maybe he would be less likely to ask her about the pills he shouldn't have been handing out willy nilly.

Exiting her room, Mina turned to the right with no clear goal in mind. There was something she wanted to do, but the thoughts escaped her. They were slippery, coming and going like dandelion seeds floating in the wind. It felt like there were several things she needed to remember, too, and those also eluded her.

What was wrong with her brain?

Maybe she was hungry? Since her guts had stopped twisting, a persistent, gnawing feeling had started up. She couldn't remember the last time she ate something. Latching onto the idea of food, Mina turned towards the mess hall at the next intersection of hallways.

The gray walls melted into the gray ceiling in her peripherals, making everything at the sides look like it was speeding past her while the things in front of her moved at a regular speed. Mina blinked, trying to clear her vision and get rid of the dizziness it was bringing on.

Food. Food would help her feel better. A gallon of water would help, too. On top of not remembering when she last ate, she couldn't remember her last glass of water either. Where was her crew tumbler? It should have been in her room, but it definitely wasn't there when she left.

Get it together, Mina. She did not need Ocean Dark Syndrome on top of everything else. If she refused it hard enough, it couldn't happen. A stupid idea, but she was going to stick with it.

A figure walked into the intersection up ahead, and it took her a moment to recognize Divya. Great. The snarkiest crewmate who outed her to the whole crew about what Mina knew was just who she wanted to see when she was feeling at her worst.

For a second, Mina thought Divya wasn't going to look down the hallway, and she was going to get away with not having to interact with her. But, no. Nothing was going to go her way today, it seemed.

Divya paused in the middle of the hallway intersection and turned to look directly at Mina almost like she expected to see her there.

"Where have you been?" Divya's accusatory tone ramped up Mina's headache. Godsdammit, she just wanted to eat. She was so hungry. "They're back and we all need to have a talk."

"What do you mean?" Her voice sounded awful: raspy and unused. It sounded as bad as she felt on the inside.

Divya waited for Mina to almost get to the intersection and then she stepped back, as if she didn't want to be too close to Mina.

"You've been acting really weird, Mina. I don't know what's going on, but something needs to be done." Divya crossed her arms and glared at Mina. "Come on."

Weird? Her? She didn't think there was anyone else who would describe her that way.

"What does that mean?" Mina asked the question to Divya's retreating back. She kept walking, so Mina followed, catching up with minimal effort. "What do you mean I've been weird?" Even though she didn't feel right, she didn't think anyone else had noticed.

Divya twisted her body around to talk to Mina and her eyes widened. Her feet stuttered and she lurched to the side to put space between them. Mina wanted to laugh. If anyone was acting weird it was Divya.

"Do you remember yesterday? After everyone left?" Mina didn't answer, unsure what Divya could possibly be referencing. "I went to the lab to look for more notes or see if there was anything else you could remember about what they said about Kraken 3. And you were just standing there." Divya glanced forward to check where she was going, but kept her body twisted toward Mina. "You didn't even realize I was there or hear me calling your name. It wasn't until I left that you reacted to anything, but I wasn't hanging around."

Mina scrunched up her face. None of this sounded familiar to her. Why would she just be standing in the lab not reacting to anything?

"Are you sure you're remembering correctly? Maybe you were sleepwalking."

Divya scoffed at Mina's attempt to grasp at an explanation. "I don't sleepwalk. It's one of the things they screen you for." Mina, of course, knew this. No one wanted an errant crew member sleepwalking their way out of a dry dock or compromising anything in the hab.

"You've been off for days and I don't know what it is." Divya sped up her steps like she was trying to get away from Mina. "Stop asking questions, stay away from me, and let's find the others."

Mina squinted through a sharp burst of pain, slapping her palm against her forehead. "Godsdamn it." She stopped walking and noticed that she didn't hear Divya's steps either.

"Has your head constantly hurt the last few days?" Divya didn't sound concerned. In fact, she sounded irritated. Like Mina's pain was an inconvenience for her. She glanced over her shoulder, then back at Mina. After a moment, she whipped her head back in the other direction.

From between clenched teeth, Mina ground out, "Yes. It got better after some pills Saul gave me, but now it's getting worse again." What the hell was Divya so focused on down the hall?

"Saul?" Divya's question made Mina squeeze her eyelids together. She didn't have the energy to remind Divya who Saul was. The pain crept into her jaw, making her teeth hurt. "Oh, Perisdo." Divya's tone was mocking, a verbal eyeroll. "That asshole. Why would you take anything from him?" How she managed to be so miserable all the time, Mina couldn't fathom. "What is that down there?" Divya's voice faded as she moved away. "What is that?" Her voice pitched to a higher octave.

Mina squinted through her increasing pain and staggered after Divya. When she caught up, her eyes snapped open.

"George…?"

A heap of black and white fur lay in a puddle of blood. It wasn't distinguishable as a cat, but she knew. Just like Divya knew.

There was a streak of blood leading away from George to a toppled over cleaner bot.

"Could the bot...?" Mina couldn't finish the sentence, pain contorting her face and making her jaw clench.

Divya hesitated, crouching next to what used to be George. "It shouldn't. Unless it malfunctioned, but even then." She reached out towards the cat, then thought better of it, pulling her hand to her chest.

Mina thought she said something to Divya, but her voice sounded garbled to her. Whatever Divya was saying back didn't register with Mina. It all sounded like static that ground into her last frayed nerves. The sounds electrified her teeth and sent tingles down into her fingers and toes. Her skin felt like it was crawling, like there were ants marching up and down the curves and planes of her muscles. A buzzing started up in her ears, and above that she could hear what sounded like a woman shouting. She didn't sound quite scared, more annoyed, but the possibility of fear was right there beneath her irritation.

Forcing her eyes open one at a time, Mina found that she was doubled over with her elbows braced on her knees, her hands dangling between her legs. The ants, to her horror, weren't part of her imagination. Her skin rippled with movement, like the insects were having a party inside her body. Mina wanted to scream, but her voice wasn't working. She looked up, trying to find Divya to plead for help, hoping that the other woman was already gone in search of it.

She wasn't, though. Divya stood several paces away, hands on her hips, her mouth moving without any sound coming out. Unless the buzzing in Mina's ears was preventing her from hearing anything.

Something cracked in her skull. There was no pain, but she heard and felt it. Divya backed up a step and Mina felt an overwhelming sense of rage rise up in her. Heat rose up from her gut, flooding every inch of her body. She felt like she was about to pass out and also, somehow, like she'd swallowed a whole package of caffeine pills.

The flush filled her head and the buzzing stopped, as did the pain. It filled her head until only one thought remained.

Divya needed to die.

Carlos

"What is so important that you couldn't wait a few minutes for me to get Divya sorted out? She's going to turn the attitude up even more for the next few days."

Carlos was over this. Over Kraken 3 and Kraken 7, being underwater, the monsters they'd encountered, the cracking noises in his neck, and about eight other things he couldn't name but was sure belonged on the list of his aggravations. Once his contract was up, he was going to put in for reassignment. There was enough money in his accounts to put his daughter through college and help with any other expenses that might come up for her. He didn't need much for himself, since all his major expenses–home, car, motorcycle–were all paid off. Being reassigned to a surface job would allow him to spend more time with his daughter and stay the fuck away from the bottom of the ocean.

"I have to show you," Asha hissed. She kept her voice low and looked around like she thought someone might be listening in, paying particular attention to corners at hallway intersections. "We can't do this out here. My office is right there."

His frayed nerves unraveled further. Was Asha acting like this because of something she found, or was she experiencing the Syndrome?

"Asha. What's my daughter's name?"

Looking over her shoulder, Asha curled her lip at him. "I'm not going crazy, Carlos." She broke his name up into two sarcastic syllables. He thought she would continue talking, since she could monologue with the best of them when she was peeved. Instead, she turned around and picked up her pace until she reached her office.

Once inside, she surveyed the area like she expected something to be wrong. He lingered at the door while she sat at her desk and logged in.

"Everything alright?" He took a seat next to her.

"Yeah," she muttered. "I wanted to make sure no one touched my stuff. I wasn't sure if they knew I was on to them." Before he could say anything, she snapped, "I am not crazy."

"I'd never say such a thing." He was pretty sure she was going off the rails on the crazy train. She sounded paranoid, and maybe even a little manic. His ex-wife would get manic episodes when she wasn't taking her meds. Not that he wanted to diagnose Asha; he just didn't want her to be experiencing the Syndrome on top of everything else that was happening. They still needed to locate Benson and update him on what happened. On the flip side, Carlos wanted an update on Zane and Mina. Especially Zane.

Asha plugged a large drive into her computer. A folder opened on her screen, and she scrolled through the icons until she found what she wanted. A paused camera view of the lab appeared, showing it empty with the lights on.

"We have cameras?" Carlos thought of all the times he'd adjusted his balls while walking down the hallway, thinking no one was watching.

"Nope." She clicked through some other videos and then fast forwarded on one. "This is the lab on Kraken 3. I took everything I could. Not that there was much there."

"Why would they have cameras there but not here?" Not that he wanted cameras at Kraken 7. They wouldn't serve a purpose. They were isolated down here, with no chance of anyone coming from the outside to steal anything or harm anyone.

On the screen, two bloody people moved into the room followed by another. Their movements were comical with the video sped up.

"We don't need to watch this part." Asha's voice was tight, and Carlos assumed she'd already watched this whole video. Whatever she wanted him to know was later. Blood sprayed around the room like it was coming out of a fire hose and Carlos looked away, tired of witnessing violence.

"I'd never seen a dead body before today." Carlos' voice was subdued. He looked at some data streaming on one of the other computer screens. Asha grunted in response. "But you have apparently."

Asha stopped clicking on things, her entire body going still. He waited, knowing that when she spoke about this, it would be on her terms, just like when she told him right before the deep walk. It was time he didn't think they had, but he needed to know.

"This isn't the time," she grumbled, still not moving. Carlos remained silent, waiting until she sighed and her shoulders dropped. "It happened when I was twenty-six. I went out with my brothers, Shane and Will, and a few of their friends to a bar with their girlfriends. It was fine, but one of their friends got into an argument with some guy, and when we tried to leave a few hours later, that guy jumped us with a few other people."

Asha closed her eyes and leaned back into her seat, tapping her fingers on her thigh. Carlos put a hand on her knee, and she swiped it away.

"At first, me and the other women were left alone, but then one of the dudes started to strangle Shane. My brother went limp and all I could think about was him dying, so I picked up a brick." She shrugged, and when she opened her eyes, they were glassy. "The dude let go, but then he turned on me, pulled a knife, and I hit him again. He didn't get up after that."

Carlos recognized that he shouldn't have brought this up but also knew he wouldn't have been able to continue on if he hadn't brought it up. What had Asha thought would happen when she casually mentioned she killed someone? That he'd forget? Or let it go? Maybe she'd just panicked at the thought of being on the deep walk and possibly dying out there. Whatever the reason was, Carlos wished he could go back in time and shut her up before she said anything.

"I was acquitted, obviously. Otherwise, Amphitrite wouldn't have hired me. But Perisdo wants to hold it over my head like that wasn't one of the worst days of my life."

Carlos paused, considered his next words hard, and then said, "So far."

Asha blinked, and it was like her eyes sucked her tears back up. "What?"

"The worst day of your life, so far." He pointed vaguely out the door. "There are human-fish creatures hunting us. I'd say that ranks as a pretty bad day." She stared at him and then burst out laughing.

"You are something else, man." Asha sniffed and rubbed at her eyes. "Thanks, though."

There were different degrees to everything, and while some people might have seen Asha in an entirely different light with this story, Carlos didn't. He would have done the same thing in her position, and he'd bet she would do it all over again, too.

When Carlos put his hand on her knee this time, she didn't push it away. Instead, she turned back to her computer screens, returning to business.

After a few clicks, she paused a video. "Okay, here." She pointed at the corner of the screen. A fourth person walked in where her finger pointed.

Carlos waited through the person rolling the bodies into the body bags and picking up bits of body parts from the floor. He could have done without having to see this part, and he withdrew his hand from Asha's knee without realizing it, crossing his arms over his chest like he was trying to protect himself from what was on the screen.

"Look." Asha paused the video as the man stood up. "Do you see him?"

Carlos squinted at the screen. There wasn't much to go on beyond the thin shoulders and brown hair that was only just long enough to brush the nape of his neck. He might've been familiar, and even though something nagged in his brain, Carlos rationalized that lots of people could look similar from behind.

"What about him?" He remained noncommittal, unsure where Asha was going to take this.

"What about him?" Asha scoffed. "I thought about this a lot on our ride home since we took the long way around to avoid whatever was chasing us between the habs." That had been quite the argument between the three of them, with Asha finally relenting that they should take the extra time to make a wide arc between Kraken 3 and 7. "It's *Keaner*. Look at his skinny shoulders. And, yeah, the hair is different, but it looks just like him! He was on Kraken 3. He was cleaning up these bodies." Her voice pitched higher and then she regained control. "Keaner acted like he had no idea what Kraken 3 even was, but he's right here, plain as day putting people in body bags."

Carlos hedged. "I'm not sure it's plain as day. Other than the hair being too short, I think this guy might be a little skinnier than Keaner. And with these cameras, Amphitrite would have known for sure that it was him if he was there. Why would they put him back in another hab if he did this?" Worry threaded its way from Carlos' stomach to his throat, tightening everything along the way. The words *Ocean Dark Syndrome* flashed in his mind, and he blinked them away.

Asha growled and banged the mouse on the desk. "It was five years ago. People change." She navigated the mouse pointer across the screen, clicking files open and abruptly closing them. "And after everything that's happened over the past few days, you don't think Amphitrite wouldn't sell us all out for another few million in their pockets?"

Carlos shook his head, trying to follow Asha' thin logic. "How does massacring a whole crew, burying it, and letting those monsters run free help them? What reason could they have for putting Keaner here with us?" Asha's angry clicking was distracting. "What are you looking for?" Carlos was trying to retain the image of the man and compare it in his head to the Keaner he knew at Kraken 7. If they were the same person, Keaner had a lot to answer for. Amphitrite had a lot to answer for, on top of that. Even if Keaner wasn't at fault for what happened at Kraken 3, he shouldn't have passed the psych eval with that much underwater trauma.

Hell, the psych guy had questioned Carlos repeatedly over an incident where a rowboat he was on tipped over and he'd needed to be rescued along with his two siblings on the lake. They were worried this would give him some sort of fear of the water that would exacerbate the risk of the Syndrome. No way they would let Keaner stay on.

But that was all assuming any of this was reasonable and it wasn't. None of this was. Yarn spinning, star sign obsessed, long-haired Keaner was not this devious murder clean-up dude from another hab.

"I don't know," Asha snapped. "Anything. There has to be something." She clicked several things in rapid succession, opening up a dozen windows, cluttering her monitors.

Carlos laughed without mirth. "Can we move on from this?"

Instead of responding, Asha clicked into more videos. "If I can just find his face," she muttered.

It amazed Carlos how she could swing from spilling her guts about a traumatic moment in her life to obsessively looking for something that wasn't going to be there. He was going to emphasize that Keaner wasn't the person she was looking for, when a video popped up on the screen of the back of a man dragging a body bag toward a group of six other body bags.

Carlos' words fizzled out on his tongue.

The bags weren't yet stacked like they were when their group had saw hours ago. Instead, they were laid out in a line with the zippers pulled down to expose the faces. The shuffling susurrations of the vinyl bags against the metal floor continued until the man laid the final body next to the others, just out of the line of sight of the camera. Standing a few feet away from the heads of the row, he surveyed his work.

"That's one of the crew." Carlos whispered, as if he might attract the man's attention through the camera if he spoke too loudly.

"Huh?" Asha didn't look away from the screen.

The man on screen tilted his head back, exposing a face that looked like it was melting; there were deep indentations where his eye sockets and nose should have been, and the pale flesh hung like curtains from his cheekbones. As they watched, his hairline started to slide towards the back of his head. The man opened his mouth and raised his arms a few feet out from his sides.

"There's seven body bags. This guy is a crew member." Carlos didn't know if he was trying to suggest this guy murdered the crew, or if he was trying to cover it up, or what. But this was definitely one of the crew stacking the bodies, even though he was doing things that should be impossible for a human body.

His mouth stretched wider and wider until there was a crack, and his jaw dropped down to the level of his collarbones. Carlos wished that when the man had first titled his head back, his features weren't already deformed. Who the hell was he?

From the gaping hole of the stranger's mouth, long tendrils of worms burst forth, stretching outward until they dropped to the floor. He splayed his fingers which looked to be growing into the many knuckled tendrils that reminded Carlos of the Mordices. The tendrils shivered, scraping the floor with a rattling like bones being shaken together.

Asha was muttering under her breath, words that might have been a prayer or just a continuous string of curse words. Carlos couldn't be sure, but he would consider either of those options appropriate.

As the worms fell from the man's mouth and struck the floor, they wriggled their way to the people in the body bags, sliding into their ears or mouths. The bodies convulsed, the furious flopping creating a cacophony of thumps and what sounded like bones breaking.

The man's jaw drew back up to his face and settled back into his skull with a click, then he tilted his head forward, his facial features still mushy. His long fingers rattled over the floor as he approached the body bags.

Carlos smashed the spacebar on Asha's keyboard, pausing the video.

"I've seen enough. We've gotta get the fuck out of here." Shoving his seat away, he spun Asha's chair so she could get up with him.

Asha stumbled to her feet, looking shell shocked, like she couldn't believe what she'd just watched. "What about the surfacers? They haven't had the required seven day–"

"Doesn't matter." Carlos chopped his hands in front of himself. He didn't care about them, whether they knew what was going on down here or not. They sure as hell wouldn't care about his crew, and didn't care about the crew of Kraken 3. "They either come, and we get them to a doctor right away for the decomp sick, or they can stay here and deal with whatever shit is down here. But our crew is leaving."

Asha pulled away to unplug the drive from the computer and tucked it into the pocket of her pants, zipping the pocket shut.

"I told Divya I'd meet her at the tool room in forty minutes." Carlos checked his watch and cursed. Almost an hour had passed since he saw her at the dry dock. She was going to be pissed. More pissed than when they separated earlier. "C'mon. We gotta go."

Divya

"Mina, stop!" Divya screamed as she ran, looking over her shoulder to check where her pursuer was. The only thing that was keeping her ahead was that she'd kicked Mina in the knee and was pretty sure her knee was broken.

How Mina was still limping after her with a jacked up knee, Divya didn't know and didn't want to find out. Blood sheeted down half of Divya's face where Mina had clawed her. She could feel the raised edges of the gouges stretching from her hairline, over her eyebrow, and across her cheek. It was a good thing the bitch had missed her eye. Couldn't be a good mechanic with only one eye.

A roar echoed behind Divya and she struggled against the closing of her throat. She screamed, a strangled sound that didn't drown out the monster behind her. Divya knew about Ocean Dark Syndrome, but she never thought she or her crewmates would experience it. As far as she knew, the Syndrome wasn't supposed to make someone this violent or out of control. They were just supposed to act weird, do things that were unsafe, create chaotic problems. There wasn't a single research article where someone suffering from Ocean Dark Syndrome became murderous.

Divya hung a left at the next intersection, aiming for the mess hall. She didn't know if anyone would be up this early for breakfast, but maybe Keaner was cooking. And at least there were knives in there.

Over the pounding of her footsteps, Divya heard another set of steps running. She had only enough time to think "Fuck" and then Mina appeared around a corner, clotheslining Divya. Her body whipped backwards and slammed into the floor, flinging Divya's head against the hard metal ground. Starbursts of color flashed in her eyes, the world above her becoming a kaleidoscope of colors and shapes. How had Mina run ahead of her like that?

Divya tilted her head up, trying to focus on Mina standing above her. There were three of her, wavering and merging. Each set of her eyes looked deranged: wide and glistening, rimmed in red.

"I only wanted to be your friend, Divya." Mina's mouth barely moved with the words. "We'll be friends, though. I'll see to it."

"What're you talking about, dumbass?" Divya heaved herself up onto her elbows and dragged herself backward, away from Mina. Her forearms slipped on the floor, and when she looked down, she saw it was slicked with blood. "We're already friends, don't be stupid. Come on, Mina."

A cackle came out of Mina. The sound shot a bolt of ice down Divya's spine.

"Mina! Snap out of it!" Divya screamed the words, trying to distract Mina and call for help at the same time. She pulled her knees up and kicked out, aiming for Mina's knees. The woman danced out of her way, nimble, as though Divya hadn't taken out her knee earlier.

"You'll be alright, Divya. It'll only hurt for a second." Mina looked up, as though she had a sudden, errant thought. "At least, that's what I've been told."

"Mina, stop!" Divya tried to put as much authority into her voice as possible. Cowing Mina shouldn't be this difficult, but something had possessed her.

Mina stepped up next to Divya and grinned down at her. Something white wiggled out of the corner of Mina's mouth and then disappeared between her lips.

"Hey! What are you doing?!"

Divya whipped her head around at the unfamiliar voice. One of the surfacers stood at the next intersection with Perisdo, Benson, and the remaining surfacer. She didn't even care what they were all scheming about and leaving the real crew out of. They might provide enough of a distraction to get Mina to stop, or the sight of an authority figure might snap Mina back into herself.

There was a dull pressure in Divya's abdomen that exploded into pain. Every nerve ending lit up like lights on a Christmas tree, rending a scream from Divya. She turned back to Mina, forgetting about the people who were supposed to be doing some sort of saving and failing epically at it.

Mina's foot was through her abdomen.

Mina's *foot* was planted straight into her *abdomen.*

With a twist of her leg, Mina snapped and crushed the vertebra in Divya's spine. Her legs stopped scrabbling to try and get away, only able to twitch ineffectively and without feeling. There was plenty of feeling left in the caved in meat of Divya's gut, though. Loops of intestine curled over the edges, forced out by the foot taking up residence in Divya. A coil of it slid out, hitting the floor with a wet *splat.* Some sort of dark, meaty organ oozed up, a sheen of blood shining in the overhead lights.

Somewhere, very far outside of Divya, she could hear the muted screams of other people in the hall. She coughed, blood spraying all over Mina's already bloody pant leg and dribbling down Divya's mouth. With a groan, she tried to push Mina's leg away. There was a foul odor wafting up from Divya's guts, mixed in with the metallic smell of blood, both coating the insides of her mouth and nostrils. She probably would have felt her stomach convulse in revulsion if she had a stomach left.

Mina smiled down at Divya, and used the leg not planted in Divya's stomach to kick the woman's arms away and push her to the ground. Mina's smile grew wide and several worms squirmed from between her teeth, dropping into the cavity of Divya's stomach. Divya couldn't be sure if the scream she uttered was one that she hadn't stopped since Mina put her foot into her stomach, or a new one. Nothing felt real and felt all too real at the same time. There wasn't going to be any escape from this hell hole for her.

But at least they would all know there was something seriously fucking wrong with Mina.

Staring up at Mina, Divya opened her mouth to launch more expletives at Mina, when someone crashed into the monstrous woman, taking her to the ground with a crash. As Mina fell, the toe of her boot tipped up and caught the bottom of Divya's sternum, snapping her rib cage open and popping the bones out of the skin of her chest. Divya gasped, her eyes rolled up into her head, and her consciousness faded.

Asha

Screams were never a good thing, whether they were ringing out on land or seven miles under. Asha would prefer to go the rest of her life without walking down a hallway and hearing screaming eve again.

She and Carlos weren't far from the tool room when the screams started, and it didn't take them long to find the gaggle of toppers congregating in the hallway.

"Move!" Asha shoved between them, clearing the way for Carlos to follow her. She burst from between their shoulders and jerked to a stop, trying to make sense of what she was seeing.

It looked like Mina had knocked Divya over and was standing over her like some school yard bully. Asha tried to reconcile this with the timid Mina that shew knew. Then she saw the blood all over Mina's leg, the pool of it under Divya. Was that…were those Divya's organs? Saliva flooded Asha's mouth and she blinked hard, clamping her teeth together.

Mina kicked Divya down, and Asha could see how the rest of this would play out in her mind: blood, bone, and a heavy *crunch* mixed in with a *squish.*

Launching forward, Asha was in motion before she made a decision on what she should do once she reached them. Hands grasped at her, unable to gain traction on her bare arms, her shirt slipping out of the grabbing fingers. She didn't know if Divya could live, or would live, but she wasn't going to let Mina plant her boot in Divya's face.

With a roar, Asha slammed into Mina's middle with her shoulder. Since Mina's other leg was lifted, her lack of balance took away any advantage her height and weight gave her over Asha. They hit the floor hard, jarring Asha off Mina. She scrambled to her knees, awkward with one knee on Mina's thigh and the other on the metal floor. Clocking that Mina looked dazed, Asha hauled herself up to straddle Mina's chest and grabbed either side of her head.

There was only one other time in her life when she had felt so devoid of any emotion. She hadn't felt any fear then, either. All there was in this moment was the knowledge that she needed to stop Mina from hurting anyone else.

Mina's eyes twitched open and she groaned. Asha snarled her fingers in Mina's hair and lifted the woman's head up.

Then she slammed it onto the ground.

The retort of sound was like when a speeding bowling ball hits a pin; sharp and dry, a heavy crack meant to destroy.

In response, Mina reached up for Asha. With a quick movement, Asha smashed Mina's head into the ground again, using her momentum to slide herself forward and pin Mina's arms to the ground with her knees. Blood gushed from Mina's mouth; she must have bitten her tongue or her lips. It didn't matter. She was still flexing her arms beneath Asha's knees, trying to dislodge her. Asha lifted her head two more times, thumping it into the floor in two successive hits.

"Asha, stop!" Hands grabbed her shoulders and dragged her off Mina. Asha let them, satisfied that Mina was knocked out. Benson and the topper named Bryan crowded around Mina, reaching shaking fingers to the woman's neck. Elio, the last topper, stood off to the side, looking very green.

When Asha looked over and saw Divya, she almost wished Mina was dead.

There was a gaping hole full of purple, red, and pink masses in the center of Divya. White bones jutted out of her chest, and her head was tilted towards Asha, her eyes blank and glassy. Swallowing hard, Asha looked behind her. Carlos stood there, his hands twisted in the fabric of his shirt, staring straight ahead with a look that told her he was somewhere far away from here. Asha smacked his leg to get his attention and then reached her hand up. It took him a moment to look down at her, and he paused before grabbing her wrist and hauling her up.

"What did you do?" There was a tremor to Carlos' voice that she'd never heard before.

Shaking her head, she saw Mina's chest rise and fall; she was breathing. Disappointment brought a sour taste to her mouth.

"This is Kraken 3 all over," she muttered.

"What did you say?" Perisdo's sudden materialization at her shoulder made her jump. He didn't look any worse for the wear, his suit still impeccably clean. Did the man not sleep?

"You heard me." Asha turned toward him and jutted her chin up. "Kraken 3. We know what happened there."

"What happened where?" Keaner appeared behind Perisdo. He angled himself to look around the man and caught sight of Divya. "Holy shit." His eyes widened and Asha scoffed.

"Don't act like you don't know what's going on, you were there, Keaner." She took a step toward Keaner. Carlos grabbed her arm and pulled her back.

"I don't know most of what's going on here, so you're gonna have to fill me in, Asha." Keaner tilted his head at her. "Just turn the hostility down a bit. What gives?" Asha wanted to scream at the smirk on his face. He hid behind Perisdo like the big man was his own personal bodyguard.

Something cracked, and Asha looked down.

One of Divya's arms was snapped up at a weird angle. Every other thought about Keaner and Perisdo and Kraken 3 withered in her brain. The bones in Divya's chest jerked down, moving back into place, no longer jutting through her skin.

"Is…is that rigor mortis?" She jerked her arms around in a poor imitation of what Divya's body was doing.

"No," Carlos said, his hand gripping her elbow. "Rigor mortis wouldn't set in for a few hours. This is something else. The body shouldn't do that."

“That’s ridiculous,” Perisdo scoffed. “This is obviously the result of natural death processes.”

The upper half of Divya’s body jerked up, as if determined to prove him wrong.

“Well, that is definitely not part of rigor mortis.” Carlos’ grip on Asha’s elbow tightened. Backing up into him, Asha felt a flash of fear compounded by the fear rolling off everyone else in the hallway.

“Is this the part where we run?” Keaner gave a weak chuckle.

“No,” Perisdo snapped. “It’s rigor mortis.” He sounded so sure in his convictions, as incorrect as Asha thought they were, that when Divya’s head snapped towards them, she didn’t dash off down the hall.

Instead, she stared as Divya’s mouth worked open and closed. Her eyes blinked, and a low moan grew from her.

“Fuck no.” Carlos jerked Asha further away. “Run!” Asha was dragged along behind him until her feet caught up with what her brain wanted her to do.

“Yep, time to go!” Keaner’s voice was high pitched.

They dashed past the small group hovering over Mina.

“Where are you going?” Benson demanded. None of them answered, rushing past. One scream turned into several and there was a scramble of noise that faded behind them.

Asha couldn’t find the breath to ask where Carlos was leading her. She didn’t even want to turn around to see who else was following them. Either those other people would reach safety with her and Carlos, or they wouldn’t.

Carlos turned right and left and left and right, holding Asha’s hand and refusing to let go, even when she started to drag. Exhaustion was getting the best of her: how long had it been since she slept? How much had she run over the past twelve hours? Or longer. She didn't even know anything about time anymore. Too much of her past few hours had been spent running and terrified.

"Here," Carlos panted. He let go of Asha's hand and spun around, facing down the hallway. Asha kept going for a few steps before she was able to put on the brakes. She staggered back against a wall, and slid part of the way down it. Glancing down the hallway, she spotted Keaner and Perisdo only a few yards away. "Better hurry," Carlos muttered while opening up a panel in the wall.

"What are you doing?" Each of her words came out on a different gust of breath, as if each one was its own individual sentence. Holy hell, she was out of shape. If she made it back to the surface, she needed to start jogging or hiking again.

When. When she made it back to surface, she mentally corrected herself.

Gesturing to the doorway with one hand, while flipping a few toggles with the other, Carlos also spoke his words on gusts of breath, though they sounded much more controlled than Asha's. "This is a watertight door. It's meant to engage if something catastrophic happens in one area of the hab to protect the other areas." This was news to her. She never thought about what would happen if part of the hab became damaged. It seemed silly in the moment, but she'd just assumed the hab was indestructible and never thought about what might happen in the event it wasn't.

Looking at this area of the hallway, Asha noticed that there was a slight ridge running up the walls and across the ceiling. There wasn't a ridge on the floor, but there was a seam running across the it that she never noticed before.

Keaner and Perisdo sprinted past them. Asha didn't bother stopping them.

"I'm manually engaging it to stop Divya from following us." His hand paused over the panel, and he leaned around the wall to look down the hallway.

"I don't think that thing is Divya, anymore." Her words were steadier, her breath coming easier. Carlos didn't respond. "What are you waiting for?"

Down the hall, a cacophony of slapping feet approached them before anyone showed up.

"Even if we close this door, the Divya thing can just walk around another way to get to us." Her extremities were tingling, and she wasn't sure if it was because of exhaustion or fear.

"I'll close another door later." The sounds coming down the hall were holding his focus more than Asha's concern was.

Huffing breaths came up behind them, and Asha spun around. She felt like a top, the way she kept spinning toward things. A petrified, spinning top.

It was only Keaner and Perisdo, but that didn't do much to quiet the roiling in her gut.

"What are you waiting for?" Perisdo demanded. Despite his being out of breath, his voice maintained its assertiveness. "Close the door."

"Benson and your surfacers are still out there," Carlos said, as if that was all the explanation needed. Asha wasn't quite sure she agreed with him. Of course she didn't want to shut anyone out of safety, but she also didn't want to get torn apart by whatever Divya had turned into.

Perisdo put his hand on Carlos' shoulder and squeezed, his knuckles turning white. "Close the door."

Carlos whipped around, knocking Perisdo's arm off his shoulder and shoving the man back at the same time. "You don't make the rules down here, big man." He sneered his way through a mockery of the words "big man". A scream echoed down the hall, half drawing Carlos' attention. Perisdo made a move to grab for Carlos, and Asha shoved him. Next to Perisdo, Keaner's mouth popped open in surprise. It would have been comical if Asha wasn't so consumed by anger corroded over with terror.

Eyes wide, Perisdo gave her a startled look before attempting to recover his authority. Asha didn't let him have the chance to get any words out.

"Shut up, surfacer." The screaming behind her was getting louder, including pleas for help. "You're in our world and we make the rules." Perisdo took a step towards her, and she shoved him again, stepping into his space. Never in her life would Asha have thought she would be going toe to toe with a boss like this. She followed rules, she liked order. But she trusted Carlos and his knowledge a lot more than she trusted this stuffy asshole.

Perisdo glanced over her shoulder, his lips pressing together so hard they disappeared.

"You know what I've done, Perisdo." That drew his attention back to her, his eyes narrowing. "Don't test me."

Asha stepped back from Perisdo and gave the screaming down the hallway her attention. Benson and the two remaining surfacers were supporting Mina between them. The sight almost made Asha join in with Perisdo and demand that they close the door on them. She'd just slammed Mina's head into the ground after they all watched Mina kill Divya. Why was anyone even thinking about trying to save her? In Asha's mind, it would have been a bit of poetic justice for the Divya monster to kill Mina.

Or eat her. Whatever the goal of that thing was.

The small group was maybe another thirty seconds from crossing the threshold when the thing they were all concerned about rounded the corner behind them.

Divya's head wagged back and forth on her neck like she–it? – wasn't quite sure how to hold it up. All of her hair was gone, replaced by a crown of yellowish antennae that fluttered around her head. The arms were kinked out at odd angles, like it was trying to hold itself up on the air. Gray skin sagged from her limbs, wobbling as she moved. Where Mina had planted her foot was a raw, red hole with loops of intestines dangling from it. Asha thought there might have been a lung, a pinkish mass, flopping back and forth in the chest cavity with Divya's movements.

No, that thing wasn't Divya anymore. It might be Divya's body, but nothing about this creature with the hole that exposed the white bones of its spine was Divya.

"Carlos." Her previous bravado when dealing with Perisdo was gone, replaced by a nervous tremor that vibrated over every letter of Carlos' name.

One of his hands was on the final toggle for the door, his other rubbing his earlobe. "Wait, just wait."

The creature behind the group staggered forward, the legs uncoordinated, jerking everywhere. Another few yards and the group would be here. Asha bounced on her toes, her fingers tapping against her thighs. Just another few yards…

"Um, guys, I think we're in danger." Keaner spoke as the monster found coordination and lurched forward. As it picked up speed behind the group, the flopping lung tore free of whatever was holding it in the chest cavity, falling into the path of the creature's foot and getting kicked forward. Skidding across the floor, the lung left a dark patch of blood in its wake.

Unbidden, the word "Hurry!" wrenched free of Asha's throat, screeching down the hall. Bryan turned back, and once he saw the monster behind them, he dropped his side of Mina and ran. Benson and Elio staggered, struggling to redistribute the dead weight of the woman between them.

Asha hissed a breath out from between her teeth. As Bryan crossed the threshold, Carlos reached out and clotheslined him.

"You son of a bitching coward!" The man hit the ground, and Carlos kicked him in the ribs, rolling him over onto the safe side of the door. A blur jumped over the downed man, snapping Asha's attention up. Keaner sprinted down the hallway, arms pumping.

Was he going to rescue them, or sacrifice them? If he was the same person from Kraken 3, Asha could see him tripping them all up and leaving them for the monster. Carlos would close the door on all of them, then, she hoped. He would believe her if that's what Keaner did.

But Asha wasn't even sure Keaner was going to make it. There was no way, with the monster picking up speed.

Keaner met the group two steps ahead of the monster. It stretched its arms out, reaching for them. If it took them all down, would Carlos close the door? Asha glanced at him, a quick side eye, before refocusing on the group. Rearing back, Keaner lifted a leg and kicked out, striking the creature in the hip. It spun around, arms outstretched and still clawing, catching on the front of Keaner's shirt and the back of Mina's. Keaner jerked back, tearing the fabric of his shirt, Mina's blonde hairs caught in the creature's claws as it lost its balance and fell to its knees with a sharp crack.

"Come on!" Carlos shouted at them. "Come on, come on, come on!"

"Just shut the door!" Perisdo screamed.

Shoving his shoulder under Mina, Keaner helped to balance out the other two. His face was a rictus of strain, his eyes squinted, lips folded into his mouth.

With a series of cracking noises, the creature stood and turned around with delicate movements, like it was trying to make sure it wasn't even more broken.

Asha stepped to the side, dragging Bryan, who was still on the ground, out of the way.

The monster took two cautious steps, then leaned forward into a run, its arms and legs working better than before to propel it forward.

Keaner, Mina, Benson, and Elio careened over the threshold, landing in a heaped pile and an exhalation of pained grunts.

Carlos pushed the toggle switch down, the tiny movement at odds with the tension of the situation. Just one little switch standing between them and safety.

The watertight door slammed shut, slotting into the seam in the floor, at the same time that the monster crashed into it from the other side. It roared, a thunderous banging erupting as the creature pummeled the door. There was no window to see on the other side, so all they could do was imagine what the rage of that thing trying to get to them looked like.

Asha heaved a sigh, not necessarily of relief, but of survival. She'd made it, and somehow, so had these other people. Just as the last of the sigh left her mouth, Perisdo started yelling.

"You could have killed me! What were you thinking?" He jabbed a finger at Mina. "And why is she here? We all watched her kill that woman." He backed away from the group. "You need to get rid of her."

"We need to leave!" Asha yelled back at him. "We are fucked if we stay down here, and we need to *go.*"

"Do you plan on bringing her with you?" Perisdo gestured at the unconscious Mina, his lip curling in disgust.

Carlos jumped in before Asha could continue yelling. "I want to make sure I'm understanding that the decision maker of Amphitrite is suggesting that we leave an injured crew member behind in a dangerous environment."

Perisdo barked out a laugh. "Suggesting it? I'm going to order it. This environment is out of control. You people have no idea what you're doing down here or how to manage an expensive venture like a Kraken lab." While Perisdo ranted, Benson stood and brushed himself off. Perisdo tilted his chin up, staring down his nose at them. "She should have been left for that creature."

Benson gave Perisdo an indignant look. "She is a member of my crew, and she will not be left to fend for herself. What Doctor Kibner did is inexcusable, and she will be dealt with accordingly." Benson glared at Perisdo. It surprised Asha that Benson would stand up to a superior, rather than groveling to him. Maybe some sense of self-preservation was making Benson appreciate his crew more.

Benson's glasses were askew, and even though he fiddled with them for a second, it didn't seem like they could be straightened. He continued, "We cannot just leave her down here, and, at any rate, we should have a better plan in place than just 'leave'. You, Mr. Edricks, and Mr. Massin will need medical care upon return to the surface because you have not acclimated properly yet. We will also need medical care for Science Officer Marsh."

"Speaking of, Mina can go with Zane for the time being." All of them turned towards Keaner. He sat on the floor, Mina was laid out across his legs, his shirt torn. "They can be crazy together." It wasn't a bad idea, and Asha felt herself nodding, despite her earlier feelings about Keaner. Maybe she was wrong?

But who was that eighth person collecting the bodies?

"That's a good idea." Benson looked around at them. "Engineer Cepeda. You still need to close off this section from that...thing out there. Take Mr. Keaner, and the two of you can bring Dr. Kibner to the lock up room. If I'm thinking of the hab layout correctly, that is on the way to one of the doors you can seal us off with." Asha was surprised Benson knew the layout of the hab that well.

Carlos nodded and waved to Keaner. The two of them bent over, each grabbing one of Mina's arms.

"So, you're saying she's got Ocean Dark Syndrome? And that's what that other deranged doctor has? I'm going to have to speak with whoever vetted this crew," Perisdo fumed. "Someone is getting fired."

"Can you just shut up?" Asha sighed. "No one said anything about Ocean Dark Syndrome, and no one cares about what you have to say. I already told you, you don't make the rules down here. So just. Shut up. We need to get this done so we can then focus on getting out of here."

Asha wasn't going to admit that it was entirely possible both Mina and Zane had the Syndrome. However, the two of them getting it at almost the exact same time? Not likely.

Addressing Carlos, she said, "I'm going with you." He started to argue with her, and she dismissed him with a flick of her wrist.

"That's not necessary," Carlos said, at the time Benson ordered, "No you're not."

Crossing her arms over her chest, Asha cocked an eyebrow.

Benson responded to her implied question. "The fewer people wandering around the hallways, the better. Besides, we need to have a chat about your little deep walk." He crossed his arms over his chest, mirroring her stance.

"My deep walk? Mine?" Carlos met her glare and shrugged, still working with Keaner to drag Mina down the hall. "I can't believe this," she muttered. "Whatever. The mess hall is down here and I haven't eaten in forever."

"I didn't say anything about eating." Benson uncrossed his arms, his control over the situation slipping away. Asha had a habit of doing that.

"And he's your hab supervisor." Standing next to Benson, Perisdo sounded haughty, like he was regaining control. "I'm going to cite you for insubordination."

Benson waved his hands in front of himself. "No one said anything about citations or insubordination. It's fine, we can eat." Perisdo's face soured at Benson's failure to agree with him. Rolling her eyes, Asha stalked off to the mess hall. They could follow or not, rules against splitting up be damned. At this point, she would welcome a citation for insubordination and being fired. The sooner she could get off the bottom of the ocean, the better.

We don't delight in this chaos. Such things never lead to beneficial outcomes. Chaos is what sent us to the bottom of this forsaken landscape, what trapped us here. Sometimes the systrarna get overexcited. Sometimes they lose sight of the end goal. It's happened before. I cannot let it happen again, no matter how the systrarna fight me.

Carlos

Never in his imagination did Carlos ever think that he would be dragging one of his crewmates to a room to be locked up. Maybe dragging someone who was injured, or needed assistance, but never like this. And Mina wasn't even the first one to be locked up.

"Pretty sure this isn't in either of our job descriptions." Keaner huffed, checking over his shoulder to see how much further they had. It was like he was reading Carlos' mind. "Think we can ask for special pay?" Carlos wasn't looking at him, but he could hear the grin in Keaner's voice.

"Keaner, at this point I think we'll be lucky to just make it out of here alive."

Carlos didn't want to think about that. He glanced down at Mina who looked kind of peaceful. Or, as peaceful as someone could look with their head lolling back at an awkward angle as they were being dragged across the floor. This was messed up. They just needed to get Mina into the room with Zane, and then get the other watertight doors closed. It was going to take some time to get to each door, and he was going to put his hours of time jogging to use. Whether or not Keaner could keep up, he didn't care. The doors needed to be closed and Carlos didn't need Keaner's help with closing them.

There was also Asha's nagging question of whether or not Keaner had been on Kraken 3 for the massacre. Which was, of course, ridiculous.

Mostly.

Huffing, Keaner wiped beads of sweat from his forehead. "What do you think those creatures are? Where'd they come from?"

Carlos rolled his eyes even though Keaner couldn't see his face. Why was it always the out of shape people who wanted to talk while doing physical activity? He was only making things harder for himself.

"Probably from some underwater volcano or something. Doesn't weird stuff come up out of those vents all the time?" He remembered reading somewhere that robots found a bunch of undiscovered species of fish and things in volcanic vents. The Mordices were a new fish, and they'd just been floating around down here, minding their own business. Like humans should've been doing. "It doesn't matter."

"If we're all dead, it definitely won't matter. Except to our next of kin." Keaner chuckled at his joke.

It wasn't much further, Carlos reassured himself. They were almost there. Please let them almost be there.

Checking over his shoulder, Carlos saw the door was just behind them. He stopped, and gently lowered Mina down to the ground, Keaner following his lead.

"Hey." Carlos looked at his partner, then down at Mina. "You've been down here for a while. How did Kraken 3 compare to the other habs you've been in? You've been in a few, right?" He kept his gaze down at Mina, hoping he was coming across as curious, rather than interrogative.

"Eh, you know, one is like the like the next. They're all built exactly the same and the view never changes." He breathed out with a "phew" sound. "Glad I wasn't in the first few. Between issues with parts of habs collapsing, and then Ocean Dark Syndrome. Never heard anything about these weird monsters, though."

Carlos grunted. It was a bland answer, and didn't help him with shutting down Asha's suspicions. "Let's get Mina in there and then I've gotta get those watertight doors shut." Waving his ID bracelet in front of the scanner, Carlos grabbed Mina's arm and started dragging her without waiting for Keaner. The tear in her shirt folded open at her shoulder and Carlos caught a glimpse of a line of black bumps running down her back. One of the bumps had ruptured, oozing a white fluid. He tried not to think about what was on her skin, and almost had her through the door before Keaner moved in to help.

Backing through the door, Carlos couldn't see the state Zane was in, but the smell in the room made him wrinkle his nose. It was heavy and noxious, rancid meat combined with week old spoiled milk left on the counter. The odor crawled up his nostrils and nested there, promising to return at the most unexpected moments. Carlos coughed, his eyes watering, and he let go of Mina's arm. She was in the room. It was good enough. He stood up and turned.

Zane was crouched on the bed, staring at them with hollow eyes and dark circles that looked to be dripping down his cheeks, melting into the burn sores on his face. All up and down Zane's arms, his burns were an oozing mess of red, white, and black fluids that were seeping from the wounds and pooling on the bed. Fluid saturated the sheets, and they squelched when Zane shifted.

"Why is she here?" His voice sounded like the meat of his throat had been run through a grinder. "What have you done?" When he moved his arms, the zip-ties dug into his skin, peeling it away. White bone peeked out of the sludge of his flesh.

This was a terrible idea.

"We don't have another pair of ties, do we?" Carlos asked.

"Nope," Keaner returned, without looking away from Zane, sounding far too unconcerned for Carlos' taste. "If she kills him, it might be a mercy."

Carlos snapped his head toward Keaner, who looked unaffected by what he just said.

"It would be a mercy," Zane growled. He bared his teeth, stained red with blood. "It would be a mercy if we all died." Stepping back, Carlos didn't know how to answer that. "You should all die. Just die, die, die die diediediedie!" Zane's voice grew in volume until he was roaring the word into a single, continuous sound.

In backing up, Carlos bumped into Keaner and for a moment, Carlos didn't think the other man was going to let him out of the room. There was something in Keaner's eyes, something Carlos couldn't be sure he imagined. It was a predatory look, a flash of the eyes that looked like they were all pupil and no iris.

Then they were both stumbling into the hallway. Carlos felt like he could breathe again, even though the smell was still mashed up his nose and sliding down his throat. That's all that was, when he looked at Keaner: too many emotions making him see things that weren't there. Keaner was fine. There was nothing wrong him.

"Jesus," Carlos moaned.

"I don't think He lives down here." Carlos blinked and looked to Keaner who stared at the door to the room like he could see through it. When he noticed Carlos' stare, he shrugged. "I'm just saying. I don't think a guy who lived in a desert could swim."

"Yeah," Carlos responded, feeling his skin crawl. Shaking his arms out, Carlos tried to recover even the tiniest bit of composure. "I'm going to get the watertight doors shut. Don't bother trying to keep up."

Carlos didn't wait for Keaner to respond. He took off down the hallway, picking up speed until he was running at a full sprint.

Asha

Sitting down didn't make her feel better. Eating didn't make her feel better. Imagining strangling Perisdo didn't make her feel better.

What Asha needed was twenty-four hours of uninterrupted sleep. And to have her feet on solid ground that wasn't underwater.

Asha would pray to whatever god would present herself if only they would take her out of here. Unfortunately for her, none made themselves available.

Leaning back on a chair she'd dragged into a corner, Asha surveyed the group. Perisdo and Benson were sitting at a table by themselves, heads together, whispering. The other two surfacers were sitting at a table with their heads down, snores rolling out of them.

Lucky bastards. Any time Asha closed her eyes, her heart rate skyrocketed, and she felt like if she didn't open her eyes she would die. Carlos couldn't come back soon enough. She wanted to drag him to a computer console, plug the drive in, and scour the data on it until they could figure out what happened at Kraken 3.

"Asha."

Blinking her eyes, Asha wondered if she had fallen asleep or just been so distracted she hadn't noticed Benson get up and stand in front of her.

"I quit." She hoped that would make him go away, and closed her eyes again.

"Communications Officer Moore."

Asha sighed and opened her eyes while looking at the ceiling.

"What do you want, Supervisor Benson? You know I don't like you." Asha looked at Benson. "You know, I'm actually pretty sure no one likes you."

Narrowing his eyes, Benson said, "While that may be true, it doesn't matter in the workplace. I'm still your supervisor, and I demand to know why you went to Kraken 3."

Asha wrinkled her nose and curled her lips to show her teeth. "That's what you're worried about right now? Not the dead people we have here, or the reanimated Divya monster, or that Mina stomped a hole in her?" Shaking her head, Asha continued, "That we can't leave? That you're going to keep us here until whenever you decide? Of course not. You just want us all to respect your au-tho-ri-tay." She mockingly dragged out the syllables of the word.

"That's right." Benson seemed to miss the mockery and disgust in her tone. Before he could continue to speak, and annoy her even more, Asha spoke over him, her anger pressing hot against her skin.

"You know what we found at Kraken 3? Monsters. Body bags. Blood smeared on the walls. There was some sort of fish creature monster that chased us on the deep walk. There's stuff out there that we have no idea about, and you want to act like you still have control over this situation." Benson's mouth dropped open as she talked. He stuttered out a few syllables, but nothing turned into actual words. "Yeah. That's why I quit." Asha stopped herself short of saying that when Carlos got back, they were getting whoever wanted to leave and going to the sub to return to the surface. She didn't care what he had to say.

"Well, I'll just have to speak to the surface and figure out what we should do about this. No one is leaving just yet. You are contractually obligated to be down here until released." Asha opened and closed her hand at him in an imitation of a hand puppet jabbering. "And Mr. Perisdo and the stake holders still need a few more days to acclimate before they can return to the surface."

"I don't care," Asha snapped. "Please go away so I can try to sleep."

Benson looked like he was going to argue with her, then decided there were other, better, battles that he could choose to fight. Sniffing, Benson rubbed his nose and walked back to his table with Perisdo.

Sighing, Asha closed her eyes and tried to think calming thoughts to keep her heart rate from spiking. If she could just get a little bit of sleep, she could think straight, could plan better. Plan what, she wasn't entirely sure, but that's why she needed Carlos here. She needed to talk about what was going on, and she wanted to watch more footage from the drive, and she just felt like she needed so much more information about what the fuck was going on down here.

Perisdo was either oblivious to what was happening, or didn't care, but how could his company be covering up so much? It didn't make sense. Why send people down here for some parasite filled fish that resembled the humanoid monsters swimming around out there? She shivered at the thought of running away from those clawed, roaring monsters, and clenched her teeth.

Sleep. She just needed to sleep.

"Here." Asha startled and almost jumped off her chair. Kneeling in front of her was Perisdo, a hand held out. Two small, round items were cupped in his palm. "These will help you sleep."

Asha eyed him, suspicion souring his potentially helpful behavior.

"What is it?" She didn't reach for the pills but tried to keep her voice diplomatic, hoping that would make him go away faster.

He looked down at his hand and then back at her, his eyes softer than she'd ever seen them. She wanted to make a face at his sudden change in disposition but managed to keep her features flat. When people made personality changes so fast like that, Asha expected nothing good from them.

"I have a hard time sleeping, and this is something that Amphitrite developed that helps. It's still in the clinical testing stage, but I've been reassured that it's safe and the rest is just bureaucratic nonsense." He moved his hand a little closer to her. The little round balls didn't look like any pills she knew of.

"Nah, I think I'm good." Asha closed her eyes, dismissing him. His presence didn't leave her space. She could tell that he was still looming there, and she sighed. "You're not gonna leave?" Nothing changed on his face, the stillness of his smile creeping her out. Reaching out her hand, Asha accepted the pills. Satisfied, Perisdo stepped back and turned like he was going to leave but paused.

Irritation curdled any good will Asha might have been nurturing for him. The man was as fake as fake could be, slimier than rotten vegetables, and she was positive that whatever it was she held in her hand, it wasn't going to help her sleep. And here he was, still hanging out in her space. For what?

Perisdo half turned, speaking more over his shoulder than to her. "Don't ever speak to me like you did in the hallway again." There was the walking, talking, dickhead she knew and hated. He didn't wait for an answer he knew he wasn't going to get. She sneered at his back, drawing a frown from Benson. Asha stuck her tongue out at Benson and flipped her middle finger up at him. He huffed and turned away.

Asha held the pills up to her face and squinted at them. Smooth, shiny, perfect spheres. Frowning, Asha thought they looked a lot like tiny versions of the worm filled spheres they encountered during the deep walk.

Plucking one of the balls out of her palm, she gave it a gentle squeeze. The surface gave a bit under the pressure, springing back to its shape once she released it. Whatever they were coated in, they would go down smooth for sure.

Beneath the pads of her fingers, the pill flexed even though she didn't squeeze it. Asha almost dropped it. She leaned away from her hand and slowly pressed her fingers together. There wasn't any resistance to the sphere until her fingers were almost together, and then something pressed back against her skin. Not letting that deter her, Asha kept pressing until the ends of the pill broke open. A milky fluid dribbled out from the burst ends, trailing down her fingers. Frowning, Asha squished it even harder.

A white tip extruded from between her pressed together fingers. This time Asha dropped the thing that she was certain was *not* a pill. Dropping the other sphere, Asha stomped on it with her boot, and then crushed the other one, grinding her shoe into the floor. Looking up from ground, she zeroed in on Perisdo.

"What the fuck?" At the same time Asha shouted, Bryan projectile vomited across the table he was sitting at. His body convulsed so violently, and the noise he made was so loud, it was like his body was trying to turn itself inside out.

The other man at the table, Elio, jumped up, slapping at the vomit that splattered onto his shirt. His slaps became more frantic and small yelping noises squeaked out of him.

Asha jumped out of her seat, along with Perisdo and Benson. Bryan's body heaved again, and a red stream of vomit spewed out of him. Chunks of darker material skittered across the table and plopped onto the floor. Dread filled Asha as she scanned the room. There was no doctor down here, no medical equipment at this end of the hab, and both scientists were deranged and incapable of making any kind of decisions.

"Get them off!" Elio shouted. "Get them off, get them off, getthemoff!" Slapping at his shirt, he sloughed off droplets, chunks of vomit, and…wriggling worms.

No one moved to help him. Benson and Perisdo backed away, putting tables and chairs between them and the two surfacers. In his panicked slapping, Elio stumbled over his chair and crashed to the floor.

Still convulsing, Bryan also fell to the floor, his limbs beating a drumbeat against the metal. The worms in his vomit writhed across the floor, heading for Elio who slipped in vomit as he tried to push himself away from their advance.

Bleach. Would bleach kill these things? They were in a mess hall attached to a kitchen. There had to be cleaning supplies in the kitchen.

"Benson!" Her supervisor snapped his head in her direction. "Bleach! Get the bleach in the kitchen!" Asha gestured with her arms, jabbing aggressively at the door behind him that would lead to the kitchen.

He stared at her, and Asha thought he might not go, that she would need to traverse the mess hall and get into the kitchen.

Then, without any acknowledgment, he darted away.

Several abrupt cracking noises, like large shells being broken open, drew Asha's attention back to Bryan. He wasn't convulsing anymore, but something under his clothing was pushing the fabric up. Elio screamed, though whether it was from the worms closing in on him, or Bryan's expanding size, Asha wasn't sure. There were more cracks, and then the sound of fabric tearing. The seams of Bryan's shirt split and light-colored shards of...something jutted from the openings. They dripped with a clear fluid that steamed. More tearing sounds released more of the shards, sharp and glistening in the overhead lights.

Asha backed up, trying to catch her breath, and bumped into something. Startled, she looked behind her and saw the case for the defibrillator the stupid company had given them.

Bryan's face cracked open and she realized that those "shards" were Bryan's skin, hardened to the point that it was cracking off his body. Bryan's face split into three pieces, and the chunks of skin peeled off from the muscle beneath and fell, shattering on the floor like some perverted ceramic. Beneath the shed skin, Bryan's face wasn't red and smooth, like Asha expected the muscle to look. Instead, it was yellow and gray, rounded ridges following what would have been the curvatures in Bryan's face if any face remained. His nose was gone, an empty space above a gaping black hole of a mouth, and above all that were two blinking red eyes.

Bryan was gone.

The scream about to claw its way out of Asha's mouth was arrested by Benson slamming the door open and lurching into the room with a bottle of bleach. He tore the cap off as he got close to Elio, ready to douse the worms in the chemical to hopefully kill them. Perisdo snapped his head towards Benson, as if noticing for the first time that he was back in the room and scrambled to get out of his way.

Except, somehow, Perisdo's trajectory put him right in Benson's path, tripping him.

The bottle of bleach left Benson's hands, spinning, flinging bleach everywhere. It hit Elio in the head, cutting off his screams, and fell into his lap. Bleach spilled all over his pants and then flowed onto the floor, swallowing up the bloody pools of squirming worms. Elio picked up the bottle and chucked it at the worms. There was still some liquid in it, and it sloshed out as the bottle bounced across the floor, splashing onto the thing that used to be Bryan.

A rattling groan came out of the creature, and its skin hissed wherever the bleach landed on it. The torn shirt and pants it wore were dampened with the clear fluid oozing up between the pieces of cracked skin, and when the thing started to move its limbs, those shards fell and shattered like the pieces of its face had before.

Asha's blood pounded in her head, and she felt a wave of exhaustion that was quickly replaced by a need to do something, to run. But where? She didn't know where the watertight doors were. Glancing down at her watch, she tried to pull up the hab map that would show her everyone's locations, but her fingers were shaking too much for the fine motor coordination operating the watch required.

The creature's groaning intensified, hitting a higher pitch. It rolled over onto its stomach, the movement slow as it peeled itself out of the shell of skin with a sticky tearing sound. Strings of yellow-gray flesh stretched between the creature and its shell until they snapped, some of them plastering to the creature's wet skin like long hairs against a shower wall. It half lifted itself up on arms that wobbled, its long fingers splayed out beneath it. Tiny yellowed claws ticked against the floor. A shiver ran down the length of the thing, and flaccid spines lifted off the back of the thing's arms.

The nightmares had followed them back from Kraken 3.

"Get out of here!" Asha stuttered over the words. Everyone looked at her, including the monster on the floor. It laid between her and the door to the hallway.

Perisdo didn't need any other encouragement, choosing to put himself ahead of everyone else as usual. Elio staggered to his feet, his clothing soaked with various fluids. Even though he had a clear path to the doorway with the creature turning towards Asha, he somehow ran in front of the monster.

Too close.

The creature struck out with its claws, hooking the back of Elio's ankle. He squealed and went down, striking his chin against the floor, spitting out blood and what looked like a couple of teeth. Elio tried to drag himself away, fingers slipping on the floor. The creature pulled him back, lifting his ankle off the floor as Elio fought to get away, its claw stretching out the tendon at the back of Elio's ankle.

Asha whipped around, tearing open the door of the defibrillator compartment which set off an ear-piercing siren. She snatched the device out of its enclosure and slammed the door shut to silence the alarm, just in time to hear Elio's tendon snap with a sound like a gunshot.

Asha yelped, her voice drowned out by Elio's scream. With a rumbling growl, the creature opened its mouth to expose rows of sharp teeth and swung both of its arms forward to sink claws into Elio's calves. It dragged itself closer to him, angling its head to chomp into Elio's foot.

Lifting the defibrillator above her head to throw at the creature, Asha didn't get the chance to complete the movement.

Roaring, Benson jumped behind the creature with a chair raised over his head. The noise disrupted the creature, which paused and started to turn towards Benson. His roar turned into a screech and he slammed the chair into the creature's back. Its body compressed and then sprang back up. Benson brought the chair down again, striking the creature in its upper back. The thing unhooked its claws from Elio and rolled over to face Benson.

Benson's teeth were gritted, and his lips were peeled back. As he brought the chair down against the creature's head again and again, his jaw flexed like he was trying to crush his own teeth with every strike.

Asha rushed forward and grabbed Elio's arm while she held onto the defibrillator. "Up we go." With a shredded Achilles tendon and claw marks in his calves, Asha wasn't sure if he was going to be able to get up, but she wasn't about to leave him.

Elio moaned and was dead weight as she tried to lift him. Something twinged in Asha's back and she let Elio slide to the ground.

"I need you to help me," she ground out. Elio was crying, tears and snot mixing with the blood dribbling down his chin. "Come on." Asha grunted when she picked up his arms again.

At Elio's feet, Benson let out a breathless whoop and dropped the chair with a clatter. A yellow and gray mess of flayed meat was where the creature's head used to be.

"Benson."

Chest heaving, Benson looked up when Asha called his name, seeming to not see her. His eyes had a faraway look, and it looked like one of his lenses were missing. When Asha repeated his name, he snapped his attention towards her. "Help. Me."

He scrambled over to her, feet slipping on the wet floor.

"What the hell happened in here?"

Asha spared a glance for Carlos standing in the entryway but didn't respond. Benson was next to her, heaving Elio up with her; the man was heavier than he looked.

A crackling noise came from the body Asha thought was dead. The creature's smashed in face pressed outwards, reforming to what it looked like before Benson went to town. Asha and Benson were almost at the door with Elio when the creature groaned.

"Alright," Carlos said, his voice tight. He reached down between Asha and Benson and grabbed Elio under the arms and hoisted him up with a grunt. Asha released her hold on Elio, clutching the defibrillator to her chest while Benson and Carlos split the man's weight. "We've gotta boogey. Next watertight door is two hallways down." Jutting his chin in the direction they needed to walk in, the three of them moved as fast as they could drag Elio. He whimpered and whined, tears still running down his face. Asha wanted to slap him. She knew he couldn't use the leg with the torn tendon, but he could at least take some weight off of them with the other leg.

"Come on, man." Carlos sounded part encouraging, part scolding. "You've gotta use your other leg."

Elio sniffled something that could have been words but didn't sound like anything understandable.

Instead of arguing with Elio, Carlos grunted, "Where'd Perisdo go?"

"Don't know," Asha huffed. "He took off after Bryan turned into the demon fish."

"A what…? Never mind. One more hallway."

"Where's Keaner?" Asha checked both ways of the intersection as if they were crossing a street, checking for monsters instead of cars. She looked behind them and saw a yellow clawed hand shoot out of the mess hall doorway to curl around the edge. Shit.

"Don't know." Carlos repeated her words back to her. "I left him so that I could shut the doors."

"And now we're shut in with one of them." Benson's voice was tight, his words coming on short bursts of air. When Asha looked at him, she caught him checking behind them.

The monster must have made it into the hallway; she didn't turn around to check.

"We've got other problems, too."

Asha didn't bother asking what this new problem was; Carlos would tell her soon enough.

Behind them, the creature screeched.

"Let's get on with it kids." Carlos huffed and moved faster, forcing Asha and Benson to move quicker. Elio kept whimpering, his feet shuffling beneath him without doing much of anything. "Just right there."

Once they crossed the threshold, Carlos ducked out from under Elio and the dead weight dragged Benson down. Asha dropped the defibrillator and tried to grab Elio, but went down too, her knees cracking on the ground. She winced and threw Elio's arm off her shoulders. Goddamn pathetic, he was.

The watertight door hissed shut behind them, sealing off the view of the monster Asha knew was still bearing down on them. She crawled away from the jumble on the floor and leaned against the hallway wall. Carlos slithered down the wall next to and put his hand on her knee.

"Good thinking with the bleach," Benson muttered. He was still on the floor but had rolled himself onto his back and out from underneath Elio who was face down, blubbering into the floor.

"Nice job with the," Asha imitated swinging a chair over her head and grinned. Benson hesitated before grinning back at her.

They sat in silence, Elio quieting down until they could hear each other breathing in the small space. Asha stared at a spot about three feet up the wall. There wasn't anything interesting or different about this bit of wall; it was just where her eyes happened to land.

"Fuck Perisdo," Asha muttered. Benson grunted, though she wasn't sure if it was an agreement or a reprimand. She wanted to know what Carlos had to tell them, but she also didn't want to know. It was only going to be bad news. There was nothing good coming down for them, as far as she could tell. What they needed to do was get the hell out of the hab and head back for the surface. Between the medical care people needed and the monsters trawling the halls…

Asha straightened up, a sudden thought pricking her mind.

"Perisdo gave me something." No one responded to her. "Perisdo gave me something," she repeated. "He said they were sleeping pills, but there was something moving inside, and when I squished them, I'm pretty sure it was worm inside."

Benson pushed himself up onto his elbows and squinted his eyes at her. "A worm? Why would he do that?"

"I don't know, Benson. Why is he even here? Why did any of these people come down here?" Asha could hear her voice pitching higher. “For that stupid fish? Or for the worms? How about for the fish monsters that you and Perisdo were so unconcerned about before?” Pushing off the wall, Asha paced the few feet from one side of the hallway to the other.

“Well.” Benson sat up further and pushed away from Elio who was finally quiet. “We weren’t necessarily convinced that what you were talking about was real.” The implication hung between them.

The watertight door shook when something slammed into it from the other side.

They all jumped. Elio sniffled loudly and Asha hoped he didn’t start crying again.

“Is that real enough for you?” She jabbed her finger at the door, extending her arm until her elbow locked out.

“That’s not a fish monster. That’s a…person…monster.” Benson shrugged, wincing and deflating under Asha’s withering glare.

“And it’s not the only one in here.” Carlos’ eyes were closed, his lips pressed into a pale line.

Asha kept her careful words neutral. “Right. There’s also Divya. Or what used to be Divya.”

Carlos sighed. “Yeah. She’s…it’s…that’s not what I’m talking about. Something came in through the emergency dry dock.”

Ice ran down Asha’s back, draining all her blood into her feet. She swayed and braced herself against the wall. “What do you mean?”

“We’re all accounted for here.” Benson tapped around on his ID bracelet. “Well, those of us that are…” He trailed off, unwilling or unable to finish the sentence.

The thing on the other side of the door slammed into it again, making it shake.

“I don’t think it was something human that used it.” Carlos used the wall to shimmy himself into a standing position. There was an audible click in one of his joints.

Asha didn’t need to ask what he thought it was. Whatever that monster was out in the abyss, it had watched them use the emergency dry dock door. If it had any semblance of intelligence, it wouldn’t be that difficult for it to open up a door after watching Carlos do it earlier.

“Cool, great, that’s awesome. Not only do we have whatever Divya and Bryan turned into wandering around, we now have another monster in here with us.” Asha squeezed her eyes shut and pressed the heels of her hands against them, creating flashes of light in the dark. From the other side of the door, a sound like nails on a chalkboard blaring through a megaphone sounded. “Will you shut up?” Asha screamed.

“I think we need to move away from the door.” Benson eyed it nervously and stepped back from it, looking at Elio on the floor. “Mr. Edricks, you need to get up.”

Elio wailed and didn’t move.

“If you don’t get up, we’re leaving you.” Carlos sounded harsher than Asha ever heard him. “And I really don’t know if that door is going to hold that thing.”

Asha cast her eyes at the doors, unsure if Carlos was being serious. If it was meant to hold back the ocean, shouldn’t it be able to hold back that monster?

As if in answer, the door shuddered at the force on the other side slamming into it.

Elio pushed himself onto his hands and knees, whimpering. “I, I need help.”

Rolling his eyes, Carlos nodded to Asha and then crouched next to Elio’s side.

“Actually.” Asha dragged out the syllables of the word. “I need to find a computer. Benson, help Carlos. Please?” She added the last as an afterthought.

“Asha,” Carlos groaned.

“Sure,” Benson slipped in before they could argue further. He bent next to Elio and nodded to Asha. “Go ahead.”

His agreeableness made Asha question his motives, but she had a drive to get through.

“Just message me where you end up. I’ll find you.”

Perisdo

This was not what he'd expected. There was far more chaos than he anticipated. These creatures were out of control. They were supposed to listen to him. *He* was the one giving these things the opportunity to return to the surface, after all.

There was a cost, of course. There was always a cost. Nothing was free in this world. It didn't matter if you were an old primordial monster. Without Amphitrite, none of these things would make it to the surface and Amphirtrite didn't give things away for free. They had contracts with various countries for the worms and the monsters. Perisdo didn't know what their plans for the creatures were, and he didn't care. All he knew were the dollar signs and the multiple zeros on the checks pending deposit into Amphitrite's accounts.

Pending the cooperation of these stupid fish creatures.

Something clanged down the hall, startling him.

He really shouldn't have left the group. There was safety in numbers and he was alone.

Not that he was scared. He was the boss. Fear was for poor people.

But he should try and find the group. Get back to the surface, report back that they needed to send weapons down here to keep these creatures in line. Send someone else down next time. This type of work was beneath him.

It sounded like something skittered down the hall, and Perisdo headed in the other direction.

Not out of fear, of course. He just had important things to do.

Carlos

Falling asleep was almost on purpose.

Almost.

It's hard to say that something was done on purpose when the exhaustion was so strong that there was no other choice but to close his eyes and drift off. Despite Elio's sniffling, Benson's thousand-yard stare, and his own fearful thoughts, sleep snatched Carlos into the dark.

His dreams were incoherent bits of colors, blood, claws, feeling like he was drowning. It felt like every few minutes he would startle himself awake and have to reorient himself to his location in the command portal. Each time he awakened, his blurry eyes would play tricks on him, seeing menacing shadows and shapes where nothing existed.

Looking at his bracelet, he noted that they had been sitting in this room for only an hour, maybe two. Where was Asha? Perisdo? Keaner?

He shivered, squeezing his eyes shut and then opening them to bleary vision. Hell, he was tired. Benson and Elio were passed out, gentle snores coming from Elio's direction.

At the very least, Asha should have come to find them. Did she really need that much time to go through a drive? Carlos was sure she was looking for something specific, something she thought would tie someone to Kraken 3. Or maybe she was just looking for clues for killing the fish things: the Mordices outside, and the monsters inside with them. Carlos just wanted to get to the sub. The mysteries of this place didn't matter to him. He wasn't going to remain an employee of Amphitrite, even if he had to swim from here to land.

An impossible task, but it was better to think about that than staying here.

Carlos yawned and checked his messages again. Still nothing. He tapped out another message to Asha, asking for an update. After staring at his watch for a few minutes with no response, he settled back into his chair and let his eyes slide closed.

It felt like only seconds later that he jerked into wakefulness.

Something was wrong. It was a feeling, more than anything else, lacking defined edges in his mind. The room seemed darker than before, like Benson or Elio had lowered the lights while his eyes were closed. It must have been Benson, since Elio was both unwilling and unable to move. They'd wrapped his shredded Achilles and punctured calves as best they could with spare uniforms kept in one of the cubbies in the control portal, but they had no pain medication and nothing that might help with an infection. Carlos hoped they could get him to a doctor sooner rather than later, but he wasn't going to leave until they had a plan in place for everyone. They could, potentially, all fit in the sub. Even Zane and Mina, though he wasn't sure how to safely get them in there.

As long as no one else turned into a "freaky fish monster" as Asha called them. The name made him smirk. Leave it to her to come up with an inappropriately apt name for something.

Carlos scanned the room again, unease still swirling in his stomach.

There. Behind Elio. Or was it next to him? The darkness made it difficult to differentiate depth and shape. But there was something there that didn't belong.

Shifting his weight, Carlos blinked his eyes as though that might help him to see clearer. He didn't know if he should call out, or even if what he was seeing was real. Sleep deprivation could cause hallucinations, he knew. Or it could be the Syndrome.

To hell with it.

"Hello?" His voice came out more of whisper than he intended. Nothing happened and he wasn't sure if he needed to be louder or if there really was nothing in that shadow.

A few seconds passed, and Carlos leaned back into his chair, still distrustful of the shadow. Elio snorted in his sleep, choking on a snore. Above his head, two red eyes blazed into existence.

"Oh, shit!" Carlos jumped up, shoving the rolling chair backwards. At his exclamation, Benson and Elio both startled awake.

"Mr. Edricks, no!" Benson shouted, his hands reaching forward. Elio looked between Benson and Carlos, oblivious to the danger he was in. He leaned forward, his face coming more into one of the dim lights.

Milky fluid dripped onto his face from above. "Oh, gross," he whined.

Elio didn't get to say anything more. Yellow claws curved around his head and sank into his face, popping one of his eyes. He flailed, opening his mouth to scream. The creature shifted its grip to slide two claws into his mouth, yanking his lips back and distorting Elio's scream.

Carlos lunged for the lights, slapping them on. The creature didn't react to the change in lighting, but it allowed Carlos to get a good look at it. It had the same gray yellow skin of the other creatures he'd seen, of the one whose claw he still had stashed in his pocket. Its red eyes weren't nearly as bright under the lights, but they held a menace that made Carlos' knees shake. He knew what those claws could do to glass after they shattered his helmet. Those claws could probably shred Elio with ease.

With a snarl, the creature tore its claws from Elio's face, ripping his mouth open to his ears. Blood sheeted down Elio's jaw, soaking into the collar of his shirt. The yellow antenna on top of the thing's head rose up and vibrated, creating a rattling sound. It grabbed Elio by his arm and dragged him, screaming, from his chair. His shoulder popped out of its socket, making the creature yank even harder to drag Elio. With a shredding tear, Elio's arm was ripped entirely from its socket, blood shooting out of the amputated limb's stump. Hissing, the creature threw the arm across the room. When it hit the wall, it left a splatter of red.

Grabbing Elio in its claws, the creature started to drag him across the floor.

"Help, please!" Elio wailed. His struggle against the creature was weak, futile, his single arm an ineffective defense.

Carlos looked at Benson, and the two of them ran for Elio. He didn't know what either of them were going to do, but how could they let Elio just be dragged away like that? To where?

They rounded the table as the creature slithered into a vent in the floor, dragging Elio with it.

Elio didn't fit into the vent, though. It was only a six inch by twelve-inch vent, meant for air circulation, not meant for humans. It shouldn't have fit something as large as that monster either, but it compressed its body without hesitation and disappeared. Elio's remaining arm went into the vent after the creature, but the edges of the vent caught him in his ribs and the side of his neck. There was a crack, and Elio screamed louder, his eyes bugging out of his head.

Grabbing Elio's shirt, Benson and Carlos tried to drag him out of the vent. The shirt tore and Benson tumbled backwards. Carlos managed to keep his feet and grabbed for where Elio's arm should have been. Instead, he sank his fingers into the squishy meat of Elio's exposed shoulder. When he reflexively grabbed, his fingers tore away chunks of muscle.

Something cracked and Elio jerked further into the air vent.

"Help me! Please! Don't let it take me!" he wailed. Part of his shoulder had been pulled into the vent, leaving his neck twisted at an awkward and painful angle.

Carlos looked at his red stained hands, bits of muscle fiber stuck in the blood. Help him how?

Elio's pleas were cut short when his body was pulled deeper into the vent and his neck snapped, his head turning to the ceiling in a way it shouldn't have been able to. His ribs crunched as his body folded in on itself.

"Oh no." Benson's words were such an understatement that Carlos choked on a laugh. He wheezed as the creature roared beneath their feet. With a series of squelches and cracks, Elio was pulled entirely into the vent.

Except for his head. As the body went down, the skull got stuck. The skin of the neck tore, and the neck bones popped as they were stretched beyond the limits of the connective tissues to keep them together. There were several wet sucking sounds, and then the head separated from the body. It rolled away from the vent while Elio's torso compressed enough to fit into the vent, followed by his legs. The creature's screech echoed out from beneath the floor.

"We need to find the others." Carlos was surprised he was able to find his voice. His throat was still tight from the manic laugh that he choked down. Elio's head sat at the edge of the vent, rocking back and forth like a gentle breeze might push it over the edge.

"And get the fuck out of here." Benson was already striding for the command portal exit. His declaration startled Carlos; Benson never swore. "Let's go." Left with no choice but to follow Benson, Carlos chased after him.

"I think I know where Asha will be. You have any idea where Perisdo would be?" Checking on his bracelet, Carlos searched the screen for Keaner. Only five dots appeared: Zane and Mina bunched together, Asha in the communications room where he expected her to be, then him and Benson grouped together. "Keaner's turned his bracelet off."

Benson didn't react to that information, still marching down the hall.

"If they can move through the vents," Carlos continued, "the watertight doors don't matter." Nowhere was safe for them. That thought sent his stomach plummeting. He'd agreed to Asha going off on her own because he'd thought they were safe. At least, as safe as they could be given the circumstances. If anything happened to her, he'd never forgive himself.

"No, the doors are still important." Benson paused at an intersection and turned to Carlos. "Asha is that way?"

There was a clattering beneath them, and they both looked down, stepping away from the noise. Carlos bumped into the wall and the contact startled him. It wasn't until the noise faded that he said, "Yeah. Yeah, she's down that way."

"Starting to rethink that whole 'no need for security or weapons' policy that Amphitrite has." Benson frowned. "I'm going to try and find Perisdo. We'll all meet back at the submersible."

"And Keaner?" Carlos looked down the hall, unsure who–or what–he was expecting to see.

Shaking his head, Benson's frown deepened. "Let him go for now. There's something not right about him."

Carlos blinked. "What do you mean?" Did Benson know something about Keaner?

The frown lines smoothed on Benson's face, as though he suddenly remembered Carlos was an employee and not his friend, regardless of their dire circumstances.

"I probably shouldn't say anything," Benson hesitated. Carlos reached up to rub his earlobe. Benson kept him in suspense for a few more seconds, adjusted his broken glasses, then continued. "But, Perisdo mentioned that Keaner had a history of acting strangely at his last placement. That he was removed for his behavior, and they considered not hiring him back." He shook his head. "I wasn't able to ask more about it, because he got up to talk to Asha and then everything with Bryan and Elio started."

Frustrated with the half answer, there wasn't anything Carlos could do about it now.

"Alright. I'm going to get Asha, you get Perisdo. We'll meet at the sub and decide what to do about Mina and Zane." Benson hesitated, then nodded. Carlos wasn't sure what the hesitation was about, but there wasn't any time. He gave Benson a half-hearted salute and turned to find Asha.

Mina

Everything hurt, and when Mina opened her eyes, she didn't know where she was.

The ceiling lacked the glow in the dark stars she'd plastered up there in her room, and the floor lacked the softness of the area rug she'd brought with her from the surface. They weren't allowed many comforts down here, and Mina maximized hers. So, this minimalist room was for sure not hers.

Movement came from somewhere behind where her head was laying. Mina squeezed her eyes together, and when she opened them, she forced herself to sit up.

"Mina."

Zane's raspy voice was even worse than when Mina last came to see him. She was nervous about looking at him, but she turned anyway.

She gasped. Everything about him seemed to be oozing, like his skin was melting off and sloughing away everything underneath. His cheeks were sunken, and he stared at her with an intensity that was unlike him. The surface of his skin shivered. Or maybe that was just her imagination. Asha had really pummeled her.

Mina gasped at the memory. "Divya." Guilt crashed over her in a wave. She'd stomped straight through Divya's gut, was going to crush her skull until that bitch Asha tackled her. Mina's internal thoughts paused. Since when did she hate Asha?

"What's that?" Zane leaned towards her, the zip ties dragging against his bones with a scratching noise that made her teeth clench.

"Nothing." Mina spat the word out faster than she could think of a better response. Hunching her shoulders, she deflected the conversation away from herself. "What's wrong with you?"

It was obvious that a lot was wrong. The smell, which she was just noticing as she woke up more, was one of the worst things she'd ever experienced, and she'd dissected and transported decaying animal carcasses.

Giggling, Zane said, "What isn't wrong with me? I've got them. And you've got them, too. It's only a matter of time." His whole body spasmed and his eyes rolled back into his head. "Don't let them take you, Mina."

"Don't let who take me?" Mina stood up and went to the door. She pressed the button to open it, and looked out into the hallway. No one was there, so she stepped back into the room and let the door shut behind her. She turned back to Zane who grinned at her with a mouthful of bloody teeth.

"Remember the wormssss? The things that started all thissss?" He dragged out the ending of his sentences in a way that irritated her. He almost sounded condescending. "You've got themmm, I've got themmm. Don't let them get into your brain, Minaaa." Zane started coughing, and the black fluid he spit up wriggled on the floor.

Something clicked into place in Mina's brain, and she felt herself drifting away. She wasn't sure where she was going, or what was sliding into that empty space. Emotions spiraled out of her like they were disappearing down the drain, taking away her guilt and remorse, her fear and concern. She didn't know how to grab onto those things, to hold them within herself. Warmth started to drain from her limbs, leaving her chilled. There was a sharp *pop* behind her eyes and Mina blinked, focusing on Zane.

"You know," she began, "if you just let it happen, everything will be much easier. You won't be such a," she gestured at the state that Zane was in, "mess."

Zane's smile disappeared and his lips folded in on themselves. "Mina?" He sounded unsure, though the person who stood in front of him looked exactly like her.

Straightening her shoulders, Mina's chuckled. "Of course I'm Mina. Just better. You could be better, too, if you'd just let us do our work."

Asha

There was a clattering in the floor beneath her. Asha jumped and stared down. There was no reason for anyone to be under the floor, and no reason to be moving as fast as that noise was. Her gaze followed the noise until it passed beneath the wall that separated her room from the next.

Swallowing hard, Asha got up and pushed the rolling chair over the single air vent in the room.

"It's just the circulation system." The tremor in her voice betrayed the lie. "Just the circulation system, Asha. Nothing to worry about." She gave a nervous chuckle and returned to her seat, almost missing it and falling to the floor. Another nervous laugh trickled out of her.

At least if she died, Carlos would know where to find her body.

If the monsters didn't get him first.

Asha shook her head hard, trying to dislodge those awful thoughts. Either of them dying was the last thing she wanted to think about. The focus needed to be on the data in the drive. She was convinced that there was something important in this data, something beyond the bloodshed that saturated the videos she and Carlos watched.

Although, she'd found nothing so far. With the limited time she knew she had, Asha fast forwarded through videos, trying to find a better view of the man she was convinced was Keaner. But he seemed to have an almost preternatural ability to avoid looking at the cameras. Asha again wondered why there were no cameras in Kraken 7. Unless it was to prevent someone from looking at footage of Kraken 7 at some future date after they'd all been massacred. Just like she was doing now with Kraken 3.

A wash of cold sent a shiver across her skin. Asha shook her shoulders and blew a hard breath out from between her lips.

The recordings were getting her nowhere. She needed to try something else, look somewhere else.

Closing out of the videos, Asha pulled up the written logs from the scientists working in the lab. Their notes were mundane, much like Mina and Zane's were in the beginning of their stay at Kraken 7. Generic dissections of the typical deep-sea creatures: anglerfish, barreleyes, the beaded comb jelly. When she read about the dissection of the blobfish she couldn't help the small smile on her face. Imagine just trying to exist and some pretentious human pronounces that you're a blobfish.

Not that the name wasn't fitting. It just seemed kind of mean.

Scrolling past these notes, her eyes skimming the words, Asha was desperate to read anything about the multi-jointed, rumbling

Mordices. She didn't expect to see that name exactly, but she knew they'd found one from the video she watched at Kraken 3.

She'd seen it on the recordings, though. Seen them dissecting it.

Asha grumbled unintelligible noises at herself as she scrolled.

Scroll, scan, scroll, scan, scroll.

Pause. *Claws.*

Asha's eyes roved back to the beginning of the sentence.

A frilled shark was pulled from one of the traps with "two yellow claws and an unknown parasitic worm" in it. Both finds were sent to the surface for testing, at least according to these notes. Yet, Mina and Zane were unfamiliar with the worm, and no one had warned them about some sort of creature with *claws* down here. The thing that had chased them across the ocean floor swam into her mind, its red eyes glowing, the yellowed claws swiping for her.

Refocusing on the notes, Asha skimmed down a little further. This discovery, if her recollection was accurate, was a little less than a month before the final video with the body bags and the stranger extruding worms from his body. She opened the notes closer to that date. It started out as general commentary on the specimens being brought in, moving on to Valla, one of the crewmates, having a headache for a few days, pills that were sent down from the surface for her and a few other crew members who were complaining about a persistent rumbling sound affecting their ability to sleep.

That rumbling noise reminded Asha of the sound the Mordices made when poked with the rod. Mina was complaining about headaches for a few days before everything went to hell. Now three people were dead, Mina and Zane were deranged, and there were goddamned monsters all over the hab.

But *why?* If Amphitrite was aware of what happened at Kraken 3–and there was no conceivable way they weren't–why send another crew back down here with no warning? With no safety precautions?

Asha paused. She was reading notes from Kraken 3, living in Kraken 7, and had found a location for Kraken 1 and Kraken 5 in the Amphitrite database. What if the person naming these habs wasn't just bad at numbers or trying to confuse the competition? What if Amphitrite was trying to hide these habs from other teams?

If that were true, was the "why" of the whole situation that they were allowing their crews to be savaged by some deep-sea monstrosities? What the hell was Amphitrite getting out of this?

Another few scrolls revealed a handwritten note scanned into the system.

I don't know who I can trust. No one believes me about the worms, the creatures I've been seeing on the other side of the viewing windows. I hear noises and I can't sleep, but I won't take those pills. Amphitrite won't remove us from Kraken 3, but they can send us pills??? I don't trust them, I don't trust anyone here. My headaches are getting worse...

[Engineer Ward]

Asha rubbed her hands together, trying to warm them up. The chill that wouldn't leave her body didn't have anything to do with the temperature in the room. She wanted to see who this Engineer Ward was. Then she could see where he was going, what he was up to in the days before the massacre.

Checking her bracelet, Asha saw a message from Carlos checking in on her. She bit her lip and ignored him. If she responded, he would want her to come back and she wasn't ready to. Asha glanced at the air vent with the chair she'd rolled over it. Had it moved? She gave a nervous laugh. Of course it hadn't moved. That was silly. Ridiculous, even.

Asha stood and went to the chair, repositioning it over the vent. There. Better. She could focus without thinking about the vent and things that were *not* crawling around in there because that was silly, too.

Sitting in her chair, Asha did a search on the drive for the crew member manifest. She should've done this from the beginning. Instead, she'd been so focused on watching those videos, unable to take her eyes away from them despite the awfulness they contained.

The door to her room slid open and Asha jumped, whirling around to confront whatever was coming through the door.

"We have to go," Carlos announced as he entered. His eyes went to the chair sitting on top of the air vent. "What's wrong?"

"Oh, nothing. Just monsters crawling around everywhere, a corporation keeping secrets and continuing to send people to the bottom of the ocean even though they know there are monsters down here." Asha crossed her arms over her chest. "I need five minutes."

Carlos shook his head. "They're in the air vents. We don't have minutes. What do you mean?"

"What I mean," Asha said, turning back to her computer and trying to not get hung up on what he said about the vents, "is that Amphitrite was sent samples of claws and worms from as early as Kraken 3, and they sent us back down here without any sort of heads up or defense against it."

"Yeah, but why?" Carlos crouched next to her instead of pulling the chair off the air vent.

Asha opened up the crew member manifest. "I don't know. Does their reasoning even really matter? They know about this, and they're still sending people down here!"

There were eight members of the crew, their names listed in alphabetical order. None of the names were familiar to her. She clicked on the first one.

"Well, yeah, it does matter. Someone outside of the company would notice if groups of people went missing at the same time, all working for the same company. *Someone* would notice. They have families and friends, Asha."

Three more profiles were opened and closed. She didn't recognize any of their faces.

"Amphitrite is like, a billion-dollar corporation. More. You think they couldn't buy silence?" She turned and glared at him. "They told us they want to use what they find for military purposes. When has that ever gone well for anyone?"

"It doesn't, but there's no way they can buy the silence of that many people. There's no way, Asha. We have to go. This doesn't matter. We just need to get to the surface." Carlos put his hand on her shoulder, his grip tight enough to tell her he would pull her out of her chair if need be.

"There's just four more, let me go through them and then we'll leave." She didn't wait for his acknowledgement. If her theories proved to be right, she didn't think Amphitrite would let them get back to the surface.

"Asha, we don't–" Carlos bit his words off at the face that popped up on Asha's screen. His intake of breath was sharp.

There was no sense of vindication, no cocky "I told you so" ready to roll out of Asha's mouth. It was only a confirmation that her fear was valid, a harsh reminder of the note she'd just read from Kraken 3: *I don't trust anyone here.* Her stomach was an empty pit swallowing her into it. The world around her lost some of its realness.

The door to her room opened, drawing her back into herself, and she turned, Carlos matching her movement.

"Good thing I found you guys. It's time…oh. Well, I guess that changes things, doesn't it?" Asha squeezed her hands over her knees, her knuckles turning white.

Benson adjusted his glasses and smiled, exposing too many sharp white teeth behind his peeled back lips.

Zane

Shrinking away from Mina, Zane didn't even feel the pain of his raw body anymore. His entire existence was pain, and he thought that might be why he was able to remain himself.

Unlike Mina.

He could feel the worms slithering around beneath his skin. Sometimes, they even poked out of the open wounds that covered his body. But he refused to let them think for him. He didn't know how he was doing it, if it was just a mind over matter thing. Or maybe he was just crazy and living in his own world while the worms puppeteered his body. If that were the case, Zane didn't want to know.

The door to the room hissed open and in stepped Keaner. He looked between the two of them and then smiled at Mina.

"It's about time one of us made the transition without completely wrecking the body." He frowned. "Why did you have to stomp through that human's stomach, huh? Do you know how much work that's going to take to fix? And now she's just going to be a secondary." Keaner glanced at Zane and then back at Mina.

Zane felt dizzy. So, someone was dead, or some sort of "secondary", whatever that meant. And Keaner had the worms? When had that happened? Zane felt a throbbing at the base of his skull and swallowed hard. He was missing so much being locked up in this room. Was it possible that he was the only holdout?

Mina shrugged. "I was mad. It's been a long time since I've felt whole."

"It's been a long time since any of us felt whole," Keaner snapped.

"Don't be mad just because I have the superior form." She ran her hands down her body and smirked.

Rolling his eyes, Keaner directed his attention to Zane. "How you doing with the children I slipped you? It'll be easier if you just give in."

Zane blinked. "When?" he croaked, his throat tight. He swallowed again.

Keaner shrugged. "After you got burned, and I tackled you to keep you from setting fire to anything else." Holding his hand out with the palm up, a forest of wriggling white growths erupted from his skin. "It was nothing to just press my hand against one of your burns and let them slide right on in."

Shuddering, Zane remembered that feeling, the white hot pin points of pain that he wrote off as coming from his burn wound.

"And Mina?" He closed his eyes, unwilling to look at either of them grinning at him like how a mean kid grins at an ant hill they're about to set on fire.

"A few days before, when the first tertiary–what you call 'Mordices' –was brought into the hab. There's a reason why I cook everyone's meals. Or, try to." Zane could hear the frown in Keaner's voice. Out of everyone, Divya, Carlos and Zane preferred to prepare their own meals. It was a control thing for him. Divya probably just hadn't wanted to say "Thank you" to someone.

Gulping, the pain at the base of his skull receding, Zane asked, "And everyone else?"

"They'll be dealt with soon enough. Come on, let's finish up." Keaner eyed Zane, winked at him, then turned away. "We'll come back for this one. In his state, he won't make a good primary anyway."

"How long?" Zane's question came out as a gurgle. Keaner turned around with a cocked eyebrow. "How. Long."

Keaner considered the vague question. "I've always been a primary here. The best outcome from Mother's little children." He again wiggled his fingers, letting the worms rise from his palm. "But, before? They got me at Kraken 5." He made a dramatic motion with his arms and pretended to fall backward. "The only one of my group to become a primary. Everyone else died. Not even worthy of being a secondary." He shrugged, laughing. Zane felt like he was going to throw up.

"Why?" Zane wasn't sure he wanted to know, but he couldn't help the question. The scientist in him was still so damn curious.

Mina sighed heavily and rolled her eyes. "That's not any of your business yet, human."

"No, no, he's almost family. Let's indulge him." Keaner stepped toward Zane, his smile full of sharp teeth. If Zane had any energy, he would have moved as far away as his tethered hands would let him. "We want to return to the surface. But the bodies we have down here, our *real* selves, don't agree with your sun. Amphitrite has agreed to send us new bodies so that we'll help them with their wars or whatever." Keaner rolled his eyes and stepped back.

"As if." Mina made a disgusted face. "We'll just take the company over, one by one. And then the rest of you who don't deserve the land." She snapped her fingers and Zane flinched. "Just like that."

The two of them exchanged smiles before Keaner said, "Catch you on the other side, Zane." They left without looking back.

Just like that, his partner, his fellow scientist and coworker, someone he thought was his friend, was gone. Not just in the physical, she's left the room kind of gone. The Mina that should have existed within that body was no longer present.

A miserable keening noise worked its way from between Zane's bloodied teeth, the shredded bottom lip he kept chewing on. He couldn't let this happen. Whatever those worm things were, with the primary and secondary and tertiary bullshit, he wasn't going to let them get anyone else.

"Fuck you," he snarled and tugged at the zip ties that kept him tethered to the wall. They were crusted over with his dried blood and whatever other fluids were leaking out of him. Zane knew that everything in his body didn't belong only to him anymore. Parts of him belonged to the worms, but if he could keep them out of his thoughts long enough, he could make himself useful.

Clenching his jaws together, he felt several of his teeth crack, and as they ground together the nerves in the roots shot lightning bolts into his brain. That was fine. It would be a good distraction from what he was about to do.

Fresh blood was already sheeting down his hands, springing forth from the unhealed wounds around his wrists. Squeezing his jaws together even harder to get that electric shock in his head, Zane drew his hands in toward himself. The outer edge of his hand and the large thumb joint at the base of his palm caught against the ties.

Zane pulled harder. More blood poured out as the plastic bit further into his flesh. The pressure against his hands built until it turned into pain, and then his hands slipped partially through the zip ties. The skin from his hands bunched up as the ties pushed against it. Zane arched his back and braced his feet against the wall for more leverage.

He was going to get his hands out of these cuffs or dislocate his arms trying.

More skin gathered around the plastic until it started to peel away from the muscle underneath. Zane could see connective tissues and flexing tendons as the ties slid further over the largest part of his hand. Panting, Zane knew he couldn't take a second to relax or catch his breath. If he stopped, he didn't know if he would be able to start again. God, this hurt.

Sucking in a huge breath, Zane released it in a scream and yanked himself back. The skin tearing off sounded like sheafs of wet paper being shredded and if the pain hadn't been at the forefront of his mind, Zane might have thrown up from the sound. The ties clattered against the wall and Zane held his hands up in front of his face.

His hands looked like something he would see in a movie: pale skin was rolled up almost above the first knuckle joints of his fingers. Bits of connective tissue were stretched between the skin and the muscle, beaded with droplets of blood like tiny gems. He was shaking so badly, those tiny drops were vibrating off the strands and spattering on the floor. When he spread his fingers, the skin was forced down. It didn't suction back to his hand and instead flowed around the meat like the hem of a dress.

Heat rushed into Zane's face and a feeling of lightheadedness came over him. He slapped his hands together and all the exposed nerve endings screamed.

He screamed with them.

When the feeling passed, Zane slid off the bed, made sure he wasn't going to pass out, and headed for the door.

Carlos

"Did you find Perisdo?" Carlos thought that question made the most sense. Despite what Asha had just shown him, despite the way Benson was smiling at them, Carlos wanted to attempt to pretend that everything was normal. If they could pretend long enough, maybe he and Asha could get out of this.

Benson's smiled widened, his eyes flashing. He was no longer wearing his glasses, and Carlos could see a weird reflection in the pupil, like there was some extra lens or something in there. His teeth were also pointy, way more pointy than they should have been. Carlos' skin crawled and his eyes hovered just over Benson's shoulder, looking at the open doorway behind him.

"What were you doing at Kraken 3?" Carlos closed his eyes at Asha's accusatory tone. Of course she would confront Benson right away. He should have known there was no way she could keep her mouth shut; that wasn't her style.

Asha stood up next to him, her chair squeaking as it wheeled away. Opening his eyes, Carlos cut them to her. Benson's photo was prominently displayed on the screen behind her, except he had a different name. Carlos wished Asha would look at him so he could try to communicate with his eyes that she needed to chill out. Carlos wasn't convinced that Benson was still human, but he also didn't know what exactly he was, either. He looked human, despite the teeth and the wild eyes. Benson didn't look like the fish monsters who had chased them across the ocean floor or through the habs. There was something about him, though, that made Carlos' brain scream "DANGER" with neon lights and a klaxon sounding in his head.

"Perisdo is being taken care of." Benson's voice took on a weird purring sound. Not quite like the sound a cat would make. More so like a large piece of machinery, something that could be felt shaking the ground as it operated. "Nothing to worry about." Benson took a step further into the room.

Asha's comms office was not a large room. It was meant for one person to handle message transmissions and cyber security of the hab. Two people was a bit of a squeeze. Three people, when one of them was threatening the others, was claustrophobic.

There was nowhere for Asha and Carlos to back up, unless they wanted to start climbing up onto the computer consoles.

"You were at Kraken 3." Asha changed her question into a statement, impressing Carlos with the smoothness of her voice. She didn't sound as scared as Carlos felt.

"I was." Benson held up his hand, inspecting his fingertips. It looked like something was bulging beneath the skin. "That was where this all started."

"Where it all started?" Asha leaned forward. "Was Keaner there?" Carlos didn't want Asha to continue this line of questioning. What did it matter? None of that was going to affect their ability to get out of here.

"He was not." The nails on Benson's hand stretched into sharp points. "He was at Kraken 5, though. As was I."

"Why is Amphitrite trying to hide them?" Carlos blurted out.

Benson shrugged, bringing his hand to his face and tapping his chin with one of his sharpened nails. "Amphitrite." Disgust colored Benson's voice. "You humans think you're so special, so inventive, coming to the bottom of the ocean and building your silly little habitats so you don't get crushed like the pathetic creatures that you are." Benson curled his hand into a fist, his nails puncturing his palm and releasing a spurt of green colored blood. "We've survived down here for eons, existed before you were even a blip on the evolutionary line. If it hadn't been for the organisms coming out of the ocean, changing the air, allowing the *sun*," he spat out the word, "to shine through the atmosphere, we never would have been forced down here, where you so willingly come to explore."

"We can leave," Carlos said, his words hurried and coming out almost as one. "We'll get on the sub and leave you alone and make sure Amphitrite never comes back. Keep the habs."

Against the wall, the chair over the air vent squeaked. Beneath it, the air vent rattled.

Chuckling, Benson shook his head. "We don't want *you* to leave. *We* want to leave. We want to return to the surface, and for that, unfortunately, we need you. Your bodies, actually, so we can withstand the sun. I think what we bring to your human bodies is quite an improvement."

Metal groaned and squealed, and the vent shot up from the floor. Benson lunged forward, clawed hands raised in front of him. Carlos jumped to meet him, unsure how he was going to fare barehanded against this monster. When they crashed together, Carlos angled his head to smash into Benson's face, hearing the satisfying crack of a nose against the top of his head. He saw stars as they tumbled to the ground, jarring the breath out of him.

Somewhere above, a guttural growl sounded.

"Carlos!" Asha grunted and something crashed against the wall.

Reeling, Carlos cocked his elbow back and punched forward into the general direction of where he felt Benson. His fist connected with something soft and Benson gagged.

"Run, Asha!" Claws sank into Carlos' side and he screamed, the creature from the air vent matching him. "Run!"

He rolled away from Benson, the stomping of Asha's feet followed by a second set of clacking steps. The monster was chasing her.

Benson crouched a few feet away from Carlos, green blood sheeting down his face from his nose, dripping onto the floor. He was massaging his throat, the air whistling out of his mouth.

"Not…nice," Benson wheezed. He dragged himself into a seated position. The metal air vent was just near Carlos and he snatched it up, intending to use it as an awkward hatchet. "We don't…want to kill…you. We're just trying…" Benson sucked in a big breath, the whistling fading. He pressed his fingers to his throat. "Better. We're just trying to use you to get back to the surface." Grinning with all those pointy teeth, he gestured to himself. "Benson used to exist on Kraken 3 as one of you. Then I found him. Within you little fleshbags, we can go back to the surface where we belong."

Leaning forward, Benson pressed his palms against the floor to push himself into a standing position.

Carlos didn't give him a chance to get up.

Darting forward, Carlos reared his arm back and slammed the edge of the air vent into Benson's skull.

The scream that came out of the man hiding a monster was high pitched and harsh, like some nightmare scream heard in the middle of a pitch-black forest. It reminded Carlos of the screech from an Aztec death whistle that people loved to make on their 3D printers. Hearing it in real life chilled his blood and made him stumble as he got to his feet.

Benson lashed out, taking advantage of the stumble, his claws snagged in the pants and skin of Carlos' calf. Grunting, Carlos jerked his leg out of the creature's gasp. He slammed into the door, hit the button to open it, and darted out.

Behind him, Benson's shriek carried his rage out after Carlos, chasing him down the hall.

Where would Asha have gone? Sure, their goal was to get the fuck out of the hab and back to the surface, but did that mean Asha would run for the sub? Carlos wasn't sure he would be thinking that if he was being chased by that creature. He didn't dare slow down to check his bracelet to see where she was; it wouldn't make a difference what her location was if Benson caught up with him and disemboweled him.

The sub. Carlos would make for the sub and regroup.

Thinking about regrouping would have made him laugh if he wasn't focused on keeping his breathing even for running and ignoring the pain striping his calf. The word "regroup" made him think they should have an actual group, not just him and Asha. There was no one else left, though.

Carlos thought he heard Benson's death shriek echoing behind him. Grimacing, Carlos slowed to a stop at one of the watertight doors. Despite controlling his breathing, he felt like he was struggling. Other than the pain in his calf, his side was sore, like he had a stitch there. He pressed a hand to his side and felt wetness. Carlos didn't bother looking at his hand, knowing he would find blood there.

Opening the panel at the side of the door, Carlos hit a couple of buttons and the door slid shut. The hissing of the door as it sealed matched the sigh Carlos exhaled, letting his head tilt forward until it made contact with the cool metal of the door.

He felt like he could breathe, even though it sounded labored. It didn't feel that hard to breathe, so why was it so loud?

Carlos sucked in a big lungful of air, and held it, his cheeks puffing out.

The heavy sound of air moving continued.

Closing his eyes, Carlos left his head tilted against the door. If he couldn't see whatever was making that noise, it couldn't hurt him. He could just refuse to acknowledge that it existed, and then maybe he could just not exist anymore.

He was spiraling, feeling crazier and dizzier the longer he held his breath and kept his eye closed.

This was ridiculous.

Carlos spun around, opening his eyes and puffing the air out of his mouth at the same time. He was met with a gust of heat that felt like it was about to singe off his eyebrows. Stepping back put him up against the door.

"Zane?" Carlos wished he could put more distance between himself and the man standing just a few feet in front of him. Zane's face was shiny with oozing sores, worse than when Carlos saw him. His clothing was saturated in whatever was coming out of his body, and the skin of his hands looked like gloves that were too big for him.

In those mishappen hands, Zane held a nozzle that looked like it had been hijacked from one of Carlos' welding tools. The nozzle was taped to a hose that curled around Zane and was screwed into the top of large hydrogen container strapped to Zane's back with a combination of straps and duct tape.

Raising his hands, Carlos saw the lighter Zane held in his other hand. If Zane didn't set him on fire, there was a very good chance he was going to kill Carlos in an explosion.

"You're not one of them." It wasn't a question. Zane clicked the lighter and stared at the flame.

Carlos wasn't sure how to respond to that. He wanted to know how Zane knew, how he had made a flamethrower, who had removed his zip ties. So many questions and not enough time.

"Where's Mina?" Carlos settled for the question that would help him figure out if there was someone else running around in the hab that he needed to be worried about. Even if she wasn't one of those things, and was taken over by Ocean Dark Syndrome, she'd killed Divya.

Zane tilted his head, his eyes blinking. A few drops of blood pooled over the rims of his eyes and mixed with the oozing mess of his face.

"She got away. I'm looking for her."

Mina

"This would have been a lot easier if you hadn't gotten rid of your bracelet," Mina grumbled.

She and Keaner walked down the hallway, looking for the others. Not that there were many left. Zane was locked up, Divya was dead along with the surfacers. Benson should have been taking care of Carlos and Perisdo. They just needed to find Asha.

"If you hadn't gotten caught killing Divya, you wouldn't have been tackled and broken yours. At least I was trying to remain incognito. You were just sloppy." Keaner didn't sound annoyed when he blamed her for their current search problem, just cocky. Mina hated that more.

"Finding George after the cleaning bot got her upset me." She didn't want to think about the mangled body of the cat.

"I killed George." Keaner said it like it was the most obvious thing in the world. "The cleaning bots can't even roll over your shoe. How are they going to kill a cat?"

Mina didn't answer, struggling with this new information. On one hand, the cat didn't like them. On the other, her primary form was still so new, human Mina's feelings for George were affecting her.

"It's your fault then."

Keaner shrugged. "Doesn't seem like my problem."

"Whatever," Mina sneered. "We'll be on the surface soon enough."

They passed a viewing window and Mina paused, looking out into the ocean beyond. The darkness swallowed the little bit of light let out by the window, so she flicked on the outside lights.

At the very edge of the light's reach there was movement. Mina pressed her hand to the glass. "Mother?" A dark shape pressed forward, still cloaked in the shadows with its glowing red eyes the only color out there. "We're going to bring you home, Mother," Mina whispered. In response, lights flared to life across Mother's neck and arms. Mina knew the light was caused by bioluminescent bacteria living symbiotically within Mother, but she liked to think the lights were Mother's own special shine, an apology from the world for forcing them beneath the waves.

None of them glowed on the surface, all those eons ago.

The lights reflected off spherical orbs clinging to her body. They were scattered all over, holding the rest of the children they were trying to get to the surface. The orbs swayed with Mother's movements, clinging tight to her.

"We *might* be on the surface soon enough." Keaner's correction of her earlier statement startled her. She snapped her head towards him. "This is Kraken 7. This is the fifth time we've tried doing this. Something always goes wrong."

Mina turned back to the viewing window, but Mother was gone, the moment ruined by Keaner's depressing take on their situation.

"Don't be such a downer, Keaner." Mina snorted and left the viewing window, continuing down the hallway.

"I'm not being a downer," he countered. "I'm being a realist. Someone has to be."

"I think we're all a bunch of realists, Kean. There's nothing wrong with a little positivity." Mina turned a corner and found a closed watertight door. "Guess we're not going this way." She looked over her shoulder, expecting some smartass remark about realistically breaking down a watertight door or something, but Keaner was staring straight ahead, as if there was something more interesting down the other hallway. Huffing, Mina continued, "We're going to do it this time. I mean, yeah, most of these people turned into secondaries, but that just means they weren't worthy to return to the surface with us."

Grunting, Keaner continued going straight down the hallway. "You, me, and Benson are hardly the number of people we would need to establish ourselves up there again. Too many of these fleshbags have weak constitutions." He affected a poor rendition of a British accent, and fluttered his hand like he was waving away a nuisance person.

"Maybe we should just take our chances then." Mina jutted her chin out. "I don't want to stay down here any longer."

"Benson said Amphitrite won't let us come up until we have a sizeable number. This time around, Perisdo told Benson something about needing some of us for some military applications." Disgust twisted through his words.

Mina wrinkled her nose. "So you weren't just making that up to upset Zane?" Keaner shook his head. She hoped that she would not be offered up for some war machine. She just wanted to return to the surface where she and her sisters belonged. It was annoying to have all these rules, all these requirements from an inferior species. What was worse, was that they would have to remain in these subpar skins because of that stupid sun.

"Men." Mina's response was as judgmental as she could make it. "We're not meant for war. Mother won't let it happen." Mina could conveniently forget her teeth and claws and extra strength. She didn't want to fight the fleshbag's wars.

"None of that will matter if we can't find the rest of the people in the hab." They turned a corner together and spotted Perisdo, walking down the hallway and wringing his hands. His head was bowed, focusing his gaze on the ground as he walked, oblivious to the two of them. "How opportune." Keaner's grin could be heard in his voice.

"I'll get him," Mina volunteered. She wanted to put some pain on Perisdo for how much of an asshole he was. "Hey!" Her shout snapped his head up. "What're you doing?"

Perisdo paused and straightened up, his hands still wringing.

"What are you doing out of the holding room?" His voice didn't start off strong, but towards the end he was sounding like his regular self-assured asshole self. "Where is Benson?"

Mina smirked as she approached him, lifting her hands with the palms facing him. "That shouldn't be your concern."

“This whole place is my concern.” Perisdo jutted his chin out. “You don’t tell me what is and isn’t my concern. Do you want to continue to work here?” Looking around Mina, he addressed Keaner. “Do you want to make it to the surface? Where is Benson? I want to speak to the creature that’s in charge, not the messengers or whatever you are.”

When Perisdo first came down to the hab, fleshbag Mina hadn’t liked him. In her current form, Mina still despised the man. Her smirk peeled up around her teeth. They were still very human, unlike Benson’s which was good because she liked to smile.

Especially when she could see the fear in Perisdo’s face as she lunged for him. He tried to run, twisting his body around to try and pedal his feet into movement. He didn’t get far.

Mina wrapped her arms around him, squeezing him until she heard his bones crack, pressing her knuckles into his sternum for added pain. Perisdo shrieked.

“Hey, hey, hey, ease up there Mina. We don’t want the children to have to do more work than need be.” Keaner made a face at her, his tone full of chastisement.

“Keaner, just do your thing. I’m doing my job, so do yours.” Mina crushed Perisdo tighter to herself for emphasis.

Without comment, Keaner raised one of his hands up, the surface of it writhing.

“What are you doing? This wasn’t the agreement. I’m not supposed to change. You’re supposed to leave me alone!” Perisdo’s air of authority leaked out of him, leaving his voice high pitched and frightened. “I demand that you let me go! The company headquarters will hear of this!”

“Blah, blah, blah.” Keaner rolled his eyes and smiled. “With any luck, you’ll be bringing us back.” From the skin of his hand, the heads of dozens of worms shot up, tiny droplets of blood spraying out from them in a fine mist.

Opening his mouth wide in his scream, Perisdo didn’t realize his mistake until it was too late.

Keaner slammed his hand full of worms into Perisdo’s mouth. The scream became muffled, Perisdo’s teeth and lips trying to work their way around the fist, flattening his tongue and pushing his teeth into his cheeks.

Mina grinned at Keaner over Perisdo’s head, holding him tighter as his body began to thrash. “Think that’s long enough?”

Tiny tears opened up from the edges of Perisdo’s mouth, splitting his cheeks. Blood poured down the sides of his face, coating his suit collar and Keaner’s wrist.

“Wait till he stops moving around so much.”

They still needed to find Asha and Carlos, and this was taking so long. This surfacer was a pain in the ass no matter what he was doing.

Perisdo’s muffled screams weakened to whimpering, his thrashing downgrading to shaking. When he went limp in Mina’s arms, Keaner removed his bloody fist, and Mina let the man slip to the ground.

“When will we know?” She stepped back from the body, the only sign of it still living was the shallow rise and fall of the chest. “Keaner, when will we know?" She stressed her words and gave him a push, as if he were ignoring her.

Shooting her an irritated look, Keaner snapped, "Have some patience. I wish you'd retained some of old Mina's temerity. You're a pain in the ass."

"I'll show you being a pain in the ass." Mina cut herself off when the body made a cracking sound. On the ground, Perisdo's body was expanding, forcing his skin to crack open like a shell, tearing through his shirt. "Godsdammit," she muttered.

"You're going to keep that little affectation?" Keaner glanced at her before looking down at Perisdo with a sigh.

"I think it's got a nice ring to it." Mina shrugged. "Of course this fleshbag would be a secondary." She didn't say it out loud, but she was glad for it. His human attitude would have come through too much and they would have been stuck with someone insufferable. More systrarna were needed, but not ones like Perisdo.

A groan exhaled from the creature on the floor and yellowish-gray skin broke through the cracked human skin. Pieces fell to the floor, sounding like bits of pottery breaking apart.

"We can use him to funnel the others to us." The faster they could implant everyone remaining, the better. "How many other secondaries are in here?"

"Divya, I think two of those surfacers, this guy," Keaner nudged the twitching Perisdo with his toe, "and one from the outside."

Mina raised an eyebrow at Keaner. Once a secondary moved outside of a hab, they never came back in. She didn't know if it was because they liked the dark, ocean abyss better, or if the habs reminded them of their past, weaker selves.

"The secondaries aren't listening well this time around. The ones in here have just been on a rampage, and the one from outside won't answer my calls." He huffed out an exasperated sigh. "I think the one from outside is trying to find Carlos. He cut off her arm with a door when we were trying to get into Kraken 3 through the emergency door."

"Can't blame her," Mina shrugged. "We'll have to talk to Mother about…" She trailed off, tilting her head. "Do you hear that?" A series of clicking sounds attracted her attention. Keaner frowned and looked over her shoulder.

Fear was not something they often felt, being at the top of the food chain no matter where they were. So, the flash of it that crossed Keaner's face before he composed it back into a half smile was disconcerting. The extra lenses in his eyes caught the light when he tilted his head, flashing purple.

"What've ya got there, Zane?"

Zane?

Mina turned around and there he was, her old partner looking haggard but determined, carrying some sort of machine that had a nozzle tipped with a tiny flame. His continued resistance both amazed and frustrated her. He would be a primary for sure, and he would make a good one. Zane wasn't an asshole like some of these other fleshbags. If he would just allow himself to change over, they could continue to be partners.

Still in the throes of his transformation, Perisdo groaned which goaded Zane forward. The bulb of fire on the end of the nozzle grew in size.

"Zane, let us help you. Your transition will be easier if you let us ease you into it." She wasn't sure if that was true at this point. He had been fighting for so long, it looked like his skin was melting off. Either way, he wasn't listening to her. Zane's lips were peeled back in a bloody grimace, his eyes shining out of the wet pulp of his face.

In the time it took Mina to say those words, Zane covered the distance between them until he was only about ten feet away. He lifted the nozzle, and shot out a stream of fire at Perisdo. The flames caught his pant legs, racing up the fabric. The heat shattered the flaking skin, sending shards of it everywhere. Perisdo wailed, his almost completed form rolling over and dragging itself away.

"Zane!" Mina shrieked. What an idiot she was, thinking she could talk to him. Zane would see to it that either he would die, or they would die. There was no transformation for him.

At her calling his name, he whipped the nozzle in her direction, his eyes wild. A bit of skin from his cheek detached, sliding off his face and dangling from his chin.

"By fire ye shall be cleansed."

The words didn't sound quite right for the Bible verses he was so fond of repeating, but Mina got the gist well enough. Reaching out, she grabbed Keaner's arm and jerked him in front of her. She had the size and strength over him, and she wasn't about to let herself greet the flames with open arms.

Keaner yelped, unable to get any words out before the spray of fire covered his body. Mina shoved him forward and he staggered towards Zane who jumped out of the way while keeping the stream of fire focused on Keaner. Metal on metal clattering to her left drew her attention to the smear of red tinged green blood along the floor leading to a vent. She watched Perisdo slither into the vent, his legs getting stuck, until he pulled enough to pop one of his legs off. It lay smoldering just outside the vent.

A vile smell filled the hallway of burning meat and clothing and hair, overlayed by Keaner's weakening wails. When she turned back towards him, Zane was redirecting his gaze to her.

She didn't wait, she didn't mourn, she didn't even think. Mina whipped around and took off down the hallway.

Asha

Benson being a part of the freaky fish gang wasn't a twist Asha was expecting, but it made sense. He never quite fit in with the rest of the crew, and he was always lording himself over everyone like he was better than them. He may have some cool abilities, but that in no way meant that he was better than the rest of them. If anything, it made him worse. There must be some creative ways to use his abilities for good. Cutting down bushes or trees or something.

Not *murdering* people.

Keaner, on the other hand… Sure, she'd been suspicious of him since the video footage on Kraken 3, but who knew a younger version of Benson could look so much like Keaner. They certainly didn't look anything alike on Kraken 7. Asha chalked it up to the video quality and wanting to find answers even when they were incomplete.

Turned out, there were two untrustworthy people at Kraken 7.

Asha's spiraling train of thought was moving as fast as her feet were pounding through the hallways of the hab. Amphitrite knew about these fish monsters, or creatures, Mordices, whatever the hell they were. She didn't have any clue what their real name was or even what they preferred to call themselves. Benson's information felt like it was missing context, like important gaps needed to be filled. Not important enough for Asha to stick around, of course.

Nope. She was going to the sub and prepping it for her and Carlos to leave. Forget about Murderer Mina, and Zane was probably on his way to being just like them if he wasn't already.

Once they got to the surface they could deal with the fallout from Amphitrite. She and Carlos would have a whole three hours to do nothing other than plan. She would have groaned if she weren't running for her life. All she wanted to do was work a good job and make good money away from people. Apparently, the universe had other ideas for her.

Just ahead on her right, an air vent exploded up. Asha ducked, throwing her arms over her head for protection. It wasn't until she heard the slithering, sucking sound of something coming out of the vent that she remembered the scene from the comms room she just left.

If it had found her, did that mean Carlos was dead?

The thing dragged the rest of its body out of the vent and hunched over, its breathing heavy and uneven. It was missing a leg, and green blood was still oozing out of the fat stump. The other one from her comms office wasn't missing a leg when she left. Maybe Carlos had done this and he wasn't dead?

Backing up one silent step at a time, Asha worked to keep her footfalls silent. She didn't know if that thing had popped out of the vent because it heard her running, or if it was just tired of being smushed in the vent. Asha never had a reason to go in the air vents, but she knew they weren't made for people to be crawling around in, not when every bit of space counted down here.

The creature's head snapped up and Asha froze. She didn't know if that was the correct response, or if her flight, fight, or freeze response was turned to freeze in this extraordinary set of circumstances. Clenching her teeth, Asha willed herself to take another step back. It was difficult to look away from the dim glow of the creature's eyes.

With a series of pops and cracks, the creature rolled its neck and shoulders, blinking in a way that told Asha it was focusing on her. Her inner voice was screaming at her to run, yet her legs had grown roots and refused to move.

Propping itself up on its elbows, the creature lurched upwards, balancing on one leg and two arms, the head craned up at an extreme angle to be able to see forward. It undulated its entire body with an accompaniment of cracks, and then it bared pointy teeth at Asha. She managed a few more steps backward, and, as if on cue, the creature lumbered forward. The missing leg gave it a rolling run, the limbs snapping out every which way to stabilize it and prevent a fall. Asha remembered a cartoon she once saw of a spider trying to ice skate, and this thing's movement looked exactly like that. The ill-timed humor of a struggling spider snapped Asha out of her stupor. Her knees buckled and she twisted around, scrambling to keep herself upright. She didn't even spare energy for a scream.

Asha had never spent so much time running in her life, and even though it felt like she couldn't take another step, she knew she would have to. Either she kept running, or the three-limbed thing chasing her down was going to make a meal of her.

Wheezing, Asha reached out to grab a corner of the wall and swing herself around it, using the momentum to propel herself forward. Her sweaty palm caused her momentum to almost send her careening to the floor, instead of around the turn. Asha managed to course correct enough that she didn't fall, but she did crash her shoulder into the wall.

Something shifted in the joint and a lightning bolt of pain raced down her arm. Snarling and gritting her teeth, Asha grabbed her shoulder with the opposite hand and held tight to it so it wouldn't be jostled by her running. Her body tilted in that direction, though, as if her wounded arm weighed more. She tried to ignore the scrabbling sounds behind her that were getting closer, tried to determine if her arm was broken or dislocated or just in a lot of pain because she'd slammed it into a wall. Pinning her eyes up ahead, she scanned the walls for a watertight door panel, a door to a room, or anything she could lock herself into. The thing would have to find an air vent to get to her, and that would give her time to get back out of the room.

In her scanning, her eyes snagged on an object hanging on the wall.

The fire extinguisher.

Lunging forward, dragging herself against the wall, Asha reached the extinguisher as the creature unleashed a torrent of crackling shrieks behind her. She grabbed the extinguisher and tried to pull it off the wall.

It didn't budge.

Asha's screams matched the creature's, and she lurched back, pain exploding from her injured shoulder. It felt like something might have torn, but she didn't care. She needed this extinguisher. If she was going to have even a chance of surviving, she needed. The fucking. Extinguisher.

Checking over her shoulder, she saw yellowed claws extended towards her on gray skinned arms. Asha dropped to the ground, her arms outstretched above her as she clung to the extinguisher. A set of claws raked over her arms, the other tangling in her hair and ripping out a chunk. Grunting, Asha pulled herself up from the ground, hoping the creature landed far enough away to give her some time.

A clip. There was a stupid fucking clip holding the extinguisher in. With shaking fingers, Asha managed to unsnap the clip after two tries and jerked the extinguisher off the wall. The force with which she used to wrench it off spun her around. She lost her balance and fell to her knees. Pain lanced up her thigh bones, matching the feeling in her shoulder.

The creature was struggling to get its footing, its claws making it unable to gain purchase on the metal floor.

Asha didn't have those problems. Pushing through her pain, she got one foot under herself and then the other, squatting on the floor. Glowing eyes locked onto her and the creature surged forward, its mouth open in a howl of pointed teeth and spraying spittle. Its hands and foot beat an ominous drumbeat against the metal floor as it bore down on her.

She wasn't ready, though. The extinguisher was in her hands, but she was fumbling to get the hose out of the snap holding it to the cannister, pulling the pin out to release the trigger. Screaming in frustration, Asha's fingers fumbled with the steps–way too many steps–as the monster drew closer. Panic seized her just as she got the pin out and the hose was jostled loose from her flailing.

Whipping the nozzle up, Asha depressed the trigger. The creature slammed into her, dragging her to the ground, and she managed to force the chemical spraying tube into the creature's open mouth. As they fell, Asha twisted, shoving the monster to the ground, keeping the cannister between them. She kept feeding the tube into the thing's mouth, pushing her hand past the gnashing teeth, a fine powder thickening the blood and saliva. The glowing eyes bugged up at her and the creature gagged, spitting up more green blood. Its claws scrabbled at the hose, oblivious to the fact that it should just slice her arms to ribbons.

She held down the trigger of the extinguisher until the creature stopped struggling. Something trickled down her chin, and when Asha wiped at it with the back of her hand, she saw blood. Testing the inside of her mouth, she found a split in her lower lip, releasing the tang of pennies into her mouth.

Asha scrambled off the creature, dragging the extinguisher with her. Standing over it, heaving air in and out of her lungs, Asha aimed the nozzle at the creature and depressed the trigger. She coated the thing in powder, and after an impulsive thought, shoved the nozzle into one of its nostrils. White powder wafted out of the other nostril.

"Worst cocaine high of your life, buddy." Asha sneered down at the creature. She probably couldn't afford to take the time to do this, was possibly putting herself and Carlos in danger by trying to desecrate this thing's body, but Asha wouldn't be satisfied otherwise. It was best to make sure it was dead. Then, she could prep the sub.

Asha kept spraying the powder until the cannister was emptied, spraying out a hiss of compressed gas and then nothing. She could bludgeon it. Even empty, the cannister was heavy. Tilting her head at the monster beneath her, she hefted the extinguisher in her hands, feeling a jolt of pain in her shoulder. Her arm spasmed and she dropped the cannister with a heavy clang.

"Asha?!"

At the sound of Carlos' voice, Asha staggered back from the creature. She looked down the length of the thing's body, noticing the scraps of clothing stuck to the wet folds of its skin.

"Asha!"

It took her a few tries to get her tight throat to work. She choked on Carlos' name until she saw him round the corner at a full sprint.

Tears sprung from her eyes and she whispered, "Carlos."

His gaze strayed from her, to the thing on the floor, and back to Asha. He slowed as he approached, and when he reached her, Carlos wrapped his arms around her and squeezed tight. She sniffed hard, trying to choke back the tears that refused to stay locked behind her eyelids. Relief at finding a familiar face in the hellscape that was her home swamped her ability to have self-control. Then again, was it so terrible to have these feelings after what she'd experienced? It would have been way more terrible if she wasn't around to experience them.

The two of them did an awkward shuffle down the hall, putting space between them and the monster without letting go of each other. They just needed to get to the sub and get out.

Halfway through releasing a sob, Asha blinked her tear bleary eyes open and was startled by Zane walking down the hallway. Asha half shoved herself away from Carlos and half dragged him with her.

"How did he get out?" Her voice pitched toward panic.

Carlos, unknowingly, grabbed her bad arm and the pain jolted her out of her spiral. "He's fine. I think." He mumbled the last part, then said, "Hey, Zane? Why don't you just stop there a minute while we figure some things out? Okay, buddy?"

Zane stopped and set down the cannister he was holding. She noticed that in his other hand was a nozzle with a tiny flame at the end of it. The defibrillator she'd dropped so long ago was tucked between his arm and his side, and he put that down next to the creature's body like he was going to revive it.

"Ummm, he has a flamethrower." Asha stepped back, unsure how "fine" Zane really was.

"Yeah, he uh, torched Keaner. Apparently." Carlos didn't sound all that sad about Keaner's demise. Asha certainly wasn't. "Said Mina got away, though, so we'll have to keep an eye out for her and the rest of the nasties crawling around in here."

Asha took a deep breath. "Come on. Let's get to the sub. We're not too far away." Zane was staring down at the dead creature, but she said the words loud enough that he should have been able to hear. Grabbing Carlos' hand, Asha dragged him in the direction of the sub. "It's not far from here."

They were almost down the hallway when Carlos looked over his shoulder.

"Jesus Christ, Zane, no!"

Zane

It looked so impotent on the floor, coated in powder and missing a leg. Not anything like the others roaming around the hab.

Nothing like what was trying to infest his brain.

There was really only one solution and he could provide that.

Zane glanced down the hallway, watching Asha and Carlos walk away. To the sub, most likely. Were they infested? Did it matter?

The risk was too great. He couldn't let any of them reach the surface. Kraken 7 needed to be a failure for Amphitrite. There could be no survivors.

Hefting the nozzle and the tank, Zane aimed down at the thing that once was human. The flame flared as he depressed the trigger by a hair. He nudged the defibrillator closer to the body, into the path of the flames.

Flooding the hab was the easiest way to destroy it, and once these dry chems had absorbed enough oxygen they were potent explosives. The battery in the defibrillator was extra explosive insurance.

Zane looked up again at the retreating backs of his crewmates. There was no guilt flashing through his mind over what he was about to do. He was doing his best to keep them all safe, and keep the devils at the bottom of the ocean.

A bit of skin fell from his face, landing on the creature and sending up a small plume of white powder.

This was the correct path.

He pulled the trigger, and the world went white.

Mina

Taking refuge in the lab might not have been her best choice. While the door was locked, there was no real guarantee that this wouldn't be the first place Zane looked for her, and that he wouldn't try to melt the door down to get to her.

And the cat was here.

She wasn't sure who brought George here, or why, or with what time. But here she was.

Knowing that Keaner killed George alleviated any guilt she had about sacrificing him to Zane's flames. There was no reason for that kind of cruelty, and Mina thought Keaner's humanity was showing through a bit there. He may not have liked the cat–who also did not like Keaner, or any of her systrarna for that matter–but the rest of the crew was fond of the animal. Including Mina, at one point.

A sheet covered George's body, so Mina didn't have to look at her while she tried to figure out her next move.

Zane was an obvious problem, the worst of the bunch. She would need to find Benson. He was supposed to be dealing with Carlos, but who knew what had happened to him. And then there was Asha. She was so paranoid and nosy, always looking over her shoulder. After digging into the crew member files brought down by Perisdo, Mina figured Asha's paranoia had to do with the man she killed in her twenties.

Shit happened. The man deserved it. Asha needed to let that go.

Leaning back in her chair, Mina stared up at the ceiling tiles. Another thirty minutes. She would give herself another thirty minutes and then she would have to venture out of the lab to find Benson.

A rumbling sound reached her ears, and she squinted at the tank room. What could the tertiaries possibly be making noise about? No one was bothering them.

A few seconds after the noise started, the hab shook. Tools vibrated on the tables, drawers and cabinets wobbled open, bottles fell and smashed to the floor, sending various liquids everywhere.

That wasn't the tertiaries. This was something worse.

Mina stood from her chair and made her way to the lab door, listening before opening it. She stepped into the hallway and listened harder, trying to hear anything, or feel changes in the air pressure of the hab.

There. Her stomach dropped, an odd feeling for a being not used to feeling fear. But the changing air pressure sweeping down the hallway told her everything she needed to know.

There was a breach in the hab.

Carlos

There was something about the way Zane stood above the monster, aiming his MacGuyvered flamethrower down at it and the defibrillator, that told Carlos disaster was imminent.

He didn't know if Zane knew how volatile those chemicals were, if he was trying to make sure the monster was dead, or if he wanted an explosion. None of his reasoning–if there was any–mattered. The result would be the same.

"Jesus Christ, Zane, no!" Even as the words left his mouth, Carlos whipped around, latching his hand onto Asha's elbow. She yelped at the contact, but he dragged her forward anyway. They made it only a few more feet before there was a heavy, muted *whumpf* and a force slammed into their backs. Heat washed over them, like standing too close to a bonfire when a large log was added; it was suffocating.

Carlos lost his footing, staggering forward. He thought he was going to be able to stay upright until Asha fell forward and dragged him down. A running monologue of curses streamed through his mind. They needed to move. There would be only seconds, if that, before the compromised integrity of the hab walls sprung leaks and those leaks would implode. Water flooding into the hab would be the least of their problems as the pressure inside and outside attempted to equalize, and the pressure outside won. They'd be like a can of tuna getting run over by a tank. At least they wouldn't feel anything.

Supposedly.

Asha scrambled to her feet, her mouth open and panting. She grabbed his arms and hauled him up, running backwards until he gained his feet. The sound of cascading water hit his ears. Eyes growing wider than dinner plates, Asha said something but Carlos didn't hear it. The rushing in his ears was either from the water or from the blood pounding into his head. Maybe there was already pressure crushing down, compressing his head and his veins and arteries and organs and making everything so much louder.

A few meters ahead, warning lights flashed on, followed by a klaxon.

The watertight door was preparing to close.

There was a sucking sound behind them, an abrupt gust of air, and the section of hab where Zane and the creature used to be collapsed in on itself.

The genius of the hab's design was that the whole thing wouldn't implode because one area was damaged. It would stop within a specific section, the crushing process halted until the next section was too weakened by the pressure being exerted on it by the billions of gallons of water. Sixteen thousand PSI of pressure just dying to get inside. Each following section would continue to collapse until the whole hab was crushed.

Or the destruction met a watertight door.

Once the watertight doors were engaged around the carnage, that section of hab became independent from the rest of it. Whatever crushing forces that were reforming the hab walls and whatever they contained into flattened layers, were stopped by those doors.

Another section of hab behind them compressed. Carlos winced, the pressure change popping his ears. He thought he tasted blood in his mouth.

The lights around the door ahead of them started to flash faster: it was getting ready to close.

There was no space in his head for anything but covering the distance to that door. Asha pulled ahead of him, the increased flashing spurring her on.

Ten feet.

The lights stopped blinking, becoming solid red.

Five feet.

Asha lunged forward and ducked beneath the closing door.

Three feet.

Carlos kicked his legs forward, dropping into a slide and crossing the threshold on his back. Pain lanced through his battered body. His nose brushed the bottom of the door–he swore it did–as he passed onto the other side and another chance at life. He sat up and whooped, the sound echoing down the hall. Bent over with her hands on her knees, Asha looked at him and stretched her face into an exhausted grin.

Another section of hab collapsed, the sound of it coming through the watertight door.

Grimacing, Carlos rolled onto his stomach and pushed himself up.

"I think it's time we made our way to the sub." Although he knew the sectioned off part of the hab should be fine, he didn't want to put that specific piece of engineering to the test. As far as he knew, there was never a need to test the collapse design in the real world, no other incidents of hab explosions that necessitated the use of watertight doors. The first time something was tested in the real world, was always when problems occurred.

Another explosion beyond the watertight door reinforced to Carlos that they needed to get out of the hab.

"Is there still a path to the sub?" Asha reached out to Carlos and helped him get up. She was still out of breath, dark circles pouching under her eyes. Looking at her made Carlos realize how his exhaustion was threatening to take him down.

Nodding, Carlos stood with her assistance and leaned back, trying to stretch out his back. In addition to his exhaustion, everything hurt.

"Yeah. The only doors that will close are the ones that will contain the damage." He thought for a moment. "We might have to open up a door or two that I closed, but we'll be able to get to the sub."

"Great." Asha started off down the hall, flinching at the loud noises behind the watertight door. That should have been the last section to collapse. Carlos eyed the door, trying not to imagine it becoming concave, getting sucked into the ocean, collapsing his world around him.

Shaking himself, Carlos jogged down the hallway to catch up with Asha.

Mina

Each bone rattling decompression of the hab startled Mina. She might not have been as resilient as a secondary, but her body could take a lot. What it could not handle was being decompressed at rapid speeds or not having oxygen. Being crushed and drowned were real risks to her, one of the downsides of existing within a fleshbag.

Irritated, she listened at one of the air vents that were spaced along the flooring. She could hear one of the secondaries traveling through the air circulation system. If she followed it, Mina hoped it would take her to Carlos or Asha. Or both. Both was better; less effort she would have to put into searching. Mina wondered if the secondaries were as concerned about the hab collapse as she was, or if any of them were caught in the destruction. They could survive something like that–she was pretty sure they could–but it would be hard to get them back in the hab to help her if they were out in the ocean.

The noises from the vents paused, so Mina did, too, taking the opportunity for a breather. In the silence, she could hear voices coming down one of the hallways. A clattering erupted from the air vent as the secondary took off towards the noise, spurring Mina to give chase.

Multiple voices made her think that Carlos and Asha were together. It was possible that Zane was also traveling with them, but this was a risk she needed to take. She would just need to be careful.

In the approaching intersection, Asha and Carlos walked into view, oblivious to Mina or the secondary closing in on them. They were heading in the direction of the sub. Thinking about the layout of the hab in her head, Mina paused, and then backtracked.

The secondary could take care of Asha and Carlos, and if she couldn't, then Mina would handle it.

Asha

The air vents were making a helluva lot of noise even though nothing was popping out of them. Asha kept shooting nervous glances at the floor, trying not think about what might be crawling around beneath them.

Neither of them had said much since walking away from the watertight door. There wasn't much *to* say. Parts of the hab were destroyed, everyone else from the crew was dead or one of those things, and on top of all that, they were being hunted. What else was there to say?

They just needed to get to the damn sub.

"Do you hear that?" Carlos didn't stop walking, his head craning to look behind them and around corners.

Asha bit her lip, realizing that there was no more noise echoing up from the air vents. Instead of making her feel more confident about their path of travel, Asha's stomach sank. This was like the silence in the woods before a predator struck.

They kept walking, speeding up even. Asha's mantra spinning around in her mind was "We just need to make it to the sub. We just need to make it to the sub. We just need to make it to the sub."

A clicking noise escaped her notice since it wasn't as loud as the clanging in the air vents. It wasn't until the creature turned into their hallway that Asha registered the sound of claws *tick-tick-tick*ing against the floor.

"Oh shit." Carlos stopped, throwing his hand out in front of Asha as though to stop her forward movement. Not that he needed to; Asha was frozen to the spot just like with the last monster she'd encountered. "That's the one from Kraken 3." Carlos flapped the arm in front of Asha and she realized what he meant: it was missing its arm at the elbow.

Asha glanced at the walls, but this particular hallway didn't have a fire extinguisher in it. The creature advanced, one clicking step at a time, its head lowering while the rattling antenna raised over its skull.

"Make a run for it?" Asha whispered out the side of her mouth. The creature reacted to her voice, tilting its head and taking a few steps forward.

"Do you know the way?" When Carlos spoke, the creature leaned forward and hissed, exposing pointed teeth with bits of flesh hanging from them like it had just eaten something. "It's not far. We're almost there."

"Yes." The word exploded out on an exhale of breath, and they turned in unison to run back the way they'd come. Behind them, the creature roared.

Asha gritted her teeth, her muscles screaming. Maybe she'd died already, and this version of hell was a perpetual treadmill, just constant running from threats. She was beyond exhausted, and she felt on the verge of having her legs just give out. Her injured shoulder sent bolts of pain into her back with each step she took.

"Come on," Carlos grunted, as if sensing her thoughts. They skidded around a corner together and Asha spotted a fire extinguisher. She didn't have the breath to celebrate, but in her head, she punched her fist in the air.

A yellow-gray mass dropped from the ceiling right next to the extinguisher. The creature unfurled itself from where it crouched, standing to its full height. It snarled at them, slashing the air with its claws before ripping the cannister off the wall and launching it at them. Asha and Carlos both ducked, more out of instinct than anything else. The canister clattered around behind them, and Asha wrenched herself around, watching it bounce into the hallway they'd just come from. It was a risk to make a run for it, a big risk. But there were monsters in both directions and a "weapon" in only one of them.

"Asha!" Carlos shouted for her as she ran back the way they came. She ignored him, turning the corner and spotting the fire extinguisher spinning in a slow circle just feet from the monster. Gritting her teeth, Asha ran forward, trying not to let the roar of the creature shake her steps.

She reached the cannister a step before the creature did, trying to keep her momentum as she crouched down to pick it up. Above her, the creature hissed, and she swore she could hear the wind part as it slashed its only arm down at her, claws ready to shear off her head.

There was a human yell, and something dark blurred past her, tackling the creature to the ground with a howl and thudding of bodies. Carlos wound up on top, one knee planted in the thing's chest, his foot holding down the single flailing arm. Adrenaline was eroding her fine motor skills, and Asha struggled even more with working the clips on this extinguisher than she had on the other one.

"Come on!" Carlos roared. The creature matched his voice, bucking its body, dislodging Carlos from its chest a little more each time. Panicked, Asha gave up on navigating the cannister's clips and hefted the thing above her head.

She didn't need fine motor skills to use an object as a bludgeon.

At least this time, when she smashed a hard object into a skull, it was a monster's, and she wouldn't have to feel remorse for it.

Asha threw her entire weight behind her downward stroke, straining the muscles of her back, arms, neck. The curved bottom of the extinguisher smashed into the creature's skull and it convulsed violently, tossing Carlos off to the side. He scrambled up as Asha landed another blow, screaming.

With its lips peeled back, baring pointed teeth and black gums, the creature's remaining limbs beat against the floor as it seized.

Before Asha could hit it again, Carlos tore the extinguisher from her and launched it down the hallway. She was about to turn on him, when she saw the cannister sail straight into the chest of the other monster lunging down the hall.

Asha grabbed at Carlos' arm and they ran together. The sub wasn't that much further. They were going to make it. They had to make it.

Carlos

Just ahead was the entrance to the submarine. Safety, sanctuary, the surface world. Carlos thought of his teenage daughter, her smiling face, of her being excited for his earlier than expected return.

He would just have to survive the three-hour return trip to the surface.

Asha slapped her bracelet up to the door to open it. A red light flashed on, followed by a harsh beep. Denied. They were so close. Through the window in door, Carlos could see the open door of the sub, just waiting for them to enter its cozy confines.

Before Asha could slap her wrist up to the panel again, Carlos pushed her aside. They didn't have time for this.

Reaching into his pocket for his auto-screwdriver, his fingers brushed against the monster's claw that he'd had with him since Kraken 3. It seemed like forever ago since they made that deep walk. Was that when things were irreversibly changed for them? Or had it been when the first Mordices was brought into the hab?

Pushing those questions aside–they were in a life and death situation after all and pondering what-ifs was pointless–Carlos pulled the small auto-screwdriver out of his pocket and went to work on taking the panel off. "Of all the days for this to malfunction," he muttered.

"I would bet money it's not a malfunction," Asha said with confidence. Carlos didn't spare her, or that theory another thought. They needed to get in the sub.

The screws popped out easily with each mechanical whir of his auto-screwdriver, followed by the panel. Carlos didn't need to study the wire layout; he knew the schematics of the hab's wiring better than he knew his own home's wiring. Just a quick changing of connections and–

With a pneumatic hiss the door slid open. Carlos didn't bother with feeling prideful of his skills and didn't take any time to revel in them. This was easy shit, and they were low on time. He checked over his shoulder to make sure the hallway was still empty, then stepped into the dry dock vestibule. The hum of the sub's electronics being on struck him as odd, but he crossed the small space to the sub's door anyway.

At the entry, Mina appeared.

Her size forced her to hunch over in the doorway, but there was no mistaking the feral grin exposing her pointed teeth. The lights of the vestibule hitting her eyes made them flash, like a predator's in the night.

"Glad you two could make it." She remained hovering in the doorway. Every second they were here was another second the other two monsters from the hallway were closing in on them. Carlos wasn't sure, but he thought he could hear them clattering towards them. "I'll just need a few seconds of your time before we can all proceed to the surface together." Mina held out her hand, the skin of her palm writhing.

"Please, Mina," Asha pleaded at Carlos' shoulder. "We'll leave the hab to you and your friends. Just let us leave." Carlos didn't know why Asha thought pleading with these things would help at all. At no point had they been willing to negotiate or ask what anyone wanted. These monsters wanted their bodies to make it to the surface, and that was that.

Mina chuckled. "Asha, you don't seem to understand. We don't want the hab." She rolled her eyes. "We want to return to the surface, but because of the strength of the sun, the way the environment changed a millennia ago, we can't return. Our bodies refuse to adapt, and unfortunately that means we need you fleshbags." Mina stepped out of the sub and into the vestibule. Carlos took a step back, aware that it felt like she was herding them back towards the monsters.

"Why don't you just ask? I'm sure there are people deranged enough to want to be hosts to…whatever it is you are." Asha tried to keep the pleading tone out of her voice, tried to make herself sound angry or self-righteous, but Carlos heard the tremor in her words.

Mina directed a sour look at Asha, and Carlos wished she would just shut up. Pissing off the giant Mina-shaped monster wasn't going to help them. He didn't think anything would at this point. Pain lanced through his side and he just managed to not wince and hunch over.

“A higher life form does not ask permission from a lower one,” Mina sniffed. “As it is, Amphitrite has not been keeping well to their end of the bargain, sending down subpar hosts. So many lost opportunities.” Sighing, she stepped toward them again. “But you two, I’m pretty sure you’ll be primaries. There are enough secondaries running around, so let’s get to it.”

Carlos didn’t understand any of what she was talking about. None of it mattered, though. They just somehow needed to get into that sub without Mina or those monsters.

When Mina took another step forward, Asha lunged at her, a deep walk helmet clutched in her hand as she swung it overhead. Mina only had time to make a surprised face before the helmet smashed into her face. Her nose exploded in a gout of green blood and several of her teeth tore from her mouth. Asha reared her arm backward and swung the helmet down again. It connected with Mina’s cheek, but this time she was ready for it.

Moving with an uncanny speed, Mina snatched Asha’s wrist within her grasp and squeezed. Asha’s scream melded with the howls of the monsters as they closed in on the sub.

Carlos spun around, intending on slamming the button to shut them out, but they were already there, crouching and springing at him through the open doorway. All he could do was drop to the ground to avoid their launch path and hope Asha wasn’t in the way. One after another, the creatures sailed through the open door and thudded into something solid. Jerking around, Carlos saw them take out Mina, dragging her screaming into the sub. Asha was holding her limp wrist to her chest, tears making tracks down her dirty cheeks.

He would only have one shot at this.

While Mina and the monsters struggled to disentangle themselves within the confines of the sub, Carlos grabbed Asha's arm. She didn't resist as he pulled her towards him, and then shoved her out of the dry dock vestibule. She stumbled and fell to her hands and knees with a yelp.

Pulling out his auto-screwdriver, Carlos used it to get to the inner workings of the dry dock's wiring. He winced in pain when he reached his arms up to pull the panel off and start rearranging the wires. The door slid shut just as Asha slammed into it from the other side.

"Carlos!" She banged her fist on the door while screaming at him. "What are you doing?! Get the fuck out of there!"

Almost like a demonic mimic, Mina's voice matched Asha's: "What are you doing?!"

Lights began to flash in the vestibule and an androgynous voice played over the speakers.

"Equalization will begin. Please ensure that all deep walk suits are closed, your oxygen is turned on, and all loose objects are secured."

Pressing a hand to his side, feeling the squish of torn flesh and the ooze of blood, Carlos slapped his bloodied handprint against the window for the Asha to see. Her tears began in earnest then, her face screwed up in what his daughter would probably call "ugly crying".

When he tackled the one-armed beast earlier, it had raked his side before he managed to pin its arm down. As he and Asha ran for the sub, he could feel the blood trickling down his side, feel himself getting weaker. Pressing his hand to his side let him feel just how deep those gouges were, how much blood was soaked into the fabric of his uniform, the dark color of it hiding the blood loss from everyone except him.

Carlos wasn't sure he would have made it to the surface even if the sub hadn't contained a monster. The least he could do in these last moments was kill Mina and these two monsters. He wasn't sure if the sub would still work after being filled with seawater, but he hoped it would, and that Asha would still have a chance to escape. He hoped these monsters trapped with him could drown. The sudden thought that he knew so little–that the world knew so little–about what existed on the bottom of the ocean, filled him with a vast sadness.

Beating her fists against the window, Asha screamed at him. Water started to rise up from the vents in the floor, and Mina shouted behind him. With the hand not pressed to the viewing window, he gripped the claw in his pocket and closed his eyes, hoping that his daughter would be okay. He thought of the last time he saw her, when they visited a sunflower field and she had gotten lost among the blooms, popping out to scare him. Her laugh that day, the way the wind tousled her hair so she looked like some sort of glowing wind-swept fairy tale.

He would miss her.

Opening his eyes, he saw that Asha had stopped banging on the door and placed her hand against his, separated by the glass. That was enough.

Turning away from Asha, with tears falling down his own cheeks, Carlos faced the opening of the sub in knee high water that was rising faster than he ever remembered it going.

Mina was rising from the floor of the sub, shoving the monsters out of the way to push herself into the dry dock vestibule.

"Fix this," she seethed, claws growing from the tips of her fingers. Green blood covered her mouth and chin, staining her teeth. "Fix it now."

The water was at his waist, and he pulled the claw gripped in his hand out of his pocket. The lights in the vestibule made the water shimmer like silver, swirling red and green with blood.

"Fuck you." There was no anger behind his words, no challenge. Just a matter-of-fact statement.

Mina lunged for him, but her movements were slowed by the water, and she fell just short of him. Without a second thought, Carlos swung his arm in a sideways chop and plunged the claw into Mina's neck. He jerked it forward, releasing a spray of green blood that mixed into the water. The water was up to his chest as Mina grabbed for her throat, trying to hold the flaps of it closed without success. She weakened quickly, her body slipping under the water even as she struggled to stay above it. The water was almost at Carlos' chin, and he was struggling to keep his feet.

From the entrance of the sub, the two creatures slithered out, hissing at him. Their movements through the water were graceful, and even knowing he was about to die, Carlos could appreciate that.

The water buoyed him slightly, and his head bounced against the top of the vestibule ceiling, Mina's twitching body doing the same.

As the water closed over the top of his head, the creatures tore their claws into him.

Asha

Staggering down the hallway away from the dry dock vestibule was all Asha could manage. Tears blurred her vision, making it difficult to see where exactly she was heading.

Not that it made much of a difference.

If the sub didn't survive, if those creatures didn't drown, there was no other chance of escape.

A wail tore from her throat and she dropped to her knees. As the water filled up the dry dock vestibule, Asha had hoped Carlos would drown before the creatures got to him. But that wasn't to be. Instead, she watched, screamed her throat raw, as the monsters tore him apart. She couldn't, wouldn't, look away in the seconds it took for those things to dismember her best friend. Each time she blinked, she saw his shredded limbs floating in the water, the creatures circling around and slamming into the viewing window. Tears built up in her eyes, spilling over her lids as she refused to close them, to witness again and again Carlos' sacrifice.

"What's all this now?"

Asha didn't turn to the voice, hoping that Benson would just kill her. Instead, she felt gentle hands grasp her under the arms and lift her up. She could have gone limp on him, let herself fall back to the floor. But she didn't want to appear that pathetic in front of one of these monsters.

Though her legs were shaky, Asha stood on her own and looked out of the viewing window that Benson faced her towards. The lights were on, sending tendrils of illumination into the gloom. At the edges of the light's reach, clouds of sediment boiled up like something large was moving around out there.

"All this fight, and for what?" Benson's voice was calm, non-judgmental. It was like the asshole supervisor he was before had melted into nothingness, leaving this skin that looked like him behind.

"For what?" Asha repeated the words, not sure what else to do. She looked at him and startled, noticing that he had a metal air vent chopped into his head. It bisected his eye, the halves drooping onto his face, the vitreous fluid already dried into flakes on his skin. Even the green blood from the wound was dried.

Benson reached up for the air vent, seeming to be surprised that it was still there.

"Whoops. I'm sure this is upsetting to see. Let me just…" He grasped the edge of the metal and tore it from his skull, green blood trickling out of what should have been a life ending wound. Handing the green stained vent cover to her, he asked, "Better?"

Despite never wanting to close her eyes, Asha blinked at his surreal question. "How…how could anything be better?" She gestured around the hallway, as though her reasoning was written on the walls. "Everyone is dead." Asha looked down at the air vent, turning it over in her hands, then back at him. The dry flaps of eyeball that had been on his cheek drew up into the eye socket, bulging out to reform an eye.

Bile roiled in Asha's gut.

Benson tutted, smiling at her with normal human teeth. "No, not everyone. You're still here. And now, she's here." He gestured toward the viewing window.

"She?" Asha still couldn't formulate a single cohesive though, something that could help her. Anything that would get her through this. What was the point? Still, she looked in the direction that Benson indicated.

From out of the shadows a giant creature approached. It moved with an underwater grace that sent goosebumps racing across Asha's skin. Like it knew it belonged at the top of the food chain and was furious that it was forgotten.

It looked a bit like the creatures that chased her and her crewmates all over the bottom of the ocean and through the hab. Muted, yellow-gray skin with long claws and glowing red eyes, fluffy yellow antenna that floated around its head like hair. It had spots of color glowing along its neck and shoulders, glimmering down its arms, each light surrounded by the purple spheres that had rained down on them on the deep walk. Each one full of those worms.

Knobby appendages, like those on a Mordices, fluttered down its ribcage like they were grasping for something. A human-like nose was set in the center of its face, bubbles pouring out of it every few seconds.

Asha almost dropped the air vent cover as the thing set its face within inches of the viewing window. It was so close that Asha could see a dark pupil set within the glowing red orbs of its eyes. The pupil was round, and around it was a white iris. Asha felt like it was staring straight through her, flaying her skin so that it could see her every thought, fear, hope. Asha wanted to run, but gripped the air vent tighter in her hands, feeling the pain of the metal cutting into her skin.

"This is Mother." Never before had Benson sounded so loving, so full of adoration, as he did looking at this…thing. At *Mother*.

"What…?" Asha wasn't capable of a full sentence. Every fiber of her being felt like strung piano wire: taught and ready to screech. "Your mother?"

Benson nodded, the gash in his head knitting back together a centimeter at a time. "My ancestor, forced down here by the changing climate up above. As the creatures of the sea came to the surface and released their oxygen, these new gases cleared the skies for the sun to come through, and we were forced down to the depths to take their place." Benson placed a hand against the glass. The gesture speared through her chest and tears welled in her eyes. "We just want to return, and you humans are the vehicles for that. Mother has negotiated this with Amphitrite through us, me, mostly."

Shaking her head, trying to clear the fog threatening to smother her, Asha asked, "Amphitrite knows about this?"

"Oh yes." Benson smiled at her. "Mother told them that when we get enough primaries–morphs like me–to the surface, Amphitrite can use our secondaries and tertiaries–the morphs chasing you all over and the "Mordices" as you called them–to sell to the highest bidder for war." He chuckled. "As if Mother would let the humans use us for those purposes. Amphitrite is only a means to an end. Our end."

On the other side of the glass, Mother hovered. Her glowing eyes flicked between Benson and Asha until she pressed her clawed hand against the glass. The skin was gnarled, like an old woman's, the joints of the fingers looking swollen. Half of one of the claws was missing, and the others looked blunted by usage and time.

"You're connected to her already." Benson's voice startled her out of staring at Mother. She turned a questioning gaze toward him. "You might as well let me help ease your transition. She knows the children are in you."

Asha's body ran cold, and she did a mental tally of herself. Nothing felt different, or like there were worms squirming around inside her. She'd never seen any of the worms near her.

How could she have become infested?

Benson gestured at her hand, and, as if reading her mind, said, "If I had to guess, that would be where they got you." Asha lifted her right hand, the same one that had been crushed by Mina only a little bit ago and which now didn't hurt at all. There was a mixture of red and green blood on her wrist, smeared over lines of scars she'd never seen before.

Then she remembered jamming the nozzle of the extinguisher down the creature's throat, forcing her hand into its mouth and scraping her skin against its teeth.

Asha felt sick.

"You're a primary, Asha. One of the chosen." Benson sounded in awe of her. "You will help return us to the surface. You–"

The metal of the air vent cut deep into Benson's throat. He gurgled around it, green blood spilling over Asha's hand and down his uniform shirt. Asha tore the metal piece out of Benson, and he fell to his knees. Glancing at the creature, at *Mother*, beyond the glass, she saw it hadn't moved and kept its hand pressed to the viewing window. A low growl vibrated the grayish flesh at its throat.

Cocking her arm back, Asha slashed the metal vent into Benson's throat and felt the hard reverberations of the metal hitting bone. Whipping her arm back a third time, she brought it back down again.

This time, it cut clean through. Benson's head tilted to the side and fell with a thud to the floor, rolling a little way from his body which Asha kicked over. She stared at the body, her chest heaving with each breath. Thin white worm tendrils wriggled out from the meat of Benson's neck stump.

She wasn't going to go anywhere with Benson. Nor would she go anywhere with the monsters who slaughtered her entire crew to further their own goals. While she still maintained control over her thoughts and body, Asha would see to it that this entire hab was flooded. She'd have to check a few of the computer processes, but it shouldn't be hard. Asha would make sure no one could salvage anything from Kraken 7.

Looking at Mother, Asha stepped forward to the viewing window. It bared blackened teeth at her, ducking down further to look Asha directly in the eye. There was a tickling sensation at the base of her skull.

Nope. Fuck that.

Stepping away from the window, Asha gave herself a whole-body shake. The growl became a high-pitched warble, and the tickling sensation became more intense. Asha pinched herself, and the feeling faded. That's how she' do it, then. There would be no hab for Amphitrite to return to, nothing for them to salvage. She would make sure of it.

Glaring at Mother, Asha snarled, "See you in hell, bitch." The creature leaned away from the window, taking its hand with it.

Turning on her heel, Asha stalked down the hallway. If she was going to blow up the hab, she was at least going to finish her book first.

WARNING

DRY DOCK DOORS OPENING WITHOUT PROPER PREPARATION

CATASTROPHIC CONSEQUENCES IMMINENT

PROCEED?

YES/NO

Acknowledgments

Big book number five! Wowie wow wow.

Thank you, as usual, to my sister who is indefatigable when it comes to my endless questions about book covers, ending choices, and just general existential spirals. She's also a very wonderful unpaid PA, so if you ever see her at conventions, give her a candy bar or something xD She gets hangry.

Thank you to everyone that is always so kind at events, conventions, online, and everything in between. I have made some amazing friends and connections through this journey and I am always so excited to make more.

If, at this point, I haven't thanked you in any of my previous acknowledgments and you think I should, let me know. I'll add you to "The List". What list is that? I don't know, maybe you shouldn't ask to be put on it.

Thank you. <3

About the Author

Kim loves Harley, Kyle, and spending time outdoors (almost definitely in that order). When she's not writing, thinking about writing, or panicking about writing, she's gardening, hiking, playing video games, or doing other sorts of artistic things.

She has authored four other books and has spoken about the impact of women in horror movies and misogyny in the genre on her social media pages, Youtube, and podcasts. She has even had the opportunity to speak to a group of adults in continuing education on the topic and they were delightful.

Find Kim on Instagram, TikTok, and Threads at ModernMonstress.

Also, this is Harley, and she would appreciate a nose boop.

www.ingramcontent.com/pod-product-compliance
Lightning Source LLC
LaVergne TN
LVHW010627110826
845149LV00014B/2795

* 9 7 9 8 9 8 9 5 9 4 1 4 6 *